Selected Works of
Na Hye-seok,
the Korean Pioneer
of Women's Liberation

Selected Works of Na Hye-seok, the Korean Pioneer of Women's Liberation

발행일	2021년 9월 17일		
지은이	나혜석		
번역	현채운	표지 삽화	Amelia Tan
펴낸이	손형국		
펴낸곳	(주)북랩		
편집인	선일영	편집	정두철, 배진용, 김현아, 박준, 장하영
디자인	이현수, 한수희, 김윤주, 허지혜	제작	박기성, 황동현, 구성우, 권태련
마케팅	김회란, 박진관		
출판등록	2004. 12. 1(제2012-000051호)		
주소	서울특별시 금천구 가산디지털 1로 168, 우림라이온스밸리 B동 B113~114호, C동 B101호		
홈페이지	www.book.co.kr		
전화번호	(02)2026-5777	팩스	(02)2026-5747

ISBN   979-11-6539-963-4 03810 (종이책)   979-11-6539-964-1 05810 (전자책)

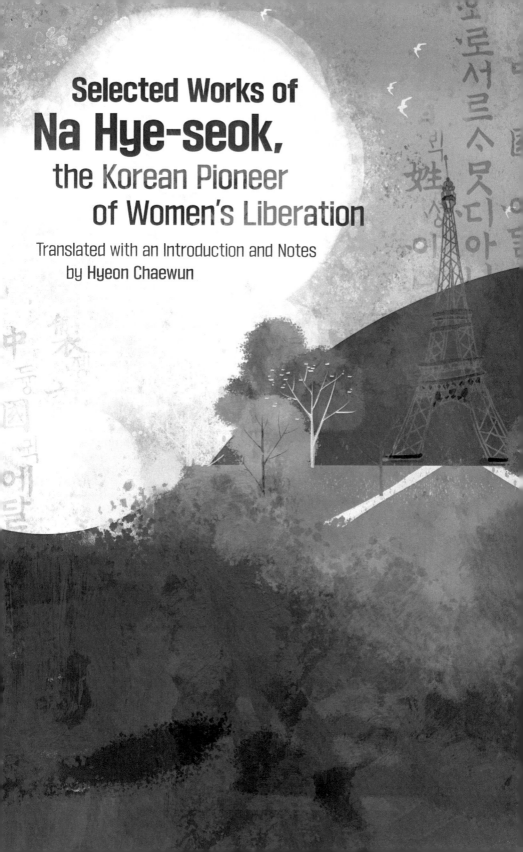

Selected Works of
Na Hye-seok,
the Korean Pioneer
of Women's Liberation

Translated with an Introduction and Notes
by Hyeon Chaewun

Na Hye-seok
(나혜석, 1896. 4. 28 ~ 1948. 12. 10)

Na Hye-seok was born in 1896 in Suwon. She was a Korean writer, poet, painter, sculptor, women's rights activist, and a journalist, who published over 80 pieces of writing, including her fiction, such as *Kyeonghee*, *Hyeon-sook*, and *Grudge*, and her poetry, such as *Nora*. In her fictions, essays, and poems, she criticized the social norm that pressurized women to be a 'Good Wife, a Wise Mother' and advocated social changes for the lives of women to be liberated beyond their confinement in chastity and beyond their devotion to their father, husband, or son. Na Hye-seok was also one of the pioneering female founders of the first magazine for Korean women called *New Woman*. She graduated with honors at Jin Myeong Girl's High School in 1913, and majored in Western oil painting at Tokyo Arts College. After graduating from Tokyo Arts College in 1918, Na Hye-seok became one of the spearheads of the women's independence organization during the March 1st Independence Movement in 1919. In 1920, she got married to Kim Woo-young, and afterwards, she went on to further study painting and learn about the burgeoning feminist movement and gender issues in the West, becoming the first Korean woman to travel to Europe and America. After returning from her trip to the West, she held exhibitions of her paintings and published more of her short stories, essays, and articles about family life as a Korean woman, such as 'Companionate Marriage, Experimental Marriage,' in 1930 and 'Confessions of a Divorcee' in 1934, where she denounced the double-standards women faced in a patriarchal society. Na Hye-seok was a woman of many talents in the arts, as a painter, a writer, and first and foremost, was one hundred years ahead of her time as the Korean pioneer of women's liberation.

Hyeon Chaewun

(현채운, Born in 1999)

Hyeon Chaewun is a student currently attending Ewha Womans University, majoring in International Studies. She graduated from Neulpureun High School in 2018. She is an avid reader, writer, and a dreamer, with passions to turn her dreams into reality and bring the creations of her story and its characters out into the world. Also, as a student with interest in gender studies and the history of Korean women writers, Na Hye-seok's short stories and essays paved the way for Chaewun's once dream-like world to become more fleshed out and concrete. Thanks to Na Hye-seok, she found a new resolve to take a deeper dive into history and bridge the past and the present by exploring English translation of Korean literature. As a student who once dreamed of the fantasy of Harry Potter, Chaewun is now further expanding her world, as she treads the path towards self-discovery with the hope, courage, and insights gained from Na Hye-seok. Now, Hyeon Chaewun has a dream of turning it into reality. A dream that as a Korean woman, with passions in the arts and gender issues like Ms. Na, she would help continue the legacy of Na Hye-seok.

Amelia Tan
(진혜린)

Amelia is a professional and multitalented visual designer and illustrator, with extensive experience in multimedia and print design. She has completed her associate degree course in Advertising & Graphic Design in The One Academy of Communication Design, Malaysia and involved herself in numerous projects from brand and corporate identity (BI & CI), publication, packaging design, advertising campaign and not forgetting, book cover illustrations. Besides that, she also possesses a Bachelor's Degree in Film & Digital Media in Dongguk University, Seoul, South Korea. With that, she is exceptionally skilled in professional design and editing softwares such as Adobe Photoshop, Adobe Illustrator, Adobe Indesign, Adobe Premiere Pro, and Procreate. Her designs and illustrations come with a specific objective in mind and she has an excellent eye for detail. Her positive attitude and effective use of communication drives her passion to create and design, has been the engine driven throughout her entire life of creativity.

Translator's Introduction in Korean

　그동안 역사 교과서에는 '신여성'이란 주로 신식교육을 받은 서양화된 여성으로 지극히 단편적인 부분만 다루어졌다. 그래서 우리들의 기억 속에 '신여성'은 1920년대~1930년대 조선 과도기(일제 강점기 시절)에, 혜성처럼 나타나 서양식 복제품인 드레스를 입고, 단발머리를 치켜세우며, 경박하게 연회식과 댄스파티를 오고 갔던 위대한 개츠비의 Daisy와 같은 그저 모던한 여성들로 일반화되었다. 잠깐 스치는 눈으로는 서구 문화 유입에 따라 물질주의를 받아들인 점으로 신여성이라고 보았으며 종종 그들의 이미지를 부정적인 시선으로 착취하는 일부 미디어에서는 돈을 사치스럽게 쓰며 쇼핑에 빠지고 외모에 집착하는 여자로 왜곡해왔다. 사실, 그러한 신여성의 이미지는 나의 무의식에서 머물곤 하며 그 당시 여성 독립 열사 몇몇을 제외하고는 일제 강점기 조선 여성의 다른 삶의 측면들, 예를 들어, 그들의 시련과 고민 그리고 혼란스러운 시대에 그들이 가졌을 법한 꿈과 야망에 대해서는 어두웠었다.

　그러던 대학교 2학년 시절 어느 날 한국 근현대사 수업을 통해 삶의 여러 방면 속 조선 여성들을 선명하게 묘사한 (그때의 여학생, 노처녀, 과부, 이혼 여성에 향한 사회적 편견을 초월한) 나혜석 선생님의 단편 소설과 수필들을 접하게 되면서 나의 어두웠던 시야가 밝아지기 시작했다. 나혜석 선생님은 시대를 앞서간 진보적인 여성, 해외에서 공부하고 구미만유를 개척한 최초의 한국 여성, 여러 성공적인 전시회를 개최하였던 한국 최초의 서양화가였다. 또한 동시에 네 아이의 어머니와 아내로서 가족과 결혼생활에 따른 다양한 시련의 경험자이시다. 예술을 불타오르는 열정으로 사랑하시고 자신의 이야기를 하는 나혜석 선생님은 각 문학 작품(소설과 수

필 등)에서 거침없는 필력으로 구시대적 결혼 관습, 여자의 정조와 순결을 둘러싼 여성 혐오 관념 등 사회적 불평등의 조각들을 선명하게 새기셨다. 또한, 가슴을 파고드는 예리함과 통찰력이 담긴 이야기들은 결혼보다 교육을 우선순위로 했던 앞서가는 여학생으로, 사회의 이중적 잣대에 시달리는 과부로, 주홍글씨가 씌워진 이혼녀로 나아가 자식에 대한 어머니의 사랑은 자연적인 것이 아닌 시간을 걸쳐 훈련된 것이라는 주장으로 무조건적 모성애를 강요하던 그 시대의 희생적 어머니상에 대한 모순과 불평등에 맞서는 데 주저함이 없으셨다.

비록 나혜석 선생님의 글에 나타나는 구시대 가부장적 풍습은 많이 사라졌기에 현시대에는 더 이상 적용되지 않는 먼 과거의 이야기로 보여질 수 있지만 사실, 오늘날 상당한 여성들의 경험에 아직도 관련이 깊다고 할 수 있다. 외부 문화와 사상의 유입이 풍성해져 경쟁이 고조로 이르렀던 조선 사회의 과도기 무렵, 신여성이 등장하여 그들의 새로운 이념과 구 관념과의 충돌이 있었던 것처럼 21세기가 된 지금의 남녀 모두 치열한 경쟁 속에 미투 운동과 같은 여권 신장 운동이 꽃피우면서 페미니즘은 여성이 남성의 몫을 빼앗고 앞질러 가 성공을 가로채는 오히려 역차별이라는 부당한 시선과 진정한 변화를 요구하는 간절한 목소리와의 끊임없는 투쟁은 계속되고 있다. 또한, 남성이 하는 여러 자유로운 행태 가운데 같은 여성의 행동은 더 큰 비난으로 향하는 이중 잣대, 육아와 일을 동시에 부담하는 어머니들의 시련, 성적 학대 피해자를 비방하는 거짓 소문들, 이렇게 빈약한 성교육으로부터 조선 여성들의 시달림은 오늘날까지 이어지고 있다. 그 당시 나혜석 선생님은 독자들이 자신의 작품과의 교감과 비판의식을 통한 사회적 변화를 굳게 믿으셨다. 사실, 오늘날, 시간의 경계를 초월하며 그녀의 글들은 현세대들에게 공감이 되며 먼 훗날의 세대에까지 울림이 될 것이다.

따라서 우리가 나혜석 선생님의 작품에서 배워야 할 점은 단지 조선 사회 남녀 관계에서 과거의 문제를 시사하는 바에 그치지 않고 세대를 걸쳐 내려져 왔던 사회의 제도 속에 묻힌 근본적인 원인을 깨달으며 어떻게 남녀 관습, 관례가 시간을 거쳐 진화해왔고 오늘날의 젠더 이슈로 형성해왔는지에 대해 알아가는 것이라고 생각한다.

　나혜석 선생님의 몇몇 작품들에 구체적으로 들어가자면, 초반 작품의 분위기, 주제, 캐릭터, 문체가 시간을 거슬러 후기 소설과 수필에서 진화한 것이 흥미롭다. 나혜석 선생님의 첫 소설은 1918년에 출판된『경희』였다. 그때는 나혜석 선생님이 도쿄 미술 학교에 재학 중인 초반 학생 시절이었기에 '경희'라는 인물은 여학생들을 둘러싼 오명과 고정관념을 깨뜨리면서 자신의 꿈과 야망을 쫓는 이상주의자로 등장한다. 그녀의 불타오르는 정신은 관습에 맞서는 것을 자극하는 동시에 집안일과 공부에 모두 다 출중해져 계속 돋보이도록 하며 가파르고 험난한 길을 걸어야만 했다. 결국, 경희는 여학생들을 험담하는 말에 대항하기 위해서 그 당시 남학생들에게는 부합되지 않아도 되는 엄격한 기준을 맞춰야만 하는 완벽주의자, 소위 슈퍼우먼(Superwoman)이 되어야 했다. 공부와 살림을 동시에 경쟁력 있게 부담하는 것은 경희의 유일한 생존 방책이었고 이는 그녀에게 전진하는 기운을 불어넣어 주었지만 동시에 조선 사회가 여성들에게 씌워왔던 높고 높은 책임감의 잣대를 보여주었다. 하지만 마지막 소설, 1937년에 출판된 나혜석의 후기 작품인『어머니와 딸』에서는 '영애'도 여학생이지만 경희와 구별되는 인물로 그려져 작가의 이상적 가치관의 진화와 나혜석 선생님이 양반집 딸로 자라며 처음에는 재정적 시련이 없었던 상황에서 나중에 경제적 시련으로 함몰하게 되었던 형편의 변화를 비춘다. 경희와 영애는 둘 다 결혼에 대한 강압을 받는 여학생으로 아주 유사하다. 두 인물을 갈라놓는 차이점은 사회·경제적 신분이다. 경희는 교육을 지원할 수 있는 양반 가족의 딸이지만 영애는 끝까지 아버지에 대한 언급조차 없이 공부를 계속할 경제적 여건이 되지 않는 여관

집 주인의 딸이다. 이 차이점으로 여성의 삶이 얼마나 사회·경제적 신분과 근접하게 맞물려 있는지 볼 수 있다.

또한, 경희와 영애는 교육의 열망이 있는 진보적인 신여성이라는 공통점이 있지만 자유에 대한 관념이 엇갈린다. 예를 들어, 경희는 하나만이 아닌 두 가지 책임, 공부와 집안일을 부담함으로써 사회에서 자신의 능력을 마음껏 펼치고자 하는 자유를 추구한다. 하지만, 영애는 집안일을 제쳐 두고 대신 개성을 펼치며 조선 사회에서 눈살 찌푸려지는 행위, 즉 자신을 위한 공부만 하며 이혼 남성과의 비밀 연애를 한다. 경희보다 영애는 경쟁심이 적고 더 느슨하며 집안일과 바느질을 능숙하게 하는 그 당시 성공적 여성의 잣대로부터 전혀 탈피한 다른 자유를 추구한다. 중매결혼 거절과 이혼 남성과의 비밀 로맨스는 그녀를 모델 부인, 모델 여성이 아닌 어머니로부터 애지중지를 받지 못한 딸이지만 오직 그녀의 자신만만한 격렬한 캐릭터는 사회적 관습에 파묻힌 많은 여성이 자유롭게 경험하지 못했을 용기로 해석될 수 있다.

1918년 『경희』에서 정략결혼의 구속을 거부한 자유의 패턴이 시작되어 1936년에 출판된 나혜석의 또 다른 작품인 『현숙』에서 새로운 자유의 의의가 등장한다. '현숙'이라는 인물은 한 남자만 만나야만 하는 사회적 구속을 넘어 여러 남자들을 만나고 자신의 처지로부터 자기 자신을 구하기 위해 바쁘게 돈을 벌며 다양한 직업, 웨이트리스, 화가의 모델, 회계원, 찻집 경영을 하는 것에서 자유를 찾는다. 따라서, 전반적인 작품들에 나혜석 선생님은 그 당시 다양한 계층의 여성들을 소개하며 관례적 성차별(Institutional Sexism)과 사회 경제적 형편에 관한 고민을 모색하였다. 또한, 조기 결혼에 경희와 영애의 "싫어요"가 자주적인 의지로 갑작스럽게 맺고 싶지 않은 관계를 미루고 자체적 결정을 하는 현숙의 "지금은 안 돼요"로 이어가며 이렇게 여성들의 목소리들이 쌓여 함께 모여 결국 오늘날의 여성들이 자신의 목소리를 내는데 길을 열어주었다.

나혜석 선생님의 소설과 수필들을 번역하면서 과도기 시절의 혼란 속에 쉽게 파묻혀질 수 있었던 그 시대의 마음을 사로잡으며 가슴을 울리는 조선 여성의 이야기들을 접하는 것만으로도 나에게는 영광이었고 큰 배움의 시간이었다. 또한, 작가의 진솔한 목소리를 들을 수 있어 번역하는 과정이 매우 즐거웠고 자신의 시련에 대해 솔직한 반면 결국 한층 밝은 미래를 위한 희망을 독자들에게 불어넣어 주시는 나혜석 선생님의 당당한 모습에 수없이 놀라며 감명을 받았다. 나혜석 선생님은 성공적인 화가에서 몇 년 후 이혼녀로서 배척을 당하고 인생의 달고 쓴 맛을 겪어 오시면서도 희망의 밧줄에 계속 매달려 있었다. 작품 출판에 쏟아진 비판, 특히, 주류 사회로부터 모성애와 결혼에 대한 그녀의 비정통적인 관점들로『모된 감상기』와『이혼 고백서』등 작품들에 대한 사회적 거부감을 받아왔음에도 나혜석 선생님은 언젠가 세상에 자신의 목소리가 들릴 것을 희망하였다. 오랜 시간이 걸렸지만 이제 나혜석 선생님의 목소리가 닿았을 뿐만 아니라 나를 포함한 독자들의 마음에 깊게 침투해올 것이다. 그분의 작품들을 번역함으로써 세상에 더 알리면서 나도 판도라의 상자에 희망을 잘 간직할 것이다. 점점 더 나혜석 선생님의 뜻이 국제적으로 넓게 전해질 수 있도록 하는 희망! 왜냐하면 세계일주를 한 최초의 한국 여성 개척자이며 서양 예술의 거인들에 깊은 감명을 받아왔던 나혜석 선생님은 글로벌하게 나아가기를 진정 원하셨을 것이기 때문이다. 끝으로 판도라 상자 밖으로 소중한 희망이 날아가지 않도록 잘 지켜지기를 기원하며…

노라*

나혜석

나는 인형이었네
아버지 딸인 인형으로
남편의 아내인 인형으로
그네의 노리개였네

노라를 놓아라
순순히 놓아다고
높은 장벽을 헐고
깊은 규문을 열어
자연의 대기 속에
노라를 놓아라

나는 사람이라네
남편의 아내 되기 전에
자식의 어미 되기 전에
첫째로 사람이 되려네

나는 사람이로세
구속이 이미 끊쳤도다
자유의 길이 열렸도다
천부의 힘은 넘치네

아아, 소녀들이여
깨어서 뒤를 따라오라
일어나 힘을 발하여라
새 날의 광명이 비쳤네

---

* 헨리크 입센의 『인형의 집』 주인공인 노라를 모티브로 한 시(1947년 출판).

Translator's Introduction in English

In Korean history textbooks, the term, New Women is cursorily mentioned, and such a tiny facet is covered that they have become generalized in our memory as modern women in the transitional period of Joseon (period of Japanese colonization of Korea) in the 1920s and 1930s, clad in copycat Western dresses, in bobbed hair, and frivolously frequenting banquets and dance parties like Daisy of *The Great Gatsby*. With a passing glimpse of New Women who have embraced materialism with an influx of Western cultures, they have been occasionally exploited by the Korean media, where their images were distorted into spendthrifts, indulgent in shopping, and obsessive about their physical appearances. In fact, such an image of New Women lingered in the subconscious layers of my mind. And, except for the patriotism of female independence activists of that time, I was in the dark about everything else in the lives of the everyday women of Joseon during the colonial period, such as their struggles, concerns, and even the dreams and ambitions they may have had in such a chaotic period.

That was until in Modern History of Korea, a class that I took in my sophomore year of university, Na Hye-seok came into my sight one day, upon reading her short stories and essays that contained the vivid portrayals of Joseon women from different walks of life, transcending the social biases against educated women, spinsters, widows, and divorced women. This was when I started to break free from my oblivion to women's issues of the early 20th century in Korea. Na Hye-seok was a progressive woman, the New Woman ahead of her times, educated abroad, the first Korean woman to have pioneered a trip to the West, the first Korean artist of Western painting who has had multiple successful exhibitions, but simultaneously, was also a mother of four children and a wife, with various experiences of hardships attached to family and marriage life. As a woman who loved the arts with a burning passion and trusted the stroke of her pen to tell her story, each of her literary works and essays are pieces that share the experiences of injustice in the face of outmoded marriage customs, misogynist norms surrounding issues of women's fidelity and chastity. The sharp and penetrating stories spoke out against injustice, whether it came in the character of a schoolgirl, prioritizing education over marriage, or a widow, afflicted with the double standards of society, and a divorcee, stained with a scarlet letter, or of a mother, criticizing the society that imposed maternal love.

While Na Hye-seok's stories touch on outmoded customs of patriarchy, many of which have faded away by now, and while readers may see them as a long-gone past that no longer apply in the 21st century, Na Hye-seok's stories are actually still quite relevant to the experiences of women today. Just as during the influx of cultures and ideas, in the peak of competition in Joseon's transitional period, when New Women clashed over their new ideals with the outmoded customs, in the 21st century, in the midst of an intense competition, with the burgeoning women's rights activism, such as the Me-Too movement, feminism has been unjustly decried by opposing sides as 'reverse discrimination,' taking away the piece of others' pie, stealing others' thunder, and ceaseless clashes with the demands for change have taken place. Also, the double standards that affront women over the same actions by men, or the issues of mothers managing the dual burdens of both childcare and work, or the slanders and rumors against victims of sexual abuse from the lack of sex education in Joseon society are still pertinent to the experiences of women today. Na Hye-seok had once said that she hoped and trusted that her readers would come to relate with the experiences she had written in her works. In fact, even to this day, transcending the boundaries of time, her writings resonate with generations of the present and would reverberate beyond.

Thus, I believe that the takeaway from reading Na Hye-seok's pieces is not solely to make a foray into the gender issues of the past, but also to realize their roots buried under the social institution, passed down over generations, and take note of how the old customs and practices of men and women have evolved over time to shape into the gender issues of today.

To get into the specifics of one of Na Hye-seok's works, it is interesting to note how the atmosphere, themes, characters, and style of writing of her earlier stories over time evolved in her later works of fiction and essays. Na Hye-seok's first fiction was *Kyeonghee*, which was published in 1918. As it was during an earlier period in Na Hye-seok's life, at a time when she was a student studying in Tokyo Arts College, Kyeonghee as a character comes off as an idealist with dreams and ambitions of her own that she chases after by breaking the stigma and stereotypes surrounding schoolgirls and educated women. At the same time that her fiery spirit pushes her to go against the convention, still, even her constant efforts to stand out by trying to excel in both housekeeping and in her studies necessitate walking along a precipitous, rocky pathway. After all, this shows how in order to stand against the ill-spoken rumors of schoolgirls, Kyeonghee was faced with no choice but to be a perfectionist, a so-called superwoman, having to meet rigorous standards that schoolboys did not have to abide by at the time. It was a means of survival for Kyeonghee to be both a student and a housekeeper, which altogether evoked her progressive spirit, but simultaneously was a manifestation of the high standards of responsibility that Joseon society put on women. However, in Na Hye-seok's later fiction, called *Mother and Daughter*, which was the last fiction published, in the year of 1937, Yeongae, also a schoolgirl, diverges from Kyeonghee as a character that reflects the evolution of Na Hye-seok's ideal beliefs and was reflective of the change of the author's circumstance from initially being in well-to-do financial circumstances as a Yangban (Upper class in Joseon) that later plunged into economic strife. Kyeonghee and Yeongae could be parallel in terms of how they are both schoolgirls who are pestered into marrying. The differences that set the two characters apart would be a difference in socio-economic status. Kyeonghee appears in the story as the daughter of a Yangban family (Upper class family in Joseon) that could afford to provide her education, whereas Yeongae is a daughter of the landlady of an inn, with her father absent throughout the rest of the story, and without the financial means to pursue further education. The difference itself induces recognition of how the education and the socio-economic status of women were closely interrelated as well.

Also, Kyeonghee and Yeongae, while both possessed of the progressive spirit of a New Woman with a desire for education, clearly diverge in terms of their notion of freedom. For instance, Kyeonghee shows the image of a New Woman capable of undertaking not just one but dual responsibilities of shouldering her studies and housekeeping, and by doing so, pursues her freedom to showcase her versatility. However, Yeongae neglects her housework, and instead, pursues education and a secret romance with a divorced man, which manifests the individuality of a woman, frowned upon in the Joseon society at the time. Compared to Kyeonghee, Yeongae appears to be less competitive, much looser, and sets out towards a different freedom by breaking away altogether from the social standard for a successful woman, which was to be proficient in housework and sewing. Turning down an arranged marriage and having a secret romance with a divorcé does not make her the model wife, the model woman, and not certainly, the apple-of her mother's eye, but her brash, impetuous qualities translate into courage that may not have been freely experienced by many other women buried under the social conventions.

This pattern of freedom that starts in *Kyeonghee*, showing the passion of a schoolgirl, driven to study, refusing to get confined into the tethers of marriage extends to a freedom in Na Hye-seok's other work, *Hyeon-sook*, published in 1936. Hyeon-sook goes beyond the social fetters that bind women into a relationship with one man, by going from one man to another man, employed in multiple jobs, busy earning money to save herself from her circumstances. That is, by working as a waitress, a painter's model, and a cashier, with plans of her own to manage a tea house. Thus, throughout the course of Na Hye-seok's works, she has introduced a wide range of women from different backgrounds, revealing their concerns in relation to both the institutional sexism and socio-economic circumstances. Whether it would be with Kyeonghee and Yeongae's "No" to early marriage, and Hyeon-sook's "Not now" to her lover, making an independent decision of her own will and autonomy to put off a relationship she did not want to abruptly dive into, at the end of the day, such women's voices have each piled up and come together to pave the way for other women to come forward with their voices today.

While translating Na Hye-seok's fictions and essays into English, I was greatly honored just to have come across such rich, captivating, resonating stories of a woman of the Joseon society, which could have been easily buried under the ravages of a chaotic transitional time. In the process of translating them, I had so much fun, getting to hear her authentic voice, and remember numerous occasions when I have been amazed and inspired by how despite being honest about her struggles, still, she managed to uplift the readers with hope for a brighter future at the very end. Na Hye-seok herself, who had her ups and downs in her life, from being a successful painter to being downtrodden after becoming a divorcee, years later, still held onto a rope of hope. That despite the criticisms that poured from the publication of her works, particularly *A Report on Becoming a mother* and *Confessions of a Divorcee*, spurned by the mainstream society for her unorthodox views about maternal love and marriage, she still hoped that one day, her voice would be heard. While it has taken a long time, indeed, her voice has not only reached but also deeply penetrated into the heart and soul of readers, including mine. By translating her works, I also set out to keep my hope safeguarded in Pandora's Box, the hope that more and more people would come to hear Na Hye-seok's voice, even internationally. As Na Hye-seok was the Korean female pioneer of a trip around the world, deeply inspired by the literary giants and artists of the West, she would have wanted to be a global figure more than ever. May such a cherished hope be secured so that it does not flutter away from Pandora's Box.

Nora*

I was a doll
A doll that was the daughter of my father
A doll that was the wife of my husband
I was their plaything

Let go of Nora, let go of her gently
Tear down the high walls
Open the deep gate of her house
Into the atmosphere of nature
Let go of Nora

I am a person
Before being the wife of a husband
Before being the mother of a child
Before being the daughter of a father
First, I am going to be a person

I am a person
The confinement has already come to an end
The path of freedom has opened
The innate strength is bursting

Ah ah, girls
Wake up and follow on
Stand up and radiate your strengths
The hope of a new day has lit up

---

* A poem written by Na Hye-seok as an inspiration from a character named Nora from
A Doll's House, a play by Henrik Ibsen(Published in 1947).

C·O·N·T·E·N·T·S

1. Fiction

2. Nonfiction

1. Fiction

Kyeonghee

Chapter 1.

"Oh my! How heavy the monsoon rain is," said the porky lady-in-law, the mother-in-law of Kyeonghee's sister, while lighting a pipe, having visited after a long time.

"Right. There would've been children falling ill in this heavy rainfall. I'm sorry that I didn't send the servant even once to look after your grandchildren," Madam Kim, speckled with white hair and a forehead manifesting a couple of wrinkles, the wife of Lee Cheolwon (the head of the house) replied, while sitting face-to-face and lighting a pipe.

"Not at all. Neither was I able to do so. My grandchildren are doing well, but their mother has been complaining of a stomach ache since a few days ago and today, I saw her wake up and set out."

"The day should be moderately hot. If something goes wrong even a little bit, it's easy to get sick. So, you must've been worried."

"She's now recovered, so I'm well-assured. By the way, you must be happy that your daughter has come back from Japan," the lady-in-law spoke, as if she was suddenly reminded of the fact.

"At first, after sending her far away, I didn't have a peace of mind, but as she comes home at least once a year, our family is re-assured," said Madam Kim, tapping her pipe on the ashtray.

"I can see that, because even if it were a son, it wouldn't have been reassuring, but to send a girl far abroad, wouldn't it be concerning? By the way, how is her health?"

"Yes, I do wonder if she was sick sometimes. She says she hasn't had any trouble, but I think she's just saying that to relieve me of my concerns as a mother, and she may have gone hungry and had her share of pains. That is why she looks haggard," said Madam Kim. Then, turning towards the backside, she addressed, "My dear child, the lady-in law came over to see you."

"Okay."

Kyeonghee replied, who had just now been sitting in the cool back porch with her sister-in-law whom she met in a long time, where her sister-in-law was sewing the beoseon (traditional Korean socks), while Kyeonghee was making the undershirt of her sister-in-law's suit with the sewing machine, and conversing about her time in Japan. About the day when she had almost been hit by the streetcar, while going somewhere, and so, how even now, reflecting back, her body still feels the narrow escape from peril. About how in winter, she did not ever sleep with her legs stretched out and when waking up in the morning, finding her legs stiff. About the day when there would be rainfall every other day in Japan, and once, the rain was pouring heavily, the school would open at a late hour, and she had been busily on her way in her high-heeled wooden shoes, when she tripped, consequently tearing the skin of her legs, her umbrella all ripped up, and as she got dirt splayed over her clothes, how embarrassed she was. About her studying in school. And, as she got to the story about what she saw, while walking the streets, sharing a story half-way about a certain time when she watched a scene in a motion picture where a child was writing an advertisement of selling one's father and posting it on a huge tree outside the door of the house, after the father deterred the child from kidding around, and right at that moment, a brother and sister of similar age to the child, of six and seven years-old were straying, having lost their parents, pulled out their remaining two pennies, knocking on the door to buy the father, accordingly with this advertisement. Her sister-in-law in no time put the sewing needle on top of her knee and she had been sitting there, joyfully listening to her talk, laughing, "Haha, Hoho," asking, "So, what happened?" and then, with a frown creasing her face, she sincerely requested, "Go and get back soon."

Even Siwol who had been sitting there, listening with rapt attention, while doing laundry and feeding the grass at the side clucked her tongue.

"Sure, I'll go and quickly come back," replied Kyeonghee and walked over to the front porch, wearing a grin, from her delight at others being entertained with her story.

Kyeonghee modestly bowed down before the lady-in-law. While she had forgotten about bowing for a year, upon her return home, last time, she bowed before her father and mother. This was why she was quite familiar with the bowing that she did this time. Kyeonghee reflected on the times in Japan when every day, she had pranced around from left to right, kidding around and now here she was, so calmly behaved, and at that, she grinned from ear to ear.

"Oh dear, how come such good looks you had turned out in this shape, how burdened you were."

The lady-in-law said in a merciful tone. She deliberately caught hold of and clasped Kyeonghee's wrist.

"Your hand really seems like the hand of someone who led a married life. Other schoolgirls have silk-like hands, but why is your hand like that?"

"It's because the texture of my hand isn't delicate."

Kyeonghee lowered her head.

"It's because she did the laundry and cooked all by herself."

Kyeonghee's mother said, lighting her pipe again.

"Oh my, then, you're doing what you're not doing at home while abroad. Does your Japanese school stipulate that?"

The lady-in-law was quite taken aback. Kyeonghee remained silent.

"No, it's not like that. It's because she put herself through a load of work. Who would do all that under someone's order? Although I sufficiently cover her school fees, strangely, she says she finds joy in being busy."

Madam Kim unintentionally told what she had heard from her

daughter in her seat last night.

"Why do you burden yourself?"

The lady-in-law tucked the strands of hair that came down from above Kyeonghee's forehead beneath her ears, touched the flesh of her back through the top of her unlined summer jacket, and caressed her face.

"I heard that in Japan, even in winter, the fire isn't lit. And, so few of the side dishes are given that they leave the appetite unsatisfied. How do you live like that?"

"Yes, even though the fire isn't lit, it doesn't matter when I could endure the cold. Also, side dishes are given in an amount sufficient for eating, so it's not really like that."

"Even if it were not so, it's a burden for everyone. By the way, your sister, due to falling ill, wasn't able to see you in the meanwhile. Maybe she will come in the evening."

"Yes, please send her. I've been wanting to see her for a long time."

"Of course. When I heard that you returned, I also wanted to see you, but wouldn't siblings be missing each other?"

The lady-in-law expressed deep empathy in these words, as originally, after getting married far-away from home, she had the experience of greatly missing her parents and siblings.

"Are you going to Japan again? Now, why don't you settle down here graciously and get married to a wealthy family, have sons and daughters, and live a jolly good life? Why would you have to burden yourself like that?"

It was as if the lady-in-law was telling Kyeonghee something that was not acted upon, due to a lack of knowledge, and directed her eyes at Kyeonghee's mother who sat facing her, as if to say, "Isn't that quite true? What I'm saying is right."

"Yes, I have to go there until I complete my studies."

"What is the use of doing so much of that studying? Is this a lad setting out to be a county magistrate? Is this to become the administrator of a district? Now, in this world, even an educated lad struggles because he is of no use."

The lady-in-law was unusually pressed with concerns. Ever since long ago, she had been frustrated as to why on earth Madam and Mr., the parents of her daughter-in-law (Kyeonghee's sister) would send a girl all the way to Japan to give her education and what she was going to do with all that studying, but nevertheless, since this was unlike other families, where it concerned the family of her daughter-in-law, she had always stowed away in her mind the deprecating thoughts, such as, 'Who would get married with that girl?' and as much as she could, she pretended to be oblivious, but today, at the coincidentally golden opportunity, she spilled the concerns that she has had.

Kyeonghee had known that this would definitely come rolling out of the lady-in-law's mouth, 'Go get married as soon as possible. What's the use of all that studying?' She thought to herself, 'Indeed, I knew she was going to say that.' Which were the words that emanated from the lips of her auntie (the sister of Kyeonghee's mother) who came over yesterday and all consistent with what her other auntie (the wife of the elder brother of Kyeonghee's father) spoke out of concern whenever she saw Kyeonghee. She heard again during the summer of this year what had been browbeaten to her during last year's summer. Kyeonghee found herself itching to talk back.

'It's not only to do with eating or wearing clothes, but to learn and know in order to be a human being. The fact that in your family, your sons have four concubines is because they've not learned, and your lack of knowledge is to blame for your suffering due to the fact. The thing is when a woman gets married into your household, you have to instruct your sons not to see concubines, and when having a wife, teach them not to have concubines at all,' Kyeonghee could barely suppress the urge to speak. Besides this, she wished to bring up many examples and explain. However, she certainly knew that what would emanate from the mouth of the lady-in-law would be aligned with what her grandmother had told her in a visit this morning, "Child, ever since the past, a woman did not have to be educated and still lived a long, rich life with many sons. A woman was blessed when she did not know the four cardinal points, North, South, East and West. Even schoolgirls who were educated ended up milling rice. Besides, if a lad doesn't even know how to have a single concubine, then how is that a lad?" Kyeonghee reflected that she would only be preaching to deaf ears, would merely tire her mouth, and that she alone would not be able to sleep this evening, caught up again in this thought. Once she would start running her mouth again, she would be so frustrated that it would be as if her insides would be burning like fire, and naturally, if the conversation were to last long, she pictured the others waiting in the back porch, and so, instead, altogether shut her mouth. Besides, she knew that the lady-in-law had a spiteful tongue, and so, if she heard one word against her, the lady-in-law would have a string of ten words that would supplement lies that if it were the remark of a schoolgirl, whatever it may be, the lady-in-law had a way with finding fault with it and springing insults on it. This was why Kyeonghee assumed that whatever excuse or explanations that were seldom made would fail to even in the slightest reach the ears of this lady-in-law. And, at a certain time, Kyeonghee's sister requested her, "Hey, don't say a word against my mother-in-law. All the more, do care not to talk about marriage. It's because my mother-in-law says, 'Schoolgirls have no scruples about discussing the notion of marriage. Oh dear, how much absurdity there is in this world. When we were growing up, where would a girl dare to speak her views on marriage.' Not only that, my mother-in-law picks up on the rumors against many of the schoolgirls from someplace that when she hears them and comes back, she alludes to them for me to hear, which is quite distasteful to me, because indeed, my sister is a student. My mother-in-law speaks ill of all sorts like if a girl goes abroad to Japan, she is bound to be ruined. So, by all means, please watch your mouth."

Kyeonghee felt her heart pounding out of her chest at what may again burst out of the mouth of the lady-in-law. So, even before another conversation would kick off, she was racing to escape to the back porch.

"I have to get going, because I have work left to do, to make the undershirt of the suit that my sister-in-law will be wearing later in a moment."

Kyeonghee said, evading the front porch with as much relief as having a decaying tooth plucked out, and scampered to the back porch, letting out a sigh once.

"How come you are so late? So, what did the child in the motion picture do to the father?"

Meanwhile, the sister-in-law had one of a pair of beoseon (Traditional Korean socks) all sewed up and put the other one of the pair to the front of her cheeks, and the moment she saw Kyeonghee, she placed the beoseon on top of her knees and closely sat right by her side, asking her, as if to prompt the ending of a story she has wondered about. Kyeonghee's eyebrows pinched together in a deep frown. Kyeonghee's two cheeks twitched. Siwol was doing her laundry and upon taking a glimpse of Kyeonghee's face, got wind of what may have happened.

"Miss, did the lady-in-law talk to you about marriage again?"

In the morning, after her grandmother made a visit, on the porch, Kyeonghee went on a parade of self-talk, grumbling to herself, "Even if I were to get married when the moment comes, now that I hear about it so many times, I hate it so much." Siwol had picked up on these words in the kitchen. Although Siwol could not specifically hear it now, Kyeonghee seemed to be saying such words. That was why she thought Miss's face denoted such a jaundiced look. Kyeonghee forced a smile. And, clasping the sewing needles, she went on with the rest of the story.

On the front porch, the lady-in-law and Madam Kim were still drinking to each other's spirits and smoking their pipes, deep in their conversation about Kyeonghee.

"Does your child do all the sewing?"

"Yes, she is quite good at sewing. Although she doesn't know how to sew a man's upper garment, she knits her clothes and wears them."

"Oh dear, how did she manage to learn sewing in such a short time? Like knowing how to make the undershirt of a suit. Do students all know how to sew?"

Indeed, the lady-in-law already knew that there were schoolgirls who did not even know how to properly hold a needle. Besides, it came as a shock to the lady-in-law that Kyeonghee, who flocked like any other schoolboy to Seoul and to Japan to study, actually knew how to sew her clothes. Yet, as expected, the lady-in-law wondered how bad Kyeonghee must be at sewing.

Although it seemed to Madam Kim that it could come off as praising her daughter, she deigned to respond to the question.

"Is there ever a time to properly settle down to learn sewing? Still, as she gradually matures, she seems to naturally develop an intent to carry it out. There was no need for me to teach her, as she came to naturally take up sewing. Doing difficult studies seemed to have brewed such an intention."

Madam Kim fleetingly halted and spoke again. In the ears of the lady-in-law, it all seemed to be a lie.

"Last summer, every day, Kyeonghee frequented the training school for using a sewing machine, needlework that was taught by a Japanese woman outside Namdaemun, learning how to make the undershirt of a suit. She knitted the suits for her niece to put them on and knitted the hats for them to wear and even the summer suit for her brother. As she knows Japanese and because she became close to her sewing school teacher, Kyeonghee started teaching even what wasn't taught to others. In the daytime, she learned more of sewing and starting from midnight until one in the morning, she drew out exactly what she saw from her learning and wrote down all the measurements. I wondered what that was and later, the director of the sewing machine company came to me and said, 'All this time, the sewing classes were in Japanese, which made it hard to teach the madams, but the sewing book that your daughter made would come to great use.' Hearing his words, I learned that it seems to be the case. It's that with a bit of education, she is quite useful anywhere. Not only that, she is held in such high esteem by the respectable Japanese folks. Even the director purposely came over again the other day after being informed somewhere of her return. Once she graduates from Japan, he said that she should certainly work for his sewing company. He said that at first, it would be easy for her to earn 1,500 nyang (a unit of old Korean coinage). As the salary goes up gradually, in 3 years, she will be able to earn 2,500 nyang. The most that other girls earn is 750 nyang, but perhaps, it must be because Kyeong-hee studied, all the way, abroad in Japan. Even Kyeonghee made that with the sewing machine."

Saying this, she pointed with her chin at the embroidery, hanging on the glass wall, facing the opposite side, which was a scenery of the countryside, where, at the front, water was flowing and at the back, it was brimming with trees. Kyeonghee's mother here did not mean to talk all the way about her daughter. Before she knew it, she had naturally babbled all the way up to talking about her daughter's earnings. More than any other madams, and even more than the lady-in-law, Madam Kim was very much of an enlightened woman. Even, it was of her intrinsic character that she resisted speaking ill of what others said, and yet, as Madam Kim mostly took so much pride in her own daughter, Kyeonghee, she deliberately set out to find fault with the rumors about schoolgirls not being able to sew, not doing laundry, and not knowing how to work on housekeeping. Still, it also had been an enigma to Madam Kim like the other madams as to what Kyeonghee would be doing with her studies, why Kyeonghee was pursuing her academics, all the way abroad in Japan, and what she would put to use once she graduates. By any chance, when the question was posed by many women in clusters, "What is your daughter going to be doing with all that studying?" she could do nothing but vaguely formulate a response that she has always heard from her son, "Who knows? In this world, even girls should be educated." Indeed, Madam Kim did know. She knew that the more one studied, the more one was treated with respect and even with higher earnings. It was the fact that a respectable director, clad in a highly polished suit and a gold watch strap, intentionally came to seek a small girl like Kyeonghee, had bowed numerous times, and despite the earnings of elementary school teachers who toil and trouble themselves from morning till' night, for 30 days, for a month, being limited to 620 nyang at most and on average 500 nyang, at his words, "While frolicking around leisurely, if Kyeonghee would nicely set up the two pairs of folding screen in a year, I will definitely offer her a salary of 40 won (2,000 nyang)," Madam Kim came to learn that indeed, education was a must and if one gets educated, rather than doing it a little, it ought to be that one should be sent all the away to Japan to be educated. Maybe, it was all because of this that Kyeonghee had uttered one day during dinner, "If I am to take up my studies, I have to study a lot. If then, not only would I be respected by others but I would be able to play a part as a person." From now on, without an inkling of doubt, and with certainty, it dawned on Madam Kim as to why her son had insisted on sending Kyeonghee all the way to Japan, and in the world at present, girls needed to be educated as much as boys. So, until now, even though when Madam Kim got bombarded by the question from someone, "What is the point of educating your daughter that much?" the beads of sweat pooled on her back, her face flushed beet red, and whenever she was in such a state, she had found herself seized by numerous thoughts that if it were not for her son, she would have wanted to take Kyeonghee as soon as possible and get her married, now that she thought about it, she reflected that it was fortunate that her son stood behind insisting against it that she and her husband did not take Kyeonghee to get her married. And, from now on, whoever it is that would be questioning her, it seemed like she would be able to clearly explain to them that even a girl needed to be educated, in order to be imbued with the intent to know how to sew on her own, and that in order to be treated with deference, Kyeonghee had to be encouraged to pursue a lot of her studies, getting sent all the way to Japan. That was why, even today, facing the lady-in-law and unwittingly speaking up to this point, Madam Kim did not hesitate in the slightest and a glimmer of happiness shone wide across her face, as if her eyes manifested the expression of, 'I'm basking in such a glory, and I take such pleasure in it.'

The lady-in-law listened to the rest of the story, anyhow, half-in-doubt. Initially, not only did she regard the story of Madam Kim as a tale of lies, but she thought to herself, while glaring at the eyes and lips of Madam Kim who was sharing the story, 'Now that you've abandoned your eldest daughter, you're now concerned about getting her married that you're embellishing this praise on her.' However, with the story becoming even lengthier, it seemed to be quite true. Besides, when she heard the talk about the director coming over, how Kyeonghee was held in high esteem, and being promised a salary of 2,000 nyang, earnings that surpassed the expectations of boys and even the normal administrators of districts, it made her doubt that Madam Kim could be lying to that extent. Although the lady-in-law did not want to see them as truthful words, the words of Madam Kim did not come off as lies. Also, the embroidery hanging on the wall was clearly within her sight and her ears right then caught the sound of the sewing machine's wheels rolling ceaselessly. The lady-in-law was thoroughly perplexed. It seemed a huge failure on her part. Her conscience stirred on its own as she repented and gave in. 'I've had misconceptions about schoolgirls. Like the daughter of this family, I really need to get my girls educated. I got to go home and soon, starting from tomorrow, I got to send my granddaughters, whom I used to segregate from boys, off to school,' she firmly made up her mind. Her vision started dimming and her ears rang. She sat there, merely blinking, at a loss for words. Amongst the cool wind that blew in from the backyard was a youthful laughter that amusingly came in engulfing as much as it could take to break the porcelain dishes.

Chapter 2.

"What are you doing in this blistering weather, miss?"

The tteok-seller put down the bowl of tteok (Korean rice-cake) at the end of the porch, utterly bereft of strength and wiped off her sweat. Her face was interlaced with a swaggering expression, with Pyongyang-styled hair, wearing a colorful towel haphazardly, made out of a silk-like fabric, weaved out of a silk-thread, and as a tteok-seller in her forties, she was in the habit of visiting Kyeong-hee's house once a day.

"I'm playing around, because I'm bored," the tteok-seller said.

In her apron, Kyeonghee was standing on the edge of the porch and was clumsily chopping off the onions.

"When did you learn how to make kimchi in a short-while? I've not seen Miss once playing around, each day that I've come over to this place. When you're not reading, you're writing, and when you're not sewing, you're making kimchi like that."

"What do you find extraordinary about a girl doing her own work?"

"It's only you, miss and what other schoolgirl would have the heart to do such an undertaking?"

The tteok-seller tapped her knees and sat closely in front of Kyeonghee. Kyeonghee put on a wide smile.

"You are quite mistaken, tteok-seller. Aren't schoolgirls also human? Don't schoolgirls also have to wear clothes and eat in order to live?"

"Oh, yeah. Who said otherwise? It's just that are there any other schoolgirls as all-knowing as you, miss?"

"Should I buy tteok, worth around 20 nyang (a unit of old Korean coinage), since I've been showered with praises?"

"Oh my, you've misjudged me. Here, I wasn't intending to sell tteok by praising you."

The flesh of the tteok-seller's cheeks, which were full of whim, sagged. And, her fat lips twitched, out of sheer disappointment at Kyeonghee's misjudgment. Kyeonghee cast a side glance at her. She assumed what the tteok-seller was feeling.

"No, I said that on purpose about buying tteok from you. It's because it felt good to be complimented."

"No, no. It's not just a compliment, it really is true."

Once again, the tteok-seller amicably sat right by her side and let out a hearty laughter, "Hoho······."

"I've never seen someone like Miss who doesn't even take a nap once and works at any cost, as I've come over and seen you every day in how many years."

"You've not seen me sleep before you came over to sell tteok and after you, tteok-seller left."

"Again, you're spewing out amusing things. A tteok-seller comes over at any time in the morning, in the daytime, and even in the evening. It's not like it is with students going to school at a set time. Yeah! Isn't that right?"

Saying this, the tteok-seller looked over at Siwol, who was grinding the starch in a millstone at a narrow wooden porch. At this, Siwol said, "That's right. If not for the times when she was ill, I've never once seen her take a nap."

"Dear tteok-seller, what if the tteok gets all spoiled, while you're leisurely sitting by and talking?" said Kyeonghee.

"No, it doesn't matter."

The voice of the tteok-seller was entirely drained of energy. The tteok-seller had a lot of gossips to share if miss would only be interested, asking, "So, what happened?" The story that the tteok-seller heard from the workers who pounded rice into flour, which was about how these days, a schoolgirl set out for school and after a few days since her disappearance, upon search for her, she was discovered having been seduced by a boy and having become a concubine, the story of a schoolgirl being brought in as a daughter-in-law and how she struggled to even find the thread to sew the beoseon (Korean traditional socks) that she suffered a mental spasm that threw her off balance, the story of a schoolgirl who burned half of the rice that she made, and such stories that attempted to denounce schoolgirls pervaded in all directions, where she heard each string of word on average, which were boundless. That was why earlier, the tteok-seller had been high in spirits, tapping her knees and sitting right up close, straining to spill the gossips, and yet, at Kyeonghee's cold, measured reply, what came bubbling up to the surface within the tteok-seller turned off like the bubbles that popped. The tteok-seller needlessly drowned in a pit of sadness, as if she had lost something. She wondered as to whether or not she should stand up, holding the tteok basket, but found that she could not. So, she sat there, dazedly with her two hands pressed against the tteok basket, and feigning ignorance, frantically glanced up and down at Kyeonghee chopping onions, at the floor, while counting the number of small portable dining tables placed on top of the rack.

"Please bring out the white tteok worth around five nyang, and the Gaepi tteok worth half of two nyang."

Madam Kim had been lying, sprawled out on top of the neat

mat, fanning herself and pulled out the money from her pocket to demand Gaepi tteok that her daughter, Kyeonghee liked and the white tteok that her son enjoyed eating.

The tteok-seller had been absent-mindedly sitting, was taken by surprise, and after repeatedly counting the number of tteok that she was told to bring forth, she pulled them out and without even turning her back, she was leaving, carrying the tteok basket, when caught up with the thought that should she not come back again to this house, she would not be able to sell tteok, said, "Miss, I'll come back again tomorrow. Ha ha ha," and setting out to the main gate, let out a deep sigh. Kyeonghee's sister-in-law who wore a patch of string (which adjusted the end of a collar and the opposite side) of a durumagi (traditional Korean overcoat) of a raw silk fabric, Kyeonghee, and Siwol looked up at each other's faces and grinned from ear to ear, without a word. Kyeonghee was basking in happiness. It was as if she had accomplished something. Now that the tteok-seller would no longer be bad-mouthing again about other school girls, Kyeonghee thought she had greatly educated the tteok-seller. Kyeonghee was deep in thoughts as she sat, holding the hilt of the kitchen knife.

"There's really nothing that child can't do."

These words simply emanated from a woman whose face filled to the brim with consternation as she sat, gloomily clasping her two fingers together and after uttering this, firmly shut her mouth again and ceaselessly sighed, who seemed to have humongous worries and sorrow. As this woman has had a close relationship with Kyeonghee's family for about twenty years, Kyeonghee's siblings called her ma'am and this woman treated them with affection like they were her nephew and niece by blood. So, when she was bored, she would pay a visit to this house and even when she was feeling upset, she would come over for a laugh. Yet, the woman's face was always scrunched up with a black cloud hanging over her and whether or not she would see good things or have joyful experiences, in the end, undoubtedly, she would deeply sigh with the sadness that piled and piled up, and if one knew the cause of it, anyone would not fail to sympathize with her.

This woman was a senile widow and so, after she lost her husband, she suffered grief and a spasm of pain in her stomach and the only fun she had and took pleasure in her life was a post-humous child that was fortunately born, named Sunam. After a day, Sunam grew bit by bit and after a year, Sunam turned one-year old. When winter came, she worried that it would be too cold, and when summer came, she worried that it would be too hot, and at night, as he was sleeping, she would pat the plump cheeks of the peacefully sleeping Sunam a couple of times. Such a precious son of hers that she cherished most in the world in no time approached the age of sixteen and from all-around, the request for marriage with his son came up constantly. Sunam's mother would find joy alone in newly having a daughter-in-law, but as she thought of receiving pyebaek (a traditional Korean ceremony for the newly-wedded couple to pay respect to the bride's family right after their wedding) solitarily, in the absence of her husband, she shed many tears in her seat. Yet, by chance, the act of shedding tears like this could be ominous to her precious son, and so, she attempted to think of her sadness as happiness, as much as she could, and made efforts to shift her tears into a smile. So, she thriftily gathered whatever money, jewelry and the like to give them for the time when she would have a daughter-in-law. There were many things that she avoided and things that she tried to attain in order to get her only son married. As it has been said that a son was bound to live poorly when a mother herself sought out a daughter-in-law, Sunam's mother entirely arranged a marriage for her son solely based on their marital compatibility. All this time, she had pictured in her head the days when her family would be rowdy and bursting with joy as she brought in a new daughter-in-law, and see a granddaughter as precious as jade and a grandson as precious as gold, which turned out to be that her imagination became a foe that was making her deeply sigh today. Since the age of seventeen when her daughter-in-law had gotten married with her son, for eight long years, her daughter-in-law failed to stitch a single jeogori (upper garment of Korean traditional clothes) and has never tenderly given it to her. She was a daughter-in-law that left a deep-rooted enmity within the heart of the mother-in-law. As it was in Sunam's mother's nature to be mild and benevolent, she made a gazillion attempts to properly teach and reform her daughter-in-law, beating herself up, unbeknownst to others. Alone, she made an exhaustive study of whether it'd be better if she were to do this and if she were to do that, whether

her daughter-in-law would be a person, admonished and coached her countless times, and yet, yesterday was like today, and tomorrow was one and the same. When she would give a needle for her daughter-in-law to hold in her hand, her daughter-in-law would soon sit dozing off, and when she would order her daughter-in-law to make rice, porridge was made instead, but to add, on top of it, her daughter-in-law was turning even more outlandish over time, with age, which left her, a mother-in-law all the more flabbergasted. As it was like this, it was inevitable that Sunam's mother, who would on occasion feel the hurt and day by day get shocked would only release a deep sigh whenever she came over to this house, at the sight of the daughter-in-law in Kyeonghee's family calmly stitching the jeogori (upper garment of Korean traditional clothes) of her mother-in-law, wondering why she does not ever get to have and wear a single jeogori, stitched by the hand of her daughter in-law, and at the sight of the diligence of Kyeonghee, she would wonder as to how come she did not bring in such a nimble-witted daughter-in-law. So, while sitting from afar like this, looking at Kyeonghee making Kimchi and after the tteok-seller chattered for a long-while, then left, she had made this simple comment that there was nothing that child could not do, and at the end of it, had let out a deep sigh, whose face Kyeonghee could not bear to see. Kyeonghee who had bent her head and had been absorbed with her chopping already was aware of the cause of the woman's sorrow and so, when the deep sigh reached her ears, she felt a tingling in her whole body that she could sympathize with the woman. At the same time that Kyeonghee felt stimulated by this, it was as if the unfortunate circumstances of many families in Joseon right then unfolded before her sight. As she hit the chopping board with the hilt of her knife, and with great force, she seemed to have made a huge determination. Kyeonghee firmly swore to herself, 'The family that I will be having will never be that kind of family. Not only me, but I won't let the family that my children, my friends, and my students will be making end up as unfortunate as this. Yes, I will definitely accomplish it.' Kyeonghee leaped into action. She went after Siwol who had been sweating profusely in the kitchen while boiling starch.

"Hey, let's do it together. Should I sit on the wood-burning stove and stir with the starch rod? Should I sit in front of the furnace and stoke the fire? What do you want me to do? I'll do whatever you tell me to do. I know how to do both of them."

"My goodness. Leave it alone. It's hot here."

Siwol had been struggling to stir the starch and stoke the fire on her own, even in the heat.

"Oh, damn you." Kyeonghee complained with her eyes wide open, and as Kyeonghee settled down to pull out and burn the wheat straw, to Siwol, this single string of words from Miss was like the wind in the stifling heat and a laughter (as a remedy) in her distress. Siwol thought to herself, 'During dinner, I got to get some tasty corns that Miss likes from somewhere, get them steamed, and bring them to her.' Reluctantly, she said,

"Then, stoke the fire. I will stir the starch."

"Alright. You who've been at it for a long time do the challenging one."

Kyeonghee stoked the fire and Siwol stirred the starch. Above, the boiling sound and below, the sound of the sparks flying up from the wheat straw, they resonated in Kyeonghee's ears as the sounds of an orchestral musical performance that she heard from the concert at Tokyo Music School. Also, within the furnace, as the fire was caught at the end of the wheat straw and its beam expanded with a gradual force, simultaneously, as little by little, it neared its way to the furnace and its flame dwindled steadily, it appeared to her as if when she was playing a piano from that end to this end, the buzzing sound gradually became taut. At the thought that Siwol sitting there and working her way through stirring would not know of such kind of fun, Kyeonghee reflected on how happy she was at being able to in the slightest know this feeling of a subtle sense of beauty. Yet, at the thought that there would be others who could feel the subtle sense of beauty tens of hundreds of times more than her, she wanted to pop her own eyes out and bash her brains in as a sacrificial offering. The red spark all of a sudden turned a bluish light. She doubted and thought, 'Ah, am I still a human being,' 'Food was wasted on me.' Unwittingly, she said, "This is rather fun."

"How come Miss finds all sorts of things fun? When you're doing laundry, you say it is such a joy to be a witness to the flowing grimy water and when you're mopping the floor, you say you take pleasure in seeing something murky at one side of the narrow wooden veranda that hasn't been mopped yet, and when you sweep the floor, you say that you enjoy the fact that there is a lot of gathering dust, and coming to think of what else you would also find to be fun later on, do you enjoy seeing the maggot getting boiled in the lavatory?"

Kyeonghee pondered, 'Sure. Indeed, I should find that interesting as well. However, I wonder as to when I would become that bright on every occasion and when my mind would be developed to such an extent anytime. I am pitiful and pathetic.'

"Hey, by the way, as you've already talked about laundry, when are you doing laundry?"

"Why? I should be doing laundry the day after tomorrow."

"Then, will it be late in the evening?"

"It will probably be late."

"Even though the laundry work may be finished earlier, come over to the stream. Then, the lady in the opposite room and I will have made dinner there and you could still come back late and eat. You should get a taste of the food I cook. Hee hee hee."

Siwol laughed along. How come a person could be so benevolent? 'I wish someone could give me sweet melon (Korean melon) for me to eat, so that I could get it to miss,' she muttered to herself. Every time Siwol heard such kind words, she could not help but be deeply grateful. And so, although she did have a mouth, she did not know how to properly express her gratitude, but it was just that knowing the fruit that miss liked eating, if she had money, she wished to buy and bring it. Yet, as she did not have the money, while she could not purchase it, in her spare time, she frequented to some place and often got corns and apricots for miss. Owing to this, not only was Kyeonghee and Siwol close, this time, when Kyeonghee came back from Japan, Siwol could not ever forget until her bones would melt how miss had bought even better toys for Siwol's child, Jeomdong than the toys of her eldest brother's children.

"Hey, by the way, I really have one thing that I want to work with you," said Kyeonghee.

"What is that?"

"Well, will you do whatever I ask we do?"

"Sure, I'll do it!"

"Why do you leave the cover of the well so dirty? I cannot bear seeing it so dirty. That is why starting from tomorrow, after washing the dishes, every day, let's definitely clean up the cover of the well. I'm not telling you to do this all alone. Would you be doing that?"

"Okay, I'll clean it up alone every day."

"No, do it with me······ with fun, ha ha ha."

"You're speaking of fun again? Ha ha ha ha."

The kitchen was rowdy. Kyeonghee's mother who had been listening from the back porch thought, 'Here they go again, bursting into laughter.'

"I wonder what she finds so amusing. Whenever she comes here, she hangs out in a group of three, day and night, and I really cannot endure all this noise of laughing, because of how distracting it is. When she was young, she even found horse dung rolling around to be amusing, and indeed, it appears to be so."

Kyeonghee's mother said to Sunam's mother.

On this, Sunam's mother said, "Is there anything that is as good besides laughing? When I come over to your house, I feel alive."

Sunam's mother once again let out a deep sigh. In the opposite room, a maiden who had been sewing alone, a distance away in the porch, upon catching the sound of laughter, wore a shoe in one foot, dragged the straw shoe with her other foot, and entered the threshold of the kitchen door, asking, "What are you all on about? I also want to be a part of it⋯⋯."

Chapter 3.

"Missus, are you sleeping?"

Lee Cheolwon, the father of Kyeonghee and the husband of Madam Kim came out of the reception room, opened the door of the main room, and stepped into the mosquito net, where Kyeonghee and Madam Kim were asleep. Madam Kim awoke, taken by surprise, and sat up.

"Why are you up, are you ill?"

"No, it's just that I'm unnecessarily having trouble falling asleep."

"Why?"

At this moment, the alarm clock that was hanging on the wall of the porch rang once.

"I've been lying, deep in thoughts and then, I came in here to discuss with missus about something!"

"About what?"

"About what to do with Kyeonghee's marriage. I've been so concerned that I couldn't fall asleep."

"I'm also worried."

"We can't miss the opportunity to get this suitor for Kyeonghee. There is really no one like him. I've been on familiar terms with the suitor's father and so, there's no need to look into it again, and the boy is decent enough, so would there be anyone else that's unique? As the boy is the eldest son, he will receive the bountiful inheritance and Kyeonghee would make a good wife of the eldest son in such a distinguished family······."

"Well, I know that there is no one like such a suitor, but what should we do when Kyeonghee loathes it? When she says she hates the idea so much, I'm afraid if I force her into it, something foreboding could happen and if then, how can I bear to be the object of resentment from my child?"

"N······o, how could something foreboding happen? Her character is good enough. We've done thousands of harvests. That is good enough. What do you say we should do then? Is the age of nineteen for a girl too young?"

Madam Kim remained silent. Lee Cheolwon clucked his tongue and began lamenting.

"It's my fault. Now that I've sent this girl all the way to Japan, here she turns up, not wanting to get married. Is there something as disgusting as that? I'm scared in case others know of this. As she's already missed some opportunities for appropriate spouses, how should we go about this? Ah······."

"Then, when should we get Kyeonghee married?"

"If only she'd agree to this, we would get her married now. Even today, I got a letter of request from a suitor····· Since the girl has been taught as much, we can't do it like in the past, when the parents themselves arranged the marriage, and so, while already, it's been four days since I've called and admonished her, she really isn't listening. How come she has such obstinate streaks inappropriate for a girl? Meanwhile, the uncle of Kyeonghee's prospective suitor had said multiple times that he shall have Kyeonghee as his niece-in-law."

"So, what did you say to that?"

"Well, I said something along the lines of it being flattering that he was asking for a mere girl. As a matter of fact, with all these insults I get about sending my eldest daughter all the way to Japan and the like, I said I would think about it."

"Then, the family over there would be waiting, right?"

"Right, already the talk about marriage had come up since the first month of the year, but here he is not getting married, putting his faith in a village maiden."

"Ah, then, in any case, soon, a decision has to be made. What should we do? She says that she wouldn't as hell get married off, before finally completing her studies. And, besides, she says that she doesn't ever dream of going off to such a wealthy house and stretching the hem of the skirt. That's why she gave away all her beautiful clothes when her sister got married. According to her, concern and sorrow underlie a silk-skirt. That is true, indeed."

Although Madam Kim had lived a rich life all this long, envying no other, when her husband was young, there were times when she was upset by his debaucheries and when he went to the district as the governor of Cheorwon, as he had two to three concubines, she remembered how much she had secretly been agonized, and so, whenever Kyeonghee talked about such things, despite Madam Kim not saying it out loud, she reflected many times that what her daughter was saying was right.

"Ah, how sickening you are. If you teach your daughter like that, then, she would turn out to be impudent that she would be of no use······ It's because she is not mature yet······ Besides, isn't it also disconcerting? What kind of a family gets the younger daughter married earlier than the elder daughter? How inferior is the elder daughter that the younger daughter is the one who gets married first? Judge Kim's family understands all that is about our family, which is why they seek to get their son married with Kyeonghee, but who else would take an unmarried eldest daughter into their family, when the younger one married first? No, this time, I shall make her get married······."

Lee Cheolwon, who had been hearing the words of his wife, which initially sounded plausible, all of a sudden felt urgent about the matter, after the thought arrived in his mind of how his younger daughter got married before his elder daughter, Kyeonghee. And, the more he thought about it, the more it occurred to him that if he were to miss the chance of a suitor from Judge Kim's family, no longer would it be possible to get another suitor with a prestigious lineage and with bountiful inheritance. So, needless to say, this time, he was willing to coerce Kyeonghee into marriage. Lee Cheolwon sprang to his feet.

"What would a girl be doing from her studies? Her education up until now is quite enough. Who would send her to Japan again? This time, her education is irrelevant. She shall get married to that suitor. Tomorrow, I shall call her out on this, and whether she listens or not, I will force her, without having to ask her again."

He was fuming. Madam Kim could not find it in herself to respond to this with, "Sure, bring it on." or "Don't do it." Yet, pressed with the thought that struck her whenever she was sprawled on her bed, sick and paralyzed, which was the fear of not seeing Kyeonghee get married before her deathbed, she would only say, "Indeed, I could only rest in peace after getting Kyeonghee, the only one remaining single, married in my lifetime."

Lee Cheolwon heaved himself up and then sat back down, asking her in a low voice.

"But after sending Kyeonghee to Japan, it seems like she hasn't been ruined?"

"No, she has become a lot more diligent than before. She would be the first one to wake up in the morning. So, she scrubs the floor, the yard, and neatly cleans it up. Not only that. Occasionally, she pounds rice into the flour until she passes it through a sieve······ That's why Siwol is so fond of her."

Whenever Madam Kim would see Kyeonghee working, she would find it more and more to be a great relief. Despite shielding Kyeonghee from the bad-mouthing of other people after sending her away to Japan, as a mother, Madam Kim has always stowed concerns within, about the aftermath of studying in Japan, where should Kyeonghee become pretentious, sit, and eat like a lad by being officious from having studied, worries about the shame that would be wreaked on Kyeonghee truly arose from a loving mother's natural affection for her daughter. Starting from the following day that her daughter came back from Japan, when Kyeonghee went into the kitchen, draped in an apron, although Madam Kim had tried to keep her from working to get her daughter some rest that she came for, inwardly, Madam Kim had earned as big of a reassurance as being able to let out a huge sigh of relief.

As anyone would know in Kyeonghee's family, Kyeonghee's scrubbing of the floor, the attic, and the closet clean-up was well-known ever since long ago. So, when Kyeonghee was attending a school in Seoul and she returned home three times a year for holiday, naturally, the attic and the closet were washed up to their core. Also, even in Madam Kim's mind, if Kyeonghee was not the one to clean things up, she would have a household that would appear to be in grave need of being tidied up. So, on occasions when the attic would become untidy, or when the closet would become disorganized, she would know that not many days would be left before the return of Kyeonghee. And, the following day, when Kyeonghee was back, her cousins, grandmother, and aunt, who came over to see Kyeonghee would once open the attic and the closet, and praise, "The attic and the closet are shiny, as if they've been powdered," and "They're so clean." This was what Madam Kim was enthused about, in the night before Kyeonghee's arrival and the prime mark of Kyeonghee's return home.

This time, Madam Kim did not expect Kyeonghee on her return from Japan to be cleaning up the attic and the closet that she had washed up three times every year. However, just as ever, after coming home, Kyeonghee would greet her parents and the first thing that she did was open the attic and the closet. And, the following day, she cleaned up the whole time.

Yet, this time, Kyeonghee's method of cleaning was entirely different from before. Before, Kyeonghee's cleaning method was mechanical. Madam Kim expected that Kyeonghee would scrub and mop the jaegi (utensil used in ancestral rites) that was placed in the east and the gourd dipper that was hanging on the wall of the west, and put them back as it is where they had been placed. Yet, this time, the cleaning method was different. It was constructive and applicative. From using the principle of order that Kyeonghee learned in home economics, organization that she learned in sanitary science, colors and the harmony of colors that she learned in art class, the melody to the beat that she learned in music class, she entirely renovated the place where the jaegi (utensil used in ancestral rites) and the gourd dipper had been placed until now.

She tried placing the porcelain next to the pottery and put the seven-dish meal into the wooden lacquerware. Beneath the brass rice-bowl, she propped up a bowl even bigger than the brass rice-bowl. She also laid out the yellowish pestle above the white, silver tray. Next to the enormous pot, she placed a bottle. And, before, in the dark of the attic, even as she furrowed her eyebrows at the odor of the dust and perspired the whole day, she had still done her clean-up, in return for the praise that she would hear from her parents. Yet, now, this too was different. Kyeonghee could not help but find moving her body here and there in the midst of the dark to be fun. She deliberately put down the broom, then held the mouse dung, and tried smelling its odor. And, the work that Kyeonghee did the whole day no longer entailed any anticipation of being rewarded. It was nothing more than doing her work of her own accord.

Like this, in every bit of conduct that Kyeonghee undertook, inwardly, she came to form a self-awareness, and at the same time that she had brought this to consciousness, even outwardly, at times, the work that she would do would grow. So, Kyeonghee had a lot on her hands. If Kyeonghee had a close peer who helped her with one of her tasks, even though the object obtained from do-ing the task was in Kyeonghee's hands, according to her, it would not be hers, but rather the peer's. On account of this, Kyeonghee could have had some good things that she wanted to get and ob-tain more than the others, but she did not by any chance pass on even the tiniest bit of work that she could easily do with her own strength to others. She would not have her share of work be taken away by others in the slightest. Ah, it was fortunate. Kyeonghee's thigh was fleshy and her forearm was thick. Until the moment when Kyeonghee would lose all her weight and consequently become incapable of walking, and until the time when her forearm would become drained of its strength that it would be drooping, there was an infinite amount of work for her to do. Kyeonghee had innumerable things that she would get. So, if she ever took a nap once, she would clearly be lacking the space of time that she could have for her work. Kyeonghee definitely grew bit by bit after working for a whole day. One by one, Kyeonghee gained even more. Driven by the desire to gain something and grow from morning to evening, she pushed herself to work with all of her might.

Day by day, Lee Cheolwon also saw his daughter working. Seeing her, again, he would internally feel a glimmer of pride. However, the reason why he had asked his wife about Kyeonghee was because like Madam Kim, Lee Cheolwon had given into their son's suggestion to send Kyeonghee to Japan, but nevertheless, it was a fact that they had always been concerned that by doing so, Kyeonghee would become ruined. So, their two smiling faces, while sitting on the floor this evening, were full of the affection of parents, with the concerns they had about getting Kyeonghee married and their concerns in case their daughter would get ruined being somewhat assuaged. What close friend, sibling, or devoted son would feel the concern and the genuine happiness that such parents felt? The anxiety that Lee Cheolwon had felt about

Kyeonghee not having any other family to get married into slightly subsided. Yet, stepping down to the porch, letting out a dry cough once, he uttered words that were formed out of his sheer determination that it seemed like anyone's order would not suffice to break it, "Tomorrow, I shall make her get married even if it means the end of the world."

At midnight, the rooster crowed, informing of a new day. The night that had been pitch-black unfolded widely into a swath of white. On the one side of the screen of the window to the east, it became steadily brighter and from one end of the mosquito net, gradually, it became dyed with the color of light green. Kyeonghee, who had been sleeping tight, blinked her eyes open. Kyeonghee once again was bursting with happiness at starting her work that she would be doing the entire day, sprung to her feet, and set out of the room.

Chapter 4.

As the time was right at noon, on the back porch, a lunch table was arranged. Kyeonghee headed in from the reception room. Without even heeding the words of Siwol and her sister-in-law, who lived on the opposite side of the room, that earnestly suggested for her to eat lunch, stepping into the small room, she firmly closed all sides of the door of the room. Kyeonghee burst into tears and started weeping. She lay, sprawled on the floor of the room, sat up, and then, heaved herself to her feet again, in the process, bumping her head on the wall. She pulled the pillar into a tight embrace and spun around and around. Not knowing what to do, Kyeonghee was at a loss. Kyeonghee's tiny chest burned like fire. Wiping her tears with the hem of the hanging towel, merely, the words that spluttered out of her mouth once in a while were "Oh dear, what am I going to do?" And, an emotion of resentment arose in her at the thought that her parents were trying to kick her out and send her away to another house, because if she were in this house, food would only dwindle and clothes would be used up on her. It was as if even above this wide, wide world, there was no space to put her tiny body. Every time a thought popped into her head, as to why someone worthless and unwieldy like herself was born into the world, the tears that had ceased burst out again like falling rain. Suppose someone were to come and try to discourage her, she might as well have gotten into a brawl with that person. And, she could have at once pulled and plucked out the hair of the person, and she might as well have scratched and torn at that someone until one would have blood dripping from the face like the flowing stream. What comes of the fate of Kyeonghee who went about crashing here and there in this small and dark room with all sides of the window firmly shut?

Two paths were laid in front of Kyeonghee at present. The paths were not faint and were clearly laid out in two directions. In one path, rice was piled up in the warehouse with an abundance of money and with red clay that could be easily trod, where it was easy to indulge in the reception of adoration, love, and where one could easily go and find their way without difficulty, which was a broad and level type of road. Yet, in the other path, one ought to pound rice into the flour until one's arms would ache in order to barely get a scrap of food to eat and go about sweating the whole day while doing someone else's work, which would only produce several ounces of penny. There, leading up to every place, only scorn would follow and the flavor of love would not be tasted, not even in one's dream. One ought to step onto rough stones until the tips of one's toes would bleed. This path had a cliff that one could suddenly fall from and a steep summit at that. One ought to cross the water and the hill, and there were too many twists in the path, with more perils ahead, making it difficult to find one's way. Today, Kyeonghee needed to choose one of the two paths in front of her and certainly arrive at a decision now. After having gone with her choice today, there would be no turning back tomorrow. It would also be unlikely for her heart that was decided at the moment to drastically change later in time. Ah, Ah, in which path of the two should Kyeonghee set foot? This was not what could be taught by teachers and even with friends, their advice would be of no use. Only when Kyeonghee herself would opt for her own path that she would take would this path be sustained for long and only when the decision would be reached in the right state of mind would no change be made. Once again, Kyeonghee banged her head and cried out, "Oh dear, what should I do?"

Kyeonghee was a girl like any other. To add to it, she was a girl that has lived in the Joseon society. She was a girl that has been buried in the conventionality of the Joseon family. It was in the societal honor code that a girl had to be of a gentle and mild character in order to be of use and it was in the family's education that taught that a woman's lifeline held onto three duties, which were to follow her father as a youngster, her husband upon marriage, and after the passing of her husband, her son. When she strained to stand up, the surrounding forces would trample her down and if she moved about, hurled from all sides would be cursing. The advice of a government official, who would amicably clasp one by the hand, would be like the words of ten people, in unison, "Like it was in the past, let us comfortably live before passing." Kyeonghee had seen clothes made out of silk and had imbibed Yaksik Jeongol (stew made out of sweet rice with nuts and Jujubes). Ah, Ah, which path should Kyeonghee naturally take? How should she live in order for it to be good? It was like slightly prodding with the end of the cane the tail of a snake that had been smoothly crawling by on the roadside, causing it to shrivel up its body that had been stretched, to occasionally roll its small eyeballs, and to often hold its sharp tongue out with spite, and whenever she thought of this, the two arms that hung from Kyeonghee's body and her two legs that had been extended would shrink closely in her chest and right in her stomach. She would turn into a toy-like object, like the one in the toy store, with a mere head and a body. And, her weight that was 13 gwan (48.75 kg) would all of a sudden be replaced with the weight of one blank sheet of paper, flapping in the wind. Again, as far as she knew her inner state of mind, she felt numb and chilled to the bone. She found herself incapable of blinking and it was as if she had pierced the wall, creating a gaping hole. Beads of perspiration formed a pool on her back and her limbs were icy-cold, much like a dead person.

"Oh dear, what am I supposed to do?"

Kyeonghee felt like she had gone mindless. She could barely speak and the only thing that she could muster were these words.

Kyeonghee tried touching her body. Touching her left wrist with her right hand and touching her right wrist with her left hand. She also tried shaking her head. This body, which is not even big, but instead is tiny······. How should I make this body stand? Where should I direct this body······. Kyeonghee caught a glimpse of her body again, up and down. Should I extend the silk skirt, have it draped in this body, and put a binyeo (Korean traditional ornamental hairpin worn by married women), made out of jade, in this hair of mine? How dignified would the wife of the eldest son of a big, thriving home be? How much fun would there be in the merrymaking of the newlywed's newborn? How much love would she get from her parents-in-law? How much would her body, which was currently unruly, be the reception of adoration by her parents? Indeed, would a relative be envious and look up to her? I did wrong. Ah, Ah, I did wrong. Why did I not say "Yes" to my father when he said, "Set your mind on getting married," and instead, said, "No. I won't." Ah, Ah, why did I say that? What was I thinking of doing in making that response? Why did I say that

I detested such riches and honors? What should I do later on if I missed the opportunity for such a position? It could be because I know nothing of hardship as my father told me. It may be because I have not matured yet. As my father had said, "Later on, you're going to regret it," already, I must be overcome with deep remorse. Ah, ah, what should I do? Before time passes even more, maybe, I should now set out to the reception room, repent, and be obedient in front of my father. "I was mistaken." Should I say it like that? No. Yes, I shall. That is a decent path. Besides, I shall also quit my troublesome load of studies. I will not go back to Japan, where I was told not to go. This must be my path. This must be the path that I must step onto. Ah, then, let me just choose this. But······.

"Oh dear, what am I supposed to do······."

Kyeonghee had her eyes wide open, absent-mindedly. Her entire body became heavy, as if a great weight bore down on her. She felt heavy, as if she had worn a gigantic helmet made out of a steel billet on top of her head. The two shriveled arms and legs in no time revealed themselves, drooping. Again, her whole body went back to being shriveled up. What was she thinking of doing when she had made such a bold reply? When her father said, "What a woman ought to do is to get married, have sons and daughters, do nothing more than serve one's mother-in-law, and respect one's husband," she would retort, "That is an old saying. Now, even a woman is a human being, and as long as she is a person, there is nothing that she can't do. She could earn money like a lad and she could enter a government post like a lad. It is a world where she could do whatever a lad could do." Ruminating on her retorts, a thought surfaced in her mind of the terrifying eyes of her father who held up a pipe, saying, "What's with this gibberish? What can a mere girl like you do? All this time, have you been learning such nonsense when you were in Japan, while not doing the studies you were supposed to do and wasting precious money?" and her body shivered.

Indeed, it was true. What would someone like her do? Was she not imitating the words spoken by other people? Ah, ah. It is not easy to play a role as a person. A girl who does all the things like a boy would be an extraordinary girl. Without breaking the 4000 years' ingrained habit, without receiving fairly good studies, and without being a prodigy in no small degree, a girl could not be extraordinary. Without the nuanced ability to understand like Madam Staël who moved the entirety of the hearts of people in Paris during the period of Napoleon, without the volubility of one's speech, and without being a prodigal societal figure, she was incapable of being an extraordinary person. Without saving Orléans in her living years and by dying, saving France, as the indomitable, brave sacrifice like Joan of Arc, she could not end up extraordinary. Without being meticulous and being organized in theory, and possessed of a firm resolve like the creator of one's thesis who could wield a facile pen, the renowned author of a clearly written book on economics, the valiant Madam Ford of the gynecocracy of England, she could not be extraordinary. Ah, ah, it was not easy. In order to accomplish, it has to involve such an extent of ability and such a scale of sacrifice.

Even as Kyeonghee tried to brush up on the studies that she had learned all this time, there was nothing that surprising. Instead, she had a moronic sense of intuition like how when others would be dancing and singing in front of her, she did not know how to truly enjoy and genuinely smile at them. In making a single reply, her face would flush red and she had a sluggish tongue that did not know how to find the right order of words. She had a pain in her chest, where a resentment would arise in her at being distressed in the slightest and when she would get hit even a tiny bit, she would drown in her tears. A weakened will crashed in, whence even as she got carried away, followed what a person would do from here and there, and accordingly with the east wind and the west wind, she would not be able to fix something. Is this a person? Could a figure of such a disposition be a human being? Merely with her studies that were more or less studying the Korean letters that everyone could do, and knowing how to hold the spoon in her right hand when eating the three daily meals that others also knew how to make, already, she was not capable. It was a preposterous vanity. If each entrepreneurial madam of all ages were to know of this, they would have snorted. It really was absurd of her.

"Oh my, what am I going to do?"

Kyeonghee, who had been in her self-regret up to this point, thought it to be even pitiful that Judge Kim's family would be taking her in as a daughter-in-law, getting her to become married to the eldest son. Also, in order for an idiot like her to be taken into such a dignified household, it was absolutely normal for her to have to lower her head, say yes, yes, dedicate herself to this family, and soon set foot in their house, but to say that she would hate it, even she thought it to be rather indignant of her. And, it seemed to be perfectly natural for her father, mother, the rest of her many relatives, like her grandmother and her auntie to worry about not getting her married, every time they would lay eyes on her.

Up until now, Kyeonghee had thought it to be very pitiful to see wives who did their hair in a chignon with a binyeo (Korean traditional ornamental hairpin) pierced in their hair. 'What did they come upon knowing to become such an adult? They don't even know of love for their husbands and they live mechanically and instinctively like beasts. Their affection for their children comes in the form of solely feeding them a lot of rice and meat, without knowing how to teach good academics. Is that even a person?' Kyeonghee had thought to herself with her eyes directed at them, beaming with conceit. Yet, for some reason, today, the wives all looked admirable. The hair pierced with the binyeo (Korean traditional ornamental hairpin worn by married women) of Siwol who was washing the dishes seemed to be a lot better than the way Kyeonghee did her hair. In between the wall, as the crying sound of the children of the farmers reached her ears, their world seemed to be far better than hers and different from hers. The more she thought about it, it appeared to be that she would not be able to grow up to be like such adults and with her body, she could not have such kinds of children. 'How come so many others get married, which is such a difficult thing for someone like me and while I make an exhaustive study of my future children's education here and there with such difficulty, how do they manage to live their lives well that easily?' With these thoughts in mind, she was nothing. These wives were a hundred times better than her.

'How did they so easily get their hair done in a chignon, with a binyeo (Korean traditional ornamental hairpin) pierced? Having given birth to so many children, they are living well in harmony. How admirable.'

The more Kyeonghee thought about it, the more she found the wives to be admirable. And, it was so strange that for her, it was such a challenge to get married. 'Are these wives praiseworthy? Or, am I? Do these wives deserve to be human beings? Or, do I?' This contradiction was a huge struggle that awakened Kyeonghee from her deep slumber. As she thought, 'Then, how do I become an admirable person,' Kyeonghee bore the brunt of the pain that made her head feel heavier.

"Oh my. What should I do? Would I have known that I would end up like this······."

The single string of words extended. At the same time, the ends of Kyeonghee's hair rose upwards. And, Kyeonghee's brazen face, flat lips, the longish feature of her whole body all disappeared and something, like a flickering flame at the edge of the tiny wheat straw seemed to be floating in the wind. The room inside was blistering. She opened the windows on all sides unconsciously.

The strong, hot rays of the sun that came sweeping in were like thugs on both sides holding six-sided clubs, saying "Come on……," in defiance as the rays of the sun shone, penetrating in an astonishingly powerful way. Above the garden zinnia, where this year's flower bloomed, crowded with the five cardinal colors, a tiger swallowtail and a sulfur butterfly ceaselessly came and went. In the nestling place of the magpie, on top of the pear tree, there was the head of a black baby crow, sneaking in and out incessantly, while waiting for mother crow to come bring it food. In the shade of the summer cypress, the pot-bellied family dog was sprawled out and sleeping soundly. Its belly was bulging. Under the fence, following one after the other behind the mother hen, which was chasing around to catch a cicada larva, were about five or six chicks. From afar, Kyeonghee sat, gazing ahead blankly, and purposefully moved her body.

There! That was the dog. That was a flower and that was a hen. That was a pear tree. And, there, what was hanging in the tree was a pear. What was floating in that sky was a magpie. That was a pot and that was a large mortar.

Like this, Kyeonghee called out the names of whatever was within her sight. She tried touching the single chest of drawers that was set at the side. She also tried caressing the Myeongju blanket that was folded up and placed on top of it.

"Then, who am I? I am a human being! Yes, a human."

Kyeonghee saw the reflection of herself in the mirror that hung on the wall. She tried squeezing her mouth and her eyes open.

She attempted to raise her arms and even held her legs out. This was definitely the shape of a human. And, she made a comparison between herself and the dog lying on its belly, the hen that went around to hack at a cicada larva, and also the crow. She had learned in zoology that those were beasts, in other words, the lower life forms. Contrastingly, she also learned that someone like her who could wear clothes, speak, walk around, and work with one's hands was a supreme creature of all creations, that was, a human being. If so, she was also such a person of worth.

'Ah, ah, I made a good response.' When her father said, "If you get married there, won't you be wearing good clothes and for the rest of your life, eating richly before passing?" while shuddering, she responded for the first time in her life in front of her terrifying father.

"Aren't there father Anja (Anhee)'s wise words, 'With coarse rice to eat, with water to drink, and my bended arm for a pillow - I still have joy in the midst of these things?' If someone were to live, solely eating, and pass away, then, that is not a human but a beast. Even if it's a boiled barley, someone who eats one's rice with one's own efforts is a human being. Merely, as it is, once again eating the rice that one's husband was straight away receiving from his ancestors would be one and the same as the dog from our house," she said.

That was right. If one were to just eat and then die, that was a lower life form. To add to it, without even moving one inch of one's finger, and instead, receiving the riches of one's ancestor, let alone failing to make them by one's efforts, there were countless unfortunate things that went on in wealthy families that did not even know how to put to use what they received that they would be uselessly wasting it on alcohol and Gisaeng (Korean Geisha), unlike a human, but like a beast, ending up on their deathbed, merely after indulging in a life of comfort from their luxury and riches. There were dozens of cases where a distinction almost could not be made with a beast. Such a being momentarily borrowed and put on the skin of a human, but was not a human being even in the slightest. Even if such a being were to abruptly lie, sprawled in the shade of the summer cypress, the dog would have snorted and would have barked that the spot was wasted on that being.

That was it. After the passing of a distressful phase, joy would be there, and after the falling of tears, laughter would burst out, which was what made a human different from a beast. A human could think what beasts could not easily be capable of thinking and a human could achieve the act of creation. Unlike beasts that would be hoping for the rice that was earned by humans, the leftovers of the rice that humans ate, and if they were given to them, the beasts would relish them, humans who were different from beasts found with their own strengths and gained with their own ability. This was the difference between humans and beasts, which was without the least bit of contradiction. This was the truth that could not be doubted in the slightest.

Kyeonghee was also a human. After that, she was a woman. If so, then, before she was a woman, she was a human being, first and foremost. Also, before being a woman of the Joseon society, she was first and foremost a woman of the whole humanity within the universe. Before being a daughter of Lee Cheolwon and Madam Kim, she was first and foremost a daughter of God. Anyhow, needless to say, she was in the form of a human being. This form was not simply a skin she put on briefly, and without a doubt, its inner structure was also not that of a beast but a human being.

Yes, I am a person. As a human, if one would not find the obscure, rough pathway, then, who else would find it! It would be a human who would climb up to the summit of the mountain and look down. Yes, what use would this arm be and as for this leg, where should this leg be put to use?

Kyeonghee raised her two arms, straight up in the air. She leaped with her two legs.

The rays of sunlight that had been shamelessly blazing started to fade out gradually. The light of the sky, which was like the hue of a deep-blue skirt was obscured by the black clouds that placidly emerged. The wind from the south came, blowing in graciously and softly. The smell of pollen swept in with the wind. Unfolded before one's vision, lightning cackled and above the shoulder, a clap of thunder stormed in. A little while later, the summer shower of rain would come pouring.

Kyeonghee was enraptured. Kyeonghee felt as if she had grown taller, like the yeot (Korean traditional rice candy) that was stretched to its core, all of a sudden. And, her eyes widened, seeming to envelop the entirety of her face. Right there, prostrating herself, she put her hands together and prayed.

God! Here is the daughter of God. Father! My life is filled with a lot of blessings.

Take a look! Aren't my eyes and ears active like this?

God! Please pass down your infinite honor and strength.

I will go on working with all my might.

Whether you reward or punish me, do whatever is in your interest to manage me.

〈*A Community of Women* (Women's Magazine published to enlighten Korean women, written by Joseon schoolgirls studying abroad in Tokyo; 1917~1921)〉

(1918. 3.)

The Anguish of a Grass Widow

As certainly the time was in mid-May, after rainfall, for it still had not cleared, the black strip of clouds swept over, circling the summit of the Samgaksan mountain, and the poplar, which liked to stand, full of spirits, and flutter did not even move a single leaf, and merely stood silently, from not even the least bit of the wind blowing. The sparrows gathered in flocks and wavering, they went from here and there, and the herons flew about, crying for the rain to fall, while passing by the roof.

At this time, six to seven madams who came to see their young children in the hall of a three-room house sat down, fanned themselves, or incapable of fighting off the fatigue from the heat, they took off their coat string for a moment, pushed it aside, leaned onto a wooden pillow on top of a hwamunseok (Korean figured matting woven in floral or other patterns) and closed their eyes lightly, or as this was a house they came to for the first time, they thoughtlessly sat, looking around the front and the back, or they talked about housekeeping, or they sat, listening. In the porch, two diapers of the babies were laid out, the water kettle was placed there, and the air, which had a bit of water drops remaining, three to four of them were scattered around. Also, the cherry seeds had fallen from here to there, and the cherry which was even short of being half-filled in a big glass bowl was wet from the water and translucently, in a refined way, reflected by the beautiful, red beam, sparkling with the glossiness of the oil.

At the time, while moaning from the heat of post-child-birth, the mother of the baby, who sat up, carelessly wearing her disheveled hair in a bun, put on a binyeo (Korean traditional ornamental hairpin) made out of the horn of a black water buffalo, and without energy, sat, leaning onto the back of the doorsill, upon hearing the crying sound of the child resonating from the reception room, far-away through the back gate that was flung open, was taken by surprise, sprung to her feet, stepped out to the reception room, and came in, holding the baby vertically in her arms. The pair of eyes of the baby partially flowed with tears, and a couple of places of the body were imprinted with red spots as mosquito bites. Clinging to the arms of one's mother, the child rolled one's clear eyeballs, as if one was taking pleasure, took a look around the mob, and grinned, seemingly knowing or not knowing. While the eyes of the mob gathered and were concentrating on the baby, they all said, "Oh dear, the baby's smiling," and wondered as to whether the child was going to smile again, caressed, patted the head, and touched the hand. The baby, pretending not to know, whirled around, turned one's lips to the chest of one's mother, and sought her milk.

In some way, when seeing a madam who sat there in the corner, staring up at the sky absent-mindedly, holding the pipe in her mouth, she appeared to be around forty, and in a certain way, she appeared to be barely over thirty. For some reason, her face, which seemed to be of a noble character, held such a trace of hardship that wrinkles could be captured here and there. No matter how much she would be scrutinized, all the more, as she seemed angered, the blackened hue of her face, which was steamed by the sunlight, went around. She, with forelocks that covered her forehead, which were measured and peppered with pomade made of beeswax and sesame oil, from left to right in a parallel, attached, braided, with a silver hairpin that pierced the hair, rather in a longish way, with the lengthy sleeve of the jeogori (Korean traditional upper garment) in the ramie fabric of unlined summer jacket plastered over the back of her hand, and with a rather gauze-like skirt made out of a ramie fabric widely attached to the waist, wearing it a little loosely leftward, was not the madam from Seoul, but for an unknowable reason, it was apparent from the fact that she appeared elegant that she had grown up in the house of Yangban (Upper class in Joseon) with a sense of propriety. Like this, while several madams came up to the babies, caressed and touched them, only one madam alone looked from afar, without a word, let out one strange snort, dropped her glance, for the moment placed a pipe that did not even burn halfway on the ashtray by the side, and knocked the ash off the pipe at the bottom of the porch in a huge yard, bending her waist, flashing a strangely sorrowful expression. This madam sat down again like before, and looking at the baby feeding on the mother's milk, said, "Hmph, look at that. Among many of us sitting here, the mother is the only one who's heard the baby crying. Like that, the affection unbreakable to the very core between the child and the mother is intertwined, and as for someone like me······." And, a lump formed in her throat, where she could not finish her sentence and tears sprung in her two eyes. The mob all found it to be peculiar and so, could not help but ask why she was flashing such an expression of sorrow. At this, without any reply, she stayed still, accompanied by her friend Madam Kim, who sat down and staring at her, said, "Traces of your wretched fate are being unveiled again. You must've been thinking about your two sons." The suspicion of the mob deepened.

They could not help but ask again, "What about the two sons?" This madam certainly sat, at a loss for words, and Madam Kim, staring at this madam again, said, "In order to talk about a personal history, it would be like an old tale, all the way back to Sukhyang jeon (Name of a late seventeenth-century Korean novel)." This led to the mob having even more curiosity and aroused their inquisitiveness. "How come? Please do talk about it," it was the demand of the mob. Madam Kim once again looked at her and requested, "Please talk." The madam indeed sat in silence and then said, "Look at this," held out her two hands, uttering, "There is no way in the world to know of one's fortune and destiny. Who would've known that my hand, which had been like the soft and smooth texture of a powder would have each one of the joints nailed, and who would've known that I would turn out to wear cotton loose bloomer shorts until the blistering weather of May and June? (Lifting her skirt and pointing at her cotton loose bloomer shorts with the blackish-red color) I too grew up with good clothes and food, with no envy of others, and even when I got married, there wasn't a time when I came down from the porch. Based on this, I was the daughter of a prominent Yangban (Upper class in Joseon) household. To speak of my personal history, it is all too dumbfounding." Like this, she started to talk about her past life, little by little.

"My father led a life as the governor of Pyongyang, lived in Bongsan valley, and also lived in Anseong valley. My uncle is from minister Lee's family. So, in the Cheorwon valley, which was our hometown, the influence of the faction of our parent's house was intimidating. In such a house, I grew up being adored as the well-grounded daughter in between four sons. Although due to all the sufferings I've been through, by now, my face became spoiled like this, when I was about twelve or thirteen years old, a maiden's appearance was stuck to me with a white hue, a lovely face, a thick pitch-black hair that was braided, and hung down loosely. So, starting from the year when I turned ten, whether it'd be from the countryside or from Seoul, marriage proposals flooded in from the houses of prime ministers. When my father would say such things, my mother would ask if it was so lamentable, having just one daughter. Then, my father would be at a loss for words. Yet, a daughter is of no use. In March of the year that I turned sixteen, I finally ended up getting married."

"How old was the husband?" one madam asked. "My husband was thirteen years old. My father-in-law, minister Kim and my father were best of friends. Perhaps, while the two were drinking to each other's spirits, our marriage must have been decided. Because I didn't want to be apart from my mother that much, I cried, while getting married off to a place that was about 31 km away. Like at my house, where I've lived without anything lacking, that house consisting of only brothers, where the last one of the sons was getting married, the family adored us, like a wedding present and silk. Who would've received the adoration from their parents-in-law like me? It was a marriage in name, and who in the world would've led a married life like mine, without knowing of difficulty and strife? Three years since getting married, there was no sign of pregnancy, they became rather worried, waited, and in the eighth year, coincidentally, I showed signs of pregnancy, gave birth to a son, and so, the happiness of the adults was beyond expression. They bestowed a small, silver portable dining table. Right in that year, my husband took up a government position in the county office of Chuncheon. So, I also followed along and did housekeeping there for three years. All the while, when my first child was three-years-old, I had another child, who turned out to be a son again. At night, when the four of us, as a family, would be sitting in a cluster and sharing cute tricks, even while we had been lonely, living in another place, we lived with joy. Yet, whether my blessings came to an end or there must have been an ill omen in the household, in November of the lunar calendar of the year when my second child had been born, because it was the Japanese Lunar New-Year's Day, my husband went to a banquet, and came back late at night, heavily drunk. Without even taking off his clothes, he lay, sprawled on the seat that was laid out, moaned about having an intense headache, and all of a sudden, as he cried, red, clotted blood came out for about two times, tangled up, and I was chilled to my bones."

Many madams who sat, listening up till' now had their hearts pounding out of their chest, and so, asked, "Then, what?" wanting her to continue the story, or some said, "Oh no, what to do about it," as if they could not bear to hear, frowning. Or, they said, "My goodness, how pitiful." Madam Lee choked up, swallowed once, and after tentatively halting her words, went on again. "At this time, after he was bedridden, starting from the following day, he sowed hatred per day, not getting a wink of sleep, let alone going out at the appointed time to work in the government position, and as his condition exacerbated more and more, he spat out heaps of red blood. Like that, without getting a rough idea of what it was, with the illness becoming graver, he fell into a pitiable state, and so, I wrote a letter to my husband's family. As I sent a correspondence, my eldest brother-in-law came to bring us all. So, we went about packing the bags, and all left immediately. Would there be any other sort of an incident like that? As I stepped into the house of my husband's family, as if I had unnecessarily committed some crime, I didn't have the dignity to face the adults. Sure enough, my mother-in-law blamed it on me, questioning me as to what I did to make him that ill, my mother-in-law and father-in-law altogether stopped eating and drinking, lay flat on the ground, and so, where else would such a turmoil be in the household? Buying ginseng, antler, and all sorts of good medicines, whether the most proficient of doctors would be from faraway or nearby, they were brought into the reception room and every day, they would check his pulse, and use the medicine, but in case it would not be effective, because not only did it cost an exorbitant sum of money, it aroused the tensions of people, how much did their hearts race. The following year in August, at last, he passed away at the age of twenty-one," she said, wiping her eyes, clasping the strap of an unlined summer jacket. The mob all said, "Oh my, what ought to be done about this?" and clucked their tongues. Madam Lee was drained and barely continued speaking.

"So, in a blooming age of twenty-five, having deserted all the delicacies of the world, where even the dead would take pity, as a woman who didn't even turn thirty became widowed, the circumstances were unspeakable. How ominous must I have appeared to be. For some reason, everyone saw this body of mine as a hapless piece of flesh that I became so ashamed that once I turned single, I lived, unable to face people. My brother came to see me, and how humiliating it was to see him in my white mourning clothes that it was as if a bonfire was hurled at me, and so, I wasn't able to lift my head right away."

According to one madam, "Really, what a person of the past. Ah, not only that. A widow in former days would be like a sinner in her lifetime. Try to lift your head somewhere, speak up loudly, raise your voice, and cry. But if she became a widow and cried like that in the past, it must be that the sky collapsed. Really – it is absurd. But how are the widows these days? Wouldn't the world come to an end when there is not one widow not wearing a red, purple daenggi (Korean traditional pigtail ribbon) and putting on face-powder?" (Meaning that compared to the past time of Madam Lee's days as a widow, there are too many widows wearing daenggi and face-powder, signifying that they are lifting their head high up and looking forward to a new beginning in life) Saying this, she lay back and then sat right up, and when seeing her bend her waist to brush the ashes off the pipe, she had a daenggi (Korean traditional pigtail ribbon) in her hair, which seemed to show that they were words of experience from this madam, who was one of the widows as well.

Madam Lee once again continued. "Now that I think about it, it was because I was foolish. Indeed, in the middle of a misfortune, fortunately, as my two sons were left there, their grandmother and grandfather were greatly consoled by them and I also leaned onto them. My father-in-law taking such a pity on the three of us, lived, finding joy in housekeeping, gave the rice paddy and a farmland that reaped three hundred seok (a unit of measurement for crops) of harvests, which had been done for the second son's share, to me, in my name as a verification, bought me a house right in front of his family's house, where he adorned it very cleanly, like a new wallpaper, so, it was always azure, in November of the lunar calendar, gave the household goods to the three of us, and all the time, came in and out, seeing us. It would be fun when from my parents-in-law taking on housekeeping, I become driven to buy this too or that too. What if I reluctantly came to buy one related to the housekeeping? Then, I would think of where I'm heading, and wonder as to how I was troubling myself in order to live like this, alone, and without the time to get it under control, sorrow would well up, from which tears would obscure my sight."

"As my parents considered me pitiful, they would regularly send fruits that grow each and every season and clothes for the children, and as I, in the absence of my husband use the money that my father-in-law earned, they considered me so poor, and they would send all the money for me to use as a supplement for daily use. Ah – how fast time flies. As the breakfast and dinner table that had the spirit tablet were arranged, as if my husband was there, living, I would be hugely consoled, and at night, when coming outside and seeing the white covering at the spot in the porch where spirits were attended to, before holding the funeral, I felt reassured as if it seemed to guard the house, but after completing my mourning for three years, what's more, suddenly and unexpectedly, I felt a sorrow in my heart, empty, and indescribably disappointed. It was a regret that I didn't follow along to die. As I couldn't die, during the time that I lived, one year passed, the two years drifted by, until it became four years. In August of that year, in the porch, alone, when I was sitting down, doing a Chuseokbim (Chuseokbim, where the child would get to wear new clothes or shoes on the day of Chuseok, Korean Thanksgiving Day) for my eldest child, the Jeomdong old lady who has been frequenting our deceased husband's family house, sewing since before, came in, carrying her grandson on her back. Unlike before, telling me that it must be pitiful and so sad that I was living alone, she said that a certain respectable person from Seoul lost his wife and that he was trying to have a lover that is a young widow, went on and on about how his family status was alright and his property was considerable. I thought she must be just sharing such a story and merely listened to it indifferently. Later, after some time, one day, wasn't it rather abnormal that the old lady came and spoke about such things again, where she couldn't dare to say what it was and was trying to read my mind? It was so detestable that I also merely pretended not to know. Ah – Look here. After a few days, she came again, asking me if I didn't even have a sense of shame, and whether I didn't have a heart. In front of her, I said to her, how could you say such things to me, and when I yelled, she broke into a run, chickened out. After that, I was so enraged that I couldn't fall asleep at night. And then, as everyone seemed to be looking down on me, it was so saddening that it was even worse than when I had first become a widow. But look here. It wouldn't be difficult to fall into disgrace. As I really couldn't forget the date, it was the 11th of September of that year. After having dinner, as it was cool inside the main room, I closed the door, and to feed my milk to the child, I was about to lie, sprawled out, holding the child in between my arms, when suddenly, from the porch, I heard the sound of a man calling the name of my eldest child, Sunyeong,

Sunyeong. Wondering if my father-in-law had come, after I finished feeding my milk and was standing up, as I heard the sound of the calling once again, while the voice of my father-in-law was shrill, his was a sonorous voice. As I felt it to be abnormal, for a moment, I looked out from in between the door. While it was a dim night and I could not see clearly, even for a moment, seeing a much taller man clasping his hands behind his back, shaking a stick in his hand swingingly, standing in the direction towards the interior of the house, he was not a person from our family. As an appalling thought instantly cropped up, in a voice that I could barely muster, I said, shudderingly, "Who must you be?" As if the man was delighted to hear my voice, he came near, and said, casually, "Yes – I came from Seoul." Once again, in a trembling voice, I said, "You say you come from Seoul, but I wanted to ask who you were." Then, he lightly came up to the porch, saying, "Right, you would've heard from Jeomdong old lady. I'm Jang Jusa from Seoul," and it was as if he was speaking to someone that he was familiar with, putting on a half-smile. As I was frightened and upset, I said, "I don't know such a person. But how on earth could you come into the hall of a stranger's house without a word?" and when we were talking back and forth, just in time, as the sound of the main gate opening rang out, my mother-in-law stepped in."

The mob all said, "Oh dear, what should be done about it?" "How is it that it is right at that moment?" and they were on edge.

"That is why, it was really like the meat that was entangled in the net. How can it leap over? So, should the guy named Jang Jusa take off outside or run inside? Not knowing what to do, he scurried into the room. I helplessly ended up being falsely accused of dishonor. My mother-in-law, seeing the man's suspicious attitude must have taken notice and followed me into the room, with her eyes clearly open, staring and saying, "Why is this person here?" and attentively observed my behavior once again. Then, what was I supposed to say in that spot? As it was such a dumbfounding situation, no words came out of my mouth and so, I merely stood there in silence. As she was such an impetuous adult, she soon rushed to me, seized strands of my hair, slapped this and that cheek, saying, "You bitch really are screwing with another's house. Having a husband who was just as sound, as if you lacked something, as you would go consorting with some man all night, and committing adultery, such lowly men would be scattered around you from the front to the back, which is why you bitch must have drugged your husband and made him ill. Ah- it wouldn't even be a relief to grind and devour a bitch like you. Don't you dare stay in my house even for a moment. Get out with that guy. Come on, come on!" As she would make her demand, like a thunder-bolt, I became frightened out of my wits, and so, who could go against it? As it was a countryside and the sound of such a high volume was made, from houses from the back to the front, certainly, men and women of all ages and the onlookers came in clusters until the porch became crowded. As the five viscera (of heart, liver, spleen, lungs and kidneys) couldn't be turned upside down and couldn't be looked inside like it was with being able to turn the ankle beoseon (traditional Korean socks) upside down and looked inside, in that spot, if I said I was falsely accused, who would listen to my side of the story? Namyeong, Mr. Hong, and others soon gathered and a stream of words claiming that the bitch should be quickly expelled flooded out. Would there be anything else as resentful as this? It is only that as I looked up at the sky, I would come to resent God. While ever since I was young, as I was raised by my parents, I didn't get even a single loud scolding, a clump of my hair was plucked out, I was beaten to the point that the left side of my body became bruised, where there would be no place that went unscathed. Take a look at this. (She lifted her upper lip, showing the fractures here and there that gleamed on her front teeth) As I had been beaten during that time so much, starting from the moment, the gum in my mouth, which was of a pure color, swelled and throbbed that in six months, the front teeth all fell off. So, I altogether put on false front teeth like this (pointing at the six front teeth). So, on that day, at that time, I was immediately chased out. Of course, my two children were taken away from me. When I got chased out, was there a place to go? First, as I felt ashamed to face others and as this was a small area, instantly, everyone within the city knew. I had no choice but to seek far-off for my family's house on my parent's side and was up all night sitting on top of the hypocaust, which was as cold as ice in the corner of the servants' quarters. My hands and legs went so cold that they would become numb, and my chest became too swollen and painful that I could not stand it. As I became desperate, tears wouldn't even come out and I couldn't even greet my parents. It was at a point, where I thought it was okay, for I am the mother, waited for the footsteps, sent a person, and had the person take my youngest child back to me. The following day, around the time of late breakfast, a sedan came in, at the back, a certain guy followed inside, and as I saw him for a moment, he looked similar to the person that scurried into the room of my house in the prior evening. When I saw the guy, as if the poplar was being felled, as angry thoughts sprung, I was seized by an urge to soon come down, grab his collar and fight a match, as much as I liked. As if with a bravado, he was paying a visit to his esteemed wife, he told me to get in the sedan. Would there be a woman as illogical and as devoid of a compass to get in the sedan? Then, naturally, would words mildly come out of my mouth? Spouting about how he was a son of a bitch who left me falsely accused of dishonor and when I had ended up in this state as a bitch, what the hell were you on about, and the like, where more and more, only my rage would burst out, and my dreary state would be in open display. As I came to see, already, from the front to the back, a dense crowd of onlookers had come. Then, what was I supposed to do? For the moment, I became busy, setting off to leave the place. Seeing the servants of my deceased husband's family huddling and watching, how humiliating it was that no sound came out, and unwittingly, I ended up taking flight, by getting into the sedan with my child. We've been travelling endlessly, for quite some time, when he parked the sedan in front of some corner of a thatched house that was on the verge of all falling apart in the countryside of a mountainous district and told me to come down. And, the son of a bitch tenderly looked up at me and asked me if I wasn't hungry. Really, if this were a dream, would there be a kind of dream like that? While I had wished to slap his cheeks, as infuriated as I was, how could I bear to raise my hand against another man? And then, because I didn't want to have my dreary situation be discovered when I was all the way in some other place……. I managed to somehow spend about ten days there."

A mother of a child who had been sitting, attentively listening all this time, grinned from ear to ear, and asked, "Then, when did you two get married? Did you get married there?" and at such perplexing words, Madam Lee stuttered and for a moment, her two cheeks reddened.

"Then, what was I supposed to do? As he already went to bed with me, I became his woman. That even now, at the thought of having given bodily consent to that son of a bitch, it gives me the shudders and infuriates me. If I had been like I am now, it wouldn't have mattered to turn my back on him. Yet, at that time, as I had only known of the corner of the main room, and all of a sudden, having been chased out of my house, I came to a wholly unfamiliar place, away from home, alienated that I thought that if I were to turn my back on the man, on top of it, what would once again become of the body of this woman? So, I've been letting him hold me hostage and devour me. Now that I think of it, I wonder why I didn't hang my neck at the time and die. It is because committing suicide is also fate·······. And then, Jang Jusa left, saying that he was going to buy a house in Seoul and bring me there. With my child, I stayed in the countryside of the mountainous district for a few more days, and one day, shamelessly, I got out, in search of my parent's home. Just in time, a person from that village said that one was going to Pyeonggang (where Madam Lee's parent's home was situated), and so, carrying my child on the back, for the first time in my life, I walked for about 20 km, and in the evening, as I reached the front gate of the house, my heart thumped, I went shuddering, and so, I could barely set foot inside the main gate, but I clenched my teeth and quickly stepped inside. My family from my parent's side did not know of the incident from outside about 31 km away. My mother came running out, on her feet with beoseon (Korean traditional socks) draped in them, and asked, "What is the matter here?" and my sisters-in-law also dashed out, taking the child in their arms, and in an uproar. My father had been eating meat as part of the side dishes at his dinner table, but he ate only half of it, and calling on my sisters-in-law, said, "Take her to Hong's sister. It is a pity that she would be oblivious to the joy of a married couple in this world," and at night, he would definitely not forget to ask me if it was cold or not in the room of the Hong family's house where I slept. Like this, during winter, I lived in comfort, eating well and wearing good clothes."

"It was the forenoon of the sixth day of early March of the following year. In a room on the opposite side, when I had been adorning the Magoja (Korean traditional outer coat worn by men over their jackets) of my father, my younger brother's face became a tad pale, and as if he were to break the sliding door, he flung it open and gruffly hurled some piece of correspondence at me. As I was blind-sided, I couldn't see what was to come. Even my sister-in-law, sitting at the side told me to show it to her. After staring at it for a long time, she looked up at me with strange eyes, saying, "Oh my. Sunyeong's father passed away, but who is this? He said he came in the name of Sunyeong's father, that he would be coming today, and that he is the esteemed son-in-law, Mr. Jang." Would there be another foe like that? Then, abruptly, outside the door, as the sound of a car blared out, a lanky man with the hem of the three-folded durumagi (traditional Korean overcoat), made out of silk that flapped, his gold-rimmed glasses shimmering, unfalteringly entered the middle gate, headed into the courtyard like a spring soaring up from deep beneath the ground, and slumped on the edge of the porch. My mother ended up putting a blanket on herself and sprawled out on the spot of an ondol (Korean floor heating system) floor nearest the fireplace. My brothers evaded to a village house and I stood in the kitchen, incapable of coming or going, and shuddered, when my sister-in-law said, "As this is a guest that came for you, sister-in-law, go out and receive him," and not only did I cave into this suggestion, but what if anyone else were to enter the house and see him? So, I forced myself out, told him to come in and brought him into the room on the opposite side. I merely stood at the place on the ondol (Korean floor heating system) floor nearest the fireplace and he stood on the upper side of the floor away from the fireplace, and I was at a loss for words. The more it went on, what with having had my time in an unfamiliar place, alienated, far-away from home, I have messed up and things have gone awry that I was helpless. Why of all times, at that moment, did my father come back from performing his ancestral rites in the house of his eldest brother, where he had set off four days ago? As he stepped into the main room, he asked why my mother lay, sprawled out. I told him that my mother suffered from aches all over her body. As he got back to the porch, and hung around, he caught sight of the casual footwear for thin feet that had been taken off, and called on my sister-in-law, asking her why there were shoes of a man. She half-heartedly mumbled, "A guest came for my Pyeonggang sister-in-law." "Why would there be a male guest for Hong's house and if it were a male guest, shouldn't he enter the reception room as a formality, and so, who the hell is the guest, slumped in the opposite room?" and called on me loudly for a couple of times to come out of the Hong family's house. Driven by fear, I ran outside of the back door of the room on the opposite side. And then, I was standing there, still, when all of a sudden, someone grabbed hold of a clump of my hair, as if one was bent on smashing the nape of my neck. I was taken aback and when I turned around to see, it was my father. Without uttering anything, he would go on beating me indiscriminately from the bottom to the top, and it was a hell of a pain. While I threw a wild fit, crying out, "Oh my, mother, please save me," who would be looking out? Even now, when thinking back to that time when I had been beaten, Jang Jusa would admit that it was pitiable. Now that it has turned out like that, it ought to have been the right thing for Jang Jusa to take action, putting forward my situation. He himself lightly sneaked out, got into the car, and set off. So, as it could not be the case that one could stay abashed with the servants in sight, my father chided my mother and sisters-in-law as to why they sent him in and told them to kick me out. That evening, I had no choice but to be chased out of even my parent's home, and aimlessly headed out, carrying my child on my back. My mother followed me all the way to about 8 km, and sobbed. In the street, like that, we had our last farewell as mother and daughter. And so, now, I was faced with no alternative but to set out to Jang's house. Yet, regardless of which area of Seoul it was embedded in, and by whatever means I could go to Seoul, I would need to know where his house was. Even if I would be damned, as I thought that at least I'd get damned with my children, I headed to Cheorwon, which was about 16 km away, took back my eldest child, Sunyeong who had been playing in the street, and came back to the inn that I lodged in. While I had been paying for the food, with the money (three won) that my mother secretly gave me when I was coming out of the house, unbeknownst to my father, really, how negligible the amount is to use. In less than ten days, it was all gone. What could be done about it? From that time on, I took up sewing at this inn, where my two children were taken in, and where the three of us as a family would live, being fed. Dear, don't you say a thing. Where else would I get treated to a bite of steamed rice? Although the free left-over rice is tough to eat, I get to more or less eat something starting from noon. What is it about it being just a cottage? Even if I were a married woman, I wouldn't be able to go around, doing stretches for my waist. Where else would I be able to undo my coat string even once, spread out my legs, and sleep in my lifetime when we, with the five members of the inn owner's family, as eight people could sleep in a single room? I've earnestly been through hardships. Even so, if I were to go somewhere, would there be anywhere else?"

⟨*New Family* (Korean Women's Magazine; 1920s~1930s)⟩ (1921. 7.)

Grudge

Ms. Lee, drained of the strength in her body, fell fast asleep in her clothes, with the blanket draped, at the cold hypocaust in the upper room of the house. "Hmph! Oh dear, oh······" saying, she held out her throbbing legs, raised her two arms high, stretched them with might, and lay back, flat on the ground. She thrashed her teeth and clenching them, she uttered, "That son of a bitch, Hmph Hmph," and let out a heavy sigh. A person lying beside her, taken by surprise, turned back to see her, but she really did not seem to have awakened from her sleep and bearing some kind of sorrow that sunk deep into her heart, the sound that came out unwittingly was fresh.

Ms. Lee was originally born as the only child, the daughter of a wealthy family. In the hands of a servant and a nanny, when it was cold, they made it warm, and when it was hot, they made it cool, gave her neat, beautiful clothes, and in case the food would become mushy and soggy, fed her clean, delicious food, raising her like the apple of their eye. Also, as she was pretty and smart, not only did she certainly receive her parent's love, but also even, no passerby did not treat her with love. Thereby, as time passed, the baby who became 1-year and 2-years of age was the bud of a flower, the sole happiness of her parents. Yet, as she went beyond 10-years of age, abruptly, they had the regrettable thought of, what if this were a son, and as the days passed by, gradually, they were fraught with their concerns about getting her married.

Kim Seung Ji who was the childhood friend of minister Lee only had one son. One day, in the reception room of minister Lee's house, drinks were raised between the two people, and so as to pass down the friendship of the two all the way to the next generation, they agreed that it would be good to become each other's in-laws and out of the coincidental words that were spoken, they made a promise of a century on the marriage between the then 11-year-old Kim Cheolsu and 15-year-old Lee Sojeo.

Ms. Lee's husband's home was a wealthy family that was just as good as her parent's home, of a good quality. Thereby, under the roof of her parents-in-law, who were affectionate towards her, a daughter-in-law, concurrently like a daughter to them, during the time that she prematurely lived four to five years, without knowing of difficulty, Ms. Lee came to have her first son. The happy occasion that this was the first grandchild from their only son made not even a single person of Ms. Lee's husband's family, her parent's family, and her relatives refuse to take pleasure in it.

Cheolsu was still far from maturity. He did not even go to the village school that he was unwillingly enrolled into, in his spare time, he would go flying the kite, and engaged in going around, gambling money. So, without a word that he was coming and going, when he went out, he would turn up in a few days, without saying anything, and then, go out again. Afterwards, following that, he came under tens of hundreds of debts from the cost of alcohol, Gisaeng (Korean Geisha), and gambling. "A lad ought to live a life of debauchery in order to let his emotions burst out of his heart," Kim Seung Ji said, and in the beginning, without a word, the family took it well. Yet, as the family fortune gradually became languishing, as the weight of the harvest that had been made now, in a span of one year, was merely middle-of-the-road, and as the household turned destitute, it started to become more and more tiresome. Once in a while, the family tried to call their son and reason with him. And then, they beat him with a whip or a club, whenever the opportunity would arise. As their rage was at its very peak, they threw a wild fit, as if on the verge of killing. While Cheolsu felt pained, it was in order to escape from his wrongdoing that he made excuses, "Oh my, oh my, oh my," making a fuss, and burst into tears. Whenever they suffered through this incident, rather than it being pathetic, Ms. Lee felt scared and shuddered. As she heard the sound of crying in the room, she would stand, trembling. And, for some reason, whenever the sound of "Oh my, oh my, oh my" could be heard, tears would fall out. Even, she would think up to the point of, 'I wish they'd stop hitting him by now.' There was a time when she felt a tug at her heart. Yet, she never once warned her husband against his debauchery. While she did think of desperately talking him out of it, it seemed as if the words coming from a woman like her, which were not even the words from Cheolsu's father, who had been having a wild fit every day, out of vexation, would only be reaching deaf ears. Cheolsu, whose eyes reddened and who was in a buoyant mood so much that he got out of breath, did not even seem to be a sound person. Not only was it awkward to go near him, by his side, but fearing that he would ask what was the matter, she only furtively read his countenance. The debauchery of booze and women only became worse day by day, and the confidence in his change of heart could not be spotted anywhere. The next thing she knew, the jewelry and the like, which Ms. Lee had received as wedding presents, when she got married were brought out, swallowed up, and disposed of. The street of the prostitute quarters that had entered in pairs, the prostitute marketplace, the silk bedding all got taken away, upon a two-time enforcement and in the corner of the room, only two desks were placed. When she would lie down, holding the youngster in her arm, and look up at the upper side of the room, for it was so bleak, the tears that fell ceaselessly wet her collar. All of a sudden, she became envious of Ms. Jang, who was among her childhood friends. While Ms. Jang's household was barely well-enough, her husband was a diligent person. Even if he was a man, he frugally took good care of the housekeeping, stood behind his wife, and loved his children so much that word of the house being always harmonious had been frequently heard from the madam of the neighboring house. She could not bear thinking that a person without much would have such a blessing and how much of a good fortune it was for the person. Ms. Lee only hoped that her husband's age would at once, quickly be way past thirty-years of age. Ms. Lee consoled herself with a single beam of hope that perhaps, if he would grow old, he might take the circumstances of life into his own hands.

One day, it was around noon. One shabby day laborer came, sneaking in suddenly, saying, "Hello. Is this Seung Ji's house? That son of a bitch, that – Ms. Lee's husband passed out over there, there, there, there. So, it's become a commotion now," and he could not afford to reach the end of his words, urgent. At this time, right in the moment, the wife of Kim Seung Ji, thinking of her son who was whipped by his father and who without even eating, left in the prior evening was wiping her tears with the string of her skirt and had been sitting down. As this was such an unexpected incident, taken aback, uttering, "What, who's that? What is the matter here?" Ms. Lee hurriedly ran out all the way to the yard. Ms. Lee had been sitting down, draped in her husband's durumagi (traditional Korean overcoat), shocked, out of her wits. The path in front was merely dark to the point that she could not stand up. Kim Seung Ji, who went outside and just in time came in, had his eyes wide open, with no clue as to what the situation was. The servants all, as if drained of their souls held onto each one of the pillars and had been trembling. Kim Seung Ji promptly ordered the servant and the neighboring house's Mr. Kim to go follow the person who told the news and to bring back his son. Kim Seung Ji also followed from behind. As they passed by, from place to place, from this alley to that alley, they reached the front of the main gate with a small but oblique plank, and stepping inside it, the day laborer said, "Here it is." While Kim Seung Ji hesitated over entering, the moment that he saw the door plate, which had 'Jeongdohong' written on the corner of a pillar, he soon made his way in. "The boy must have at last passed out on the knees of a Gisaeng (Korean Geisha)," he uttered and fury welled up, bursting out of his chest.

Cheolsu had been sprawled out, unconscious, with his two legs extended on top of a purple fancy mattress of the Five Blessings symbol (longevity, wealth, health, love of virtue, peaceful death) that had all faded out in the dark corner of the room. The three to four Gisaengs (Korean Geisha) had been massaging the legs and arms and upon seeing Kim Seung Ji arrive, there was one who stood up to bow, and one who deliberately, exhaustedly sat down and needlessly massaged the body here and there, with a gleam of the utmost concern. Kim Seung Ji stood, looking down, at a loss for words. And, he wore an expression of, 'I knew as much.' He called the servant over and gave an order to carry Ms. Lee's spouse and to go to the back of the alley.

The name of the disease of Cheolsu became a subject. Typically, at dawn, he would go drinking and not being able to earn even twenty won that ought to have been there last night, he was in such a state of only being beaten to a pulp that he ran to Doheung's house, brought alcohol by buying it on credit, and was in the middle of drinking for a long while. Drunk out of his mind, as he collapsed for a moment, all of a sudden, he was foaming at the mouth and as he uttered a piercing cry, his eyes turned white, lopsided, his breath became cold, and his entire body turned rigid. This sent chills to the Gisaeng (Korean Geisha) who had been laughing and playing flat out up until now.

Without once having been happy nor having had fun, the one who had only been afflicted with sad and worrisome incidents was solely Ms. Lee. It was appalling, as if she became stuck with a wound inflicted by a blade when she saw the left side of her husband's body, whose entire physique had been fine before, being moved around here and there, entrusted in others' hands. According to the doctor who felt his purse for his diagnosis, he was addicted to alcohol. After getting a few shots, his breathing became light and he started to moan. Like this, while it seemed like he could recover, his condition went back to worsening more and more. The entire family was impatient and took pity. At that time, he began to severely discharge blood. Thereby, his body became emaciated and his sickly complexion became deeply ingrained. With an earnestness that soared up, Ms. Lee steadfastly nursed him. Yet, cruelly, there was no potential efficacy. The prolonged illness lasted for three years and at last, at the age of nineteen, in November of the lunar calendar, he lost his blooming youth and ended up dead.

Ms. Lee's age was twenty-three. She was like a flower that had been in bloom since a long time ago. An untimely frost fell on top of the peony blossom, which had been in bloom. As Ms. Lee was still in sorrow, she did not know of the blessings of a new year. It was just that it was as if her deceased husband who had been bedridden was lying in the room and at some time, she found it ominous to step into her room. And, she was embarrassed as others all stared at the white mourning clothes that were draped in her body. When she was not busy and deeply dwelled on his death, rather than missing her husband, her tears streamed at the thought of herself having gone through such an agony. Everyone that met her said that it was pitiful, what a shame, and asked again what the reason was. It merely seemed like the aftermath of intensely banging her head somewhere.

The time that swiftly flew by, in no time, went past three years. Ms. Lee came to feel more and more of loneliness. While scrubbing with soap, she would quickly leave it alone and would be looking at the far-off mountain. While going on about unnecessary things without worrying, when she would come to think of her circumstances, unbeknownst to others, she would even cry heaps of tears. Kim Seung Ji and his wife, as if they had directed something that was of ill-fortune, could not bear to see their widowed daughter-in-law and could not help but take pity on her. So, they did not really intervene in Ms. Lee's behavior and left her alone to be free altogether. They thought such an attitude would be a way to console their widowed daughter-in-law. Whenever Ms. Lee could not overcome her loneliness, she would go to her parents. Even when she would go to her parents, there was nothing much to be consoled. It was merely that going to her parents was one excuse. When she would come out of the main gate, it seemed like she was refreshed, just as she got swept by the cool wind. Just seeing people seemed to give her some mental comfort. Like this, when she had gone out one or two times, by now, with the least bit of complaint inside the house, numerous times, she spent the year, without reserve, getting out of the house, as if there was something to make a big fuss over, and went on a search for her relatives from far-away she had not known before, saying this and that, such as madam, sister-in-law. Yet, there was no one who would interfere with Ms. Lee's behavior.

At the opposite side of the house of Kim Seung Ji was the house of Park Champan, who had a friendly relationship with Kim Seung Ji. Earlier on, Park Champan had taken up a public office and by his own efforts, became a substantial man of wealth. As he was in the middle of making a fortune with honor, while it was not really out-of-the-ordinary, he was currently of the same age as Kim Seung Ji, fifty-four-years-old, but still, his presence was dashing and he had somewhat of a great strength. He was a covetous person whose insides would ache, when a young woman was in his sight, even when he had two concubines that were around the age of his granddaughter. One day, when he would set out to the gate to visit the second concubine's house, on the opposite side, he saw a young, mourning woman coming out of Kim Seung Ji's house. As the face that was not even pretty nor hateful, which was good-natured, of a white hue, and a beautiful attitude stood out in his eyes, he was entranced by the sight before him. While he would covertly get behind Ms. Lee, his heart would be beating, and the fiery greed radiated all the way from beneath his jaw. If it were a deserted street, with his two trembling hands, he would have pulled Ms. Lee from behind into an embrace, wrapped her up inside of the durumagi (traditional Korean overcoat), and would have amply satisfied his greed. Yet, at the front and back of the street, and to the left and right, to no end, it was brimming with people. From afar, turning around, after learning as far as the house that Ms. Lee was entering, his heart was still beating. As she had come out of and gone into Kim Seung Ji's house, the only thing that he wondered about was whether she was the wife of Kim Seung Ji, the head of the house or whether or not she was the widowed daughter-in-law of Kim Seung Ji, which he had no way of knowing for sure.

Later, on a certain day, as Park Champan coincidentally brought it up to his wife, when it reached his ears that as much as Kim Seung Ji's widowed daughter-in-law did not have such a flaw to be a young widow, that no matter how much she would be scrutinized, she had a satisfying character and attitude, he thought inwardly, 'Then, the woman must be the widowed daughter-in-law of the house in front,' happy and relieved. While he was wandering in the yard outside, holding his pipe in his mouth, still in doubt, he paid attention to the gate of the house in front. While he was doing that, one day, like the day before, sure enough, a young, mourning woman came out through the main gate of the house. With the thought of, 'Okay, the time has come now,' he attentively looked Ms. Lee up and down. He watched her like this, for two to three times. Ms. Lee did not know that she was being watched until the second time. At the third time, it became so suspicious that once, she thoughtlessly looked back. Thinking that this would be a good opportunity, he put on a slightly odd smile in his eyes and expressed some kind of ambition. Ms. Lee felt a prick in her chest. And, her heart would be throbbing with apprehension. Later, for several days, she was in misery. She was terribly infuriated and sad, because it was as if she was being looked down on by everyone, treated as an object without its owner. Yet, the thought of his needless smile in his eyes would come back up that she would chide her mind and would spring insults on it, but it would surface again and again. She made up her mind that she would now no longer go out. However, before she knew it, she would be heading out to the main gate, where her heart would thump with apprehension and the first thing within her sight was the main gate of the house in front. That day, he was not seen there. She thought it to be rather fortunate. Yet, from the back, a freight-carrier had been aimlessly treading on an inwardly empty manure of a living corpse, oblivious to the point that a wagon-puller screamed, "Dear. Dear."

It was the night of the 14th of August of the year. She had been making Songpyeon (half-moon-shaped rice-cake) till midnight and went back to her room. While she had been sleeping, wheezing, along with the angelic little one that she had, the room was unexpectedly bleak. The moon of the autumn was rather unusually bright like glass. Whenever the cool wind would pass by, once in a while, the cacophony of the sound of the leaves of the tree pushed its way into the quiet of the night, when all of the creations should be asleep. As Ms. Lee drowned in the depths of her apprehension, she would brusquely turn off the light and lay flat in the corner of the chilly room, but the moon cold-heartedly reflected on her, fueling her emotions. It seemed like just letting out a wail, unrestrainedly and heavily would still not be relieving. So, she lay back, tossing about here and there, and while thinking endlessly of the incidents that have passed by, the esteemed God of sleep firmly cast Ms. Lee into a deep sleep.

Without knowing whether this was a dream or a reality, Ms. Lee vaguely realized that someone was tightly embracing her, as if to break her body. Ms. Lee's body itself, frightened out of its wits, had been pressed up against a stranger of a person. And, her body shivered. So, when someone's hand reached her chest, at last, it occurred to her that it was not a dream and Ms. Lee, taken aback, sat up, abruptly. In front, a man, who was keeping a straight face, sitting there was clearly seen in the light of the moon. Ms. Lee unwittingly cried, "Ah-." Yet, the sound was not loud enough to be heard in the main room and it was low, as if to take caution. The man was still sitting there nonchalantly, and wearing a smile in his eyes, he lightly coaxed Ms. Lee. Now, he told her that even if she were to throw a fit and let the whole house know, as she would have no other alternative but to be falsely accused, she had to stay still, listen to him, that he was Park Champan, who lived in a house, in front of hers, that after having seen her once, as if he had gone insanely sick from the weight of concern over seeking her, tonight, not being able to resist, he had trespassed, that if she was not going to save him, he was not going to leave her alone, and for her to keep that in mind, he threatened her. Ms. Lee could not say anything, sat, crouched in one corner, like a bird in a net, and shuddered. She wondered as to what would be good for her to do, for if she were to bawl, she would be overcome by shame, within sight of the servants, and if she were to open the door and run off, he would grab her, and so, she was flustered, not knowing what to do. When the man grasped her wrist, she would only shove it away, and when he would lunge at her, she would only avert her body. All the while, fearing that someone would see through the glass, she would look furtively at the side of the glass, and would be on edge, from someone's footsteps seemingly approaching, as if their sound could be heard. Thereby, fearing that anyone would hear, she could not speak a word and she would only avoid him, here and there, shaking off his hand, and thought that he would not dare win over her. Yet, the man had already made up his mind, regardless of life or death, with greed that reached the stage that could not be radiated more, like that of a beast. It was all too familiar and easy to get a small woman, who would be trying to evade here and there, within his clutch in an open room and do whatever he liked.

She stayed up the remaining night, with her eyes open, and heaved herself up early in the morning. The flames of the morning sunlight that rose up initially looked frightening in Ms. Lee's eyes. And, the pair of eyes of the people appeared to be too big and bright. With such eyes, she attentively looked down at her body. It was the same as when a criminal who had committed some huge crime would be frightened out of one's wits as the spear and sword of a constable was raised. It was as if it had happened inside of her dream, and it felt out of place, as if her body had turned noxious. All the while, whenever she would be in a state of shock, as if some huge botch formed on her body, it was itchy and if only she could sever her filthy body, she wished to do so. She also wanted to go on gnawing off, tearing the man apart, dragging it on, all the way through. Like this, she spent a couple of days, huddled up and hugging her chest with all sorts of thoughts that cropped up. In the meanwhile, seeing that there was not much change in the attitudes of the people in the house, she would let out a deep sigh of relief. It was as if she had carried a huge load and put it down. Yet, strangely, Ms. Lee could not forget the impression of that night. The more she thought of the warm hands, the friendly eyes, they unfolded before her sight vividly. Yet, when the thought came up, "But with someone like an old man," as if she had suffered a severe offense, she was terribly infuriated and was ashamed of herself.

One evening, Kim Seung Ji took away the dishes after eating dinner and visited Park Champan's house to play baduk (a game of Go). As he briskly entered the reception room, he saw one pair of a woman's shoes placed there on a flight of stone steps. Knowing that the village Gisaengs constantly came over to play in this house, Kim Seung Ji did not really take it as strange, and thoughtlessly opened the door of the reception room, in search for the owner. As he brought one foot into the doorsill, he yelled, "Ah⋯⋯." After taking a step back and halting, he soon turned around and exited. Where in the world would there be another one of such absurdity! What is with this – his widowed daughter-in-law whom he had trusted to the very core, earnestly taken pity on, and was affectionate to, was sitting on top of Park Champan's knees and hastily came down, not knowing what to do, helpless. Kim Seung Ji still doubted what he saw. He tried not to believe in the fact. He rubbed his eyes, wondering if it was a dream, and tried shaking his head. Soon, he went to his house and called her, "Daughter-in-law." According to his wife, the daughter-in-law ate dinner and went out to visit her parents. Kim Seung Ji came out once again and was keeping an eye out on her movement. In about thirty minutes, indeed, when seeing a mourning woman come out of Park Champan's house, furtively glancing around the front and the back, and going into his house, his mind reeled. It turned out to be that he could do no more than believe in it, even if he did not want to.

From that day forth, complaining that he was in a frail state, Kim Seung Ji lay in the reception room, only sowing hatred, and refused to altogether enter into the other rooms. Among the members of the family, there was only one person who knew why.

That night, Ms. Lee had been sure enough on her way to go to her parents. The moment that she made her way out of the gate, just in time, as if he had been standing there, ready for her, Park Champan, with the expression of surprise and delight, with a sense of familiarity, grabbed her wrist and dragged her off to his reception room. As Park Champan was rather out of his mind, without hearing the sound of the arrival of a person, in his unruly state, his secret was spilled, unexpectedly, right in front of Kim Seung Ji. Park Champan, in fact, did not have the dignity to face him, from having lured Kim Seung Ji's daughter-in-law, when they had been friends. However, on the one hand, as he thought of this, he found it rather fortunate that it had been revealed, even a day sooner. As a matter of fact, he would only ponder over what he should do to make Ms. Lee always sit by his side. So, when Ms. Lee, who had not been subserviently listening to him, all of a sudden clung to his chest, uttering, "Old man," and crying, he was infinitely happy. "Okay, don't cry. Starting from today, won't it be best if you don't go and if you just stay with me?" when he would say this, among his sadistic nature, the triumphant pride would have emerged, where he would go, "I knew it. Finally, you're also going to be mine." When Ms. Lee was setting out to leave, he tenaciously held onto her. As he held her, he realized that there was no need for him to do so. This was because she did not have anywhere else to go now, and she would have no choice but to come to him.

In the mind of Kim Seung Ji, who was infuriated, he wanted to wreak a big humiliation on Park Champan by accusing him of the sin of seduction and to chase his daughter-in-law out. Yet, first, he could not help but think of how his wield of his power and his reputation would be hindered, and of his Yangban (Upper class in Joseon) family name. He could do nothing but endure and it was merely that in the space between his eyebrows, the depths of anxiety would not ever leave.

Only three people knew of this secret and thinking that no one else would know, there was not a single one of the three that spilled the beans. Yet, strangely, in no time, crossing from one mouth to the other mouth, the wife of Kim Seung Ji learned of it, the wife of Park Champan came to know, the two servants of the house became aware of it, and in Wondong-ri, it ended up becoming a gossip. Now, Ms. Lee did not have the sense of shame to remain in Kim Seung Ji's house any longer. Besides, she did not have any place to set foot in this wide world, when her parents were in a frenzy, saying that they would kill her. Even suicide was short of a blessing. Incapable of doing this or that, she was faced with no choice but to leave her child, whom she has raised, in the absence of his father, and with her head lowered, step into the house of Park Champan.

Ms. Lee became the third concubine of Park Champan. Yet, as a matter of fact, she did not know how many of the concubines would come to be there. Anyhow, for a brief time period, as a concubine who was favored the most, he did not let her leave his side. Yet, Ms. Lee who was hapless would face the fate of not even receiving this love for long. Park Champan who had solely been engulfed day and night in love, in less than two months, became more extreme in his access to concubines. One day, sending Ms. Lee away inside, he brought a woman similar to a female student with hair done up in a Western style and forced her not to leave his side, like he had done with Ms. Lee. The woman was a beautiful female who was also around twenty-five or twenty-six, like Ms. Lee. When seeing the woman take her place, rather than being angry or jealous, Ms. Lee felt sorry for her and as if the woman's future could be vividly seen, Ms. Lee took pity on her. And, when some kind of opportunity would arise, Ms. Lee wanted to give her advice.

Ms. Lee became a handmaid, like the legal wife of Park Champan. Ceaselessly, she would massage his legs and arms that ached from nervous disorders, light up the pipe and have it ready, scoop up and present the water for washing up, read aloud a story-book every night, smooth clothes by pounding on them, sew, and without even a brief moment of goofing off, she was thriftily shoved around to work like a horse. Even when Ms. Lee had led a marriage life for seven years, it was the first time that she was maltreated and undertook difficult tasks to such an extent. Yet, thinking, 'Who could I blame, this is all my fault,' she went on to endure it. She had decided that whatever she would do, she would become the ghost of Mr. Park's house. All the while, she suffered through all sorts of mistreatment. What was more, if she made a little mistake, Park Champan's wife would say, "You bitch, if you're going to be like that, get out," and when the wife was striking Ms. Lee's hand, the spot where it had been struck seemed to be on fire. It was an offense that a person could not bear to suffer from. Ms. Lee, who grew mad, bore a heavy grudge. And, she came to make a different decision.

In a year, Ms. Lee got out of the house of Park Champan. She spat at the lofty gate. She cursed, glared, and clenched her hand into a fist. Still, there was nothing to be relieved about. While she was able to escape from that hellhole, when she was wondering as to where she would head off to in the future, as the grief, which was beyond expression from among all the embittering experiences she has had until now, bubbled to the surface, the tears that could not be contained flooded out like the shower of rain in the month of May and June.

Indeed, Ms. Lee, who was said to have smeared the Yangban family name, did not have a place where she was accepted. To her mortification, while she was able to wash away the dishonor of a concubine, the joints of her hands thickened and her body had only deeply stained red. The woman who still had not turned thirty was wandering the street and sobbing.

Ms. Lee earned fifty won from a loan at a high interest rate, and on the basis of it, started a business. She sold Hankwangwoori rice, Hankwangwoori adzuki beans, Hankangwoori soybeans, stacked them up, carried them upside down, until her head would shrink, and from here and there, she went on a search for the lively market, hoping for a penny, two pennies, and endured through the cold and hot days, going around, bellowing, "It's cheap, cheap." Even today, she walked about 24 km, travelling back and forth to the marketplace, and came back, having a bite of the rice that lost its steam and fell into a bitter, fatigued sleep at the cold hypocaust of the upper side of a room. "Oh my, Oh my, my leg, my leg, Hmph······That son of a bitch."

⟨*The Joseon Literary Circles* (Magazine; 1924~1936)⟩ (1926. 4.)

A Single Woman's
Theory on Chastity

"Sis, please write one love letter for me."

Just now, K, who was an employed woman, came to S, her elder sister, for a request. As K was S's most loved younger sister, K occasionally played on S's affection and when K shared the story with her elder sister all the time of her romance with Y, her fiancé, her husband-to-be, S has been attentively listening to the story, treating it with adoration and interest.

"Kid, I'm having a headache."

"Why are you like that? You've aged."

"Although I've aged, it's because I got cross."

"Why?"

K's eyes were wide open.

"Why can't I be? It may be because despite being physically aged, my mind is still young."

"If so, does that mean you're basking in the memory of romance in your period of youth, dear sister?"

"While that may be so, do you think that I'm not experiencing any romance now?"

"Oh my, how disgusting. You, an oldie."

"Yeah, I'm worried."

"Right. Are you, sister, also worried like I am, where I get so agonized over wanting to see my lover that I could not sleep at night?"

"That is the romance of youths. The romance of people in their mid-age is different."

"How is it different, sis?"

K closely bid defiance to her.

"I'm going to tell you that later."

"Spit it out now, please, sis?"

"This isn't what you need right now and because I would most likely be preaching to deaf ears and you wouldn't even be able to understand, let's call it quits."

"Then, write one letter for me."

"That is, to Y."

"Yes."

"Until when?"

"Until tomorrow morning."

"That's rushing at most."

"Sis, you saw the letter from Y last time. This is supposed to be a reply to that letter."

"Then, I should write long."

"Since the letter that came was long, the letter that should be sent ought to be long."

"By the way, although you're not aged, you act senile."

"Why?"

"Who has her love-letter written by someone else?"

"Who doesn't know that?"

"It's like having one's eyes open and falling into a hole."

"There goes my annoying sister's theory again."

"It's not a theory but isn't that so? Isn't a love letter the byproduct of writing out of the blood boiling from within one's chest with soft hands?"

"Who doesn't know such a thing?"

"Hmph, then, does that mean everyone knows that?"

"Yes."

"If I can't do it······."

"Sis, don't you say that but instead, please, just this once, write one for me."

K clung to her elder and coaxed her.

"You mean that if you yourself write the letter, the level of your intellect, which has usually stayed hidden, would come to the surface."

"Right, my sister knows well. By now, I'd have nothing much to write."

"Yes. With such a teeny tiny bit of your learning."

"Right, I can't handle this letter-writing to Y, considering the state that Y is in."

"Kid. Having seen Y's letter, I can tell that his character is complete. He is a person with a considerable mix of humanity and philanthropy."

"That may be true. So, please write as it is."

"Should I write it?"

S glanced at the wall in front of her fleetingly and blinked.

"Oh my, how wonderful."

"This is a bit of a difficult request."

"While it's a difficult thing for me, it's easy for you, sis."

"That is, if I were to write to my lover, it would be easy."

"Write with the feeling of you writing to your lover."

"Then, won't that become wildly out of control?"

"Certainly, my sister is a passionate person."

"Even though I'm aged, the passion still remains."

"I know. That's because you're an artist."

"You exceed my expectations, knowing all that."

"Sis, you also tend to look down on nerds like me."

"That's not something to get angry about. It's because you're cute."

S patted K on the back.

"Then, sis, please take good care of the letter."

K headed to the hospital, where she had her job and frequented every day.

Sending K away, S sat obliquely and grinned from ear to ear. This was because she found the honey-like whispers between K and Y at present to be cute and lovely, and the future path, where they would be making their step-by-step progress passed by lambently like the film of a motion picture.

And, another reason was because predicting in their future path all sorts of tragedy and comedy, a sense of watching a single act of a play was formed. S opened the desk drawer, pulled out the letter paper, and held her pen.

Dear Mr. Y!

Is it already spring? Spring may have come. Has it arrived? Well. Indeed, spring has come. Ah, ah. It's already spring.

The spring of the city, the spring of the farm village, warm spring, beautiful spring, the spring of the screeching and weeping of birds, the spring of the flower-plant field, the spring of pipe, the spring of people, the spring of beasts, the spring of happiness, the spring of melancholy, the spring of the river with the willow trees in the long bank, the spring of the Hwahongmun Gate, the spring of Banghwa Suryujeong (architecture located in Gyeonggi, Suwon, Hwaseong Fortress, set up by King Jeongjo of Joseon in the year of 1794), a complete spring has arrived. How happy is it that we, a couple, have both the spring of nature and the spring of life? Seeing that nature, which is seemingly the simplest, doesn't give us a feeling of aversion, the power of nature must be profuse with its intrinsic force.

Until today, in a very remote distance, under the high sky, I couldn't lift my head, and due to not being able to lift my head under the sky that was as high as 500 km away, somehow, unwittingly, the surrounding felt uneasy, and yet, starting from today, my mind is at peace, I feel energized automatically, and my will springs up. As you are already a person with a combi-

nation of humanity and philanthropy, I know that you've been
assuming all this, and I trust that you would eternally love me,
care for me, and with the best of my sincerity, I will come to
receive this love and care and pull them into my embrace. Upon
respectfully reading your esteemed letter once again, there are
a lot of things that I could feel. That is true, indeed. Without
knowing of hardship, a person could not acknowledge the other
person's circumstances well. In other words, such a person could
not be of good taste. You've experienced trials yourself of starv-
ing and cutting wood. Which is what has made you of today.
Although I'm not a match for your tribulations, I also more or
less have had my share of burdens. Despite not knowing how
to acknowledge other people, I do understand the words they
speak. Considering this point, I know that our future path is a
sturdy road that would suffice to guarantee our happiness. By
all means, please guide me well⋯⋯.

So and so forth⋯⋯.

K budding from the ninety days of spring.

In the morning of the following day, K visited S.

"Sis, did you finish writing?"

"Although I did finish writing, I don't think I could hand it to you just like that."

S, who was an expert at kidding around, joked again.

"Then, what am I supposed to do?"

"Who just writes a love letter for someone? This is a decision made out of blood and sweat."

"You mean I should pay you back again?"

"Is there any room for doubts?"

"I will pay you back."

"How?"

"Once Y gets his salary, let's go eat rice cooked in the temple (Buddhist temple)."

"That sounds nice."

"Now that the conditions have all been attached, give me the letter."

"Kid, I almost died, trying to squeeze them out by force. Are there any words to write? I just droned on and on about innocent spring."

"Let me see."

K held the letter and looked at it.

"This really is talkative."

"Now that I've gone to great pains writing this for you, you go about making some noise, without crediting me."

"No, no, sis, you wrote brilliantly with such craftiness."

"If that's the case, that may be true."

"You wrote all that was in my mind, how splendid."

"Even when in the very least, the person who wrote this letter is me, an oldie, you still think that?"

"Yes, even now, you still write a passionate letter."

"Right."

"Should I also try my hand at writing?"

"What would you do with it then?"

"Why?"

"That's because writing is burdensome."

"It may be fun."

"Despite having physically aged, I'm young at heart. This indeed would not be tasted by those who never had a taste of the artistic sensibility."

"If so, such a person with an artistic sensibility must be happy."

"Such a person would suffer a lot of pains in the heart."

"Sis, how is romance in your mid-age?"

"Well, I keep telling you to call it quits."

"Please, do tell me."

"The love between young adults is like a bonfire and the love between middle-aged people is like fire made with the hulls of rice that gently burns and is a relationship, where one gets to have all the sleep they would have."

"Is that really so?"

"Do you get it?"

"I don't get it."

"Are you going to send the letter today?"

"Yes, it should be quickly sent. Thank you."

K set off outside.

In a spring day that was neither cold nor hot, at 5pm, when the overripe cherry blossoms bloomed in the government office (government office for the advancement of agriculture and stockbreeding) at Hwahongmun Gate, after their departure, the taxi that gave K and Y a ride arrived in front of the door of S's house. K swiftly came down and went inside.

"Sis, come on out."

S, who had been preparing just in time, came out. Y was standing, waiting at the gate section.

The taxi that picked up the three people rushed to Bongnyeong-sa temple. The fragrant smell of the grass that got carried by the wind cooled the head of S who had been in a sullen mood. In a flash, the taxi reached the top of Bongnyeongsa temple, which was less than about 3.9 km from the fortress. The three people climbed up the flight of stairs and after looking around the Buddhist sanctuary, they chose a quiet room and went inside, ordering dinner. Soon, the food was all done. Oil was plastered in the gourd dipper, fried kelp was smashed and added, Gobi-namul (Asian royal fern herbs) and Doraji-namul (seasoned bellflower roots) were put in, and Dubu-jeongol (the soup of the tofu hot pot) was included and mixed in.

"It really is delicious."

K spoke, while enjoying her meal.

"Eat up."

"It is tasty."

Y chimed in.

"Indeed, it is tasty."

They set out, after paying for the food.

The sun was setting and as it was the fifteenth night by the lunar calendar, a full moon was high up in the sky.

"Let us talk, while we leisurely walk."

"I'm feeling really good."

Y smiled with satisfaction.

The three people lightly walked.

Above the black pine tree, a white moon was up and a shadow wavered.

From the ground, the smell of wormwood came rising up.

"Don't go ahead like that."

"As a Westerner once said, when one sees Easterners accompanying each other, one gets a sense of which country they come from."

"How so?"

Y who had been walking ahead halted and asked.

"The Westerner says that when one sees people standing side by side, talking, they must be Japanese, and when one sees people standing apart, scattered, and walking without a word, they must be either Chinese or Korean."

"Hahaha Hohoho."

"Sis, share a story."

"Shall I? Should I get into my story so that we become oblivious to how far of a distance we're walking?"

"I'm up for it."

"Upon visiting the historical site of the volcano in Pompeii of Italy, among its customs, it had a custom 2,000 years ago, where there was a tiny gourd-shaped bottle and when mourning took place, they brought a person there, made one cry, placed the tears inside the gourd-shaped bottle, and put a price on it."

"Oh my, how amusing."

K burst into laughter.

"And, a single piece of mural remained in someplace, which was covered, where only an image of a man could be seen, and I thought it was of a person drawing something, but when I came to see, there turned out to be a scale that weighed the male genital."

"What is the use of weighing such a thing?"

K laughed again.

"It must be for measuring its weight."

Y went on to casually talk about what meaning it contained.

"In that period, the customs of Pompeii were extremely extravagant and obscene, and so, in the eating places, there were paintings of birds, in an assembly room, paintings of a goddess, in the bedroom, paintings of pornography, in the children's room, freehand drawings, a room with the wall on all sides in the color of black, a room in the color of pure dark red, and a room solely in the color of dark green."

"Isn't Pompeii where God sent down punishment, because of it being extremely extravagant and obscene?"

Y, who had some common knowledge, spoke.

"It doesn't end there. In the peak of the Roman period, at a feast, some eating their food put their fingers in their mouths, threw up, went back to eating again, and again."

"Oh my."

K was quite taken aback.

"In Paris of France, in the archaic museum, there is a famous waistband of a woman, and in the past, while the husband was out participating in a match, the behavior of the woman was so unscrupulous that around the time when the husband was going to the match, he tied the waistband around the pubic area of the woman, which would just leave room for peeing, locked her up, and went out with the key."

"My goodness, how come? How disgusting. There are all sorts of customs."

"If the stories were brought up one by one, there would be all sorts of customs."

"Right. Since civilization and history are lengthy, various kinds of customs would exist." Y spoke.

"Hey, K."

"Yes."

"Have you seen a fart?"

"How can one see a fart?"

"You've never seen one?"

Y said, grinning widely at her.

"You're such a pretentious know-it-all."

"Then, you don't know?"

"Then, come on, speak up."

"You should be the one talking first."

"No, since you're the one who claims to have seen it, you should be the one talking first."

K and Y stealthily moved their body, bumped into each other's backs, pinched one another's flesh, and relished playing for quite a while. S, the one who raised the question about the fart, furtively took side-glances at them and put on a broad smile. As each one of them all pulled their shadows along, which were lightening and darkening, while strolling in between the pine trees, the three people heading for the fortress, who whispered amongst themselves and taking a walk, were free and amusing.

"You're quite shrewd."

"Why?"

"Since you don't want to say that you didn't see the fart, you're suggesting others to be the one to speak."

"That's not something to be delayed by shifting the responsibility onto each other. Let's just do rock, paper, scissors."

"Okay, let's do that."

"Rock, paper, scissors. Oh dear, it's a draw."

"Right, it's our principle that boys lose in this game with a draw."

"I'm totally screwed."

"Go on, do tell me."

K pinched Y.

"Ow, ow, as I've been sticking out my mouth like this, now, talking seems a bit bland."

"Can it be tolerated, if you're not talking at all?"

"Then, I'll talk."

"Go on."

K clasped the shoulder of Y.

"Why are you grabbing someone's shoulder, as if you're bidding ill-will?"

"Go on, speak."

"Have you ever farted inside a bathtub filled with water? How was it?"

"Okay, okay, Right, right, the fart simmers, bubbling up to the surface."

"Hahahaha, Hohohoho."

"How was it? You didn't know that?"

"Now I know."

The three people held their waists and rolled around and around. For a brief moment, they were silent, and then, the subject matter entered into their perspective on life.

"When are you having your wedding?"

As the grown-up, S asked.

"I am the happiest in this time now. The longer the period of engagement is, the more one gets to know the taste of life."

"Yet, since marriage is not the whole of your lives, without the need for Mr. Y and K thoughtlessly and mindlessly spending time, it would be good to quickly get on with the wedding celebration and be well-assured."

"Why is there a need for that?"

"That's because it's easy to develop a distaste. In other words, before a flaw is seen, it would be good to come to a decision."

"Isn't it more dangerous to develop a distaste after marriage?"

"Whether it is before or after marriage, at any time, everyone is bound to suffer a distaste for the other person at least once."

"Why is that?"

"Love, admiration, and sympathy are around when they are getting to know each other. By the time they know each other, the emotions would wane and flaws would be seen. It's like the temperature of the thermometer going all the way up to 100 degrees and then going down to 0 degrees, and if worse, it could go down to below Celsius."

"Would it be like that?"

"Certainly, yes. It's not that there is no limit to the affection of humans, but rather, a limit exists. The degree of the highs and lows should once more deeply take root."

"It may be so, but it all depends on the person."

"People share similarities."

"Then, how should one live, in order to live well?"

Y entered into the fundamental problem with great interest on which he had been racking his brain alone, all this time.

"I know. While it's such a short life, how many of them are there who fall into the pitfall of love and end up having their body shrunken up and unable to run?"

"That's because at the end of the day, the purpose of life is to become ordinary."

"That is true, but before becoming ordinary, there is a way to make life richer."

"How?"

"After getting married in the name of love, don't wives give birth to children and live their lives, cooped up, struggling hard to lick the boots of their husbands before passing away? This is the so-called ordinary."

"Then, is there any other course of action? The purpose of life is reproduction."

"Right, eventually, one would all step into each list of things, but there is no need to quickly step into it, because the social system has even that much space for freedom."

"I don't know what you're talking about."

"To put it in other words, at the age of puberty for men and women, they aren't satisfied with the love from parents and friends, miss their partner, worry themselves sick, while confining their body early on in the name of love, and end up falling into a hellhole where they get huddled up in their twenties or below thirties, where they cannot run."

"Yes, sure."

"Instead of doing that, there is a need for them to first think about what they're suffering from or agonizing over, solve them, and improve from their life of confinement."

"A majority of people may be worried about how to release their sexual desire."

"Doesn't the social system already have that covered for single people?"

"Do you mean red-light districts?"

"That's right, while living a single life, one could enter the red-light districts, that is, after one would be able to easily guarantee an unmarried life."

"While venereal diseases could be scary, at least, one doesn't become desperate."

"One could be considerably careful of that. That's why I once told a young person that it's better to go to a different place than always go to one place."

"That is right. There seems to be no need to confine one's body, just because of sexual lust alone."

"There's never any need for that. That is why not only is there a need for licensed prostitution for women, but also a licensed prostitution for men."

"There is a licensed prostitute quarter for men in Paris."

"While there is one in Paris, I heard as a true story that as it is on a large scale, spinsters, wives of soldiers, and widows make their entry."

"Then, there seems to be no sense of chastity there."

"Instead of having a nervous breakdown from trying to abide by the principle of chastity, and thus, becoming hysterical, contemporary people would also need to learn to relieve their sexual lust by paying money and living life exuberantly."

"It will be like that little by little."

"That is why with the advancement of the humanities, there would be a lot more single people and as long as sexual desire is fulfilled, the time as an unmarried person would be lengthier, as much as possible, without the need for a family with one's beloved."

"Then, where would single people get solace?"

"Those who entered the frontline of life could not afford to feel such loneliness and they'd wind up finding solace in what they do."

"What if they get tired of what they do?"

"Such a thing could just be under self-control."

"Could one keep living a life as a single person like that?"

"I'm not encouraging life as a single person, but rather I'm saying that it would be good for one to be single as long as one could."

"With the slightest mistake, could this lead someone astray?"

"That may be so, but it's a difficult issue."

"This is giving me a headache, so let's stop."

"Then, how could one have a peaceful family?"

Y had a bountiful of huge ideals about a new family that he would be having in the future. Yet, he wanted to hear the views of S, who already had a lot of experiences.

"According to the Western proverb, in order to have a peaceful family, the husband should treat his wife like a flower and the wife should be aware that the flower bloomed."

"Indeed. That sounds reasonable."

"The sweet home of Westerners is not solely from the strength of a husband and a wife but freedom in who they go out with. It would be easy to get tired of one another when a husband and a wife always see each other every day. Before getting tired of each other, accompanied by his wife, they would go out and the husband would set out to dance with the wife of another house, and the wife would go dancing with the husband of another house, having a conversation, which would make them feel fresh. That's why whenever they go somewhere, it becomes a thing of discourtesy for a married couple to be just dancing with each other and having their conversation."

"That seems to be quite plausible."

"Isn't that quite true? Going out, one could import a sense of novelty and come back home, using that emotion, and so, how could that not be a sweet home?"

"Would it gradually be like that in Joseon?"

"It would take a long time."

"As the husband gets all the bitter and sweet taste of a complex society and as for the wife, cooped up in a cramped household, she replays the same thing over and over, every day, as the wife doesn't get the husband's emotional cycle, and the husband doesn't understand his wife's emotions, wherever they are, they become scattered apart that the family would become dull and would become fatigued."

"That is true, indeed."

"That is why when she gets married from dating him, at first, there is a curiosity over what may happen to her in its wake, and yet, soon, the bottom of her marriage life becomes see-through and the woman becomes literally dried up, but as for the man, he continuously gets his social training, from which he goes on to grow, and so, what would the result be? They end up vacantly staring at each other and getting fatigued."

"Then, it sounds like the man elevates his status earlier than the woman?"

"That is true. The woman matures reproductively, and the man matures in terms of knowledge. That's why as far as knowledge is concerned, a twenty-five-year-old man is a match for a woman of thirty or forty."

"Is that so?"

"Then, if a man of thirty meets a woman of forty and they get married, they would have an ideal family."

"That can be true, but since a condition of beauty is attached to women, no men would think transcendentally to such an extent."

"Didn't people like the genius artist, Raphael in the Renaissance, or the 19th century prodigal artist Renoir exalt their mid-aged wives, and so, went on to draw only the nudes of their mid-aged wives?"

Y talked about what he had heard from an artist in the past.

"Upon inspection, the beauty of a mature relationship between men and women in mid-age is better than that in young adulthood."

"Then, what should families in Joseon do to have a peaceful family?"

"Right. Although they say it is gender equality, since they think of every sort of workload to be equal between men and women, there are countless cases of grievances. As for the husband, he could feel superior to his wife in some respects and so, aside from something inevitable, he himself could deal with work that could be more burdensome for his wife, which would instead cause no grievance. For example, couldn't that be seen in how a lot of conflicts take place in a new family, while peace is preserved in a family that has aged?"

"Miss K, listen and keep this in mind."

Y tapped K who was walking beside him by the shoulder with his hand.

"A person with a withered hand like you won't be able to say that."

K spewed out.

"How can you not get my intention that much?"

"How can she not know? She's just playing on your affection."

S suspected the emotional rollercoaster of the ups and downs between Y and K and mediated.

"Then, instead of fumbling an attempt at being a new woman, wouldn't it be better to act like an aged woman?"

"But is there anything else besides being more knowledgeable as an aged woman? It all depends on whether the man is well-rounded."

"Mr. Y, listen and keep this in mind."

K tapped Y on the shoulder with her hand.

"A person with a withered hand like you won't be able to say that. This is like cornering you with your own words."

"Hahahaha Hohohoho."

"You two are really enjoying yourselves. It's a good time."

S spoke like a grown-up that she was.

"Does it seem fun?"

Y said, scrutinizing S.

"Sure."

"What, sis? You're the sister who's had such fun yourself back in the days when you were our age."

"How do you know so well?"

"How can I not know?"

"By the way, Ms. S, you should've shared your history."

"Instead of talking about the long-gone, stale past, it's good to talk about the things that will be coming in the future."

"I've heard a lot of really helpful words from you."

Y abruptly paid his respects. S could not help but follow along and pay her respects.

"While pretending to know something, all high and mighty, may not be all that good, it is more or less different in my case."

"I know it is."

The new long highway in no time reached the East Gate. The East Gate, which was all in ruins, was protecting the old castle and overseeing the straw-roofed houses, stood grandly, while listening to the sound of the quivering pine trees, which were bent under the moon.

"Oh my, already, we've reached the East Gate."

Taken by surprise at seeing the East Gate that she tapped, K said.

"You wish that it would be a bit farther away? Miss K."

The moonlight at once shone on Y's face, flush with excitement.

"Well, we're nearing home."

The lonely room of hers surfaced in S's mind.

A whole day passed by today. From hour to hour, the course of one's life went hidden in the midst of time.

Face-to-face with a new fact, the past memory itself stayed hidden. Although she left the 40 years of her life above the flow of time, she realized that S's past was vanishing into thin air from S's present.

S felt greatly the freshness of the evening air of late spring. Entering the East Gate, the Yeonmudae (army training center in Joseon) that seemed high up left the past shelter for shooting arrows remaining, and in between, solely, the several pillars that commanded a view of the white sky were reflected in the moonlight. Sure enough, the car lane that had been made at the side seemed to be waiting for the footsteps of the lovers and companions, Y and K.

As they whirled around to take the path, what emerged were the white overripe cherry blossoms that bloomed under the moonlight. In between the flowers, Banghwa Suryujeong, (architecture set up by King Jeongjo of Joseon in the year of 1794) and the Hwahongmun Gate could be seen. With a mere piece of newspaper that had a leftover of lunch eaten by people blowing in the wind, the surrounding was tranquil. The three people stayed for a while and returned home.

The time was 11 at night. When they fell into a deep sleep at each one's dwelling, Y and K's soul went back and forth.

Although flowers may wane, a new spring will arrive again. Who would say that waiting for it is not a wonder? Waiting for the day. Waiting for the day.

⟨*Samcheonri* (Magazine; 1929~1950)⟩ (1935. 10.)

Hyeon-sook

Chapter 1.

It has been half a year since the two people met.

While the man was invited by the woman, originally, the man had been waiting for this opportunity to arrive. Of course, they shared all sorts of stories, such as the talks of their peers.

Now face-to-face, the aromatic, chiseled cheeks, the lips like an azalea, the warm sound of breathing like the taste of mahogany, the things that he had forgotten for a long time imbued him with a peak of excitement.

She certainly was not the woman of half a year ago. In the countenance of the woman who was capable of drawing the fondness from anyone of the opposite sex, the index of her finger, which could be extended to its utmost, was without reserve, waiting to be stretched.

"……Whatever it is, your attitude was no fun. Like how you quit working at store A in 3 days or how you became a waitress at a café……."

"……It was because I could not stay there for one more day.

Right, it was because being a waitress seemed to be reasonable. And, I always passed as the model of the Western-style painter, Mr. K. Mr. K brings disgrace to himself. I tell you about Mr. all the time. While Mr. always does make me feel unpleasant, there are lots of things that couldn't be done if not for me……."

"Right, okay, let's drink."

He directed the woman's attention to the black tea, which was placed there.

"And, I am recently living life like a cash register. How simple, effective, and how 100% clear people's reactions are, hahaha-ha……."

As it seemed like she was acting up, she blew on the hot tea, for two to three times, and as if she were to say in her expression,

'During the course of half a year since you left me, you must have been rather forlorn? Now, enough of this and come to me,' and looked thoroughly at the man's face.

At the age of twenty-three, clad in white-colored clothes that fitted his body, with the thick nape of his neck, the man facing the woman was a journalist of some newspaper. It was still early morning at 9am, in a small tea house, in the vicinity of Namdaemun station.

"I brought a good plan today. But you shouldn't get jealous like before. Haven't you already become sick of it?"

"Well, what would it be like! This time, would it not matter whether or not you set foot in it?"

He smiled for a moment.

The plan of the woman was to have the tea house, the store to be handed over to her. The location was Jongno-1-ga, and while she wanted to take over and manage it, she needed to have 400 won (The past value of the won was a lot less than the current value of the won). So, in case someone was to apply to claim 1 share in the property for 10 won, and in case a willing person was to apply to claim more than 10 shares in the property, she had been waiting for an appropriate night to discuss this for just the two of them.

"Wouldn't it be good to find a person you've been close to until now? So, how many shares did it turn out to be?"

"6 shares for 25 won. Because, as everyone says, it's an economic depression."

"So, how many people did it turn out to be?"

The man opened his huge eyes.

"That's it. That's a gentlemen's agreement. Whoever it may be, they think that they're all alone in this! As for you, since before, you had nothing that you were involved in. Haha······."

The woman burst into laughter.

"Yet, you told me a while ago that you lived a life like a register? That is, for instance, when treating a man who applied to claim 10 shares in the property, you would treat him to the extent of 10 shares, and when treating a man who applied to claim 20 shares in the property······."

"You're not smart. If you hate service that much, why don't you get shares at the maximum limit? So, apply to claim up to 30 shares of the property. As for the money, it would even be good to pay the second time around⋯⋯. How's that? Okay?"

"Someone has been talking about what you said, that you got a good patron? How envious is it to have a patron?"

"It's not that much. If I make a call, the elder sometimes goes to a restaurant in Jeongjaok department store and just buys me lunch."

As expected, she was thinking of the elder. When she would speak to the elder, it seemed like a lump of money could be made. The woman knew that the man approved of this plan. So, she threw a couple of the letters that she had on top of the table.

"Is there also a love letter?"

The man spoke.

"Yes. While there are a lot of love letters, the problem is not that. It is that I want you to write a reply. These days, I cannot write even a single short sentence in my reply to the letters of young men in pure love. Okay, although I try to write well by thinking of a phrase, I can't. Okay? Please write for me! I beg of you!"

The woman was not lying. Really, she could not even write a single short sentence and so, until today, she had been delaying the response.

All the while, the man read through the letter. It was the letter of a young man who was lodging with the woman.

It went along the lines of, *I'm speaking of my love for you. Already, for a long time, I have been resisting it, but I could not for the life of me bear it. I'm not even deciding tonight on a letter that meets my satisfaction, but instead, waiting for tomorrow⋯⋯.*

The man's eyebrows were furrowed. He took out a fountain pen from his pocket. At the same time, the woman promptly pulled out a letter paper from her handbag and in order for it to be written soon, talked about her current life in the inn. The young man was in the outer-wing room, the woman was in the room next to his, and an elderly poet was in the room next to hers. Two to three months prior, the young man came up to the capital from the province and as he was in the midst of preparing for a submission for the Joseon art exhibition, he had written in his letter to the woman that he hoped to be selected by all means.

The journalist spread out the line of the letter paper that had been bent and went on, writing. Really, after having put it off and then having a grain of understanding, he was agile.

'While I also love you like you love me, whether it is light or dark, I'm busy trying to earn money. Now, I don't even have enough time to write this letter.'

Like this, in minute detail, he scribbled down words that seemed like those of a woman and wrote the letter.

"Make a clean copy of this."

"Okay, it's all good. I will copy it neatly. Really, you are a liar."

"You who's using the liar is more of a liar."

The woman smoothly read the response. At the very last, it said in the letter, 'With my love for you in dear friend's inn.' While it would have been amusing to write on, 'following that······' the one line of the letter was written as such.

"Hey, I'm going to die if I write such a thing."

"That doesn't have to be written. This is enough. That person would read the response, while taking a deep breath. He would be hurt. It would be amusing if it was said in the letter that it was ghostwritten. If he were confronted with it, there, for the first time, he would suck in a deep breath and let it out."

"What? If on the other hand, he gets to overcome it, his heart would be pounding, what with the rising heartbeat."

"It would be because that would be in your handwriting. He would think that this is someone's ghostwriting and so, wouldn't trust it."

"Then, wouldn't it be good not to reply? It's because just leaving it, as it is, would be a good expression of one's feelings."

The more the woman thought of the emotions running about in the young man's heart, she became driven to eventually head for the opposite direction. Thus, she put the letter paper that was folded in the Western-style envelope.

Wondering how a person could change this much, the man glanced at his clock.

"Tonight at 7pm, let's meet at the crossroad of Jongno,"

he spoke. The two people stood up.

Chapter 2.

The Angukjeong boarding house was gloomy and murky in a cloudy day with the autumn rain. The elderly poet's room was mountainously piled with the old newspapers and old magazines, without the space to set foot. The poet himself put a package right in the middle, instead of a desk, sat, facing a company of three students, and was talking in a loud voice. The three students who wore the student provincial high school uniform spoke in a tone of sincerely paying their respects to the destitute but famous elderly poet, "The lyrics of the school song that teacher wrote half a year ago has just recently been made into a song. It is a composition of Mr. S. Today, as the representatives of the alumni association, we came to inform you, teacher. We will go and soon present the song to the entire student body. Teacher, we're going to try singing it."

The three people paid respects to the utmost and in small voices, sang the school song. With an enraptured face, the elderly poet was keeping pace with the beat with his index finger.

However, honestly speaking, as if the elderly poet was listening to someone else's song, he was forgetting that he had written it. Yet, excited by their eloquent singing, there were two to three phrases that he remembered.

"Okay! That! That! It's definitely that!"

The elderly poet caressed his bald head and nodded.

"It is a really good melody. I worship Lord Byron. In this school song, I could smell the poetry of Lord Byron. Please sing again, let's learn it together."

At the passionate words of the elderly poet, the students little by little raised their voices. The elderly poet wavered. Up until that point, on the one hand, in the corner, a pale and grimy young man, an artist, wearing a Western-style shirt, who had been wholly neglected, heaved himself up.

"Teacher, I will give you a treat."

He opened the torn window and placed the five to six beer bottles that had been put inside in front of the elderly poet, in his traveling outfit.

"Mr. L, thank you for your effort. It'd be good to drink."

The elderly poet had his eyes half-shut and was enjoying it.

"Mr. L, later, I'll be heavily drinking to your spirits."

The elderly poet has become a model for Mr. L's painting. For three to four days, their schedule did not match, and so, today, awash with a pleasant feeling at meeting his student, the beers had been bought with the model fees and kept, in advance. Certainly, so as to make the elderly poet happy, Mr. L took out all the beers that had been brought.

At the suggestion of the elderly poet, the students each had a drink. While the elderly poet clung to them, urging them to play around more, as they said they were going, with his drunken, tipsy moves, the elderly poet followed the three people to the highway. Mr. L was left alone. The old newspaper that was laid out in an awkward manner was rough-hewn. L drinking, said,

"······Young people full of hope······."

After two to three times replaying in his mouth, once again, he came to feel the misfortune of the present, which was far from his hope.

Hyeon-sook's reply to the letter······ why didn't he realize Hyeon-sook's feelings earlier on? It was because he had failed to do so that he asked about her feelings. Wasn't it because of her living conditions that Hyeon-sook's reply was sent to trifle with him like that? When thinking of it in such a way, he could never get angry at her.

'Hyeon-sook is really busy, as written in Hyeon-sook's letter. Yet, the rumors on Hyeon-sook are very bad.'

With a pained heart, he took pity on the rumors about Hyeon-sook that occasionally reached his ears.

While it was a coincidence that at present, the elderly poet, Hyeon-sook, and himself, the three people were living together in one inn, cordially like this, there was a time when it had been discomfiting. The elderly poet was inebriated all the time and if there was no money to pay for the alcohol, even for a few days, he starved.

"A gave a poem to me. Although I speak as if my spirits were all taken away by alcohol, even when I'm old like this, my blood is still boiling."

The elderly poet, who has been single for over 50 years, wore a lonely expression.

Hyeon-sook bought the poetry book of the elderly poet in the bookstore as she had a love of reading, watched over the elderly poet, and whenever she had money, she would undoubtedly buy him a drink, pour it, and give him advice that the life of the elderly poet, which had been dreary, was refreshed by the goodwill of

Hyeon-sook. Hence, following this, the three people's lives have reached the point of not even a single person being able to live apart from each other. This year, with the anticipation that L's work would be selected and publicized, the elderly poet became the painting model of L.

"Whoever serves as your model makes you special. Okay, are you always going to treat me to drinks? If you draw me drinking smoothly, I'd be in a good mood."

Thereby, L burned his boats. If he became selected this year, he thought he would be throwing away the painting brush. By giving away the books that he had already read and clothes, he borrowed some money and came, having bought the 50th issue of a canvas, painting materials, and two bottles of beer. While it was not even the season of beer, it was because merely seeing the beer excited him.

For 2 hours a day, 3 bottles of beer, and the subject was 'Aged poet Y,' which was what the elderly poet himself had chosen. Initially, for the four to five days, it was implemented according to the rules, and it beamed with sensuality. After the elderly poet drank 3 bottles according to the rules,

"Ah, how tasty," he said and went outside. Among the three fellow lodgers, Hyeon-sook, who always carried with her a sunny breeze said,

"What? Teacher, I also know how to do sewing. Teacher's clothes became dirty."

As Hyeon-sook spoke, she looked into the dirty room and

leaped towards L's side, like the wind blowing at the hill. L, infatuated by her appeal, rolled around, once again.

"A while ago, I opened your room. You seemed to be writing some kind of diary. Doesn't everyone think that, right? Well, wasn't the reply I made to the letter quite interesting? Really, it was more about figuring out how to manage my finances, accounting than it was about emotions, and you know what, in terms of accounting······ well, what do you think······ It is good for the entry of a relationship to start from accounting. Right. Until now, I have failed in everything, from sinking into emotions. That is why I find nothing difficult and frightening to deal with a young man in pure love like you."

"I'm just satisfied with lodging together with Ms. Hyeon-sook."

"But Mr. L, I'm going to be leaving this house in the near future."

"······."

"You're wearing a disappointed expression. You shouldn't be disappointed. Although I cried a lot of tears, I wasn't disappointed. Now, I will notify you and the teacher of some good stuff. I am planning something really fun right now. I have to leave again. I have something to forget a bit."

Once more, Hyeon-sook fixed the hair that hung down from her neck, half-closed her pretty eyes, and was adorning her body in front of the mirror.

"I'll come back in the evening."

She said to herself and set out to the main gate.

Chapter 3.

The next morning, as the elderly poet had opened his eyes early, he was sucking on his pipe, when there was the sound of someone's footsteps. It seemed to be a woman.

"Is this Hyeon-sook?"

he asked. However, without responding, Hyeon-sook went into her room.

"She must be drunk again."

The teacher uttering, "Something must've happened again," was too worried that he stole glances in between the door. The teacher came out and went to the room of Hyeon-sook. Hyeon-sook lay, sprawled on the spot that L spread out for her and looking up at the ceiling, spoke.

"Teacher, is it fine for me to also drink? How much did I crave to drink······ What? Teacher, what would be good for me to do?"

Without being able to finish all of her words, she lay flat on the side and wept. Hyeon-sook tried to forget the unpleasant incident that happened, from last night until this morning. ······Mr. K, an artist breached the new contract made with Hyeon-sook. That was also why behind her plan, she could not help but imagine 4 to 5 men. Besides that, in her room that she came back to, someone had laid out a seat for her.

"Thank you! Thank you. Teacher, please tell me to remember these tears of mine."

While the elderly poet did not have the foggiest idea as to

whether she was miserable because she was drunk or crying because she was lonely, whatever it was, he went outside, put water in the washbasin, and laid the wet towel on top of Hyeon-sook's forehead. As water was sprinkled, Hyeon-sook muttered that cold water was flowing down her neck.

"Well, it's because I don't know how to do it," the elderly poet was abashed.

At that time, L came in. After standing and staring at this bizarre drunkenness of Hyeon-sook for a long while, he whispered to the elderly poet.

"Something happened to the great master, Mr. K from somewhere."

"Somehow, it struck me as odd. I don't know if K would be like that. I need to know for sure. Anyhow, I should make sure that at least there is no way for Hyeon-sook to go corrupt."

The elderly poet with a solemn expression glared at Hyeon-sook.

The following day, in the afternoon, without even discussing with L, the elderly poet ran to K's house in Sajik-dong. The elderly poet steadily brought himself to speak and talked about Hyeon-sook.

"These days, Hyeon-sook has changed very much. Based on a lot of things, shouldn't you have a responsibility for Hyeon-sook? Didn't she drink here until late last night?"

"No, you seem to have some kind of misunderstanding here."

A porky and well-mannered K unpleasantly touched the bald head, where his hair had been cut, and said,

"What the heck is the meaning of the responsibility you're talking about?"

"Is that something to ask me?"

"Anyhow, you seem to have had a misunderstanding. Hyeon-sook got into contact with a lot of artists and is each getting 3 won, 5 won, 10 won for a model fee. While I can't entirely say that I don't know, the responsibility for Hyeon-sook should not just be placed on me. No, it couldn't be said like that."

"You shouldn't make that excuse. Hyeon-sook is a well-behaved woman. Still, if you are a man, what about guiding the woman to a path worthy of a human? Seeing Hyeon-sook who came back this morning, a thought popped up that she may have gone corrupt."

"It really is a strange thing. I don't have that responsibility. There were a lot of men behind Hyeon-sook, and so, there is nothing to be troubled about even. While you solely put the responsibility on me, what rights do you have to that?"

"What?"

The two cheeks of the elderly poet reddened and he abruptly stood up from the chair.

"Whatever it is, go. If you want money……."

K pulled out a crumpled-up bill from a partially grimy vest. It was 10 won.

"I was wondering what you'd be stuck with now that these days, even your poem is screwed and is not selling well, hmm, hmm."

The elderly poet, who heard these words, was roused to action like fire. He tore up the bill that K was giving him, and at the same time that he threw it over the table, he turned the chair and the like upside down, and got out of the door. The elderly poet's heart thumped.

"Not only Hyeon-sook, but he is even insulting me. Let's see here, if that man doesn't end up a mere sham, pretending to be a great master······ I can't stand the fact alone that he is flirting with a maiden······."

Saying this, he was in a fit of rage and went inside a nearby bar, and drank for four to five hours. Later, the elderly poet, who was out on the highway, was swaying, drunken. At the time that he came back to the lodging, it was already 12 at night, and Hyeon-sook and L, both, each one of them were struggling to sleep. The elderly poet, receiving the support of another person, came all the way to the doorsill of the lodging, but his face and his head were wrapped in bandages and his durumagi (traditional Korean overcoat) and beoseon (Korean traditional socks) were covered in dirt. According to a nearby person, he was fortunately pulled out of some pit that he had fallen into. Hyeon-sook stood up from the spot that she had been sprawled out on, pulled the hands and feet of the elderly poet, dragged him to the spot, and laid him there. In the meanwhile, the elderly poet in a half-vague voice said,

"That skank, that skank was also nothing much······ When he takes off the mask of an artist, I'm going to completely strip the skin off of it."

Seeing him replay like that and curse, Hyeon-sook instantaneously knew.

'Teacher must have undoubtedly gone to Mr. K's house,' and Hyeon-sook could not help but shed tears at the injustice. Hyeon-sook changed the elderly poet into night clothes and washed off her tears. Somehow, dirt got into her eyes. That had been smeared from the hem of the durumagi (traditional Korean overcoat) of the elderly poet. Hyeon-sook laughed.

"What is so funny?"

The elderly poet had his heavy, drunken eyes wide open.

"Look here. The next thing I knew, I washed my tears from the hem of teacher's durumagi. Take a look at this. Wasn't it smeared with dirt like this?"

Hyeon-sook rolled around, laughing. L, who was supporting her at the side, also grinned from ear to ear.

The next morning, with a pale face, Hyeon-sook looked out of the window blankly, as if she was ridded of her soul. When she was in such a state, just in time, the elderly poet, clad in his night clothes, came in and in a tone like that of a father,

"Being poor is really troubling. One needs to bow to shitty guys and one could not help but do things that one doesn't want to do. Okay, as I've been thinking about the incident, I woke up early. From now on, you, Hyeon-sook, also shouldn't be coming and going to see a useless man."

he spoke, imbued with strength.

"What? Teacher, I'm not miserable. I live frivolously. If I don't, won't there not be a way to live?"

"Okay, sure."

"So, beyond what teacher is thinking of, I'm self-possessed······ A woman like me doesn't like to cry if it is not for something I'm grateful for. I don't cry from others being heartless!"

"Yes, because we're poor, we should cry, when we want to cry. It is because to some extent, it relieves the chest to cry!"

Thereby, as if the elderly poet was acknowledging the feelings of the young woman, he smiled. To fall back into a morning sleep, he went back to his room. As Hyeon-sook had a lot of sleep, she stood up to do make-up accordingly.

'What a great teacher.'

She could not help but say to herself.

'While he doesn't say a word, and so, I find what the teacher does to be amusing, what if the teacher seems to get a sense of my life right now······ While I'm uselessly suffering, the teacher might be despairing about me·······.'

Chapter 4.

It was several days later, in the afternoon.

"Teacher!"

As Hyeon-sook was arranging her baggage, she said,

"I'm constantly walking diligently in the direction towards hope. So, even if I leave this place, please don't worry. I think that there would certainly be something to be celebrated in a few days."

Afterward, Hyeon-sook said she was going to share her address but stealthily moved away.

While this was what he predicted, L was really disappointed. As the elderly poet only kept going in and out, drinking, in the long run, he failed as the model of L.

A thick piece of letter without the name of an address written on it came to L who had been waiting for Hyeon-sook's letter every day. When he ripped it open, there were two pieces of envelope. The one piece had the name of L written and the other piece did not have anything but the bearer, Mr. L written.

When L first opened the one that came for him, it was written, "I would really like to once meet with my hyung (Referring to a Korean form of address to another older male) concerning Hyeon-sook. When it comes to you, hyung, Hyeon-sook is passionate. Tomorrow, at 3pm, go to the place where it was written, bringing the enclosed letter······."

L did not have a clue what was going on. Yet, of course, at the same time that he suspected that Hyeon-sook's recent news was hidden among this letter, he was flustered and the next day, before 3pm, he set off to the place of appointment.

As he went there, indeed, as there happened to be the appointed place, he knocked on the door. When he positioned his ears on the door and listened, the indication of the presence of someone was heard and before long, the door opened. When thinking that it would be a stranger of a man, the person standing right in front of him was Hyeon-sook. Ah! Taken aback, the two people stood, staring at each other.

"Ah! Was it you? Who taught you this place? When I didn't even tell you, how the heck did you come here?"

Hyeon-sook spoke, with the feeling of being displeased. L, in order to explain that he came, because of a letter without a name of its address, was taking one step forward, when Hyeon-sook all of a sudden was closing the door. Consequently, L urgently threw the strange letter at Hyeon-sook.

The door was shut. For three to four minutes, he stood in front of the door absent-mindedly. Unexpectedly meeting Hyeon-sook here, the fact that Hyeon-sook was greatly angered, where he didn't have a clue what was up······ what was the matter with this······ Hyeon-sook seemed to be misunderstanding something, and if not, it would be neglecting their friendship too much······ Once more, he knocked on the door and tried to criticize her, but drained of strength, he set out to go back.

At that time, from behind,

"Wait! Mr. L," she called.

L did not turn his back. Hyeon-sook, who chased him, held L's hand, and went into the room.

"Hello. Mr. L, because I really had someone to meet at 3 o'clock, I didn't have time to talk to you. But now that I came to realize, that person sent you instead. So, come on in. I have a lot to talk about."

Thereby, L was prompted by Hyeon-sook and stepped inside. The single room, possibly because of the household goods that were placed, appeared really narrow. The atmosphere of summer that was reflected in the window to the south was abounding. Hyeon-sook sat, wearing a black skirt in a red jeogori (upper garment of Korean traditional clothes) and told L to come to her side. A rattan chair was placed at the side.

"This is my bedroom, which is concurrently a study. How is it? Isn't it quiet and good? ······I tend not to call anyone into this room."

L turned on the light and once looked around the interior. As it was different from the room, next to that of the elderly poet, here, it was bright and orderly. One dressing stand, which looked good was placed there, a mirror was displayed like it was one of the household goods, and the small and big jars for cremation were arranged. When seeing this, L somehow could not feel good.

"Pardon me. I came to know after seeing this letter. I ran out, because I thought you were leaving. It really turned out well that you came instead. Did this letter come to you? This person who sent the letter is someone I've already ended my friendship with. Could you read this letter, please?"

Hyeon-sook forced the letter that L had thrown at her to come into his sight. The three to four sheets of the letter were crumpled up. Hyeon-sook must have tightly clutched them and crumpled them up.

To my dear Hyeon-sook!
All of a sudden, I couldn't help but go to Yeongnam province.
I occasionally come up to the capital. Yet, so far, we didn't get
to do what used to be a pastime for the two of us. Besides, I'm

disappointed that I could not even go to your place at 3pm to-morrow.

But I thought. I thought of the young man that likes Miss Hyeon-sook, the young man, L that loves Miss. While you love L, you're avoiding encountering him in your current life. That is why I thought of bringing Miss Hyeon-sook and Mr. L together.

Miss Hyeon-sook!

Doesn't L naturally have such a right? It is the vested right of L to eternally make you belong to him, starting from the beginning. It is for this vested right to be wielded. Certainly, Miss Hyeon-sook would clap her hands and be happy about L's rights. If you're also like a human being, I imagine that you're going to be fine with it and come to smile from the bottom of your heart.

Dear Miss Hyeon-sook! I brought this letter with such an intention. Now, I bring my whole-hearted blessings for the two people. Bravo! Bravo!

Hyeon-sook stood beside L, who was reading the letter in front of the window. The strong eyes that lit up looked vacantly at L's eyes passing through the letters, in anticipation. When she was thinking of the pleasant moment when L's black and fresh eyes would shoot at the inclined plane of the atmosphere, he rushed at Hyeon-sook.

The two people embraced each other. It was already as if from prior, the opportunity had been reserved.

"Well? I never imagined that the entry to accounting that I had said one time would soon make the two of us this happy. Our emotions are already sufficiently ready! That is, it doesn't matter for us from now on, even if it's an excess of emotions. Mr. L, now I'm not going to call you, Mr. L. Instead, I would call out for you, bravo. Bravo, bravo!"

Yet, some huge lump was stuck inside L's throat. It was a joy that he had not known of until now. He could not help but devour it now.

"And, please come here at 3pm! At any time, I will leave the key at the landlord's house. The two of us cannot live here. Please comfort the elderly teacher well. Okay? It would be good not to tell the teacher for the time being about us having turned out like this. Let's have a secret relationship for half a year. After half a year, we need to think again about the new contract of our relationship. We need to first prepare for that in advance."

"If you say it like that, it's amusing."

L quivered with a bleak joy and smiled.

"Of course, we don't need to prepare for that in advance."

Hyeon-sook spread her two arms and bravely extended her passionate hand in the direction towards L.

⟨*Samcheonri* (Magazine; 1929~1950)⟩ (1936. 12.)

Mother and Daughter

Chapter 1.

"I'm not jealous of those distinguished women."

The landlady who in every spare moment stepped into the room of Hanwoon and guffawed, "Hee hee hee hee hee," once again, tonight, sitting face-to-face with Hanwoon and Lee Gybong intentionally spoke loudly for Madam Kim in the outer-wing room to hear.

"Why?"

Being aware of the judgment of the landlady quite well, Lee Gybong questioned her like this to listen to what she was on to again.

"As for what a woman is, she must do sewing, weaving, carry on with her household chores well and must eat the rice of her husband."

Today, facing Gab (The most powerful person), Eul (Middle-of-the-road), Byeong (Inferior to Gab and Eul), and tomorrow, sitting in front of Iroha, and at times, discoursing with ABC (Penname of a person), the landlady of this inn had picked up on an abundance of controversies surrounding New Women at a number of places. This was how, of them, these words were what had been most stuck in her head.

"Why so? Can't New Women know how to sew and weave? The food would be a lot tastier if she were to eat hers, instead of her husband's."

Lee Gybong, who had been divorced a year ago and now, again bristled with curiosity about New Women retorted like this. At this, the landlady did not have the strength to rebuke with the same strong tone as initially.

"I told you to listen," said Hanwoon (Pointing his finger at the outer-wing room).

Hanwoon said this, firmly poking the side of Lee Gybong.

"By the way, what is she doing alone, day and night in the outer-wing room?" said Lee Gybong.

Keeping pace with the disposition of the landlady, Lee Gybong again proceeded with the subject matter.

"She says she's writing a novel or something."

The landlady who pouted her lips had no way of knowing what kind of words were cursing and what their meaning was.

"What is there for you, landlady, to feel that jealous, whether someone is writing a novel or something?"

The landlady seemed to be on the verge of saying something, and closed her mouth.

"Well, why are you like that?"

Above all, Lee Gybong wanted to hear more of the landlady boldly pretending to be all-knowing.

"If a girl is distinguished, she is of no use."

"If a boy is distinguished, is he of use?"

"If a boy is also too distinguished, he is of no use."

"Then, he must be moderately distinguished. How difficult."

Lee Gybong smacked his lips together. Once again, he sat closely right up.

"Landlady, why is it that a girl or a boy is of no use when one is distinguished? I want to hear your words on this."

"While I, being ignorant may not know much, if a girl is distinguished, she cannot be submissive to her husband, and if a boy is distinguished, he troubles the girl."

"That must be right. As I know by now, Madam landlady is a great philosopher, a literary woman."

For quite some time, he flattered the landlady. And, this was a reality that took place when the other person, the landlady's character was lacking, and although he wanted to explain that in the city or in civilized nations, the notion of denouncing distinguished people had somewhat been dropped, whereas uncivilized nations and rural places in a period of transition still preserved it as truth, it seemed like the landlady would not understand, which as a result, halted him from explaining and instead, he solely went for the words of flattery.

"You got a point there."

Hanwoon said this, while blinking his black eyes and stroking the hair that came down once.

"Why is that? Let me hear the reason."

At Hanwoon's words, Lee Gybong rejoiced at opposing him.

"Isn't it true that a distinguished woman gets divorced, as well as the distinguished man?"

"That's not because they're distinguished, but because they're not right for each other."

"At the end of the day, isn't the fact that they're not right for each other because whoever it may be, one is distinguished?"

"It may all stem from the instinct of humans to try to make progress."

Lee Gybong who had a history of having divorced replied a bit weakly.

Hanwoon, as an unmarried man and dreaming of his future prospects, wished to reject the notion of divorce through thick and thin.

"Can't one progress without divorce?"

"For those who are haplessly stuck in marriage life, they can't, because they are trying to find satisfaction in a place that they are dissatisfied with."

"If so, then, people should live alone in the first place. While it may be sensible for one to find satisfaction in oneself, it doesn't make sense to find that from dealing with someone else."

"If you get into that degree of difficulty, by living alone, the sorrow that may be needed to be known would not be there and it's not necessarily appropriate to say that people should be living alone. It's such a difficult issue."

Lee Gybong sunk into his sullen mood, and with the fact that he was now idling away, without an occupation, he mused over what woman on earth would be his wife and make him happy. Seizing this opportunity, the landlady spoke again.

"Well, ever since Madam Kim came here, my girl has refused to get married. Instead, she's saying she wants to just keep on studying. So, what to do about it?"

"If only she could do it, it would be good to make her do more of her studying."

"What would be the use of pursuing more studies? Her education at girls' middle school is enough for her."

"A girl should also receive professional education. Is there anything as precarious as the life of a girl?"

"That is why it is good for a girl not to be distinguished."

"Likewise, eventually, without the profession to care for oneself, if one reaches a state of misfortune, one might as well distress one's parents, siblings, and friends."

"One does not reach a state of misfortune, if one is not distinguished."

"No? Then, how come Dolsoe's mother parted from her husband for life and is a housemaid cooking food at the inn?"

"It's all because of fate."

The landlady said this, as she did not have any other words to reply with.

"If you speak like that, then that must be true for everyone."

Lee Gybong said simply, as it seemed like even if he would talk more, they would not be able to understand.

"Let's just play hwatu (traditional gambling card game in Korea)."

As if he detested hearing all of this conversation, Hanwoon pulled out hwatu from the desk drawer.

"What about making a bet on hwatu for Macaw (name of a cigarette)?"

"At the end of a score of two hundred, one packet of Macaw."

The three people all sat, each one of them holding their cards.

Chapter 2.

Early in the morning, the landlady entered the room of Madam Kim.

"Welcome in. Come down here to the warm spot, this way."

Madam Kim said, putting away the script that she had been writing.

"What have you been writing there day and night?"

"What? I've been taking it lightly to no purpose."

"Aren't you lonely being alone day and night?"

"What? I've graduated. And, I'm doing my studies, which work to overcome loneliness."

"You're different, being such a cultivated adult."

"Not exactly."

"How come you've studied so much?"

"What do you mean I've studied so much?"

"You're brilliant as a woman."

"Not at all."

"Who wouldn't all study to be educated and become like you, Madam Kim?"

"Why?"

As Madam Kim had overheard the conversation in the upper room last night, she wondered, 'What is up with the landlady being so capricious again?' and asked.

"Madam, why don't you join us in physical labor? Sitting here and just writing graciously is only a fresh diversion."

"……."

Madam Kim wanted to say (ironically) 'You lot are blessed,' but as this could prolong the conversation, she did not make any response.

"If you write a novel like that and send it to the magazine company, how much do they give you?"

"I'm writing, because I'm bored."

She did not mention that she was writing a prize novel worth 150 won.

"But from what I hear, you're earning a lot of money."

"That's a lie."

In the past, her writing had been chosen as a prize novel, which had produced earnings of hundreds of won, she had earned hundreds of won from writing a full-length novel in a newspaper, and she had procured a sizable amount of earnings from her submitted manuscripts for the monthly magazine, and yet, she did not speak of them, as they sounded like boasting about herself.

"Isn't it because you had made a lot of earnings that you're able to travel around like this?"

"Yes, I have in my savings account around thousands."

At a question that was raised, like the cross-questioning of a prosecutor, she replied as if she could not be too bothered by it, and so as to make the landlady feel relieved. Originally, Madam Kim was the type of person who would shake her head at the talk of money.

"Oh my goodness."

"Don't worry about the costs of the food not being repaid."

"Oh dear, no. Anyway, Madam Kim."

"Yes."

"Wouldn't it still cost you a lot to live in this inn?"

"As for that, it's something that I'd have to know how to take care of."

"I did speak to someone about getting a single room for you."

"Then, are you telling me to get out?"

"If you get a single room and make food there, it won't cost a lot. You should awaken yourself to this time of economy."

"Thank you, but as a landlady yourself, there would be no need to worry that much about your guest."

Madam Kim's face was somewhat colored with fury. The landlady feeling sorry said, "That's because we all think of each other as siblings."

"When I'm paying for the costs of the food like the others, is there a need for you to say that I should get in or get out?"

"……"

"I'm not going to move to some other place. I'm typically the type that firmly remains if I have one place where I chose to stay."

As Madam Kim very well knew that having barely settled here and having been patiently working on her creative writing, once she would set off, leaving, she would not be able to write again for some time, she felt more or less displeased, but spoke like this.

"Why on earth are you telling me to get out? I really want to know."

"Even though I was aware that it would be an offense to say that to a female guest, I said it."

"What's the reason?"

"Well, let me see. As the saying goes, 'He who touches pitch shall be defiled therewith,' after your arrival here, my daughter, Yeongae has been saying that she won't get married, but instead, saying she would study more. I mean, what would a girl be doing from studying more?"

"Then, can you pay for the school expenses?"

"While there is no money, even if there is, I'm not going to let her pursue more of her education."

"Why is that?"

"It is enough for a girl to feed on the food of her husband."

"What if while feeding on the food of her husband, she ends up getting cut off from it?"

"That happens only to distinguished girls."

"What if that happens to foolish girls?"

"I would get her married to someplace where that wouldn't happen."

"Who gets married like that early on?"

"What would a girl do when she educates herself more?"

"The more she learns, the better. Is there anything as good as knowing a lot?"

"What would she do from knowing a lot? It is enough to give birth to children and do household chores."

"Yes, that may be right, but this isn't a world, where one could live, solely trusting tyrannical men."

"As Madam Kim has always been spewing out such things to Yeongae this year, the pity of it."

"I have not talked to her about this, but speaking of which, it is what it is."

"Then, why is she saying she won't get married?"

"How am I supposed to know that? She must be doing that, because she must have some thoughts of her own. This isn't something that could be taken out on me, and not what would get me kicked out of the inn."

"Well, Madam Kim. If I were to miss the opportunity to have a promising young man like Hanwoon as a spouse for my daughter, where should I go to search for one?"

"There must be another one if you were to search."

"Well, I've been to his place once."

"The house of Hanwoon's family?"

"Yes!"

"How was it?"

"A sack of rice was piled up, wood was accumulated by loading it on the backs of horses and oxen, his father is a scholar, his siblings live in harmony, the status as a Yangban is great, and he himself is gentle. Is there anyone else to choose?"

"Do you say that to your daughter?"

"Of course."

"What did she say?"

"She said she hates it."

"Why does she hate it?"

"You, Madam Kim must know the reason more than I do."

"Would she talk to me about things that she couldn't say to her very own mother?"

"What would she even say to an ignorant mother? That's because you, Madam Kim and my daughter are in cahoots with each other."

"Don't take this out on me and try to comfort your daughter."

"Would she listen to me? That is, I'm not the one she speaks to."

"Is there a need for her to tell me anything?"

"Madam Kim messed with my daughter."

Finally spitting her words out, the landlady heaved herself up. Madam Kim pulled at the hem of her skirt, and said,

"No, what are you talking about? If so, then, I will move to another place."

"……."

"Why not just drop it and instead comfort your daughter and

ask her if there is someone she likes?"

"She is not the type to go around dating."

With these words, the landlady slammed the door shut and left.

Madam Kim sat alone and stared blankly at the ceiling. It was amusing, funny, and even infuriating. Yet, she pictured her daughter in her head. She thought to herself, like the mother and the daughter of this inn. What if Madam Kim were to take a liking towards a certain somebody for her daughter, but what if instead, her daughter said she hated it? She tucked the misfortune spurred by the injustice that she suffered in the program of all the misfortunes of her past.

"Should I stay here longer and watch it unfold?" and later,

"Oh, it's all so bothersome. Who knows if I fall into some other misfortune again?"

Talking to herself, she decided to leave the inn and packed the baggage that was strewn about in disarray.

Chapter 3.

"Ma'am."

Saying this, Yeongae came in. The traces of tears she shed were in her eyes.

"Quickly, come in."

"Ma'am."

Yeongae said, sprawled on the knees of Madam Kim. Her shoulders throbbed.

"Don't you cry and say all that you want to say."

"......."

"Yeongae."

"Yes."

Sitting up, Yeongae wiped the tears that trickled down with the hem of her shirt.

"Is there a promise of marriage that you made with someone?"

"There isn't."

"Well, I also could see that there isn't."

"No."

"Then, why are you saying that you hate it when your mother has found a good person for you to get married to? Why?"

"I hate it."

"Are you saying that you don't want to get married, or are you saying that you hate Hanwoon?"

"I don't want to get married and I hate that person."

"Then, what are you going to do?"

"I just want to die."

"If that is really something to die for, then, one could."

"Ma'am."

"Yes."

"I want to study more."

"Do you have money?"

"I'm going to work my way through school."

"Do you think you can do whatever you want? Something that

you're dying for is not up for discussion with others."

"Oh, ma'am."

Once again, tears brimmed in the eyes of Yeongae.

"Does your mother not have the ability to finance your education?"

"She doesn't!"

"Isn't there anyone from your other relatives who could pay for the school fees?"

"There's no one!"

"It would be a waste to throw away the opportunity for education, seeing your talent."

"I wish someone could please pay for it. So that after I graduate, I can earn money and repay."

"There's no way to know if you could make money to repay someone and would there be any kind person out there?"

"Ma'am, wouldn't there be any person who would do that?"

"Even though one were to pay for it, such a person would lend if one has the money, that is, one should have the money."

"I wish some rich people could lend me some money."

"If you were to study, what are you going to specialize in?"

"Literature."

"Literature? That's good."

"Is it difficult?"

"Although it is difficult, it'd be good to be proficient at it. It would be great to study literature, since you, Yeongae, read a lot of books. That's because at the same time that a person lives individually, living a life socially has the taste of being alive. There would be nothing happier than presenting a good creative work and becoming a socially accomplished figure."

"Oh dear, this is killing me."

"Rather than getting caught up in your daydream, take the near and easy road."

"What road?"

"Because without money, you won't have the means to study, won't you have to get married?"

"I don't want to."

"Perhaps, do you hate Hanwoon?"

"Yes, I hate him."

"Why? What is it about him?"

"He's not up to the mark."

"But your mother really does have a soft spot for him."

"Although he may have a role as an individual, he won't be a societal figure."

"It is enough to play one's role individually."

"Ma'am, what did you just say now?"

"If one plays one's role individually, then, one in other words gets to be a social figure."

"Then, you and I are all figures of society?"

"Though it's not like that."

"I hate that person."

"Why is that? To me, he looks great."

"He is a boy lacking will."

"He is young, I must admit."

"He's a complete botch of a person."

"Then, tell your mother to find someone else."

"I don't want to."

"What are you going to do, if you hate this and that, and everything?"

"I just want to die."

"That's also delusional. Anyhow, you should soon go on to make your decision in order to be secure. Even others beside you are on edge."

"Oh my, mother is coming down."

Yeongae stood up in a rush.

"Quickly, go on. She must think you discussed something with me."

"She hates it the most when I come to this room."

"I know."

"Ma'am, I'll come back."

Yeongae hastily got out.

Chapter 4.

"You bitch, how come you're lying here, all sprawled out, sleeping at this hour?"

As soon as the landlady stepped into the room where Yeongae lay sleeping alone, she seized the blanket, tearing it off, and grabbing Yeongae, beat her, and exclaimed with her raised voice.

"Bitch, when you've been sleeping, sprawled out like that for half a day, eating the food that I've made for you, and just reading books day and night, would clothes or food appear out of thin air? I hate seeing a bitch like you. Just go away."

"Oh my, oh my, mother, I'm sorry."

"Bitch, how would a stuck-up girl like you have something to feel sorry for?"

"......"

"Bitch, I don't want to see a stuck-up bitch like you. Just go away right now."

"Where should I go?"

"Just go wherever you want. Go to the man you're dating."

"Mother, you're also out of your mind."

"You're not getting married, because you have someone you like?"

"No."

"Bitch, I've been sending you to girls' middle school to make a person out of you, but now that I'm suffering like this, I'm deeply regretting it."

"......"

"Bitch, what use would a child be who doesn't listen to her mother? Didn't Sim Cheong sacrifice herself to help her father open his eyes? You and I have nothing to do with each other. If you could, get out now, starting from today."

She whipped Yeongae again.

"Owowowow."

"Bitch, just either die or get out. I don't want to see you."

"Ow, I won't ever do that again."

"What do you mean you won't do that again when I'm telling you to get out?"

Fed up with listening to the conversation, Madam Kim opened the door and said,

"Hello, hello, please do come here."

Chapter 5.

One day, it was past dinner. Hanwoon came into the room of Madam Kim and said,

"I came over, because I was bored."

"I'm glad you came. Please sit."

"In the daytime, while I go to the office and spend time there busily, at night, I'm bored."

"What kind of office work do you do?"

"It concerns agriculture and forestry."

"Right, you graduated from a school in agriculture and forestry."

"Yes."

"You work in the provincial government building?"

"Yes."

"Are you busy?"

"Yes, I'm quite busy."

"Now, you would have to get married and have a family."

"I personally would like to live my whole life single, but my parents and siblings wouldn't tolerate that."

"Why is that? The joy of a married couple is the best in life."

"Is that really true? I think it's going to be more tiresome than it is when being single."

"While it's tiresome, it is fun."

"I don't know why God has brought into the world men and women."

"As men and women were brought in, a peculiar and wondrous world was formed."

"I think living alone would be most comfortable."

"But what should you do about the fact that when a man and a woman merge, a unity of life and a unity of character take place?"

"Is that right?"

"That is right. What should you do about a single man lacking patience?"

"That must be right in that respect. I must admit, it is lonely."

"Go get married soon."

"Could that be easily done?"

"How is it going with Yeongae?"

"I don't know."

"If it's not working with Yeongae, you should go look for somewhere else to ask for someone's hand in marriage."

In order to get a sense of what he was going to say to this, Madam Kim asked this question.

"If I wanted to get married somewhere else, I would've already done it."

"Then, do you really want to get married to Yeongae?"

"……."

"You should go all out to get your sincerity, in other words, dedication to your utmost to the point that a deity would answer you, and get it heated up to 100 degrees. Is there anything that one cannot do if one were to aim for it?"

"She says she's going to study."

"She needs to pay for her school expenses."

"Wouldn't it be possible if I pay for some and her mother pays for some?"

"Really? Did you bring that up to the landlady?"

"She says there is no way she's making her daughter study."

"She must be very fond of you, Mr. Hanwoon."

"What's the point of her mother liking me? It is a matter of the parties between themselves that are concerned."

Hanwoon, who still didn't have the foggiest idea said.

"What if Yeongae doesn't want to get married to you?"

In order for him to take notice more or less, she said.

"……."

"Let's call it quits with that conversation and let's just play the recorder."

Madam Kim, who feared malicious gossip about other people's business, cut off the conversation.

"Let's hear a piece of Western music."

Hanwoon did not want to say another word, as well and so, put in the phonograph.

"As that is the piece, please carry on with it."

Carmen, Juasdo, Hamlet, Marseille. At every finale of the sound of the music that burst out sonorously, Yeongae's thin laughter came flooding in from the room of Lee Gybong. Although Hanwoon attentively pricked up his ears, the expression that flashed across his face was of nonchalance. Madam Kim who had been needlessly on edge and sitting face-to-face said, "Ah, ah. What a naïve young man."

〈*Samcheonri* (Magazine; 1929~1950)〉 (1937. 10.)

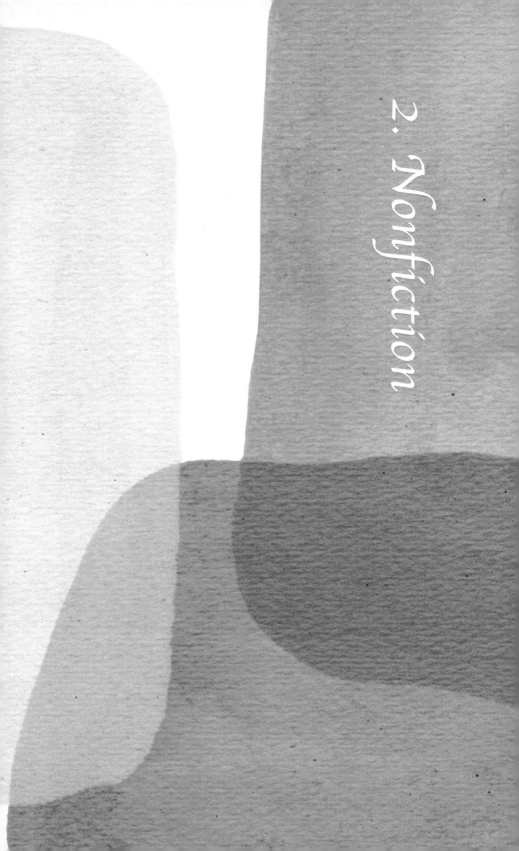

2. Nonfiction

Ideal Madam

First of all, what would an ideal, a so-called ideal be referring to? In other words, an ideal is the idea of desire. If an ideal were to be called an emotional ideal, this so-called ideal would be a numinous and a peculiar ideal.

Then, who could be called an ideal madam? I do not think that a madam that would be said to be an ideal madam has existed throughout the past and the present.

I have not sufficiently studied the unique disposition of madams yet and my sense of an ideal exists at an extraordinarily high station. Katyusha (Main female character in *Resurrection* by Leo Tolstoy, published in 1899) who idealized God, Magda (Main female character in *Magda: A Play in Four Acts* by Hermann Sudermann, published in 1895) who idealized self-profit, Madam Nora (Main female character in *A Doll's House* by Henrik Ibsen, published in 1879) who idealized true romance, Madam Stowe who idealized religious equality (Harriet Beecher Stowe, the author of the book, *Uncle Tom's Cabin*, published in 1852), Madam Raicho (Hiratsuka Raicho; 1886~1971, a feminist who founded the first all-women literary magazine) who idealized being a prodigy, Madam Yosano (Yosano Akiko; 1878~1942, Japanese author, poet, feminist, and social reformer) who idealized having a well-rounded family, and like these people, even now, there are no small number of madams who work for the various kinds of ideals.

I cannot worship these people in every aspect, but currently, in my case, I consider them to be the closest to ideal, and thus, partly worship them.

Why is that?

The ordinary kind of people become dominated by fate, fearing growth, and development, in other words, they are afraid of fully discovering themselves, and so, besides doing their plain, fixed housework as usual, they are the weak, without complete ideals.

Although we may be young, considering that we should get this point in all matters, extracted from one's conscience that has been fostered every-day, one should grow and advance closely to the best of one's ideal from one's novel imagination. One cannot refer to a madam who out of habit was moralistic, in other words, one who only completed her own secular duty as ideal. Without getting into the pace of running neck and neck and being more than prepared for this, I doubt one could be called ideal. Merely being a good wife and a wise mother and choosing it as her ideal does not surely make her ideal. It is just that I suspect that those who proclaim this making them ideal may scheme to appear good by doing the current educator's business of artifice.

Men are husbands, fathers. They did not get an education yet on how to be a good husband and a good father, and a mere adjunct to education limited to women exists. Although these words may be brought up for psychological cultivation, in fact, they are not amusing. Also, when a madam has a mild and compliant character and calls it her ideal, she would not surely have become an ideal madam, and speaking of which, it was in order to turn a woman into a slave that an encouragement of these womanly virtues had been necessary with such a principle.

In the meanwhile, the wives of today for a long time have been fostered under the principle of exhausting themselves by solely working for men, which as a result turned them excessively mild and compliant that such an ideal has almost led them all the way to not knowing how to tell right from wrong. If so, what should be done for each person to become deserving of an ideal woman?

Certainly, knowledge and possession of talent must be needed. However unforeseen the event is, it ought to not be the case that one is deprived of the ability to deal with things from left to right with common knowledge. I am of the belief that without being a madam, possessed of the self-awareness to meaningfully manifest her uniqueness with a consistent purpose, without an understanding of the contemporary society, without becoming the period's pioneer in knowledge and character, without having the ability and the power, and also without being an ideal madam having the mystical beam of inner hope, it is not right to say that she has lived up to her ideal.

Then, when we at present gradually expand our knowledge and with the very best of our own efforts, take responsibility, fulfill our duty, grow from the trouble that we have suffered, become pressed to assess, study, cultivate, and from developing our conscience, we get closer to achieving our ideal, the day-to-day would not needlessly disappear, and afterward, while one may have a life tomorrow, today, at the present hour, we would be living up to an ideal life.

Therefore, at present, with an acute personal desire of mine, I am heading towards a path, where even a shadow cannot be glimpsed and battling my eternal pain, I am putting the very best of my efforts in the arts that I have directed.

Written on the 5th of November in 1914

⟨*Hakjigwang* (Magazine for overseas Korean students in Tokyo; 1914~1930)⟩

(1914. 12.)

Painting and Joseon Woman

Among the same arts, because literature and music are quite pervasive, while literary magazines and music concerts open occasionally, it is quite disappointing that only painting lags behind this much. While it isn't that other arts are not also treated poorly, when it comes to painting, ever since the past, it was said, 'If one takes up painting, one would be poor······' and as painters were called 'daubers,' they have been much too mistreated and scorned that naturally not only for women, but also for men, there were few who studied this professionally. As a result, leading up to today, only a scarce number of people ended up being qualified enough to pass on the talent of painting, which is ranked as the first of the ancient arts of Joseon.

Really, of the same arts, painting endows the general people a feeling of happiness and beautiful thoughts the most widely and the most easily. Along with music, painting is needed in our lives. Therefore, while it may be childish, starting from primary school, shouldn't the changga (Love song, Korean traditional folk song) and the practice of painting on ceramics be definitely taught?

Regardless of which family, at times, when the sound of a piano would burst out and a single piece of a beautiful painting of a scenery would be hanging, the family's intuitive and peaceful news could be certainly obtained, heard, and seen from the echo of a single melody, and the one breadth of painting.

Like this, how could it be that painting, which most fundamentally endowed a sense of beauty in our lives and made us enjoy intangible happiness was scorned that much, and while madams who made poems or women who wrote words existed, a pitiful thought roams around a lot of times in my mind about whether there was no single madam who sat holding a coloring brush, facing the canvas. However, it is because Joseon women never try to learn painting, but if they try to learn, for instance, certainly, I discovered their characteristic that foreign women could not easily catch up to, while I was teaching painting on ceramics in a girls' high school.

Not only that, I have seen how generally, students quite enjoyed listening when I told them a fun story about painting or when talking about my impression of setting out to do sketching. Hence, it is because our various circumstances are still blocking the opportunity and the convenience to bring interest in painting to Joseon women, and if from now on, a movement that instills a hobby in painting for the general women takes place, surely, I believe that female artists would be produced. Therefore, while it is beyond my own power and my talent is small, I am going to soon open an independent exhibition and I hope that a lot of groups of madams, in general, would come and watch.

⟨*Donga-ilbo* (Newspaper; 1920~Present)⟩ (1921. 2. 26.)

A Report on Becoming a mother

In the dead of night, forgetting everything from before and in a deep slumber of spring dreams, suddenly, at my side, the cries of the little children that broke the quiet of the night struck like lightning. At this time, my soul had been ceaselessly laughing with my friends and singing the song of 'peace' in the flower garden, when I cruelly got kicked out. Already, after a year, not even a single day passed without suffering from this trial every night and once I heard the first sound of "Ah," unwittingly, what came out of my mouth was, "Oh dear, not again," and a frown creased my forehead. In order to promptly get away from this, throwing out all the choice of the rules to set up a new method, I breastfed my child. The child swallowed a few drops, let go of my nipples, and fell into a deep sleep, wheezing. As I at last felt relieved, I lay back, but my sleep soon had already gone far off. So, merely, directing my sight at the brightly lit lamp, hanging loosely right in the middle of the room, I would only roll my eyes frequently and with the period of my past life as a student to the current family life, I would wonder what would once again come of my future! In this way, although it started out from bitterness with such a big question about my life and my ignorant answer to it, at last, pathologically, I got into the habit of staying up all night with joy.

To honestly make my confession, while there are not just one or two contradictions between what I had thought before and what I am going through now, the next thing I knew, how did I become a wife and a mother? As soon as this thought pops up, it really is like being in a dream. The simple words of awe that I say at times, "There is also a limit to daydreaming!" are a remainder of a statement after having had more or less a mostly bitter and sweet taste of the society and family for two years. In fact, rather than what I have dreamt of, a so-called love from which one tears one's heart out, goes shuddering, gets heated up, and becomes feverish, personally stowed in such a life are concerns about the side-dishes, concerns about the clothes, concerns about rice, concerns about the trees, concerns from the fight with the servants who are dirty, lazy, and like to deceive, concerns about the decorum of receiving guests, concerns about the loyalty to my relatives, and who would have known that it was going to be a so-called family, where I had to live for every other being, watching every word that I speak and every movement I make, and besides, not even having the time to wash the diaper when it gets wet all the time, having a so-called child that wakes me up in a crying, humdrum voice that gives no heed, where my body has become frail, my mind has plunged into a fuddled state, and who could have imagined me saying, "My lifelong wish is that I could at least have plenty of sleep!" Yet, rather than wanting to complain, as doubts about life grew, I do not regret but I know of it as happiness that I was able to get one more kind of taste than others.

That is why at the same time that I look forward to more pain, more hope, more disappointment in the future, in order to cultivate and put habitual efforts that are sufficient not to lose out against it, among the strange psychology that is or is not present as the mother of my daughter, Nayeol (Meaning of the name in Chinese characters, 'Radiant Stage') which is the byword for my pen name called Jeongwol (Meaning of the pen name in Chinese characters, 'Radiant Moon'), from 'the time of learning to become a mother' to the point of 'when I become a mother,' I will find the psychology that 'was present as the mother of my daughter' and would like to ask various new mothers, "Isn't that so, no, wasn't that so?"

The year before the last, that is, it was around mid-September of 1920. At that time, I lay in bed on the second floor of my house at Gyeongseong Insadong and rejected visitors. While originally even in normal times, I had irregularity in breathing and indigestion, which was not much to worry, strangely, not only did I start to vomit, became sensitive to touch, slumped in my desire for food but also, I became too precise in distinguishing between the food that I liked and did not like. So, at some time, I prematurely slipped into a talk about my symptoms and at the words of an experienced madam beside me who said, "That is a sign of pregnancy," I was taken by surprise and wished to take back the words that I spit out. Yet, this was not because I was embarrassed, and not the case of realizing at last what I did not know at the time. However, from that incident, I ate rice that I could not eat, did things that I could not do, endured as much as I could, and afterward, 'the words' did not altogether slip out of my mouth, and wondering what I could do to relieve their suspicion was my only concern. Yet, as the symptoms became worse, now, not only was I not able to endure, but simply trying to endure and not speak about my conditions failed to become a shield that could block what would come out of their mouths. Yet, I still hated it. The more I came to know one more person, I hated it with a vengeance. Eventually, from the words coming out of their mouths, it seemed like they were trying to specify what they were fantasizing in their minds as being 'probable or not' as 'something like that.' How so detestable, hateful, and disappointing they were! So, what if this were the work of a dream! Anytime, would I have hoped to swiftly wake up from this dream in a flash and say, "There's no way that happened." Not only did I really hope for that to be the case at a certain time, but I wanted to trust it. However, soon, the dream that I trusted became shattered, little by little. Without the courage to be stubborn like, "No way in hell," even to this point, I hated pinpointing that I was having a baby, that it was a sign of pregnancy, that I was pregnant. In the meanwhile, as I realized that in no time, something was moving in my stomach, I felt a chill in my body, and heard whatever was falling from my chest as a sound that was like a clear bang.

I did not know what the reason was. Everyone seemed to curse me in their words and the laughter that I heard, which got carried in the wind, seemed to be scoffing at me. I wanted to hit hard, wished to cry hard, pinching, tearing my flesh hard, and wanted to see the red blood flowing, one after the other, all vividly. Ah, Ah, rather than being happy, I would merely drown in the depths of anxiety and rather than finding it amusing, I would only feel my chest burning. The act of my siblings who compelled me to get married in order to avoid responsibility is disgusting, my husband who sweet-talked me, "I would die if it isn't for you," and eventually, satisfied his sexual lust is reproachful, to my friend who hoped for even one person to soon, promptly secure a livelihood, as much as I wanted to resist openly, saying, "You must be feeling all relieved now that you could see the state of my body," I merely became exasperated. How could I have easily predicted at that time with my dull brain, the pain and the confines that would come striking in the future? It was just that I have frequently heard these words from various madams. "What would a woman do after studying? She got through all of her business if she just got married and gave birth!" Whenever they would say this, at any time, I would only reply with a snort, and was of the belief that not only did their claim not deserve to be heard, but also it was out of the question. This was not a fantasy, but as this could be seen from the activity of the madams from each Western country and even from Japan, the nearest place, where seeing Yosano Akiko, the mother of ten children on a monthly basis write a thesis, create poems, and read, I clearly had in my mind, 'It's because people are not making an attempt. How come when we are all the same person and all the same woman, only such a person has the ability?' and so, the more I thought about it, the more it seemed like I had thought well. That was why the more there were madams making an assertion about solely getting married and giving birth, the more I denied it, and eventually, I pretended to be a person above their station of ability, but each time, an uneasy assignment went rampant in my brain. However, the madams would say in every one of the words they spoke and in every one of their movements, "Your thoughts are all fantasies, after all. Okay, you go on and suffer. You too have no other alternative," and rejected my views. Even seeing the new women who received high education, who until several years ago used to sit with me and condemn the madams, saying, "I'm not going to live like that," not only is it that they do not look particularly different from the madams, but seeing that they are usually spending their one year, two years on the same housekeeping as the old-fashioned madams, no matter how much I could not trust the old-fashioned madams who before had made their argument, at least I wanted to believe in the household of this new madam. Such a household was not by a long shot deprived of the ability, knowledge, and courage to improve. Then, whoever it is, if one gets married and gives birth, would anyone end up like that kind of household, or wouldn't it be possible not to end up like that?

Then, I am standing in the early stage of lapsing into such anguish. It was as if while I had my eyes wide open, I was falling into the water. In fact, when the path forward would darken, tears flowed ceaselessly. So, even when I was taking a nap, fast asleep, forgetting the things in this world, I would all of a sudden, wake up, astonished, as if someone at my side was stabbing me with the tip of the needle. At this time, my temperature went cold and hot, it was dry and then clammy, and becoming anxious, it was as if when the object is weighed by the scale, like something placed on the plate being dipped, and then doubly raised all the more, my body seemed to leap up into the air, but my head ended up being of a great weight, too heavy that it would sag.

It was too unfair. As nature would send a gale, which would cruelly snap the bud of the flower that partly opened, although there may be somewhere to plead to someone again, still, I wanted to make a plea as I thought that at least 'nature' would not surely have done that; 'What else would be unfair and bitter like this!'

I had a lot of things to do. No, the things that I really had to do were innumerable. Besides, it was the time when my eyes were just opening. As to what art is, as to what life is, as to how people from Joseon ought to do, as to how women of Joseon should carry on, and I could not put all these things off by placing them in the hands of others, but they were things that I really had to do.

I narrowly came all the way to learning that this was not the issue of duty nor responsibility but one's original purpose that came about as a person. At the same time, I thought that the twenty years of life in my past were all acts of falsehood, indolence, ignorance, lack of freedom, and vanity. Indeed, I went all the way to graduating namely, from a professional school, but to the point that I feared that others would know, it was actually a period of idling away in my school days, and eventually, ended up as someone who could not evade being merely nominal, lacking in common sense. I was critical of life, cursed the people of Joseon, and was disappointed in the women of Joseon. I unnecessarily advocated criticisms of this lack of freedom and many times delayed the things to do today to tomorrow. When I would find all these flaws in me, I could not see the least bit of promising things nor any merits. However, I had my one and only strength of love at my side, and as a woman at the age of twenty, the far-off future days and time were all too sufficient for me to live as much as I liked. Thus, a hope that was enough to overflow from me surfaced. A firm tension that seemed like it would not pop radiated. I began to have affection in all of humanity, a sense of duty towards my comrades, and a responsibility to the like. There was not a time like this that I submitted my work, not once in my past like this that I read books, albeit being short-lived. I really had the faith that while my mind could be firmer, it could not be weak, while my hope could be newer, it could not be fixed. That is, I asserted that the path that I would be taking would be the starting point now. Besides, as I had a daydream that I could not let go of, I was able to help myself to a great degree. Seeing that I had little experiences of all sorts of many peculiar things, like in the midst of misfortune, fortunately, while living in prison for half a year, even while suffering through all the restraint, the custody, the penal servitude, and the punishment, tearing the lower ends of my clothes, writing a letter with my fingernails and hurling it in the time of the Independence Movement, "as long as a person just has the heart to do something, all sorts of strength are gained, and there is nothing that a person cannot do." After certainly having had a taste of this alone, I had this thought, which has unforgettably dominated the entirety of my life. This was why the contents of my life as a single person also turned a leaf (although I still have that self-deprecation in my mind). Like that, it was a time when I lived running about in the middle of hope and courage.

Every one of you by now could make a just and reasonable judgment of me. It really had been unfair. It had been embittering to have all these hopes gone. At this time, in my self-deprecating state of mind, rather than the meaning of suicide out of secularism, I had made up my mind on one that was idealistic, tenacious, and born out of grudge. I even wondered how much of a relief my dying mind would be to take my own life.

The connections in life are indeed peculiar. Of them, a hope that was not up to the mark formed in me that I would live again. 'Would a child really be inside my tummy? What is beating now is the beating of my heart. Without the least bit of change from before, I could go around without being tied down, with plenty of time, could make a sketch, and could also read books.' As I thought of this, despite my anxiety, I could see a little bit of the beam of hope. Yet, the next thing I knew, everything that I had patiently organized like this, inside of me, flew away one by one, two at a time, and like an inwardly hollow old tree living inside of me, I, starkly empty, was floating up in the air, and I merely ended up entrusting my lifeline to the circulation of my blood.

Now that I think of it, in order to save me at most, God seemed to have been awfully burdened. Therefore, from the previous life, I must have received some kind of destiny of an upper grade from God that when I set out to the later life, I should not live like that in self-deprecation and came out into the world. That is because among such experiences, I have been reading a certain book. But one day, in the middle of the night, as I was reading the book, I was struck by surprise that I woke my husband up who had been sleeping soundly beside me, told him the state of my mind after pregnancy, and the moment that I said that if he did not send me to Tokyo again to stay there for just two months, there was no way for me to come alive again, he whom I am grateful to cordially assented. The moment I received a willing permission, I felt an unpredictable, double happiness, thinking, 'I will go on living well with such a thankful person as much as I can.'

It seemed like I had strangely gone, running from my world of daydreaming to the world of reality. No, I was able to jump over. It was rather at this time, which was the moment that I had pre-cisely gone over and stepped on the boundary of these two worlds, more than when I had made a promise about leading a life with my partner in the hall, in front of the preacher. At last, I could consult my interest in time and economy. While I could not pre-dict the rest of all the other things, if I have a child, I could at least gauge that half of my time would be devoted to the child. Thus, at the moment, it was my motivation to make up for the time that I wasted before in the slightest, even if it were for a minute, when I could have sufficient time. Therefore, my trip to Tokyo was relatively patient, tense, and saving each and every minute, I devoted my one and only attention to just my field of expertise. The four to five years of my study abroad in the past were utterly fruitless efforts, and I had only these two months to say that I had studied in Tokyo. Even now, my impression from that time is the only thing that remains. Yet, when seeing those of my alumni that were unmarried, I was envious and what was more, when I saw their vigor, their healthy complexion, and their physique, I found it detestable and upsetting. While in the midst of a state of sorrow, which was swept up in such depths of a deep anxiety, unbeknownst to others, a friend, thinking that I did not get married yet, teased me, "Ms. Na would also have to get a lover." While I reluctantly replied, "Yes," inwardly, I thought, 'I am someone who has already gone from the starting point of a relationship to reaching the stage of having a child.' Somehow, it seemed like I had even lost the qualification to share a seat with such unmarried women. How envious and covetous their naivety was, and if it were some sort of an object, I would have committed the act of stealing, regardless of whatever punishment I would get. In this way, rather, I myself became struck by the emotions of dislike and hatred that I had towards married women when I had been a single woman. Yet, somehow, I already became 6 months-pregnant.

Then, I would say through my lips, "It's because a person doesn't try to do whatever it is and so, there is nothing that cannot be done," and reflect, 'What was there to worry about having just one child? Wasn't the original purpose of what I said to do what others could not do among things, the more there are children hanging by, in clusters?' Yet, first, I need to talk more about what kind of world I lived in.

In truth, I was someone who has lived in my daydream and ideal world. Thus, as this was widely different from the real world, like the great discrepancy between the East and the West, no, even farther than that, it was as if someone like me could not for the life of me go all the way there. Yet, from what others could see, the moment that I had entered the world of marriage was when I had before long, come halfway to the real world. However, the state of my mind was not like that, and even, the contents of my marriage life have dwelled as well in daydreams and ideals. Originally, before I became someone's wife, I had found this prospect of being a wife to be frightening and difficult. That was why it seemed like there would never be a time in my life when a person like me would be someone's wife. When it had been like that, more so than from self-awareness and resource, it was from a coincidental opportunity that I ended up becoming someone's wife, and marriage life seemed to be quite easy. The biggest condition that made me not want to have a married life was that I did not want to leave the world of daydreaming, but for some reason, after getting married, the world of daydreaming only became wider and bigger in scope. So, it looked too easy and ridiculous to be advocating a life as a single person. Also, when I had the second condition that had made me evade marriage life, 'It's because I will be tied down,' for some reason, all of a sudden, all the world's creations whose mind and body have grown very patient seemed to be submitting themselves in front of me and there was not the least bit to be tied down by. I could use enough evidence for this with the fact that after getting married, I travelled around the street of Gyeongseong every three months, along with going for work at school every day, and made dozens of my artworks that were filled with heat and affection. While I do not know if the fact that it has become like that could be that in other words, I have gone over to the real world, I know that that if I had left the world of daydream and ideal, such a vigor absolutely would not have been sustained and I would not have had such a magical life, which I am confident about. However, even having come all the way here, the thought of being a mother was not in my dreams. By any chance, if there was a time that I had thought about it, it was just seeing something like the magazine on wives, and later briefly drawing it, dream-like. Thus, when I dreamed of being a wife, while I did not have much trouble arranging here and there, from the first to the second thought, the second to the third thought, when I dreamed of being a mother, one thought cropped up and it was after a long time when the second one would emerge, and later, from the third one, it would not ever surface. Then, without thinking about it more, the thoughts that were bubbling up would be erased. However, compared to the times in which I had been pessimistic and had thrashed around when I had been so frustrated and in the dark due to other things, here, I was being too nonchalant and optimistic. Thus, it was too much of a far-off world that I could not calculate with numbers the distance from me to the world of 'mothers.' In fact, there was so much to learn and know concerning the infinite matters that were before my eyes. Therefore, not only did I think that it was too embarrassing and disgraceful from now on to bring up the matter of the far-off, other world, I thought it to be needless. Thus, as I thought that possibly, such a needless thing could come to be of a detriment to me and my brain, when it seemed like I was showing any sign of being a mother, I promptly stopped thinking about it. If so, someone may dismiss what I am saying here as false (because anyhow, I ended up being pregnant with my child). It indeed is a contradiction. But thinking of it, it also seems natural. That is, this was a fact that could not be discovered from mere knowledge and imagination. In other words, this was the inevitability of love, and whether it would be the result of not having the will to be pregnant or the result of coincidence, as a married couple, we did not have the desire to have children nor did we have the desire to become parents.

Every time a period of delivery was drawing near, this thought cropped up. Uttering, 'Does a person like me deserve to be a mother? But I must be having children, because I'm deserving,' no matter how I pulled out seeming justifications from here and there, besides the qualification for biological structure, and not being modest, I could only say that I did not have any psychological qualification. As I was of a quick-tempered disposition, it seemed like I could not wait for my child to grow little by little, and because my overly sensitive nature always found something of a solitude, it seemed like I would not possess the perseverance to endure the irregular sound of bawling out, crying. Besides, as I was utterly ignorant and lacked understanding, what should I do to unfailingly open up and guide the natural talents and gifts hidden inside the child, and in case of misfortune befalling my husband who fends for the child, how could I preserve the life of the two, me and the child? Moreover, I would become neglectful of painting and I would not have the time to read. In other words, I needed a great deal of time for patiently meditating, studying, and putting things into practice in order to cultivate myself and prepare for the contents to live worthy of being a person, a woman, and individually. However, as I would come to have children, it really did not seem like I could afford to do it and so, the more I thought about it, to me, it seemed to be a needless work and a huge obstacle to my personal improvement. Although I knew that this could enable a life of understanding, freedom, and happiness between two people, a creation of love that could not be found again, an actualization, a solution, how sad it was not being able to feel the happiness and pleasure soaring up from my heart.

My conscience really did not let me play the role of an undeserving mother. It seemed like committing a sin against the child. Also, I did not have the dignity to face humanity. At my wit's end, I thought of having a miscarriage by artificial means, after all. Although legally and ethically, I would be called a criminal and get punished, it seemed like I would not regret it in the least. However, this was nothing more than a tentative moment of hideousness that occurred at the moment when I actually suffered, and at the same time that I was regaining my composure, as much as I became oblivious to the existence born of me and him, who had the combination of the characters of the two and the harmony of love, I realized that the thought of a miscarriage was a mere delusion that I could not easily predict at the moment that my body and soul stood before distressing circumstances. It was simply that I let out a wail after learning the truth that I had slighted myself and affronted my husband in doing so. To speak of this anatomically, I always had the reasoning power and ideal that at the same time that a wife who lives for herself has an important calling, a wife who lives for her own kins also has a great ability, and so, what was said about the individuality of a wife being sufficiently manifested as long as first, a wife was sexually liberated in marital relationship, and which was said to be true turned out on the contrary to be too contradictory and conflicting.

As I began to have a little bit of self-esteem, the anxiety and nerves in my mind that would make me cower surged, like the spark of fire. Simultaneously, conditions that I would absolutely make demands on surfaced. If I were already under the circumstance of giving birth to a child, I did not want to have one that was ordinary nor less than ordinary. I wanted to have a child endowed with the aptitude of having an above the ordinary beauty, an attractive facial expression, a prodigy that could not be found, with an extraordinary individuality, and the courage to dash forward. Then, would I want a son? Would I want a daughter? Whatever it would be, it does not matter. Yet, since it is said that there are a lot of so-called well-rounded men, I would like to have a daughter and make her do tons of things I did not get to do. I wished to make at least one woman a well-rounded person. Then, if a daughter were to be born, I prayed for her to come out, endowed with a lot more. Yet, to no avail. It was disheartening and disappointing. The one in my stomach was disabled, a handicap, let alone ordinary. One would make all the ruckus, frolicking around inside of my stomach, but after birth, what should have been going around stirring up insanity was silent before my eyes. This really is my crime. While during pregnancy, when I should have been laughing and been happy, I was always crying and being sad, when it was good to be at peace and sleep well, I lived as an insomniac while incessantly suffering, and when I was supposed to eat a lot of nutritious foods, I was lacking in my desire for food. From having done altogether a bad job of prenatal care, how could I have dared to hope that a well-rounded child would come out? With the eyes stuck crookedly, the mouth which was ripped to the left, and the waist bent, as such a demon-like kid came out, I could not help but think, 'This is paying for my sin.' I got goosebumps all over and my legs and arms shivered. The deeper this thought became, my mind reeled and my vision blackened. Ah ah, my body quivered like the poplars quivering.

However, the days do pass by swiftly. In the meanwhile, when I genuinely have not felt hope and happiness even once, the last month of my pregnancy arrived before I even knew. A truly, greatly, unexpectedly odd incident took place. I really want this fact alone to be known. It was the following year in early April. With my husband out at work and so, not at home, it was a peaceful night at 12, when the lamp, which was hanging down the middle of the wall in a two-compartment room reflected brightly to a degree that it had never done before and when the whole world was asleep. I was drying and sewing a pair of clothes for my baby to wear after birth, made out of a snow-white gauze. As I could not make the measurement, as an approximation, I was making the place where the arms would go in and where the legs would go in, as if to dress up a tiny doll, laid it out on the floor of the room and looked at it. Unwittingly, all of a sudden, happy thoughts soared up in a deluge. The sort that was coveted, which was wondrous hope, anticipation, and the thoughts of joy were felt. I wanted my child to come out soon and wear this, how beautiful the child would be, how lovely? I could not bear it, out of curiosity. I genuinely wanted to see the face of the child. I was folding and unfolding, letting go of and touching the clothes that I made and happily laughing. My husband came back and upon seeing my complexion, basked in fondness and happiness together. The laughter between the couple continued on, in the midst of the silence throughout the night. It was not that I was intentionally trying to be happy, but it was a momentary emotion. At least, I would like to not cause a paradox in this and would want to let it last naturally as it is. I have never once had a time like this in my pregnancy, and since giving birth, it was an experience that I never had before.

It was the 29th of that month, at 2:25am. After having gone through for about ten hours a suffering incomparable to the pain from all sorts of illness I have had until now, I have been utterly exhausted when as if this world was somewhere worthwhile to see, the baby came out deliberately, at last, crying. How many times did I cry at that moment, had no clue how the midwife was doing, what the nurse was doing, and rather than it being relieving or painful, for some reason, I burst into heavy sobs. It was simply that it was sad and embittering. Afterward, at the hospital bed, I wrote this on my sketchbook.

It is painful, hurting
Truly painful indeed
Sure enough, it is painful
Could I say that it is deeply throbbing
Could I say that it is stinging and stinging
Could I say that it is like getting closely jammed
Could I say that it is like being piercingly stabbed
Could I say that it is like being prickly pinched
Could I say that it is tinglingly numbing
Could I say that it is surprisingly sore
Could I say that it is so painful
No, this also isn't it.

It is like the bones being scratchily raked out
It is like the flesh being vehemently torn
It is like the tendons being strained to the very edge
It is like the blood vessel being plucked out into shreds
It is like the piece of meat being covertly sliced
It is like the five viscera being turned upside down and gushing
It is like the head being bashed in with an axe
Should I say that it is painful like this
No, this too isn't it.

The tiny, vivid yellow sky shaking
the high sky is lowered and
the low ground becomes higher
Without a wall Without a door
passing through, it becomes wilderness
An object inside of it
Spinning around vigorously
As if it is there
As if it isn't there
In no time, as it roams
with all sorts of light that shone bright
with such a beautiful color
coldly covering it
with the black veil that obscures
My tiny body
Seems to be floating in the air

Seems to be stuck in the corner

Seems to be squeezed beneath the bed

I shrunk and then stretched out

I sweated It was chillingly cold

How agonizing it was!

How painful it was!

Instead,

If it were a pain that would incite a flurry of running

If it were a pain that would be of crashing in with a thump

If it were a pain that would be like waveringly passing out

If it had been like that

It wouldn't be that much of a pain

Once in 10 minutes

Once in 5 minutes

While in any minute, it seems like my lifeline would get cut off

While I had strangely been in pain like that

Like the sunlight about to emerge in a foggy day

My mind turned fresh in a flash

As if to wonder when had I been in pain

What was it with me like that

Adding all sorts of seasonings

They are as tasty as they are painful

Mother, I think I might die

Dear, please save me

As I was terribly begging

My husband who had been standing beside me with arms

crossed

At his words, "Bear it"

"I don't want to hear, you wretch."

As I bawled out and wailed

How did my body

End up like this.

1921, May 8, Quilt Used at Childbirth

24 hours after giving birth, the midwife who had been holding the baby in her arms on the other bed tucked the baby gently at my side with a casualness. "Now, it would be good to breastfeed." As I was taken aback and asked, "Yes? What?" she smiled sweetly and said, "Is this your first baby, perhaps?" I did not make any reply, because it was embarrassing and strange. Having already taken notice, with her hand, the midwife pulled my breast out, gave it a massage, loosening it up, saying, "Feed the baby like this," and laying the head of the baby on top of my arm, let the baby's mouth make contact with my nipples and taught me how to breastfeed. Somehow, I felt very fresh. It was as if cold water had been poured onto my back. My parents who gave birth to me and raised me, my siblings who were my flesh and blood, and my ride or die friends did not yet see my breasts and of course, I kept them secretly hidden, out of the fear that they could be seen in whoever's

eyes. The commander who boldly plowed her way through my chest, which had been wrapped up, blowing her breath on it, and commanding the two breasts that she still had not seen to proceed to be in midair, in front was one lump of blood that just opened her eyes to the world at last.

What was the matter? The flesh is definitely a flesh attached to my body, but its absolute owner is that tiny lump of blood!

Thus, the moment that the owner came out of the world, as if she was seeking her own object, without inquiring into the right or wrong, she was in pursuit. A laughter burst out of me. "How absurd the ways of the world are⋯⋯." And, with a brusque thought in mind, along the lines of, "Oh well, take them," I bestowed the two breasts that I had kept until now to this tiny owner. And, I sat, waiting for the aftermath. The tiny owner quite casually held the nipples in her mouth and incessantly, as much as she wanted, with all of her might sucked on them. My huge body was directed towards her tiny lips and it was as if when a multitude of arbitrary dots became connected, they reached the focal point, the blood vessels of each part of my entire body gathered around the focal point of the little one's mouth. Thus, I was already pronounced a mother.

However, there was misfortune on top of misfortune. While for sixty days, it barely went on, sustaining it with considerable difficulty, after that, the milk did not come out altogether. While this was common for mothers with anemia, not only was it not that easy to find a nanny whose milk was agreeable to the taste, but during the middle of the night, the child was pale in the face, as if on the brink of death, when I lit the charcoal so that I could with ease make my child fall asleep with my milk, brought the bowl, and while heating up the milk, which caused a tumult inside the house. Yet, after having barely fed the child and having made her fall asleep, it was common that when I lay in bed, I could not for the life of me go to sleep for approximately two hours, but somehow, if I was about to drift off, once again, she would dazedly wake up and trouble me. As this irresistible pain persisted for a period of certain months, the fatigue of the mind and the body by now reached the point of the extreme, my mind radiated lunacy, and my body was a big sore, without an end. My eyes were always the eyes that wore a sifter and my body like a Dokkaebi (Korean traditional goblin) only had a skull remaining. More than all that I had hoped and wished for before, I just wanted to from morning to evening throughout the day, no, even though I could not hope for that, if I were to get plenty of sleep for merely one hour, with my mind at peace, I do not think I would have anything that I would want, even if I were to die right now. While before, when my sleeping time had been too ample, I had not quite known the meaning of sleep, now I know that there is nothing as deeply meaningful as 'sleep.' All the roots of success, ideal, studying, efforts, economy, and optimism are only this, 'sleep.' After getting sleep, there is a great desire for food, when the desire for food is present, many of the side dishes become useless (compared to the main dish), as one would digest well, one would be healthy, and a healthy body is the essence of a sound mind. Like this, wherever it is seen, one could not live without 'sleep.' Honestly, sleep is a treasure, an article of value. If one were to have a child that would take that away, there would be no greater foe. Therefore, I invented a definition called, 'A child is a demon that tears off a piece of the mother's flesh,' and every time I contemplated this repeatedly, I thought that there was no other masterpiece like this. There was a time when I wrote down this prose about having a baby.

According to people,
as broken-hearted as me
pitiful and poor
a miserable and unfortunate person
there would be no one like me again.

Go on quickly and talk
They are words spoken in luxury
Here, like me
When my eyes became closely pinched
When my body became abruptly stuck
When it couldn't be helped
Open your eyes Rouse your body
As I receive this command like lightning
An adjective about you
I'd hate to even use it

There would not be something as unfortunate and painful as not being able to sleep when sleep washes over. This is in fact even more of a cruel curse than the cost of the sin, the wrath of God that Eve paid for from plucking out and eating the fruit of the tree of knowledge. Based on this first experience, I realized how pitiable all mothers were from the ancient times until now. Moreover, when it came to women from Joseon, it was unspeakable. When they would be bringing up their child under strife, they would be chided because the child was not a son, but a daughter, and as a result of the punishment, the husband would even keep a concubine. Living in this bestial scorn, how would this sorrow be? Yet, out of necessity, there was flesh on their body and a smile on their faces. In their life, there was no path of living other than to sacrifice their present and to hope for their future. Indeed, while I would wonder as to how they could continue with such a life, it was an emotion of love that was spawned from a place of genuineness, and when thinking of their hope and pleasure from soon raising their child and going on to 'live in luxury as a result,' actually, for them, the pain of not being able to sleep and eat is not pain, the anguish in raising the child is absent, and having forgotten the sorrow from being chided, there is no loneliness to make an exhaustive study of. Speaking of which, as it was with a deity as natural as the deity was, and as it was with one's body as it was, it was a good and beautiful life of happiness. Therefore, it could be said that more than it was for a mother of one child, the more she was to become a mother of two, three, she could transform it into the life of heaven.

When in the middle of the night, forgetting sleep and on edge, as this thought started emerging, I formed my hands into a tight fist and sprung to my feet.

"Okay, now I know! As to why parents love their child. As to why people complained that I didn't give birth to a son but a daughter." Although this was coming from someone like me who would go against nature, no, going against it, as someone whose blood of sin became addicted to the whole body, which came up in a moment of antipathy, I pride myself on how it really is truthful in one aspect. It is said that parents loving their child is a soaring up of affection. If so, they ought to love their sons and daughters equally. How come starting from birth, a discrimination of love, conditions, and demands on the child of the parents arise? As it is a son, he is adored and as it is a daughter, she is said to be lowly, and more than a girl, a boy, more than the weak, the strong, more than the victim, a simpleton is preferred. How come this absolute calculation gets formed? Seeing this fact, I cannot believe in their so-called soaring up of affection. It is definite that as much of a certain secret is being hidden in their inner side. Until now, all the time, I have absolutely praised the love of parents. It is said that while the love of a couple and the love of friends is compensatory, the love of parents alone is an eternal, absolutely non-compensatory love. Therefore, losing my parents early in life was sorrowful, upsetting, and bitter that whenever I would feel the grief at the thought of not being able to get a taste of such an eternal love again, I could not hold back from being at a loss. Yet, as I came to realize that this was my misunderstanding, I was discouraged. I was disappointed. I was put off. They demand absolute filial piety on us, children and give orders to repay the kindness. A filial piety is originally the basis of engaging in a hundred of good deeds, and as there is no bigger sin than committing impiety, when a father passes away, for three years, the child would leave the work that one's father had done while living right where it is, unchanged, which was rightly referred to as filial piety. In this way, the child was the absolute slave of one's parents, an accessory, and ended up becoming a sacrificial object for one's parents for a lifetime. Like this, while the amount of love and the amount of compensation were always parallel, at some time, rather, it became weighted towards the side of compensation. Therefore, incomparable to the love of friends and partners, it was an absolute compensatory love, a vicious love. That is why an absolute calculation was formed, selfishness was radiated that it was said that more than the rise and fall of a country, the parents cared about living in ease, where the number of sons had to be greater than that of daughters, that while a daughter could be ignorant, a son had to be smart, in order for them to experience luxury in the latter years. As they found with their son such an infinite hope and pleasure in their future, they have lived a life of forgetting even the pain and sufferings. This is a fact that is conspicuous in those who are incompetent than those with talent and is present a lot more in parents from uncivilized countries than those from civilized countries.

I do not want the love of my parents again. Losing my parents early on meant that my body became liberated with freedom, that I became someone full of happiness, as one whose work would become a work on behalf of my country and humanity. Although this is bold of me, I wanted to finally speak my words on such an impression.

While people say that always, the love of a mother is furnished in the heart of someone who just became a mother from the very beginning, I cannot altogether arrive at such a thought. If I did have that thought by any chance, it was when I was a mother for the second time. In other words, it seemed like I had to pass through experiences and time in order to have a mother's love. There seems to be some truth in the proverb, 'Love for the child is the elders' love for the young.' It could be that the first person who said this could perhaps have said it with the same emotions as me. Instead of being endowed with a mother's love from the very beginning, at least, during the lengthy period of five to six months feeding and raising, the mind and body of the child undergoes a peculiar transformation so that when the peaceful smile of an angel arouses the mind of a mother, this has become my flesh and blood, and the moment that I became conscious that the child was created from my soul, it was then that I could not help but feel the electrifying love of a mother for the first time ever. (Based on my experience, this is generally similar in the traits of mothers) As such a bud opens in the heart of a mother, the possibility that it could little by little widen and grow bigger forms. Therefore, 'the soaring up of affection' is not a sense of purity, that is, it is not a sense of nature, but it is a sense of cultivation. This could be seen on occasions when a mother's love does not quite soar up when the child was raised in the hands of a nanny. In other words, it is not a love that is endowed intrinsically but radiated from training in the midst of the time of mothering. That is, this is not a theory of denial that claims that there is no such thing as a soaring up of the sense of an instinctive affection, but what I want to say is that the affection for one's child is not something special.

Next, I would like to understand by whatever means as to the need of having a child. Yet, I could not easily comprehend. 'Producing the next generation and thereby cultivating the successor is the calling that has been passed down generally on wives. It is the claim of nature, an advancement.' This conceptual reasoning power was far too remote from the emotions that I went through. 'It is because organisms live and survive with the purpose of the reproduction of their species.' This statement as well does not seem to matter to me in the least. 'It is because if the family does not have a child, it becomes too simple.' Unlike this saying, there are a lot of ways to live a more complicated life. 'It is because when one becomes old, one would rely on one's child.' If I were to get old and become incompetent, I will be taking my own life above the comfortable grass of the green cassia trees within the deep forest. I would want to get more of a taste of solitude so as not to hear this sound of bawling out, crying, and if I would not have this obstacle, I would be able to submit a work of patience, and if not for the fatigue and poor health due to a child, I would still have a lot of stamina, but solely because of this child, it is not like so. In this way, as the inverse proportion of the absolute need, the absolute needlessness comes forward. This is not a common trait but something arbitrary. In the meanwhile, I gained a bit of relief from the need of a child.

A person is hidden among very unfair contradictions. Although one's psychology could eternally grow and one's ideal could infinitely be drawn, only the time of one's lifeline is too finite and brief with one's energy becoming incompetent and too finite. As God who created such an infinite psychology and a finite body also must have come to think, as humans did not seem to have a lot that they do, God must have passed down a child, and must have told them to make their child fulfill an ideal that they were in the middle of implementing but failed to do. That is why among the ideals of a person, while one would want to do art, literature, music, medical studies, philosophy, and study whatever one could see and hear, not only does one lack the talent, but as one's energy cannot be furthered, in the end, one could do only one or two, in other words, could go so far as to solely being a literary person, and knowing a little bit of music. The leisure to dedicate one's time to do all of the rest becomes void. At this time, if one could have a daughter who likes art, a son who likes medical studies and philosophy who would grow up, one would have the desire, efforts, and courage to make one's 2nd-self fulfill what one liked, but merely was not able to put into practice. Hence, I think that the meaning of raising a child has not a single, but double meanings.

Even if one psychologically was endowed with all the hopes and had the confidence to further one's energy, when the body becomes frail, and when one could not leave one's bedside from illness all the time that the ideal and the implementation seem to have nothing to do with each other, such a thing like hardship would not have any meaning in enhancing our life and would not have value. In other words, after turning out to have an unhealthy body that could not be controlled by knowledge and cultivation, saying such and such (about people having physically withered), "It's because such a being is not a human······" was also a fantasy. It was a delusion.

Written by the mother of Kim Nayeol on her 1-year birthday on the 29th of April in 1922
⟨*Dongmyeong* (Magazine; 1922~1923)⟩ (1923. 1.)

Response to Baekgyeolsaeng

(Baekgyeolsaeng is a critic who published his criticism of *A Report on Becoming a mother* by Na Hye-seok)

While it may not be up to the mark, it is such an honor to have received the attention of all of you, readers. Seeing that it (*A Report on Becoming a mother*) was said to have "momentarily drawn the audience of the society," and on top of it, from having learned a lot from Baekgyeolsaeng, I express my gratitude.

Originally, it was not my intention to write this response. I hesitated a couple of times, because it seemed like I was making an excuse for some reason. Yet, "Simply, my concern is that while the author of *A Report on Becoming a mother* says that the old notion is mistaken and grasps the new notion, if that is also bound to be mistaken, idling away, without the least bit of worrying about the new notion is worse than the harmful consequence of the old notion, and as a so-called rookie, the author seems to have the tendency of straying ideologically." Such an outrageous thinkpiece of Sir on the conclusion about the connections I have made written in my report (*A Report on Becoming a mother*) absolutely cannot be overlooked. That does not mean that I am trying to avoid the responsibility as someone whom Sir called prejudiced and dogmatic. Also, that does not mean that I am not accepting Sir's rebuttal but rather, I am very happy. It is just that I am trying to talk about Sir rather being the one prejudiced and dogmatic, and as Sir had been concerned all the time, due to words that grate on the nerves of the public, indeed, I cannot help but worry that by chance, I might augment the straying of rookies who are ideologically straying. I will discuss Sir's think-piece on so-called rookies that stacks up to other criticisms by seizing a different opportunity, but here, I am merely trying to write my response about Sir rather simply, at the same time that I am going to transcend the attitude of excuses as much as I could.

To my regret, I could not help but say that most of all, Sir cannot distinguish between the form of a 'thesis' and a 'report,' and cannot make the distinction in the method of reading or in criticism. I would think that with a lot of learning to polish and hone in on, a thesis which leaves an ideal alone, sets up an advocate, and presents it with words has reasons, conditions, rights, duties, and responsibilities, while a report, which expresses the instantaneous intuition in words, out of a simple instinct that is manifested from moment to moment, without it being fictitious would be absolutely, unconditionally irrelevant to something like rights, duties, or responsibilities. It is just that it could not be forgotten that the sole purpose of a report alone is not for a conclusion that synthesizes the experiences, but for honestly and simply writing about what one realized intuitively at that time, without a priority. Therefore, when reading a thesis, based on seeing the examples made, one could comprehend, grasp the logic, realize it, and figure it out. On the other hand, when reading a report alone, merely based on the examples, one could not comprehend and even based on logic, could not grasp, in other words, without the readers themselves also experiencing almost the same emotions in a similar circumstance to that of the author herself, it is an enigma that absolutely could not be understood. If so, when criticizing a thesis, there would be a question, an opposition as well, and so, not only is it is natural that duties and responsibilities are pressurized, but also, it could afford concerns about the social, ideological field, and it allows for the time to call for a reflection, whereas for a report alone, originally, it does not even make sense to rebut it, and besides, would it be anything worthwhile to idealize and ideologize it? Sir putting the absolute responsibility on me and on top of it, sweepingly taking it out on me by going on about it being ideological, and it being about new women is a slander, without a cause altogether. It would seem to be the most reasonable thing to argue against nature rather than talk about this with me. While these are futile words, I am advising against Sir focusing too much on the ideological field solely, as you would be in need of cultivation to treat others with humanity and philanthropy.

Driven by the motivation that in order to learn, I needed to talk, starting from what I do not know, and in order to listen to other people, I needed to speak my words first, I plucked up the courage and after releasing, *A Report on Becoming a mother*, all the time, I silently looked forward to the thoughts of my readers. I believed that I would gain and learn a lot, if among mothers with the extent, circumstance, and experiences like mine, one person would write her thoughts on how it was after reading my report. And, I was worried about what I should do in case a person from an entirely different world, without any understanding, would drone on and on about this or that. To me, it is because I believe that this emotion alone is not something to be understood as the theory of a philosopher or a physiologist, but rather, this experience would resonate with women from a deep valley in the mountainside and from a village, who are utterly ignorant. It became a case of a slander like, "Why do you go around stepping on dirt?" from a yangban (Upper class in Joseon) in the clouds. Seeing the words of Sir, "Pregnancy is not that much of a comfortable thing," it is unforgivable that Sir is pretending to know a fact that Sir would not easily know.

Of my report, alluding to a few lines, "To avoid responsibility……", "A child is a pregnant mother's……" "A mother's love……", Sir elaborated with whatever phrases he knew, such as, "As the author of *A Report on Becoming a mother* has no intuition, is subjugated, turns her back on the old morals and embraces the new morals……" and tried to make them the important point of the rebuttal. Sure. The important statement of Sir's rebuttal was, in other words, among the texts of my report, on my most precise emotion. They were my most irresponsible words, my most childish words, my most offensive words. However, some of these words were my most honest words and the bravest words. Okay, if my pain and sufferings that had existed to a certain degree at the time were contained in these words at a scale of one to hundred, my report was a success. Thus, as I did not have that much of a falsehood, my conscience is innocent and certainly, I was only trying to write about an irresponsible, momentary intuition. It is simply a pity that Sir's oversensitive nerve, profuse learning, and lofty ideology were abused.

As I have said before, just seeing a few points, wherever I read Sir's statement of rebuttal that was under the pretext of talking about my report, not only does it have no relation whatsoever to my report, but unexpectedly, I could easily get a sense that Sir personally has some antipathy towards generally women, especially Joseon women, and among them, as Sir himself called, new women. That is, I could get that from Sir having to set at the forefront scornful words like "the pioneering of the new woman of Joseon," or "flattering herself as a new woman……" or "the face of a rookie," or "a new woman who demands liberation……" in order to say something, which are a kind of a curse, a slander, and up to this point, only when Sir mistrusting women themselves, covering the entirety of the character of the new women of Joseon and scorning it, what is there that would make your statement of rebuttal shine? I am not going to write the modest words, "That is because women themselves deserved to get such a scorn……" Based on Sir's self-esteem being excessively high, prejudiced, and dogmatic, I could not help but say that Sir lost the qualification of a critic who needs to have a fair and just attitude. At the same time that my report did not pose as a thesis representing the realm of the ideology of new women, Sir was shameless in setting me up as the representative figure of it, saying, "While through her malicious gossips, she makes an all-out effort to cry for freedom, when entering into her real life, as it is the actual state of a new woman that she still could not go beyond a subjugated life, ⋯⋯" is too much of a discourtesy. I would demand asking the general female readers, students on this. Sir spoke of this so-called subjugation in the words of, "How could there be freedom when she shoulders the responsibility of caring for food and clothes by herself?" Bringing up words that are behind a century once again and seeing the words that suggest to take steps backward, I get that even with knowledge like that of Sir, you are in the dark about issues on madams. We women have not found ourselves unfortunate to be women and we have not looked up to and envied men, have not tried to get into a fight over our rights, have not made demands about equality, and do not know absolutely about freedom. It is merely that we are no different in that we hope to live for "true love" and to fulfill it. Look, while the everyday sort of women made an uproar about the equal rights movement, didn't extraordinary women try to partake in universal love? Also, at the end of which Sir brought up another woman's marriage issue that is completely different from my circumstances and emotions, Sir said, "Not only is it certainly when women have a multitude of work, but also when they suffer an unfavorable circumstance, they

have the weakness of not being thorough, evading that responsibility." Saying such and such, what is the need to shoehorn the
entire women of civilization in an individual Joseon woman's report? While I have room for tolerating them as they are senseless
words, I do not contain my rage, in order to respect Sir's character.
Based on this, Sir's statement of rebuttal is quite separate from my
report. This indeed could seem like an excuse, but by any chance,
I am writing for reference. Whoever it is, women during pregnancy, whether physiologically or psychologically, even more than
regularly come to have an ideal, and while there may be a difference in adjustment, there is no mother that does not experience
it. Thus, during pregnancy and after giving birth, until a certain
period, no matter how dense one is, one becomes sentimental, it
becomes very easy for one's sensitive nerve to be excited and so, at
this time alone, one gets angered even at unnecessary things and
becomes quite happy even at small things. These are in fact words
and if it were really like my report, who would want to give birth?
It is simply that when I was writing it, as I was writing about my
excited emotions during the 1-year timeline of being 10 months
pregnant and post-birth, it may well be suspected what I was going through. That does not mean I was also making an assertion
about 'limiting childbirth,' and it was not that I was saying that
whoever it is, one should not give birth to a child. As I have written in my main text, "I had the reasoning power and ideal that at
the same time that a wife who lives for herself has an important
calling, a wife who lives for her own kins also has a great ability,"

"Producing the next generation and thereby, cultivating the successor is the calling that has been passed down generally on wives. It is the claim of nature, an advancement." Bringing back these words, I want to clarify that my ideals collided with my emotions.

Finally, what I request Sir to know is that I have never once flattered myself as a new woman, and I do not really think of it as an honor for Sir to say that I am a rookie. I am not an ideologist nor an educator nor an artist nor a religionist. It is just that I wore the mask of a human, was born a woman, and merely was trying to find my way to live with love. By any chance, at a different time, even if a connection is made, I wish for you to take this into consideration. Sir, is it that much of a bad thing to ideologically stray? Isn't it a bad thing to say that one should not stray at a time when one ought to stray? Is there a reason to be on edge and get worried? What would that be if one does not even stray and starts out from being fixed? Wouldn't that be a shadow of a fossil?

I definitely have faith. I have faith that *A Report on Becoming a mother* will resonate with some mothers. If there is a mother who denies this, I believe that before long, at the same time that her vision of mind is awakened, there would be an inescapable, inevitable agreement. I really hope that there will be. Rather than a few, I hope for there to be many. Only when we would have this experience, we would definitely know how to set out on the path of living resolutely. By all means, I hope that there will be.

⟨*Dongmyeong* (Magazine; 1922~1923)⟩ (1923. 3. 18.)

The Q&A between a Husband and a Wife

Wife: That is attributed to the fact that the husband originally doesn't truly love his wife. Also, he doesn't respect her character and that would be because he looks down on her. So, that is merely an ignorance of the man and may not be an issue of whether there was understanding or not.

Husband: Then, do you mean to say that the understanding of a husband is absolutely unnecessary?

Wife: Are those even appropriate words? A married couple would have to understand each other. That certainly is how a meaningful life of one family could be formed.

Husband: What I mean to say is, what if no understanding is reached?

Wife: Well. If it had been a man or a woman who sufficiently had been awakened to the meaning of freedom, equality, and understanding, one would not get married to a person who doesn't understand like that in the first place. Also, with the education and character that would be sufficient for one to receive considerable treatment, one would've gotten enough trust to earn the admiration of the other person. So, whenever one wants, one could manage things accordingly with one's own rights.

Husband: What if the married couple who seemed to be living like that, in the middle of it, experienced discord?

Wife: As for that, there won't be any other way but to try to turn the system upside down or to change one's mind.

Husband: It would be easy, if one were to literally do that⋯⋯.

Wife: Yes, if one were to do accordingly, there would be nothing difficult and so, whoever it is, if the woman sets a purpose and always has a committed attitude towards it, except for men who intentionally behave perversely, wouldn't the man be moved by the woman and would there be something that could not be understood? It is all up to the woman herself.

Husband: Ah, how admirable.

Wife: Yes, of course, it is admirable. Soon, women would all become aware like me. What is up with the men who only know one thing and cannot think of two?

Husband: Why? Would men stay where they are? Men would still keep progressing.

Wife: While I don't know about men from other countries, when men from Joseon aren't able to break away from their fetters, how much worth would it be if they do make progress? Among them, the more perverse they are, the more they aren't able to fend for even one thing for their future, but every time they speak, they end up going on and on about how women are, and seeing them doing that, the pity of it. It's as if the Songpyeon (half-moon shaped rice cake), made out of early ripening rice that I ate 3 years ago would all come barfing out. Actually, men with intellect and character are all fending for their own future and so, when would they have the luxury to complain about women?

Husband: ······.

Wife: Hello, why aren't you responding to me? Am I right?

Husband: Yes, yes, it's certainly right.

Wife: I'm genuinely speaking, but don't my words sound like words? Why do you sound like you're joking about it?

Husband: What do you mean I sound like I'm joking about it? I really meant that it's right. Like what you said, is there anything that a man could complain about a woman, or anything a woman could complain about a man? In just fending for their future, they all are burdened and have no time. If everyone fends for themselves sufficiently, in the long run, well-rounded men and women would come flooding out. When I see those without work, studying about the dilemmas faced by wives or something and wandering around, I could clearly see through their faces and find them ludicrous.

Wife: That's because recently, after the first world war, the three issues, dilemmas faced by wives, labor problems, issues affecting children have become prevalent, and he wouldn't have been able to stand still, which would've pushed him to study them.

Husband: Then, what is the point of fussing about how the more they lack in character to fend for themselves, the more they complain about women? They are doing that, because they don't have work to do and food to eat. Now, let us stop talking about this head-aching story and continue finishing what we were talking about before.

Wife: Right, the story's gone off track. Okay, because the husband is oh, so generous, people say that the wife of such a husband, that is, I go around freely.

Husband: Did they say that?

Wife: Look at that. How lucky you are. As you spend your time in the house comfortably and your status becomes gradually higher because of me who goes around, working tiresomely, as such, when I go on a business trip several times more, you wouldn't burden yourself but still, even your dignity will soar up at a certain day. Instead, a badge for the collection of my services will be hanging from my chest, and so, how huge my contribution would be and how high your status would be.

Husband: So, what the hell do you expect me to do?

Wife: So, if you want to elevate your status, send me on a trip to someplace with a different culture and a different view two times a year in spring and autumn.

Husband: Who would send such a trip? As you said, it is freedom, where one is supposed to do it with one's own strength.

Wife: Still, it requires a lot of strength from you.

Husband: What sort of a contradiction is this?

Wife: No, what I mean is that since I'm elevating your status, I need to get that much compensation in return.

Husband: What a stingy person.

Wife: How ungentle you are!

Husband: Okay, an ungentle person like me also won't have much need for status and so, stop going around working, and at a time when you're young, as you are now, you should devotedly take care of your children in your family, while I will earn money, and after we get old, let's go on a trip around the world as much as we like.

Wife: How distasteful would it be, going on a sight-seeing, being aged? Going on a sight-seeing is also about energy. When one is young, at a time in which the emotions of joy, anger, sorrow, and pleasure are as sharp as the blade of a sword, at a time in which all the things that one gets to see and hear are poetry, music and art, at a time in which the various kinds of impression that are like boiling water turn into ideas, prediction, and maxim, which are only at that time, the time when one could go around for how much distance, respectively 4 km with sturdy legs, while moving one's waist and hands, running from right to left, and seeing a variety of things, but throwing away all those times, instead, how could I go around and let my wretched state be in open view for others when I would be sapped of energy, my waist would ache, it would be no fun, and I would be yawning as an oldie who couldn't pull her legs apart? When I get old, in the corner of the back room, finding joy by replaying the things that I've seen and kept when I was young would not hinder other people and would be good.

Husband: Whether in the past or in the present, your reverie is one and the same.

Wife: When I'm trying to take pleasure in my reverie until I grow old and die, what would I do if I don't already fall into such a reverie?

Husband: Okay, how is Harbin?

Wife: In which direction?

Husband: General destination.

Wife: Just speaking of it, as it is in Siberia, I'd know that it would have a feeling of being large and wide, even without asking.

Husband: Then, how is the general appearance and attitude?

Wife: It is free, laid-back, and active.

Husband: What about the relationship between men and women?

Wife: Although I wouldn't know much in the short time that I've been there, upon seeing the motion picture a couple of times, once one becomes fond of someone, even if he was a married man, or she was a married woman, one knows how to devotedly love to the point of risking one's life, and if there is a single mistake, it is no more than asking when did you know, and turning around, which is endowed with such a daring mind of letting it go. While their way of seducing women in their twenties is skillful, the means of escape in order not to fall into the pitfall by handsome men is also admirable. It should be to that extent that the relationship between men and women would be fun, meaningful, free, and equal at last.

Husband: Then, how is their family?

Wife: Yes! Oh! What I wanted to first talk about was their family.

Their family system is very firm, very neat, very orderly. The way they live is actually living for the sake of living. This is completely different from our way of life, which is that one lives because one could not die. What makes Western people most psychologically progressive is that they know the principle of peace. Originally, in order for people to live with others peacefully, the strong should protect the weak. Yet, they know this truth. Not only do they know but they also put it into practice. The husband and the son do whatever it is that is difficult and distressing, but the mother and the daughter do things that are suitable for their strength. This is the complete opposite of the family system in our country. When I was there, what I actually saw was, in the morning, upon waking up early, in my next door, a Russian man presumably around the age of forty, clad in his pajamas, holding a big bucket in each of his two hands, gathering water, and every-day, he is the first one in his family who certainly wakes up and does that. Afterward, I ate my breakfast and as I went on to see, the door of that house from a while ago opened and a prominent gentleman wearing a frock coat and a high hat came out and looking at him, he was none other than the man who went to gather water. I stood there, where he wouldn't notice me, stared at him, and I couldn't help but admire how peaceful their life is, at the end of which, thinking of the families from our country, no matter what, I couldn't help but bitterly think of the grievance, dissatisfaction, and discord that arise from our men being deliberately ill-mannered. When I shared the story about the gentleman with another person there, the person would look rather skeptically at me as I was speaking and said, "What is so strange about it? In the Russian family, the wife is like a sovereign and so, we just do all that is a part of our duty, the daughters spend their time playing the piano and dancing, and the husband and the sons do all that is difficult." Upon briefly introducing the families from our country, the person was taken by surprise and said, "If vulnerable women are shoved around that much, how would there be peace?" and went on laughing. As the men and women are in harmony, know how to love each other, care for each other, are repulsively calm, sophisticated, orderly, and neat, how can there not be world literary giants like Tolstoy, Turgenev, and Dostoevsky?

At some time, when I went somewhere with someone, upon being asked the question regarding my impression, I said, "After seeing the family system of the Russian people, for the first time in my life, I realized how much family has such a great impact. The individuals know as much how to truly love others, the wind of peace blows in the family, which is how global literary giants and global ideology are produced." Actually, I think I got to know the deep meaning of family. Dear, of the people in our country, would those who've had an experience of the European culture all have gotten the same impression like mine? After seeing the Russians live their lives literally like the saying that their sweet home was as sweet as honey, as much as I found myself automatically doing a hula dance, the people of our country who've seen the Russian family in Harbin would've also done that and they would've been so envious that they would've been salivating. Yet, I wonder why not even one of them implemented the family lifestyle they've seen, how peculiar. That would be so as when their counterpart, a man or a woman would have grown, seen, and heard things in the completely opposite world from them, how would their goal and thoughts match? On the one hand, while they would be aware of that and fret over it, on the other hand, they would be coolly indifferent and so, after raising the family greatly in the way they had learned from the European family, once they would fall flat, they would just go back to the family life they led, once again. That is why day and night, the complaints are one and the same complaints. Although it is an unavoidable fact in the transitional period of Joseon that as long as they could do whatever they want, the family gets on well when men with the ideal that they are the Gap (The one with power), and women with the ideal that they are the Eul (The one who's subjugated) get married, there are countless cases when a couple is not even of that extent and as a man or a woman, each lacking something get married, anyhow, a harmony ought to be found in the family life so that there would be color in it at last. Wouldn't there be vigor in that? In my opinion, I don't know how much of a huge enterprise it would be to do an inspection into families in places like Shanghai or Harbin, which are near, where the Western culture could be seen, and thereby implement a fundamental method for an improvement of lifestyle here, rather than recruiting a tourist party of dozens and making them go on a sight-seeing around Japan's Fuji-mountain or Nikkô Matsushima. To add to it, I don't know how much the husbands' frowning face would become flushed when their wives of the intellectual class, who have the rights and the responsibility to proficiently hold sway over their family, are encouraged to do an inspection once into the foreign family's lifestyle. What are those without a clue on the meaning of life doing with what they have studied and when they have visited the tourist attraction, what on earth are they going to use it for?

Husband: It shouldn't all be viewed positively, just based on it being a Western culture.

Wife: Yes, you're right. There are a lot of cultures that are inferior to the Eastern culture. That is why what I'm saying is that whoever it is, one should become a well-rounded person in the East before going to the West. If one goes before one becomes a well-rounded person, one is bound to turn into a lost doll that converts into the culture from there, in other words, gets exported there, but if after one becomes a well-rounded person, one goes there, one would become a creator that could understand the place, in other words become someone for other countries to import. So, although I may be needlessly talking about the West, as those who didn't go over to the West could be even better than those who went to the West and graduated from a university there, whoever it is, there is no way but first to be a well-rounded person.

Husband: Now, let us sleep. Already, in just 10 minutes, it's going to be 1am.

Wife: Right, I've been running my mouth well. But this is just one-sixth of my travel story. Really, every time I saw all sorts of things, I added logic to them in various ways. I wonder if I would've had great success, being an explorer as I've always wished.

Husband: You're trying to do everything!

Wife: No, although there is a possibility that I could do everything, I especially want to be an explorer.

Husband: You can!

Wife: Because I am a damn woman⋯⋯.

Husband: Is there something that a woman can't do?

Wife: It isn't that I cannot do it, but it's that it would be nothing more than passive.

Husband: Why?

Wife: Even if one were not to care for the social disapproval and the violation of the cultural habit, the biggest reason is because of the feebleness of the physicality, along with how uncomfortable it is physiologically.

Husband: Why don't you do it as your strength grows?

Wife: Preferably, rather than not doing it, I should be able to do all that I want to do.

Husband: How did you form such confidence?

Wife: It wasn't formed, but rather, I naturally had it. Thinking of my route from when I was young up till' now, I had quite a lot of perilous adventures. To bring up one example, whichever road it was, I never came back to the road that I had once taken. And, there was a time when I went to a dark alley in the middle of the night, thinking that a tiger would be there, and even a time when I hoped to suddenly meet a thief somewhere.

Husband: It would've been seriously troubling if you were born a boy.

Wife: That being so, consecutively, in Donga-ilbo, under the title, 'If I were born a boy,' 'If I were born a girl,' the words of some people were written and unanimously, men said, 'I would've become a woman that would curry favor with her husband.' Women said, 'I would've become a man that loves his wife.' However, if I were to write, I wouldn't have gone for what anyone could do, but would've written that I would've become an explorer, an adventurer that would otherwise be a bit uncomfortable if one wasn't a man. But in my later years, I have something that I will definitely be trying to do.

Husband: What is that?

Wife: Let me get on with it later.

Husband: Talk all about it at the end of the conversation.

Wife: Because if I were to say it in advance, the emotions would all wane. I will do it when the time comes for me to speak about it. By the way, when I grew up, I used to quite enjoy the silence and so, I was always alone, going around studying, taking a walk alone, and also, was going to have such a lifestyle in my later years, but as I think about the busy lifestyle like I'm having now, it is amusing and strange. That is that, but earlier, didn't I talk about my thoughts on family?

Husband: Yes.

Wife: What do you think?

Husband: About what?

Wife: Don't you want us to live like how others live a life that is worthy of living?

Husband: How?

Wife: For us to live in harmony, knowing how to love each other, care for one another, and help the weak!

Husband: Why? Aren't we living a life as good as that? Our lives are better than those of the prime ministers and owners of fields yielding as much as 10,000 seok (Korean unit of measurement for crops) of rice. How many new families in Joseon are there that have the most simple, neat family, where we could spend when we want to spend money?

Wife: It's all because of my efforts.

Husband: Whatever.

Wife: But don't be all talk and no action, and instead, let's put it into practice starting from tomorrow.

Husband: How?

Wife: First, starting from tomorrow morning, you clear up the spot where you slept. And, you scoop up water for washing up with your own hands. Like this, let's all begin a life of autonomy.

Husband: What use would you be then, when I have you?

Wife: Look at that. How can something good even splutter from my mouth when such a fuss comes out? It seems like we won't even get a taste of peace.

Husband: Don't get all angered at the slightest provocation and let's do it the way that would be good. Okay, how difficult would that be?

Wife: The problem is that you're trying it just because you know it's not going to be difficult nor something that you cannot do.

Husband: I'm going to do it but why?

Wife: What if you're not going to?

Husband: Punish me.

Wife: How?

Husband: Whip my calf.

Wife: That would only be briefly painful and you would call it quits.

Husband: Then, what punishment would be good?

Wife: A punishment like the one I gave you in the daytime would be good.

Husband: That is too extreme. Okay, do whatever you want.

Wife: Instead, it would be the wisest thing not to get that extreme punishment.

Husband: Certainly.

Wife: So, what I'm saying is that whatever it is, each one of us should all live, always preparing as much so as not to have our future lag behind others. The more we live like that, the more inseparable we become. As the wife lives, always getting dragged by her husband, and her husband always looks down on his wife, there, at the slightest slip, a fight is bound to happen and if it gets worse, generally, they get to the point of so-called divorce. Anyhow, whoever it is, it is known that in the place where one aggressively takes action, freedom, equality, and peace are preserved.

Husband: Okay, do you live with such an attitude?

Wife: Of course. I'm always mentally ready. If you, my husband, had some huge complaint about me, if there was no reason for me to work to do away with it to a certain extent, I would never try to get into a fight over it. As this fact shows that already, the power of love for a woman like me has all but dissolved to that degree, that it is your attitude of repulsion towards me as much, and you wouldn't even know of such things, what am I to do? Avoiding would be the wisest thing for you and me. That doesn't mean I want to always live in a state of anxiety. It would be nothing more than being mentally prepared for what would happen if it were to lead up to that circumstance. Whoever thinks to the extent of the misfortune that would strike in the future at a time of giving and receiving love? If there was a person like that, it would be as inferior as not being mentally prepared.

Husband: Yes. It seems plausible.

Wife: It doesn't just seem, but it really is. That is why the more it is for a new woman with a bit of knowledge, the more difficult it is for her to play her role as a human being without great diligence and efforts.

Husband: That would be so.

Wife: That is not only for women, but also the same for men. It's just that the scope is wide for men.

Husband: Let's stop and go to sleep.

Wife: I'm also up for it.

Husband: Let's turn off the light.

Wife: Turn off the light.

Husband: You turn off the light.

Wife: The person who said to sleep first should be the one to turn it off.

Husband: That is what women should do.

Wife: That won't cut it.

Husband: Then, to be fair, let's do rock, paper, scissors, and the one who loses would be turning it off.

Wife: Sure.

Husband: Rock, paper, scissors······.

Wife: Look at that. What would be better about turning it off from losing?

Husband: After all, I get to turn it off.

(The lamp that had been turned on, isolated, in the quiet of the dark was turned off. As the lamp flickered and died, the room inside darkened. The two souls plunged into the dream of peace and the beautiful and soft sound moved to and fro! To and fro!)

Written on the 11th of July.

⟨*New Woman* (Magazine for New Women that Na Hye-seok helped found to foster a Korean feminist literary tradition; 1922~1923)⟩ (1923. 11.)

My Experience Raising a Child

Without any preparation for raising a child, I already have become a mother of two children. Considering this point, it is really an embarrassing thing and I do not have any qualification as a mother. It is merely that as I have coincidentally become a mother, I am trying to write about my experience of ordinarily raising a child.

Still, I attempted to pay much attention to prenatal education, which I have heard from here and there. That does not mean that I particularly did things that I came up with. It is simply that in order not to excite my nerves as much as I could, I tried not to encounter objects that could be provocative. In other words, whether it would be a banquet table, a play, or a motion picture, if it was not going to be beneficial, I did not go. And, as I had the thought of wanting to give birth to a diligent child, I took no rest and was active.

Finally, after giving birth, I really did not have a clue as to how to raise one. During the time that I would breastfeed at most, as the doctor said, I would feed the child once in four hours. Within the time, I knew that one's crying was not because of being hungry, but because of wanting to pee, being sleepy, being sick, or being thirsty. Thus, as it was when an adult became thirsty after eating, when the child was thirsty and I gave warm water with a spoon, the child seemed to like gulping it very much. And, when the child cried, depending on the sound of crying, when it did not seem like one was crying because of being ill, I let one cry until one would stop, from not wanting to cry anymore. Just as an adult gets ill after only eating and not exercising, a child would also get sick if one were to merely eat and lie still. Therefore, I know that a child whose hands tremble, wriggling and crying is the law of motion by nature. Like this, it is when the child cries for a long while that what one ate becomes digested, one's legs and arms thicken, and one gains flesh on one's body. Thereby, one's vocal cords also become developed well. While there may be a time when it would be difficult to bear hearing the sobs bursting out, the child should be left alone in an apathetic and a cool-headed manner. What should be born in mind the most is to occasionally feed the child hot water. Based on my experience, raising a child, which seemed as if it would be difficult, turned out to be unexpectedly easy. For 100 days, first, I breastfed at a set time, second, I made one cry a lot, third, when feeding a lot of hot water, for sure, the child did not have diarrhea even once, and grew up well.

After 100 days, once the child starts to crawl little by little, it would be a huge trouble for the child to pick up and eat something carelessly. At this time, there is no other alternative than to make sure that a dangerous object is not placed within the reach of the child. When the first birthday comes, one starts to walk tot-teringly. Accordingly, there are numerous moments any time that a child stands up and falls, walks with faltering steps, trips and topples over, falling flat on one's face. At this time, the adults who see this, at the side who are taken by surprise come over, running, and help the child up. If so, the child would make a big fuss and cry, opening one's mouth wide. This attitude of an adult is the least appropriate. Despite not trying to fall, there are innumerable times that the child nevertheless falls due to being surprised at the sound of an adult bawling out. And, even when the child is not hurt, a big fuss is made.

Not only that, this is the least appropriate in terms of education. If the child falls, it really should be that one should stand up alone. An adult heaving the child to one's feet makes one ill-mannered and fosters dependence. We, people up until now have depended too much. Subjects have depended on the nation, children have depended on their parents, and women have depended on men. From now on, we people should utterly call it quits. One should foster a sense of independence to do one's work. While it may be a trivial affair to help up the young one who has fallen, the child should be fostered with the sense of independence, starting from this time when one is beginning to sprout. Of course, while in a risky circumstance, the child should be promptly embraced, there would instead be a lot more harm in coming at the child, bawling out than the child getting hurt from falling. When my children trip, the members from my family altogether sit with their backs turned. Then, the child quickly looks around and as if it was dumbfounding, brushes it off, heaves oneself up and sits. Starting from early on, I have not once picked up the child and so, when one tumbles, naturally, the child knows how to stand up without saying anything. At some time, once, when my eldest daughter, Nayeol was three years old, she fell with a bang after losing her footing by the deep furnace in the dark kitchen. At that time, I calmed myself down and said, "Nayeol, what a talent. Go on and do it again." When she was about to cry, she halted right then and while laughing, she slowly stood up, as if she exercised her best talent. Our family members all laughed.

After that, the child learned how to speak. Children really could make up bizarre and nonsensical words. This is something that could not be told and corrected one by one, and even if one is corrected, one does not even understand. After letting it be until a certain extent, once one reaches the period of one's speech development becoming finalized, one should be taught smart words. Suppose one were to call, 'Papa,' 'Mama,' one should be taught to say, 'Father,' 'Mother,' and as much as one could, be corrected from papa, mama to calling, father, mother and in the first place, make them say, father, mother. As I have read in a certain book, first, in educating, what is most needed is that in terms of an object, there should not be a difference between the words spoken when one was young and the words spoken when one was a grown-up. In my perspective, from now on, children have to know and learn a lot, and need to economize time and economize brain use for keeping a sharp memory. And so, if the child from early years is taught a great deal of words addressing a child and the words addressing an adult, later, when picking up the child in school, there would be no need to tell one to do this or that. When my Nayeol was three years old, I taught her every time she ate. "To your mother and father, respectfully say jinji jabsuseyo (Courteous way of saying 'eat' to one's elders in Korean) and to Nayeol and your younger brother, it is to casually say, bab meog-eo (Casual way to say 'eat' to people of the same age or one's juniors in Korean)." Like this, I taught the child to make the distinction between junior and elder accordingly with our family members. At first, she said, "Mother, bap (meal in a casual way in Korean) jabsuseyo (eat in a courteous way in Korean)," and she said to her younger brother named Seon, "Jinji (meal in a courteous way in Korean) meog-eo (eat in a casual way in Korean)," and after teaching for a couple of times, she spoke, fully indicative of the person she was addressing. Now, she is five years old and if she would be speaking it for ten times, she would speak for ten times, "Father jinji jabsusigo (Courteous way of saying 'Father ate and' in Korean) he went to the office." Like this, even at bedtime, I taught, "To your father and mother, jumusyeoyo (Meaning 'please get some sleep' spoken to elders in a courteous way in Korean), and to Nayeol, it is to say, ja (Meaning 'get some sleep' spoken to one's contemporary or juniors in a casual way in Korean)." If it is not made into a habit like this since the early years, it would not be easy to correct it.

There is one thing I forgot. After about a year, there should be a preparation to stop breast-feeding. So, little by little, its frequency should be lessened and the child needs to be fed rice or cookies. At this time, when breast-feeding is not ceased, the baby gets to know of the taste of a mother's milk, and once one gets the taste of being in the embrace of one's mother, it becomes very difficult to put it off. I stopped breastfeeding my first child in 1 year and 2 months, and as for my second child, in 1 year and 6 months, but being in one house together, it is utterly difficult to put it off. Thus, I made up my mind and was out of the house for three to four days. While I have had some hardships, because of my breasts becoming swollen, when I come back, the child absolutely does not think about mother's milk. While it is said to be good to feed a mother's milk for as long as possible, based on my experience, the mother merely lapses into fatigue from suffering, and even the child just behaves disgracefully. Rather, as breastfeeding is ceased, the child eats a lot, and when giving cookies that contain two to three ounces of nutrition each, one gains quite a lot of flesh. And, as much as the child plays alone and does not cling to a person, one becomes well-groomed.

There is no one as monotonous and obstinate as a child. Whatever it is, the child definitely tries to do what the child set out to do once. At such a time, it is good to leave the child alone besides when doing dangerous things, as much as possible. When a child tries to eat soy sauce or red pepper paste, I just let it be and look on. Then, the child eats it and cries. Afterward, if I give it to the child for one to eat it, one does not eat it for life. Also, the child pierces the door (sliding paper door), creating a gaping hole. I left the child alone and once a day, I placed the child's finger inside the hole of the door and blew wind on it. And, for a couple of days, I tell the child that this is what you did, but isn't your finger cold. And, when I put the finger of the child on the door, urging one to pierce it again, the child adamantly backs away, without piercing it. Afterwards, the child does not pierce it again. Also, the child scratches the wall with a pencil. At such a time, I sit still and look. After that, I call the child to come over, make one stand there, and pointing at the white wall that was not scratched and also pointing at the dirty wall, I make the child listen to what is clean and what is dirty, once a day (for about four days). While it does not seem like the child would understand strange things, afterward, when I give the child a pencil and stay still, looking, the child never plays a prank again. Also, children like toys. When the toy is bought and given to them, they break it on the spot, and end up doing away with it. Once a month, I also brought my kids to the toy store and bought them several kinds of whatever we picked up. Yet, there is not a toy to play around with according to age. While I would like to choose for them one made out of wood with an artistic value as much as possible, as really, such things were not there, I have been disappointed many times. When I bought them toys like that, every day, they would greatly spread out the toys in the room and play. I do not clean up the toys nor do I order some-one else to clean them up. I definitely make my kids who play with them put them back in the spot where they had been placed. As I always make them do that, now, they surely tidy up what they played with. Even when they sleep at night, I urge them to take off their clothes, to thoroughly fold them up, and to place them at the direction of their feet when they lie down. Whatever it is, I make them put it back at the spot where it had been placed. When eating fruits, I teach them to put the peel on a separate spot. Like this, I teach tidiness and orderliness. Also, it is fun that whatever I teach is put into practice.

In terms of clothing, I foster a habit of the child wearing thin clothes as much as possible. If I make them wear clothes that would be too hot, they become sweaty, and when it gets chilly, it is easy for them to catch a cold, and also for the young skin to get very weak. And, I make the color and shape of the clothes simplistic. In terms of the color, I do not usually make them wear white and black, and I always make them wear clothes with a change of colors. And, whenever I make them wear them, I give them an education on colors, such as this color is red and this color is blue. While the clothes of Joseon have a uniform shape, when making them wear suits, I craft them in a simple way and make them wear them. While this may seem amusing, the brain of a young child is simple. Thus, when choosing a color, instead of a halftone, it is better to choose a primary color and in terms of the shape, as much as choosing a simplistic shape brings harmony to the brain of a youngster, it has a great impact on the child in terms of education.

What is most difficult to deal with is the child not listening to what one is being told not to do and crying. At this time, there is no way but to hit with a stick. According to a certain physiologist, after hitting the child once, the blood that circulates becomes discolored and it becomes a detriment to the brain that much. Even as I know of this, I sometimes hit. And, I lock the child in a quiet room. Knowing slightly of the great efficacy of hitting with a stick, I cannot figure out by myself how to not hit and achieve the efficacy. Also, there was a time when the child needlessly became despondent, fretful, and cried, seemingly without a reason. This is not for any reason other than because roundworms are moving inside the child's stomach. At such a time, I soon became patient, bought a medicine for roundworms called Se-enne, dipped it on my hand about two times, and lightly applied it in the child's mouth. Then, extraordinarily, the following day, two, three, and up to five roundworms came out. Once a month, I feed the child like this and take out the roundworms. The children tend to have a stomachache, get diarrhea, and also catch a cold. When I feed the children three daily meals, I rub the food with soy sauce and for a while put in oil, with the base of a white radish and give it to them. And, I for sure have them drink cold water. Also, two times a day, at around 10am and 3pm, I give them cookies that I made myself, in which I put a lot of eggs and milk. While there are moments when I am not able to carry out what I planned to do in time, except for days when they get a stomachache, I give them to my kids as much. The cold water seems to make their stomach healthy. After making them drink cold water, not once did they get a stomachache. Also, it is very easy to make them not catch a cold. Based on my experience, after getting sweaty on their backs and as the sweat cools, they tend to catch a cold. And, amid wearing at night the clothes that they wore in the daytime and after sleeping, wearing them again in the daytime, not only is there no new stimulation on the skin, but as the dust gets in and it becomes filthy, they tend to catch a cold. So, while it may be tiring to separately choose the clothes to wear for being active in the daytime and the clothes to wear when going to bed at night and to replace the wearing of clothes day and night, it would be good to make them change into pajamas and go to sleep. Also, the thinner and the more one-layered the nightclothes are, and the wider and longer they are, they seem to be good.

The experience of raising a five-year old daughter and a two-year old son is roughly in such a way. Gradually, in order to educate them from kindergarten, primary school, middle school and beyond, accordingly, I predict that the issues of family education would become complicated. I still have not thought about it up to that point and I am trying to put it off as something to be encountered at the time. Merely, I am thinking in advance that accordingly with the children growing up, as much as I trust the lessons of a parent as an educator and have an understanding of the period as someone who has become a mother, certainly, I will not take a break from studying. As I have said previously, I am raising my child with a cool-headed attitude according to the flow of nature.

⟨*The Chosun Ilbo* (Newspaper; 1920~ Present)⟩ (1926. 1. 3.)

Companionate Marriage, Experimental Marriage

Date: 1930, April 2, 3pm

Location: Interview in Gyeongseong, Insadong

Journalist: For a man, is the purpose of marriage to have his own wife and for a woman to have her own husband, or is it to have sons and daughters to pass down one's bloodline?

Na Hye-seok: That would be to have a husband or a wife. The children are no more than a byproduct of them.

Journalist: Then, 'sexual desire' and 'reproduction' must be entirely different.

Na Hye-seok: Although it cannot be said that they are entirely different, they cannot be confused for each other as much.

Journalist: Then, if the main purpose of a marriage already is to have a wife, if there comes a day when it turns out that the marriage has gone wrong, wouldn't they of course have to get a divorce?

Na Hye-seok: They may have to. But I know that in Europe, an experimental marriage has recently been held to determine whether the marriage would turn out happy or not, on account of divorce not being easy.

Journalist: The one where they would try living for three to four years and if they end up hating it, they would separate, and if they end up liking it, they grow old together and become buried in the same grave?

Na Hye-seok: Yes.

Journalist: Would such a marriage style be appropriate in Joseon?

Na Hye-seok: Aren't the new couples that have partially walked the up-to-date path already implementing it? It seems like it.

Journalist: What is the distinct feature of an experimental marriage?

Na Hye-seok: As it is experimental, no one side carries an absolute duty about its outcome. To simply speak, even though suppose one talks about getting a divorce, the issues with alimony and the violation of chastity would not be attached. A marriage based on the premise of an agreement is good, because divorce rights are reserved in the first place.

Journalist: It would be good to teach such new morals to many schoolgirls of today. When it comes to sex education, as educators know only how to teach the physiological side, and not know how to teach the new path in terms of ideology and ethics, it is a huge, common evil today.

Na Hye-seok: I agree. In terms of the issue with both sexes, while it would be good to instruct on the physiological side, scientifically, instead, even more fundamentally, the enlightenment on morality and ideology that would concern for example, how birth control is, and what experimental marriage is, would be much more of a needed work, which is why it would be right for the focus of educators to flock to that realm.

Journalist: Then, the experimental marriage, which necessitates a method like birth control would help to prevent divorce each time and would have the effect of making the sincere meeting and parting between men and women a lot freer.

Na Hye-seok: Yes, it would.

⟨*Samcheonri* (Magazine; 1929~1950)⟩ (1930. 6.)

Happiness in Not Forgetting Myself

Whoever it is, we wish and hope to live with fortune, in other words, with happiness. Also, we want to do it the way it is done.

It is said that if one were a housewife of fortune with the mountain at the back, water flowing at the front, the sound of the nightingale in the season of spring, the sound of rain in summer days, with a great atmosphere and scenery, at the center of the second, third floor Western-style house, with the male and female servants standing in a continuous row, with flourishing children, eating to one's heart's content in glory, one would indescribably become a person with the so-called happiness. Like this, if we make a very uneventful life the focus of our happiness, certainly, happiness would cause our life to become fixed, without vigor, make us lazy, and lead us to become regressors and losers.

Among us, there would not be a single person who wants to live, forgetting oneself. Therefore, we try to eat well, wear good clothes, and live comfortably. However, Joseon women surely, from the past up until today have lived, forgetting themselves. There was not a single time when they worked for themselves, sought out things for themselves, experienced agony alone, and had nothing that they earned for themselves. It is a pity. Living in oblivion to oneself, isn't this a thing of melancholy?

Why didn't we ever become conscious of the infinite ability hidden inwardly and make the attempt to test the manifestation of our ability! In the world, in the midst of being ordinary, as there are many who take solace in themselves at least having something that seems to flexibly secure some future, very much so, it is a fact that there are a multitude of women among them.

Look here, doesn't even a life that one treasured and protected come to an end one morning, overnight! Doesn't the heart of lovers and comrades who once made a rock-solid oath change? Doesn't the best of happiness disappear as if it had been all for nothing? Even though one were to receive the fiery love from lovers and gain the deep trust from friends, after a period passes by considerably, there is bound to be an aversion and a change of heart. One should presume in advance that at the end of it, the path would no longer be there. It is because the moment that one loses happiness, one would only be a person of incompetence and would merely consider oneself a person of disappointment.

Therefore, whenever happiness would be taken away, on this occasion, at any time, it becomes the greatest work of ours to always prepare for happiness that would be enough to mend the hurt. This would also be contingent on deciding on a goal to live, not forgetting oneself. In other words, amid having lived unconsciously, forgetting oneself, I think it is for us to live consciously, not forgetting oneself. In other words, even though misfortune, which we are most frightened of, were to invade at any time, we could overcome it without concern. Despite whatever pain being there, although there may be a new side to it, of all the pain, the logic of being defeated would be naught. That is, whether one would get the kind of happiness of the exterior or lose the kind of happiness of the exterior, it is for us not to forget the wellspring of happiness, our mind alone. Whoever person it is, one has the strength. The person becomes conscious of that strength, reaching a certain period. Anybody would all become aware of one's own strength, once or twice. One who gets that would be namely, the one who feels the happiness in not forgetting oneself. Also, in one's heart, there is really a self that one does not even know. Finding the self that is not seen, that is to say, is not forgetting oneself. To sum up, besides the faith and happiness of the current and future goal of life being about living without forgetting oneself, there would be nothing that would make us happy. As much as this would secure the unfolding of one's inner life, it would be a fruit that would be reachable.

Hence, what we have to do is to outright face this reality, and to make the roots of the future life spurt, raising them. While thinking of this, how could one lose one's footing even for a moment and live, forgetting oneself?

After a day, after a year, I had been in a constant state of regret at every passing moment. However, how much of feeling the past had, which had become one giant past? Also, among them, as I look back from afar the bits and pieces, how enjoyable the time was. The reason why anytime we could not live in the bliss of the present that is reflected in front of us is because we at once make the nearby past the present. Therefore, as a matter of fact, the present ends up becoming void. Looking at it after it passed, I have made my way to a safe place like this, and thus, the path midway that I took was something that was needed for me. I am endowed with the things I need, but not only that, when it comes to the past, from time to time, how greatly narrow the path has been!

Written on the 15th of October in Tokyo in 1931

⟨*Samcheonri* (Magazine; 1929~1950)⟩ (1931. 11.)

Family Life of a Western Madam

Cordial and Practical French Madam

When I was in Paris of France, as Mr. Gou (Pen name of Choe Rin) happened to be there, bringing a French translator, who was recommended by an influential person, the three of us took the train by the countryside and sought out the house of Mr. Saleh, the vice-president of the national conference for small nations. As it was of a distance like that of going from Gyeongseong to Yeongdeungpo, full of villas, Mr. Saleh's house was also a villa that was given when Mr. Saleh's father passed away. As I pulled on the rope of the main gate, as the meeting had been already promised, Mr. Saleh amiably came out and flung the door open. Upon stepping in, from left to right, the dense trees stood, with all sorts of flowers that bloomed above the grass, and the sounds of the dog barking and the rooster crowing. It was an elegant Western-style house, and when I opened the door and headed inside, a pleasantly plain but respectable madam came to meet me and ushered me into a study brimming with books piled up like a mountain, all sorts of antiques, and flags from various countries. After a friendly conversation between the Westerners, Mr. Saleh ventured into his impressions on his two-time trips to Japan, where among them, he remarked about how the cherry blossoms and the figures of Japanese women were pleasant, and among his impressions of the visit to Joseon he had made once, I heard with interest of his talk on the time when he saw the sword-dance, he could get how the people of Joseon are that much virtuous and peaceful, based on how they made a scary object like a sword artistic by performing a dance, and Mr. Saleh was particularly fond of Joseon, had a lot of sympathy with it, and knew much about the March 1st movement of 1919.

As a member of the French suffragette movement, the Madam was a wise, resourceful wife who was devoted to her family, and a committed social activist. After spending time that day, later, once I came back, as I expressed my wish to be with a French family, without question, I was told to come and stay in their house. I soon moved, out of happiness. At that time, my husband was out in Berlin, Germany. Since then, for 3 months, I stayed with Mr. Saleh's family, and had dinner together.

The household had 50-year-old Mr. Saleh, 40-year-old Madam Saleh, 18-year-old and 16-year-old daughters, a 7-year-old son, and me, six members. The house was made of timber, which was nothing but practical. The lower floor had a study that could concurrently be an emergency room, an eating place, and when climbing up to the second floor, where the fruits from Namyang that Mr. Saleh collected during his trip were hung, there was my room, the room of the daughters, the room of the husband and wife, a bathing room, and a toilet. On the third floor, there was the sewing room, the room for the child, and the wall, chairs, desks, bookshelves were all decked out in the color of dark red that they served as an education of the color.

In the morning, the daughters would be the first to wake up, and when I brought them barley porridge and tea, they ate them in their seats, washed their faces, Mr. Saleh went to a conference hall or a school, the Madam to her own office, and the daughters off to middle school, and when I went out to my research laboratory, the whole day, a 7-year-old boy and a dog would be watching the house. When coming back in the evening, the dog would be the first to bark and a child from the third floor opening a push-up window, saying, "Who's there?" is indeed lovely. For lunch, on ordinary days, I packed a bento and was on my way and on the first Sunday, a woman who worked on a daily wage basis would come, riding the bicycle, only doing harm, and without even turning back, would take flight.

At the dinner table, the family sat in a row. My seat was at all times at the high table, and as for Mr. Saleh, he was perched on the right side.

When Mr. Saleh would kindly say,

"Madam Kim (The French family referring to Na Hye-seok as Madam Kim because her husband's surname is Kim), has your painting gone well today?"

Madam Saleh would promptly say,

"Of course, as she's painted today, it has turned out well. She must've had a lot of influence from Bissière."

When the subject would kick off like this, the husband would talk about his time with his friends, the Madam would get on with a story about her work with her peers, the daughters would share a story about what they saw in the street, while making the hand, foot, nose, and eye gesture, and when they imitated it, the family would laugh until their backs might break, and at times, they would laugh at my incoherent reply from not being fluent in French. Every time they did this, Mr. Saleh, out of fear that I would consider it to be shameful, would feign indifference, cast his eyes down, and would stifle his laughter. Even now, when this thought occurs to me, there will be a time when I occasionally laugh.

After having dinner, I would take a walk to the garden or play the piano and dance. When I enjoyed dancing in a duet with Mr. and Madam, the couple liked it very much. Also, while listening to a radio, the couple would glance at the clock and when they say, "It's time," the son would come out with the daughters, give a greeting kiss to their parents, and each one of them would all go back to their rooms, while the husband and wife would remain in the study. Because I was curious, one night, I pretended to go to the kitchen to scoop up and drink water, and stood there, watching. The couple sat, attached to each other like pigeons, and were heavily chattering about some kind of story that they were gushing with fun like the sesame that was about to be spilled. They seemed to be making a confession to each other about what they had gone through that day. In front of them, the day's newspapers of a wide range were laid out. Like this, everywhere I looked, it was a harmonious family.

Particularly, to talk about the family life of the Madam, among French madams who were coquettish, who recreated themselves, with childishly bright smiling features, exquisite, and thrifty, she was a madam who was modest, pleasantly simple, and patient, but for some reason, had appeal, and so, with the balance of the strong and the weak, with the rules and regulations thoroughly in place, without the space for a gaping hole, the Madam did her housekeeping, and the life without a feeling of aversion and without being taxing has become, in other words, an art. I could not help but be moved by her being friendly to her husband, being rigorous to her children, being kind to her friends, being generous to her servants, being benevolent to her livestock, and on top of it, as much as the family custom was the life of a scholar, it was pleasantly plain and autonomous, and so, even the children under the authority of Mr. Saleh still scooped up water for washing up by themselves, and brought every one of the dishes from which they ate to the kitchen. At times, when an invitation for a theater, opera, or cinema came, I would request the dog to keep a good watch of the house, close, and lock the door and go watch the event. After I am done watching, while on my way, I go into a café, drink tea, eat some food, and come back. When the child would leap up with glee, the mother would give a kiss to the child's cheek, the father would smile brightly, come to my side, and stealthily ask, "Kids from Joseon are also like that, right?" I reluctantly said, "Yes, they're the same," and burst into laughter. The two daughters mimicked what they had seen of the play in the dark roadside (as it was in the countryside) now, and holding each other, broke into a dance. Mr. Saleh clapped his hands and said, "Excellent, excellent." Like this, the atmosphere of this family is exuberant and delightful any time.

To briefly touch on the social life of the Madam, not only does the Madam write an article for the monthly news magazine, she wrote a book on the suffrage of women. I was nothing but moved after seeing her signature on the news magazine and the book, and it was a huge pity that I did not know how to read the contents. The Madam frequented the assembly banquet, and clad in a dress coat, she would without a doubt come into my room, ask, "How do I look?" and when she would slightly twirl around at my side and flirt, I wanted to take her flair, swallowing it up, and make it mine, as much as the entire body would become chilled to its bones. Certainly, the husband and the wife accompany each other and when they return, they bring amusing toys that they bought, placing them on the table, and induce the laughter of the family. As someone who likes to dig up theory, if I had been proficient in the language, there would have been a great many benefits, so it is a huge regret that I was not able to do so as I liked.

Lastly, to talk about the education of children, I could not help but be astonished at how they conceived of making their child wear whimsically when it seems that a majority of French women's clothes are inexpensive. On Sunday, the daughters in this house lay their clothes out on the floor of the porch, dried their coat, wore them, and set out, or having made a hat and worn it, it would not lag behind one bought from the store, and thus, as French women first know how they look, even from someone wearing clothes that are in harmony with one's physique and one's face, the fact that such a person, that is to say, is a work of art is that the quintessence of King Louis, the 14th is closely rooted in the French national character. There is a little girl who lives next door, of the same age as the young son. I have gone over to the children playing, and seeing them slip past the fence, spread out the sheet to sit on, where this child sat in this side, that child sat in that side, their hands swaying to and fro, and their mouths moving up and down, I could get that the neighboring family has a huge knack for things. As the spring of next year was the boy's admission period for middle school, for preparation, every-day, each hour, his mother taught from a French reading book and the neighboring girl also studied with him. When the time would come, seeing him come into the main gate and without fail, make an official greeting was unusual in my eyes. And, starting from when the boy was young, he was infused with the notion that as a boy, he would be made to set the dining table all the time, divide up the dishes, if the daughters would wash the dishes, he would wipe them with a dishcloth, and even in the cold morning, mop each flight of steps.

Also, as the livestock was a dog, chicken, rabbit, cat, and the like, every morning, whenever the madam awoke, she would feed them, caress them, give them a kiss, and when they would get sick, she would give them a pat, as if to take pity on them.

Even now, once a year, the family sends a New Year's card, which is why I know of their news, and this time as well, a lengthy New Year's card arrived, and they said that they would once come visit Joseon.

〈*JoongAng* (Magazine; 1933~1936)〉 (1934. 3.)

If I become the Female Mayor of Seoul?

1. I will manage the affairs of the state by changing the tram that goes between the Seodaemun line and the Mapo line, between the Dongdaemun line and Cheongnyang-ri line, between the Gwanghuimun line and Wangsimni line to a tram for one connected district.

2. Like it is in Bonjeongtong (Past name of the Chungumuro district), the urban district of the people of Joseon, I will make sure to have electricity installed.

3. I will establish a women's organization and encourage the thoughts and behavior to come together in terms of the circumstances of the period and in terms of correcting the unjust habits and custom.

⟨*Samcheonri* (Magazine; 1929~1950)⟩ (1934. 7.)

Confessions of a Divorcee

To Mr. Cheonggu (Pseudonym of Na Hye-seok's husband)

At the age of forty, nearing fifty, having received professional education, having gone on a trip to the West, which others could not easily do so, and having been in an enough of a state to instruct juniors, indeed, it is not only such a shame for the two of us ourselves that we were not able to unify our character and our livelihood, but also, it is that we lost face in the general society, ashamed and apologetic.

Mr. Cheonggu!

This shock that I was under for the first time in my life was too hurtful and deadly. Grief, wailing, anxiety, anguish –in this entirety of track and path, as I meandered in life, Mr. who has thrown a piece of me into the bottom of the abyss, I will call again Mr. Cheonggu.

Mr. Cheonggu! As I call out, my eyes brim with tears. Would the world call me 'The weak!'?

When you and I, who's lived, coping with things every day, shared a deep understanding, specifically knew every situation and circumstance, and had confidence, how could I see the experience of hurt in our fate as the fact of reality, which we never imagined even in our daymare? My honest sincerity is that I wish to deliberately call everything a dream, a nightmare, a past tragedy.

At the very least, shouldn't a 'good husband' put on a stance of showing up to the route that would wind back to the past life between you and me? Since the 'good husband' incident, although I have tried so much to deny it, eventually, such a stance has made Mr. Cheonggu rise again in my wounded chest, as of now.

Since the incident, in my chest, which has suffered a blow, the impression and the memory of the 11 years of our married life between Mr. and I flicker. Whatever it was, didn't you not have a single discontent, complaint, and anxiety in the slightest? Didn't even one part of Mr.'s life not have any suspicion and disgust at me as a wife?

Come evening, after work, didn't Mr. get right back home? And, Mr. smiled a smile of affection to me and the children. Although Mr. smoked a small amount, you did not drink, even a tiny bit. In light of this meaning, I cannot not say that Mr. is a 'good husband,' rare in this world. As much as you were such a husband, I could not help but trust Mr. No, I really trusted you. On the other hand, who would ever dream of a terrifying nature hidden inside of Mr., who would scrape me out and split from me and Mr.'s nature of callously deserting me like I was a mere repulsive spit, without even turning back to see how I am doing? Wasn't Mr. the one that did not even give me the brief opportunity and space to reflect and repent? Didn't foolish me, at least wondering if Mr.

would get my apology, beg earnestly?

Although I am indeed unfortunate, with an unheard-of ill-fortuned event, for I have lost all my credit in the world, got denounced by public rage, was abandoned by my parents and relatives, lost my good old friends, Mr. who has executed all this would not be short on grief and despair. Merely, I am wandering the wilderness, looking forward to the emptiness and loneliness of a dark night, and in a state where my soul has left me that I am forgetting my existence.

Am I moving into the dark, holding a painting brush and a palette in my two quivering hands? If not, am I searching for the moment that a beam of light would shine on me? As someone who has suffered the shock of being too hugely and too gravely hurt, I feel like hour by hour, my chest is bursting from the impulse of hearing the desperate, lonely cries of life, weeping and collapsing.

Was our marriage a 'marriage of lies'? Or, as we came together from the understanding and love between you and I, and we went with the flow of life, did our marriage end up falling into the crossroad of 'lies'? I do not want to deliberately call our marriage, our life 'lies.' That is because already, in the period of our marriage, all the preparations, all the oaths have been established, and they have already been put into practice.

Mr. Cheonggu!

In this state of hollowness, losing my wits, where I lost both the light of hope and darkness, I think I need to pause and stand, introspecting once again, more in detail. As much as I am bearing this in mind, I am standing in the face of a woeful resolution. Enduring all the jeering and the chastisement of the world, I am turning my back on the cross and silently heading on. While listening to the quiet whispers of life flowing beneath a race that does not know whether it is the light of hope or darkness, and while being absolutely concerned underneath, once again, I head towards rehabilitation, resolved to continue my march.

My Personal History until Engagement

Already, it is about the time when I was nineteen years old in the past. A lover that I had been engaged to passed away from tuberculosis. At that time, the wound in my chest grew worse and for a brief time period, I had gone mad and so, my nervous breakdown became chronic. During the summer of that year, I returned home from Tokyo. At that time, the one who came over to the reception room as a modest guest in our house to seek out my brother (Na Hye-seok's brother, Na Kyeongseok) and also to see me was Mr. It was a very lonely period for Mr. as at the time, it had already been three years since his wife had passed away. I was playing in the reception room with my niece, when I bumped right into him. Seizing this opportunity, my brother got me to greet him. After a few days, Mr. went over to Gyeongseong and wrote me a long letter. It was honest and written with passion. He said that first of all, because of his environment and the loneliness of his mind and body, he needed a wife and hoped that I could be that partner. Of course, I did not reply. It was because I did not have that much of a presence of mind to do it. The second letter arrived again. I made a simple reply. A few days later, he came down again. He bought fruits like pineapple. I did not see him this time. As Mr. came down to his hometown (a hometown called Dognae), he sent word suggesting that I write him a letter when I go to Tokyo.

Afterward, when I set off to Tokyo, I unconsciously made a postcard.

In the middle of the night, as I passed by Osaka, a student wearing a square hat greeted me. I did not recognize who he was (He turned out to be Mr.). I had four to five people who accompanied me all the way to Kyoto and went straight to Tokyo.

It was a time when in Tokyo, Higashio Okubo station, I lived a life apart from my family, renting a room with the people that accompanied me. Having bought a local product, Hazbashi (Japanese cookies), Mr. came over, bringing them. Mr. had come as the orator in the speech contest for the association of Tokyo's young people discharged from the army. In the daytime, I definitely made a draft at my desk and at night, when I went back to the rented room, I decidedly wrote the letter. One night, it was when I would be going back. In the train station, I handed out my hand. Mr. shook hands ardently and accordingly suggested that we go to the nearby bush and there, he prayed to express his gratitude to God.

Hence, Mr.'s letter, Mr.'s words, Mr.'s behavior was an emotion that transcended reason and was nothing short of heat. Whenever I got this heat, I was happy. Unwittingly, I got the sense of melting into the heat. Like this, as Mr. was in Kyoto and I was in Tokyo, I came up once a day, got cautioned by the police while taking a stroll, had a day of mirth, riding a boat, and in search of a snowy landscape, travelled.

Like this, for six years of delaying, several times, Mr. proposed marriage. Yet, I did not want to take decisive action. Above all, this was because the hurt that remained in the one side of the corner of his heart that others would not know did not yet mend, the other reason was because despite the love of Mr. transcending reason, it was a love that was unconditional, in other words, it was a love that did not go beyond the instinct of the opposite sex and I suspected, 'Would he understand the unique work that I do?' So, although it could be an instinctual love, it would not matter if it were for other women besides me, and I thought that there was no need to be seeking for me. Why of all humanity would you be seeking me? And in partnering with you, without finding and gaining a single reason as to why you are someone that I cannot help but have and why I am someone that you cannot help but have, the marriage life is not bound to be lasting and I realized early on that I would not be happy. But still, I did not want to let go of him and Mr. did not let go of me. It was just that I did not take decisive action.

After going on like that, upon the suggestion of both sides of my relatives and out of my sense of responsibility, I set the date and got married. At that time, the conditions that I demanded were such.

Just as it is now, please love me for a lifetime.

Please do not interfere with my painting.

Please keep my mother-in-law and your former wife's daughter separate from each other.

Mr. gave unconditional consent.

As I demanded, as a part of our honeymoon, finding the grave-yard of my former lover who had passed away in the Gungchon Byeoksan mountain and even setting up a stone monument for me is a fact that I could not forget in my lifetime. Anyway, it is an indubitable fact that Mr. loved me with all his heart.

Marriage Life for 11 years

Over the 3 years in Gyeongseong, 6 years in Andonghyun, 1 year in Dongnae, 1 year and a half in the West, as I led a married life, I had one daughter and three sons, in total four. As a lawyer, as a diplomat, as a tourist, as an educator of my son, as a father, as an artist, as a wife, as a mother, as a daughter-in-law, we led a life of leaping around from this life to that life, from that life to this life. In the economic matter, it was stable, I did all that I was willing to do, and accomplished all that I put my efforts into. To be this much, I could say that it was a happy life. Mr.'s person-ality was emotional wherever to the point of departing from a reasoning power and so, I could not predict what would be held in store in the near future. As a social figure and as a housewife, I wanted to live well, worthy of a human being. In order for that, economy, time, efforts, and diligence were needed. Although the incompetent aspects were not few, it was because the motivation, the impudent ideal of living life well, deserving of a human being had not been rooted out. Also, each time we clashed as a married couple, later, one by one, a child was born.

The Life of a Painter as a Housewife

When the art that I submitted was specially selected and awarded, Mr. was as happy as me. Everyone showered me with praises that it was because I had a good husband with me. I was satisfied and happy.

While the understanding of other people and my husband is needed, self-understanding is also necessary. The starting point of everything is all in the self. There would be no one who would be against having the household covered agilely and then, using one's spare time. I have never once been sloppy in my housework while doing my painting. I have never worn clothes made out of silk and have never played for a minute. So, the most precious things for me were money and time. Now that I reflect on it, I think what took away the happiness of family from me must have been my art. Yet, that was because, without this art, there was nothing that would make me happy.

A Trip to The West

Of the sponsors who enabled a trip to the West, not only were there certainly those who prayed for the success of Mr., but also there were those who wished for my success. That was why our trip to the West was unexpectedly easy. As a person saw one more thing, as much as a person saw more of it, life expanded, becoming profuse. After the trip, Mr. formed a political view, and my perspective on life turned out to be more or less arranged.

1. How should a person live a life? While a person from the East looks up to the West and is envious of the Westerners' life, when one goes to the West, the Westerners look up to the East, and are envious of the life of Easterners. Then, whoever it is, there is no one that is satisfied with one's life. Merely, it depends on making up one's mind. It is to do with getting a knack for something, among earning a lot of money, gaining ample knowledge, doing many enterprises, and feeling satisfaction from it. In other words, it is to feel a satisfaction in merely seeing the comings and goings of a divine being between a person and an object.

2. How could a husband and wife live in harmony? Unless the uniqueness of one's work and the other person's work could be merged, it is not something that one could cling to alone. It is just that the point is not to forget self-control. And, in life as a married couple, there seems to be three phases. The 1st phase, during the period of dating, without the space to see the partner's flaws, only the fortes could be seen. It all is up to purifying, beautifying it. The 2nd phase, a period of fatigue, getting married and over the 3 to 4 years, as children are born, making it impossible to forget fatigue, the fatigue

becomes worse. The partner's flaws become prominent and start to become tiresome. According to statistics, at this time, the number of divorces is the greatest. The 3rd phase, the period of understanding, already at a time when the husband and the wife know of each other's flaws and fortes, the bond deepens and a new love forms so that one would want to close one's eyes to the flaws and encourage the fortes. At this time, whatever obstacle there is in the relationship between the husband and wife, they would not leave each other. In this, at last, beauty and goodness show up, and a significance in life as a married couple would exist.

3. How is the status of Western women? The general psychology of a Westerner is that one appreciates the small things more than the big things. One cares for the weak more than the strong. In whatever get-together, without a woman, centrality is absent and the emotions are not in harmony. She is the main character of a society, she is the queen of a family, she is the self as an agent. That does not end at so-called big, powerful men supporting her, but a woman herself has that much of a great appeal and a mystique. That is why instead of equality and freedom as something to be abruptly demanded, intrinsically, equality and freedom have been feebly kept alive for a long time. It is just that we Eastern women have not become aware of that. The power of us, women, is great. The more civilized it becomes, the more those who would come to dominate the civilization would be solely us, women.

4. What other point is there? It's Dessin. Dessin is not only to do with the image of the contour, but it is the harmony of colors. So, in the end, it becomes a daily chore to be able to draw the Dessin precisely and to proficiently draw a model. Although I may be ignorant, I more or less covered the four issues. So, it seems like the list of my life would be unfolding from now and my starting point would be from my work. Accordingly, my ideal was big and I even had a specific plan. Anyhow, although I had been infinitely optimistic about my future prospects, I am not ashamed of whatever result I came to face.

Conflicting Lifestyle with My Mother-in-law and Sister-in-law

After getting married, for a year, after living together with my mother-in-law, in order to guarantee the future of the young married couple living prematurely, she came down to her hometown, Dongnae, bought a house, and saving the money that she would send every month, purchased a few acres of the field. Her only wish was that her son and daughter-in-law would come back to the hometown when they would get old and live, fending for the relatives, and she would bestow the property that she had amassed little by little since the former times to her son, whom she had raised in the absence of his father. Thereby, this property had three people in coordination, amassing it (although it was not much). In no time, one person earned, one other person saved money and sent it, and another person collected money and made purchases. So, without the space for a crack in the livelihood of the two houses, it was tiring but fun. An incident that wreaked turmoil to such a harmonious family arose.

In a month since we came back from our trip to the West, the third uncle of my husband gave up his farm-work from the other province and without any preparation for work, trusting the eldest son of his eldest brother, in other words putting his faith in us, found his way to his hometown.

In just a few days since we have been dumbfounded, the second uncle of my husband brought with him again five family members. As it was a time when he came back home and was not employed, we could not help him and upon seeing him, he was pitiful and actually in an awkward position. Inevitably, we took the two uncles for a year into the outer-wing room and the cousins all found work to do. With the way things went, naturally, words between near relatives that had been scarce became lengthier and conversations that had been absent started to form, and the big incident was of putting the cousin's son who did not have much of a future closely ahead of him, without any budget into high school and us being entrusted to pay for the school expenses.

We could not even afford to treat our acquaintance's friends when they came from various places to hear us talk about our impressions after our trip to the West. Although to live a life pretending to have something that was not there was vanity, in order to follow the policy of success, a social life was inevitable. They were not of the type who could understand this. Out of necessity, I demanded that they withdraw just for a year until my husband could find a job. My uncle threw a fit. At any rate, if we were to do this, there was no money, if we were to do that, we lost others' sympathy, and there was really nothing we could do.

At that time, Mr. turned down being the deputy director of the government-general from the Ministry of Foreign Affairs, even rejected two telegrams that suggested him to administrate, and being stubborn, he started a business as a lawyer and became the guest of an inn in Gyeongseong, as he got seduced by beautiful Gisaeng (Korean Geisha) and wealthy prostitutes. I sent a letter to a certain gentleman, which became a scandal, and it was at that time when my husband hung out at bars, revealing his intention of divorce to his friends. Completely faultless for his motive, unaware that the account of the divorce had shortly been revealed in Seoul, I added fuel to Mr.'s anger, saying, "You fool, with no damn foresight of the near future. What would you do about things later on when you shouldered the burden of a scholar (by starting a business as a lawyer)?"

The one who indirectly had all the power over our housekeeping was my sister-in-law. Not only did she coach my mother-in-law in all aspects, even when my mother-in-law came back from Haeundae with a guest from Seoul, without a doubt, tomorrow, my sister-in-law would go to Haeundae and come back, even if she were to exorbitantly spend the money that my mother-in-law does not have. Everyone would say that this was all a result of my lack of virtues, but as a person who has seen and learned a lot more than others would acknowledge, although we may have been lacking compared to others, it was because we could not afford in the least to rise up from this predicament.

On my way back from my trip to the West, I brought some specialized products from there to various relatives and friends. Yet, I did not buy and bring them to my mother-in-law nor my sister-in-law nor my other near relatives. This was not because I was careless but because there were no suitable items for them. It was that my plan to buy them something upon returning to my home country had gone awry. When seeing that the two pairs of baggage coming from France were all merely posters, postcards, records, and painting materials, they were disappointed and scoffed. In truth, while the world that we lived in was one and the same, the world of our minds were different, which was how there came to be numerous hardships. As a result, in the midst of the absence of conversation about emotions with my mother-in-law and sister-in-law, a distance was formed.

Mr.'s uterine brother and sisters were three in total. There were two sisters and one was an idiot, the other was my sister-in-law that I was speaking of just now, who was extremely smart and so, was a woman that spotlessly dealt with her work. Although after being a young widow, the woman remarried, she came to foster a daughter that had been born somewhere, who was not even a speck of her flesh and bone, and whom she regarded as the apple of her eye. As she poured her remaining affection to her mother and her brother, the money that she saved little by little since the former times was also for her brother. Thus, she made up her mind that as much as possible, she would live in her hometown near her brother and then finish the rest of her life. At one time I said to her, "I hate Dognae. By all means, I would like to go live in Seoul." At the end of which various things were considered, the conclusion was made that her brother's wife (Me) was a restless person who was impious to her mother, was in a feud with her relatives and hated her family's hometown. Who would have known besides God that this would come up at a certain opportunity and become a supplement to the divorce statement? Indeed, the emotions of a narrow-minded woman are terrifying and men who do not suspect that and who overlook it are much too foolish.

With two housekeepers doing the housework, my mother-in-law called it 'my housekeeping,' the family's other daughter-in-law had a separate budget, my sister-in-law intruded, the missus who did her housework had some tricks up her sleeve, making things up and from the front to the back, from the left to the right, siblings and relatives brimmed, which was why only the state of a mere housekeeper who was not tender nor shrewd, without money nor a course of action to take, young and not having been trained in the old customs was awkward. While people all had outer appearances that were the same, how complex their inside story was and how entangled and tied down the movements of emotions besides reasons were?

Relationship with C

Although I had heard of the reputation of C (Choe Rin) from

earlier on, the first time I met him was in Paris. The first ever greeting, "Hello" that he said to me when I was cooking to treat him, when hearing it closely, had power in it. With my husband in Germany, as C and I did not know how to speak French, we had a translator and each time, the three of us accompanied each other, went to the restaurant, the play, did boat-riding, and went sight-seeing around the countryside. That was how while discussing the past affairs, the present affairs, the future affairs, there were a lot of things that resonated, and we came to understand each other. After he went sight-seeing around Italy, he left Paris earlier than me and set off to Germany. Afterward, we met again in Cologne (City in Germany). At that time, I said to him,

"I love you. But I'm not going to divorce my husband."

He tapped me on the back, saying, "Indeed, that is what you have to say. I'm satisfied with that."

In Geneva, I said to a friend from my home country, "If one likes another man or woman and spends time together, on the other hand, one could enjoy life even more with one's husband or wife." My friend agreed.

While perhaps, having such a thought could after all mean that one is tricking oneself, I was never trying to deceive my husband nor trying to love another man, that is C. Rather, I trusted that I would grow to have more affection for my husband. Generally, in the West, between a husband and a wife, it is natural to see that there is an open secret, for them to also have one, and I think that such a behavior within bounds, where one keeps an open secret that does not bother one's husband or wife is not a crime nor a mistake, and is a justly needed emotion for the most progressive person. That is why when one reveals this fact, it is something to laugh over and not something to deliberately catcall. I am reminded of Jean Valjean. Not tolerating seeing his young nieces not being able to endure through hunger, he went to a neighboring house and stole one loaf of bread, which was why he ended up around this time in prison for 19 years. How beautiful was his motive? Wasn't his conscience deceived, with the ethics and the law to blame for? Doesn't the cause and the effect come about separately? Due to such ethics and law, how many are there who have faced bitter deaths and borne grudges?

Misfortune of a Family

When we had been financially stable at the time that my husband lived a life as a so-called administrator, we spent 20,000 won on making a house in the hometown, on buying land, and on the trip to the West, and when the 2,000 won that we received as a royal bounty all went into starting my husband's business as a lawyer, he did not reap a single earning and day by day, the economic depression aggravated. Without any other course of action to take, I had to set out towards the frontline of my job. However, the barrier of fate was blocking even this path. In 8 months since my return to my home country, I became frail due to overworking my mind and body. And, my stage as a painter was in Gyeongseong. Yet, due to financial issues, we could not have a household in Gyeongseong. Also, I could not leave my young children, dismiss my housework, and set off on a departure. In the middle of a desperate crisis that paralyzed me, I could not help but be solely on edge. If at the time, there was no child to breastfeed and if a job was found to make a living, perhaps, such a tragedy would not have crossed our path forward.

It was at this time around. It was the so-called incident of the letter. I had no one to help me but C. So, in order to run a business, I told him to come down. And, I said that I hoped to find him again and for him to keep me company. Due to the distortion of the devious middlemen, this became 'I will always give myself to you,' which wreaked in Mr. a huge fit of rage. Instead of trusting my words, as he believed other people's words, the bond between husband and wife became tilted, and Mr. started having a change of heart.

Even in Joseon, the competition over survival intensified and the survival of the fittest exacerbated. Besides, as people enjoyed seeing others going down, instead of faring well, already, after the news of divorce propagated from the mouth of Mr. and the incident of the letter arose, the devious people, who solely devoted themselves to the gossips about others, without any cause, questioned my husband as to why he was living with such a crap of a woman like me and threw insults around, calling him an idiot for living with me. Of them, there were three to four people in a strong, coaching group, and based on their so-called ideological standpoint, out of their curiosity to see me live alone, they persistently urged me to divorce, got me sponsors and designed a plan for before and after. In their judgment, rather than a sense of humanity that would empathize with the rupture of a family and the future of the children, they wanted to watch what would happen to the relationship between me and C after divorce, and like watching a play, they wanted to see the downfall of the future of a tough, relentless bitch.

At the same time that one knows only one's own happiness, one only gets to know one's own misfortune. While asking about the intention of divorce to this person and that, and displaying the flaws of his wife who lived for 10 years together to many other people could not be said to be the act of an ordinary person, it is also not the act of an ordinary person to be led on to do it, to divorce, and his resolve to do so becoming firmer.

Anyhow, at the same time that Mr.'s family was faced with misfortune, it led up to the peak of his own adversity. Although there was a case, as his client had no money, he failed to extract it, in the inn, as Mr. could not pay the rent for three to four months, all the time, he did not have the dignity to face the owner, censure from society was widespread and he did not have the face to wield his authority due to the divorce scandal, as he was lacking judgement in terms of personality, he wavered over things, the bones of the both sides of Mr.'s cheeks were skinny to the point of protruding, and numerous times, he could not fall asleep at night up to the point that his eyes became pinched. On nights when he could not sleep, Mr. fell into a deep musing. First, his face would become flush with the outrage aroused from jealousy. Also, as he thought of himself, and as a result of having had a taste of the world, he would realize that there was nothing as difficult as earning money. He would regret having used up the money during his days as a vice-consul of Ahn Donghyeon (Currently a location called Dandong in Manchuria) and found the brush and palette that his wife bought for painting a waste.

The mind of a person was such that just like when the mast of the boat was furnished with the wind, it would follow the wind, fleeing, once one fundamentally had a thought hanging in one's mind, the entirety of one's thoughts would take flight to that side. The more Mr. thought about it like that, the more the emotions arose in him like fire, where he did not even for a moment want to continue to have such a woman under the name of his wife. Simultaneously, he had one friend, a married man, playing with a Gisaeng (Korean Geisha) and comfortably eating. As a thought registered in him that this way could be what could make him come alive again from his predicament, as the divorce scandal was out in display, from here and there, many prostitutes with money petitioned to be his sponsor, which is how he came about choosing one of them.

It was a time when he made a request for divorce to his wife and if I was not going to accept it, he threatened me that he would sue me on charges of adultery. Ah ah, when men usually look down on women, they take sufficient pleasure in the affection that women dedicate themselves to, but once men get cornered into a formalistic restraint concerning the law or their honor, they turn their back that until a day ago was arrogant and hedonistic but today that pretends to be the noble man, a genteel coward. Aren't they tyrants? We women should all stand up and curse such men.

Divorce

It was a time when I brought my children and was in Dongnae. A telegram came that notified that Mr., who was in Gyeongseong, would be arriving. I went all the way outside of the gate to meet him on his arrival.

Upon seeing me, Mr. sulked over his enmity towards me, looking at me as an eyesore. The complexion of his face was pale and his eyes were pinched up. I was taken aback. My heart thumped, as it seemed like there must have been some kind of mishap. As Mr. went over to the opposite room, he called me.

"Dear, come over here."

I came over. Without a word, I sat down, only trying to read his mind.

"Dear, let's get a divorce."

"What do you mean? All of a sudden."

"Didn't you send a letter to C?"

"Yes."

"Didn't you say in your letter, 'I will give myself to you for a lifetime'?"

"I didn't."

"Why are you lying? Anyhow, let's get a divorce."

He aggressively pulled out the important documents and insurance rights that he had put in my cupboard, each divided them up, went into the main room, and left them to his mother.

"Hey, tell your aunt to come. Tell your uncle to come."

Soon, one by one, in pairs, they gathered.

"I'm going to get a divorce."

"Hey, what are you talking about? What about the kids?"

My mother-in-law, who had seen the letter that had come in advance from Gyeongseong and had been lying like she was bedridden, dissuaded him.

"Ah, you, what nonsense."

His brother spoke.

"What are you saying, brother-in-law?"

"How can I live with someone who's committed adultery?"

Ildong went silent.

"If you're not going to let me divorce, I'm going to die."

At this time, Ildong came together with others and they muttered amongst themselves. As the sister-in-law made her claim, they came to a decision.

"Do whatever you want. It would be impious to your mother and would cause a feud with your relative."

I leaped into the company of people that was present.

"Let's divorce if you want. There's no need to go driveling about this or that, and no need to try to catch a fault that isn't there. But I made this house, made money from selling my paintings, and since you can't say that you earned money alone, let's split the whole property in half."

"This property is not my property. It is all my mother's."

"Do you think I'm a living corpse? You mean that you don't want to give it to me."

"How dare you, a woman who's sinned has such nerve?"

"What sin? It's because you make things up about it that it becomes a sin."

"I'm only going to give you this, so sell it and go."

Mr. handed over one piece of dissertation that was worth 500 won.

"This piece of crap isn't what I'm getting."

Mr. stood up, saying that he was going to Gyeongseong. Through that path, he visited his sister's house, held a discussion, and set off.

I could not fall asleep at night and deeply ruminated.

"No, No, I should apologize. And, I should say that my motivation wasn't evil. It's not fun when things become more serious. I'll give in, for the sake of my children's future."

On the spur of the moment, I headed to Gyeongseong. Making my way to the inn, I met him.

"I'm sorry for everything. My motivation alone was never evil."

"After all this time, what are you saying? Just quickly stamp the divorce paper."

"What about the kids?"

"I will raise them well, so don't worry."

"Let's not do that. If we cannot live with the strength of you and me, let's have faith in religion and live by the strength of religion. Didn't Jesus Christ get nailed on the cross in every person's stead for their crimes?"

"I don't want to listen."

Although tears sprang, I laughed inside. What is with crookedly entangling the things of this world like that? Wouldn't he remain intact in everything if he were to just once laugh over it like a man? I knew that Mr. would be unshakeable.

I ran to a certain person.

"Sir, my husband is telling me to get a divorce. So, what should I do?"

"Get a divorce. Since you don't know of hardship yet, you should try to at least experience it."

"I can't do it considering my children's future."

"Didn't Ellen Key (Swedish feminist writer and early advocate of a child-centered approach) say that rather than a child being raised by a married couple in a feud, it is better to raise the child in a new family after divorce?"

"That's nothing more than a theory. It's because a mother's love is high, noble, and great. Not only is it unfortunate for the mother to lose a mother's love, but it is also unfortunate for the child who couldn't be raised by a mother's love. As long as I know this, I cannot get a divorce. Could you please mediate, sir?"

"Then, starting from now, would you absolutely go on to become a good wife and a wise mother?"

"Until now, as there wasn't a time that I myself wouldn't be a good wife and a wise mother, I will do as Mr. demands."

"Then, I will try mediating."

He picked up the telephone and called the business director, the president of a bureau. It was about suggesting to mediate. The answer to the call came. As there was no hope of a compromise, it had to be capitulated.

As for him,

"Just divorce, do it. What would be the need of not hearing out your husband's request that much?"

As he was a novelist, instead of relating to the inner pain of life, he had as much curiosity about the unfolding of the events.

I failed to gain satisfaction even here and returned. That night, at the inn, as I was rolling back and forth, incapable of falling asleep, in the reception room, the sound of the guffawing of my husband, who brought in a Gisaeng (Korean Geisha), playing around, and crying, 'How exciting. Oh, it's exciting' flooded in. What an absurd irony. While complaining about the loose morals of their partner, under the pretext that it is a natural thing that men themselves would be pure, men have the bold rights that it would not matter for them to play and sleep with whomever of the opposite sex, which turned out to be that the social system itself was absurd as well, and at that, a laughter sputtered from me. It was nothing more than a behavior of also doing this, because you did that, like children kidding around. As it was Mr. who did not even directly experience the internal complexity of life, early on, and could not even easily imagine it, I suspected that he would soon regret it, but as he was already immersed into his Gisaeng (Korean Geisha) lover, and would be obstinately insisting on divorce, bringing up the past event as an excuse, there was no way to change his mind.

I inevitably left to set out for Dongnae. Should I run away to Bongcheon, should I take flight to Japan, and if I would just get over this trial, I was confident that I would come out of it, intact. Unfortunately, I did not have that much travel expense in my clutch. Not being able to endure the pain, I came down to Daegu. When I went over to Y's house, he welcomed me and I passed the day, without a wink of sleep, with him and his wife, us, three people in the play, in the food place, drinking alcohol, and smoking cigarettes. Y was fraught with concerns about getting a son-in-law and asked me to find an intellectual one. The pain that only I would know ceaselessly spun around and around and around in my heart. I had no choice but to come down to Dongnae. As usual, Mr. issued a reminder once every two days.

"Stamp the divorce paper. If you don't do it in fifteen days, I will sue you."

Here came my reply.

"It is a reasonable logic for estranged people to come together, and although it is also a reasonable logic to leave each other, there are four conditions as to why we cannot separate. First, we have an aged mother of 80 years old, which would be why divorce would be impious. Second, we have sons and a daughter, in total four, and as much as they are youngsters of school age, we need to care for them. Third, as much as it is the joint life of a married couple in a household, not only is production a joint work, at the same time that it becomes divided, as a single household turns into two households, we should make ends meet. Isn't it the duty of a person to arrange for such? Fourth, considering our age, whether it would be from experience or from the time period, rather than living solely for pure romance, in other words, love, we should be living for understanding and righteousness, and I already apologized, my motive was never evil, and also, according to Mr.'s request, I will be a good wife and a wise mother."

This was Mr.'s reply.

"I'm not the type of person who thinks about the past and the future. I'm merely living for the present. If you really cannot forget your children, after divorce, it's fine if you live together with your children and it doesn't matter if you live like it was before, all the same."

Regardless of whether this was trying to trick me or whether this was how the beginning and the end of divorce was going to be, as expected, they were senseless words. It had been almost a month since going back and forth between "do it," "I won't do it."

One day, my uncle, who had asked for my married status to be suspended, fraught with worry, took the lead, with the brothers and sisters of my husband, and closed in on me.

"Stamp the divorce paper as a sign that you've done wrong. We're going to all safely take matters into our hands for what comes later."

"Because when getting married, it was something that the two people did, even in divorce, it is what the two would be doing, so don't fret over it and go."

At night, I could not sleep a wink and thought.

'Things have already gone awry. He has another woman and it is useless for me to try not to do on my own what his relatives agreed should be done.'

Inadvertently, thinking of it this way, I wrote two pieces of an oath.

Written Oath

I pledge that the husband and wife for two months would not get married to another man or woman and considering the behavior of both sides, a reconciliation between them could be possible.

Husband ○○○
Wife ○○○

The brother of my husband who had gone up to the capital to arbitrate came down with the seal of my husband. He spoke.

"Dear madam, please stamp the divorce paper. What is with such a piece of paper? Since you have four children, sons and a daughter, would your rights over this house go away? And, they are mere words of my older brother. Would he really go through the legal procedures?"

Even my mother-in-law, who sat by the side said,

"Does it end at that? I'm greatly worried that he might get sick as things keep going on like that. Stamp it and he may or may not live with another woman he has and you could bring your children and live with me."

I laughed inside. It was revolting and distressing. I quickly brought out the stamp and said,

"Is there a reason to waver? I will stamp it ten times if I can."

How could one piece of paper move a person's heart? As the unpredictable things come up by ones and twos, would my expression that shifts depending on the times, be seen as crying, or laughing? In my absolute non-resistant attitude, and in my silence, I endured through the emotions and matters conveyed by others, experienced them one at a time, and merely put them aside.

After Divorce

A letter came from H.

A call came from K (Referring to Na Hye-seok's husband) and he's announcing everywhere that he has completed the procedures for divorce. What an amusing person. You did well, divorcing such a person. Get up, put it out of your mind, and come on out.

However, as I have sacrificed myself for my four children, I stayed stock-still. I was like this for two months.

The atmosphere changed completely. Although Mr. occasionally came down from Seoul, he did not go to the house where I was staying and visiting his sister's house, he asked for his mother, his children and saw them, my mother-in-law glared at me, my sister-in-law tried to lure me into something, the brothers of my husband called me stutteringly, and my mother-in-law held absolute power.

The village people said, as onlookers, "Why isn't she leaving, when is she leaving?" The grandmother bought the children cookies and candies, and brought the children to my room, where they slept. As such, it was as if after the war, I became a captive, in between a winner or a loser. A thought popped up suddenly.

'Should I save my children or should I be the one alive?'

I stayed up all night for three days with this thought in mind.

'Okay, after I was here, creations came into being. My children were born. My kids, you go through hardships earlier on. Above all, you are going to be human beings as you are. Living is not living for academics or knowledge. One lives, for one is a human. According to Jacques Rousseau, "Rather than fostering scholars or soldiers, I am going to first cultivate a human being." The day that I leave the house, it will be the day that seven people meander in hardship.'

Whatever this was or that was, in order for my individuality and in order for the general victory of women, I packed my bags and set off on my way to leave the house.

I took the northbound car.

'Where should I go? I am alone, without a house nor parents nor children nor friends. Where should I go? Where should I go?'

I went to the house of my brother, who was alone, making his living in Gyeongseong. Because just in time, it was the period of an ancestral rite, my brother came back from Bongcheon (Located in the capital of Korea at the time, Gyeongseong). Although I already talked about the situation from the beginning to the end through a long letter, for this incident, he did not take the lead altogether, and instead, sent his wife to bargain for a compromise.

"Anyhow, for the time being, come over to Bongcheon and stay there."

"I shall make up my mind once I meet C (Choe Rin). As things have turned up to this point, and as long as I've split from K, isn't it natural that I connect with C?"

"Stop with the nonsense. As K is acting like that, because he is at a loss now regarding his reputation, if you go to Bongcheon and stay there, he might also have some thinking to do."

At this time, a couple of friends were entirely against me leaving Gyeongseong.

As there were a lot of single women with money in Seoul (Another name that refers to the capital of Korea, Gyeongseong), he was saying that they were seducing K (Referring to Na Hye-seok's husband). My brother spoke.

"If he is having another woman, K's character is all knowable. Just leave it up to fate, and let's go, go."

I went to Bongcheon. I could not stay calm. Of course, I could not draw, and could not just kill time as it was. I organized the scripts that I drafted in order to get a sense of my past life. Among them, a writing about maternal instinct, a writing about marriage life, a writing about reminiscing on my lover, a writing about suicide, and it seemed like it foreboded all that I would be suffering now. Accordingly, I was able to delay what I had thought of prior, and put my mind at peace. In less than a month, a letter arrived.

K has got a new wife. He says that he is bringing his children.

All along, I thought, 'Would he really be going all the way through the legal procedures? If we could only save face in society, we could reconcile,' and had been trusting that I was taken aback. My brother came in.

"Why are you not eating?"

"Look at this."

He looked at the letter. After seeing it, my brother scoffed.

"I was mistaken. The great man knew everything. Give that shit up and live your life, painting. Don't you know if a masterpiece will come out?"

"I need to go."

"Where?"

"From Seoul to Dongnae."

"What could you do, going there, when it's all over? You will only be jeered at."

"But how could he do that as a person? What is up with not even giving away a single penny for my living expenses and just divorcing? Whatever happened to the pledge about us, living apart but legally married for two months?"

"He must've had his way, rescinding that too."

"He must be out of his mind, how insane. I'm going to be making a claim for the bills for my living expenses. No, I will be seeking what I earned."

"Then, when you go there, you need to take things cautiously to avoid being mocked."

I took the train bound for Busan (but headed back to Gyeongseong, in search of Mr. who was not in Busan).

As I landed at the Gyeongseong station, T, who received the telegram, came out. I went inside T's house and first, asked for the owner of the inn where Mr. had been lodging. That was because I knew that the behavior of Mr. was not a self-act, but out of an impulse from his surrounding friends, including the owner of the inn.

"Hello."

"Yes."

"Would you want the family of your friend to be unfortunate? Or, would you want the family to be happy?"

"Yes, I get the meaning of you asking me this. Please don't misunderstand too much. While I didn't have a clue, one day, he took his bags and left."

"Also, I know his girl well. I will stay here for a couple of days."

T said.

I was accompanied by a couple of friends and headed to Buk-michangjeong (Past name of the location in Gyeongseong that is currently Bukchang-dong, Jung-gu), Mr.'s private home. As I stood outside, Mr. reluctantly came and without going into his house, he passed by, ahead of me.

"Dear, let us go into a tea house and talk."

The two went inside the tea house.

"Shouldn't you help set up a way for me to live?"

"Would I have a clue? Wouldn't C (Choe Rin) be the one, asking to be saved?"

"Don't worry about others, and do what you are supposed to do."

"I don't know."

On the way, I headed into the government administrative office of the district, went through the formalities to restore our marriage, brought the papers, and made my way into his office.

"Dear, please restore our marriage."

"What the heck are you talking about?"

"Forget all the things from the past and let's start our life anew. Otherwise, you would be ruined, I would be ruined, and the others' lives associated with the two of us would also be ruined."

"Why are you doing this?"

"Let's live on little by little. Your pain would be worse than my pain."

"Who said to worry about such a thing?"

He promptly set off outside.

It was the following day. I went into the office, in search of Mr. He was on his way to his house to eat lunch, just in time.

"Let's go into the tea house and talk."

Without a word, Mr. ran and slipped into the gate of the house. I also unwittingly stepped inside. I came into the room, following him. Mr.'s second wife had been scrubbing the household goods when she said, "Who is she?" The three people sat, staring at each other, face-to-face.

"I'm thankful that you take care of him a lot. Today, I didn't mean to come all the way here but I was just suggesting we go inside a tea house and talk, but he just went his way, so I followed him here."

"I think I saw you quite a lot of times in the street."

"That could be possible."

"The reason why I came here is because I had no clue that it would quickly end like this. Now that it has ended like this, shouldn't you at least set up the means for me to also live? If not, I'm also going to be living in this house. How could I say my greetings to someone who doesn't even greet me?"

Mr. went out, without saying anything. My conversation with the second wife started.

"Really, what is this all about?"

"What is there to ask me? You would've heard it all from your thrifty husband."

"Okay, since you have the talent in painting, you wouldn't worry about making your living."

"Is there a business that could stand without a supporting cane?"

"Although I have been ill-fated as to be living as the second wife, how upsetting you must be when you have your kids. When you want to see your kids, you could come see them any time."

"As for that, I will do whatever I want."

"While the pine trees at the peak of the Namsan mountain may appear lofty, when you climb to the peak, likewise, it would have dust and dirt as well."

"Do you mean that this would be the same if I were to live as someone's concubine and then, turn into one's lawful wife?"

"That is up to you to interpret."

Mr. came in again. The three people exchanged words again and started off with their conversation.

At this time, a certain friend stepped in. He was the one who had tried hard to help make peace for this incident.

"What are you people up to?"

"It's about dividing up the money that the two people earned."

"Leave that issue to me and come on out with me, Madam R (Referring to Na Hye-seok). Let's go."

Because it seemed like by staying here longer, I could find no other alternative, I stood up, making an excuse. I had dinner with Mr. and talked about a lot of things.

The following day, I came down to Dongnae. Seizing this opportunity, I was determined to throw myself into the sea with my four children. My mother-in-law and sister-in-law, who must have noticed that my attitude was strange, pulled the children to their sides. Even though I tried to seize the opportunity, I could not. In order to clean up my luggage again, I opened the door of the wardrobe that I had locked. I was taken by surprise, seeing that half of them were gone.

"Who unlocked this door with a passkey?"

"I don't know. Last time, the master of the house came and opened it."

"Okay, so what happened to the items that were here?"

"He took them and put them in the main room."

"Bring all of them out here."

How hateful and distressing Mr.'s judgement was when he must have danced to the tip of his new wife's tongue and unlocked the door that I locked and taken away my important items? I calmed my heart and thought about it. Really, it was a senseless and inhumane act. He became uselessly cunning that much and I thought it pitiful that he suffered through economic oppression as much. Making up my mind again to leave the house at last, I headed to Gyeongseong. I was a lonely figure, standing in a precipitous desert.

Where Should I Be Heading?

I made every effort to hold onto my maternal instinct. Considering this, there was nothing about my conscience to be ashamed of.

I ended up becoming a person that could only die. It is easy to die. Once one makes up one's mind, what comes after is paradise. However, it was as if I had my calling. I had my own strength to find a path that was not there, and I had my own strength to form hope.

The know-how of a person going through adversity was effort. It was about diligence. When one goes through anguish solely, time would pass and that time would bring on nothing but despair and destruction. First, I set out with the hope to have my title art piece selected. I borrowed money, using my paintings that I was selling as a security relief, and travelled to Geumgangsan mountain. While living for a month in Manmulsang, Mansangjeong (An area in Geumgansan mountain), I gained twenty big pieces of art equipment. Here, I coincidentally met Mr. Abe Yoshie and Mr. Park Heedo.

"Ah, what is the matter here?"

Upon seeing me, Park Heedo was also astonished.

"Here is Madam R."

Mr. Abe perched on the threshold of our room and attentively stared at my face.

"Are you alone?"

"It is natural that I am alone here."

"Let's go."

Mr. Abe spoke, filled with empathy, in a strong tone.

"I have a painting that I will be finishing until tomorrow."

"Then, I'll wait at the hotel."

"By all means."

Mr. Abe dragged his one foot and perched on the chair, which he frequently went to sit on.

"Even a person up to this point is doomed."

"Madam, don't mention it."

The following day, as we met in the hotel and talked, a conversation proceeded that I would participate as a part of a company of people that would be going on this trip to the upriver of Amnok-kang (Yalu River). The next day, Mr. Yang went to the hot spring from Jueul and I went to the Haegum river from Goseong. As during my days of studying abroad in Tokyo, I was friends with the wife of the governor of the Kosung County Office, I went over to her private residence, enjoyed a feast, and meeting a friend in Haegum River whom I had also known, I had a sumptuous meal of raw abalone.

Going to Bukcheong, I met a company of people and headed to Haesanjin. The view of the thick hill of the mountaintop was like a strip of Chinese painting of the Southern school. Of the company, since Mr. Abe and Mr. Park Yeongcheol, the two people were there, we were welcomed everywhere and the banquet was grand. The scenery that circuited from the upriver of Amnokkang (Yalu River) to Shingalpo was indescribably good. The company crossed Sinuiju, heading for Gyeongseong, and I set off for Bongcheon. There, I held a painting exhibition and went all the way to Dalian. Through that path, I prepared for a trip to Tokyo. In Daegu, I met Mr. Abe, went on a sight-seeing around Kyeongju, and heading to Jinyeong, I went sight-seeing around Bakgan farm, passed by

Tongdosa Temple and Beomeosa Temple by car, crossed Dongnae and reached Busan, riding the ferry.

C (Choe Rin) met me on my arrival in Tokyo. He was taken by shock at seeing me come unexpectedly.

I submitted *The Garden* as a title art piece that I drew in Paris, which to me, is worthy of being called a masterpiece. One night, I could not sleep from happiness at the thought of being selected and the other night, I could not sleep from concerns about being rejected. My artwork was selected, where 200 pieces were chosen out of 1224 pieces. I was bursting with so much happiness that my whole body shivered. The newspaper cameraman knocked on my door in the middle of the night and a radio broadcast was made, becoming news, and so, I shook the whole of Tokyo. From this, I was able to be in a dignified position and could make my own living. Regardless of whether one is a man or a woman, a person all comes into being with strength. Reaching up to a certain period, a person becomes conscious of that strength. Whoever it would be, once or twice, everyone becomes aware of one's own strength. For the first time in my life, I became aware of my strength. At that time, I was very happy. Ah, Mr. Abe is my savior who helped me have a fresh start in my life. There is no way that I would forget his kindness, as whether psychologically or materialistically, he worked so hard for me.

Maternal Love

Thousands of years ago, starting from the past, millions of

women gave birth to a child and raised one. At the same time, they had instinctively, indiscriminately, and unconditionally dedicated their flesh and soul to their children. This was a moral, a duty that starting from their birth, women carried with them, and there was no calling that went beyond this. Therefore, while the love of lovers and the love of friends is relative and conservative, the love that mothers have for their child alone is absolute, unconservative, and sacrificial. Thus, the highest and noblest of things ended up being maternal love. Many women would have felt so much satisfaction and happiness from this maternal love that they had. However, also, at times, there is not a lack of women who are cooped up in this maternal love, which keeps them from doing what they want to do and makes them weep inside of their miserable fate. Then, at the same time that this maternal love becomes the best of happiness for women, it has ended up becoming their worst misery. While a certain woman could have been infinitely comfortable and happy when she lived her life, forgetting her individuality and getting all the security in living from a man, when such a woman who has lived her life like that also makes a claim about her human rights, tries to show off her individuality, and sets out to the frontline of living today that does not rely solely on men, there would be a time as well, when she feels an infinite pain and unhappiness.

In no time, I ended up being the mother of four children. Yet, it remains a huge fact that I had worked hard to conceive, give birth, breastfeed, and raise my child. In *A Report on Becoming a mother,*

I said, "the meaning of raising a child has not a single, but double meanings." While raising one to two kids, indeed, I came to feel an affection that I had not gotten a taste of from my lover nor my friends. After coming back from my trip to the West, I came to have ideals about my child. The individuality of my children could be prominently seen and I gained the confidence to guide their path forward. Thus, I strove so hard to beg, apologize, and reconcile with my former husband in an attempt to raise them. However, everything turned out useless.

Ascetic Life

When in the middle of the night, my eyes blinked open, a gust of wind came blowing in from the corner of the void, somewhere unknowable. I realized that at that time, loneliness spread in my chest. The loneliness that I had felt up until now had been painful, but nothing of a detriment. I realized that the loneliness that I felt now was the trace of a pain from getting pricked by the poisonous plant's thorns. In the middle of not knowing where to come from and where to go, whatever it is that I do, its aftermath is lonely.

Rather than committing to the so-called chastity, as for me, I try not to lose my focus until I remarry. In other words, it is not to forget my mind alone. I already had wound up being a person who had lost her solid core. That was why the day I would lose my focus, the way ahead for me would be destruction. In order to hold onto a sense of focus alone, I led an ascetic life.

Not only is it in a relationship between a man and a woman of course, but during the period of pregnancy, an ascetic life is not easy. During this period, I had also lived my life, dreaming of the forthcoming conception of my baby and in pain.

Occasionally, there were times when I felt like a maiden and times when I felt like a widow. And, one should not forget that such an epigram exists for a single person; "Should I give a nod to everyone, or should I reject anyone?"

The love of the opposite sex is frightening. Rather than one's passion infinitely going up, as it is with the temperature of the thermometer climbing up to 100 degrees and then, going back down, if one were to call the focal point of love 100 degrees, it does not go above that and goes back, declining. Therefore, when one's passion is high, the other person's behavior becomes beautified and purified. When it declines, beyond any doubt, it turns filthy and gets worse. I know this well. Thus, when love was going to sprout, I would break it right then. I am frightened of the loneliness that would come after love wanes. I hate it. That is because this time, on the very day that I would get hurt like this again, I have nowhere to go back to but a perilous place, where I would be on the brink of death. Ah, how frightening!

A person is bound to be forlorn. Therefore, the fact that a person is living could not be thought of meaninglessly, but is bestowed with an overly deep sensation. Wherever one rolls around and however one does, a person that manages to go all the way there is a blessed person. It could be that returning from our forlornness is our hope. Ah, a person is too small to be living alone. While one day is short in time, the time that continues onward for 1 year or 2 years is long.

My Thoughts After Divorce

I regret being born a human. I was not born a human, because I wanted to be born a human, but rather I was born, not knowing what a human is, and what kind of place the world is. This life has become more hideous and miserable, and even though I may have become all the more despairing, I do not hold a grudge. I think dying and living would be one and the same. Death must be frightening. Whenever I am like this, I try to see if I genuinely saved myself or not. I am not afraid of death when I have genuinely saved myself. It is just that I become afraid of death when I have not completely saved myself. Hence, every time I realize the horror of death, I acutely feel my lack of virtue.

At the same time that I do not want to make myself shallow, before I hold a grudge against the other person, I want to reflect on myself. A person who knows of a shallowness inwardly forming in one's heart and could not stand not correcting it is the treasure of civilization. Such a person, already forgetting the weed inside of one's heart, goes on to spread good seeds wherever one goes, which becomes the common sense of one's mind. In other words, such a person is like Confucius or Buddha or Jesus. Although the sun does not try to heat up all living things, it heats up nature. Whatever comes, it transforms nature with the ingredient of the sun that reflects on it. No matter how something putrid floats on the sea, that does not make the sea itself filthy.

As one thinks about the cases and circumstances of everyone, from there, at that moment, one finds oneself. One realizes love. Therefore, the person who makes one's demand would be first making oneself. A person really has a self that even one does not know inwardly. It is the work of a person's lifetime to search for the self that one does not see and know. That is, self-discovery.

A person is subject to a lot of restraints from the useless formality, from the reputation of household goods, and from the studies that one knows roughly half of. The more one has, the more one wants money. The higher it is, the higher one wants one's status to be. As much as one has, what turns into a yin energy is one's studies. The happiness of a person is not when one earns wealth, it is not when one makes a name for oneself, but it is when one has a determination in something. In the moment that one becomes determined, a person realizes happiness, as if one has one's entire body cleanly washed up. In other words, it is the moment of realizing an artistic feeling.

It could be that life is undergoing pain. Pain is the fact of life. The destiny of life is pain. One could deeply have a taste of chronic sickness for a lifetime. Thus, I am precisely letting this pain be known to people. A criminal gets dominated by pain and a genius sets up a way to reap glory and prestige with death, defeating pain. This is attributed to the fact that beyond pain and pleasure, the genius has a sense of mission for oneself. Therefore, at last, one ends up making something that is beyond pain.

Even during one's agony, one makes up the roots of an incident and forgets.

I need to find the path that I would be taking and earn it.

Whoever it is, a person does not know what will happen to one's fate. Fate made an inner knot. It is the chain of fate that cannot be broken off. Yet, such a miserable fate betrays the weak. Almost, without an ounce of energy to bounce back, I turned out to be on the receiving end of beatings, insults, and curses. However, in the long run, although I could be tied up in the rope of fate and disappear, I will try to bounce back, even when I am desperately dragged by my struggles, tear my heart out, and suffer.

Mind of the People of Joseon Society

Although before our trip to the West, it had not been as intense, after coming back, it could be pinpointed that the general level of our country has become a lot more advanced than before. So, at the same time that men of learning became numerous, the competition over survival became much more exacerbated. There were no few of the twenty million people who stood in the frontline of life, straying in the path, without savings nor the ability to live, having no choice but to move to Osaka, Manju, and setting out on a vagabond life. Even in Joseon, now, one could only live if one had the money or the ability, in other words, talent.

When seeing this in terms of an ideological sense, when an international figure travels, various kinds of beliefs and ideology become imported. Thus, as those who know narrowly are not able to see widely, it is of a natural logic that they would be straying to acquire such a know-how. They merely eat Bibimbap (boiled rice with assorted mixtures of meats and vegetables), and among them, the majority does not know how to get a refined taste of it. Therefore, today, they play with this belief and tomorrow, they play with that belief, today, they become close to this person and tomorrow, they become close to that person. Without a consistent belief being established, and without a solitary outlook on life standing, they end up spending their days like the reeds getting blown by the wind. Although it may be mostly because the path to politics has been blocked and they have become tied down by the economy that they could not follow their heart according to their whims, it has become too desultory.

Joseon's male intellectual class is pitiable. The best stage, which is the path to politics has been obstructed and the use of academics that he had learned and accumulated has vanished, and when he would speak of this theory or that theory, as this was a society that did not understand, at least, he would wonder if he should live for love, but because of a wife that has a lack of sympathy for a family that is shackled by the family institution, he would furrow his eyebrows and life would be nothing but filled with trials. He would enter a vague food place, grumble all about guiltless alcohol, get a shameless Gisaeng (Korean Geisha), and enjoy it, but that as well would not give him satisfaction. Despite wondering if it would be better to go this way or to meet that person, what remains is mere loneliness.

The female intellectual class, in other words, new women are also pitiable. Still growing under the family system of the feudal age, getting married and doing housekeeping, the complexity of the contents of their life is an indescribable crisis. The academics that they more or less know only half of causes the merging of the new and the old ways to be lost and could merely stoke a yin energy. But didn't they learn life philosophy at their university and their profession, and watch the families from the West and Tokyo? Doesn't one's spirit and will exist in the sky, but doesn't one's body and labor exist on the ground? Although she married for sweet love, as each one of the married couples plays according to the whims of you are you and I am me, the meaning of life disappears and from morning to dinner, doesn't she end up with mere worries about the side dishes? Soon, getting hypersensitiveness and a nervous breakdown, doesn't she become envious of single women and make her assertion for celibacy? Although it is commonly said that women are the weak, they after all are the strong, and although it is said that women are small, the ones who are great are women. Happiness is the ability to rule over everything. Please rule over the rest of your family, your husband, your children, and all the way over society. Isn't the ultimate victory in the hands of women?

The judgement of Joseon men is strange. Although they themselves do not have a sense of chastity, they impose it on their wives and generally women, and also, try to take away female virginity. As for the people of the West or of Tokyo, if I did not have a notion of chastity, they would understand and admire someone without a notion of chastity. As long as the men of Joseon lure their women into chastity, shouldn't it be commonly recognized that they ought to love their women so that such a chastity could be adhered to? Suppose a woman had loose morals, when men themselves directly taste pleasure, there are no few cases that the men indirectly annihilate the woman and gnaw away at her. What an absurd, barbarous immorality.

The general mind of the people of Joseon is that as much as it is a period of transition, they cannot set out forward, but demand such a thing inwardly. As they are withdrawn and cannot run about, because of being constrained by the economy, they do not have anywhere to relieve their boiling emotions, they condemn the person if there is someone who blocks their way, regardless of the right or wrong, they do not have a solution for matters without a precise outlook on their life, and devoid of sympathy and understanding, they wind up straying from here to there, upon whatever arrival of circumstances. Without the least bit of thought to help save other people from their suffering by setting up some way, they take pleasure, scoff, and reprimand, as if they are an onlooker of a play or a motion picture, and isn't this making a promising young man, who put his mind to being the first to set out to see something, a cowering cripple? Look here, in each country of the West, doesn't one make a trend out of a person who leaps into the air, doesn't one encourage that and call that an intellect, a genius? So, as one fights one's way forward, and presents one's creative work, couldn't a steady progress of the society be seen? What about Joseon? If there is even a little change to one's behavior, it is quickly annihilated and is kept from bouncing back, as seen in the instances of the past and the present. Not only is it that a genius cannot find satisfaction with the cultural custom of one's contemporary, but it is that one could predict the subsequent period and create, and so, how could we ever see such a person who carries out change as imprudent? Manufacturing things is breaking the bud of a genius. Therefore, in Joseon society, from now on, although we need a person who could act in the front-line, we are in need of a supporter who could help pave the way when a promising young person is in a predicament due to falling back on the second, third rate, and we would need a person with an understanding, who would carefully inspect the cause, the motivation of a matter, and not make someone a huge criminal out of a trial over useless morals and the law.

To Mr. Cheonggu

Mr., while we've been apart, you would know just to this extent my thoughts and my life, which have changed. But excuse me, I still have not found where an appropriate, happy path would be for me. I do not know if I would have been happy living with Mr., where sometimes, our ideas would be in conflict with each other, where we would spend our days sloppily with the children and on housekeeping, or if I would have been happy with this life as a vagabond, carrying a sketch-box, canvas, and going around painting. However, life is not merely about family. Life is not merely about the arts. Life is a merging of here and there. It is like water, which is the merging of hydrogen and oxygen. Pardon me, this is my belief. Among people, suppose there are those who live ordinarily and those who live beyond ordinarily. Then, the person who lives beyond ordinarily has the stamina and individuality that goes beyond ordinary people. Besides, the best ideal of a person of the modern times would be to do all that other people do and with one's remaining energy, exhibit one's individuality. Such a person is not only theoretical but also a concrete example for many and so, the lives of great people, heroes would be such. In other words, just as it in the past, which was that in order for one to fare well and cultivate one's body and one's mind, first, one ought to take care of one's household, subsequently, govern the country, and then, make the whole country peaceful, it is no different now.

For 10 years, with this ideal, I have continued to do my work in my family life and even had the confidence to earn money. Hence, it is hardly possible that it would just be short of a partial happiness in my life, but rather, this may have been the path of happiness that I have really been demanding as a whole. What a pity that this ideal has come to be destroyed.

If the circulatory system of emotions is 10 years, one could come to like a person that one hated and one could come to hate a person that one liked, a person whom one was close to could put up a distance and one could become close to someone who had been distant, a good person could become evil and an evil person could become good. What would come of the emotions of Mr. after 10 years? As I have said previously, in order for the life of a married couple to really have meaning, they need to go through the three phases. As long as I already knew of your fortes and flaws, and Mr. knew of my fortes and flaws, weren't we supposed to mutually support each other and live on?

Anyhow, as I have said before, just to caution you, the divorce was not my intention, it was Mr.'s extortion. As I have non-resistantly given way, even after thinking of it for ten million times, it is a shame that under our circumstances, we were not able to unite our characters and unify our lives. Also, what I would want is for you to make the remaining years of your 80-year-old elderly mother comforting, to fully pay attention to raising my four children, and as for the rest, to wish Mr. a good health.

Written in August of 1934

〈*Samcheonri* (Magazine; 1929~1950)〉 (1934. 9.)

Entering a New Life

"I will go."

"Where?"

"To the West."

"Where in the West?"

"Paris."

"To do what?"

"To study."

"What would you do with studying when you're aged?"

"In youth, one should play, and when aged, one should study."

"That may be right, because the work of an old master with white hair has value. But don't you find it tiring to even budge?"

"I have done a fair amount of packing but still, I have fun just packing the bags."

"You could live anywhere. But you're aged."

"Living is not to live for the body, but to live for the mind."

"If the body is aged, then, the mind also becomes aged."

"No, as much as the body grows older, the mind becomes younger. Oscar Wilde once said in his poem, 'The tragedy of old age is not that one is old, but that one is young,' and so, Westerners, without a sense of aging are able to live with the feeling of being young indefinitely, but as Easterners always think about aging, they become old."

"However, it is a fact that when the body is aged and withers, the mind and the feeling also become drained of spirit, and what would you do about the fact that experiencing a lively, young feeling is like being in a dream?"

"That may be so, but it merely depends on making up one's mind. It's just that the concerns are with age, as one becomes older, one's thoughts lengthen but one's energy falters."

"Well, that is what I'm saying. That is why I'm telling you, my friend, not to wander around here and there at the age of forty, and to settle down in Seoul, as it is."

"I hate that. I hate Joseon, which knows all of my past, present, and future. I hate people from Joseon."

"Hmph, that is something that you wouldn't know. If you, my friend, leave Joseon, do you think that the past, present, and the future wouldn't follow you?"

"Well, while the past could chase me around anywhere, at least the present and the future could be changed with the environment."

"But what could you do about the fact that no matter how the environment changes, the past would always interlope and would blur the renovated environment? That is why a person who once had a past could not easily pluck out one's roots."

"Sure, while the roots may not be plucked out, depending on

how one pioneers, one could conquer the past with the environment."

"Yet, to be doing that, how much of a sorrow would there be to heal such a pain?"

"As for that, if one just makes up one's mind, it could be endured, but it is indeed difficult."

"If your mind is resolute to that degree, I am relieved. Do whatever you want."

While I got the permission of my friend, with the pretense of being strong, my heart was again filled with an emptiness at my friend irresponsibly turning back on me. After the incident of the divorce, I was recognized publicly in my relation between me and others as a person who cannot be in Joseon, and for the four to five years, in fact, I was in pain. First, not only was I ostracized socially, but with my career being of seniority, it was hard to sell my paintings and difficult to get a job, which was why my living could not be secured. Second, as my siblings, relatives were near, they hated seeing me, pitied me, and thought me pathetic. Third, my close friends and acquaintance attentively inspected my behavior and kept an eye on my attitude. No, with regard to all these conditions, if first, I am here, I could win over them. Worse than this, there is a pain, like it is when I get my flesh sliced and my bones raked out, which is the letter from my daughter and son, occasionally sent by the mailman. The words are 'Mother, I miss you.' The environment is amusing and also, scary. At the same time that the environment changes completely, the contributions of the past become gone, and instead, the facts of the past only heavily lag behind. That is why I cannot help but start the list of my life from the void while embracing the past that follows me.

Temptation

Wasn't the blunder of laying her hand on the apple, when she was said to never touch it, the temptation of the snake and the curiosity of Eve? How strict was the punishment of the deity, because of this? There seems to be nothing as scary and of a pleasant appeal as temptation, which is the joy of temptation, and the anxiety, apprehension, and concern were thrown out by curiosity.

Whatever the motivation was, the world that was wide open was strangely good and moreover, how could they, Adam and Eve not come to have such an emotion of freedom in their unrestrained, solemn hearts? I really had been tempted and indubitably had had curiosity. We discovered a bed of roses that were not thought to be in the rough thorny roadside. We were enraptured in the midst of moving in a certain direction, with things that were sealed off from us. Regardless of what the result would be, I could not help but try to put up with it in the process of making my progress. The route of progress for people has various kinds of patterns. There are no few who under a happy environment and conditions, live thoughtlessly, without any suffering and trouble. Yet, a majority ends up yielding before they carry out their goal. In whatever way one suppresses, is led astray by, and ends up breaking, couldn't we try to live, being of one mind? Look at the streams that are frozen in winter. How did the water that had flowed filthily get frozen white and beautifully to such an extent? This shows precisely that its natural constitution had not lost its purity and beauty. I come to think of the person who is making progress based on this point. For this person, the filthier the falling water and the deeper the path of temptation that one fell into, one would experience a more severe, complicated reality, and based on this, although the more such a person would be led astray, the more one would be in pain on the outer surface, inwardly, one could live emotionally rich. And, such a person manages to turn all of the things in the world into positivity.

A Single Person

The love between people of the opposite sex is said to be pure love. One who loses such a pure love is one who got hurt. One who had a taste of this hurt does not have the bodily will and is not possessed of the will of the mind, in other words, lacking the resilience, one loses the sense of intermediacy and does not have a sense of harmony. Therefore, the one who got hurt, that is, if this were the case of a single person, the emotions become paralyzed, the boundary of joy, anger, sorrow, and pleasure becomes obscure, and simultaneously, one gets tired of objects and does not find attachment. That is why for those who got hurt by a relationship between a man and a woman, certainly, if one were a man, he should choose a virgin woman as his partner, and if one were a woman, she should choose a virgin man as her partner, and that way, a sense of harmony could be maintained.

Should I live a life of momentary pleasure by giving permission to many people, or should I reject anyone and live, securing my heart? In the end, as I have come to put it into practice, as I have been brought under the conventionality of family education since young, and so, would feel a prick of conscience, and besides, as my conscience would not let me, I could not carry out the former, and in putting the latter into practice, it is indeed difficult. One could not have a close friend and would lose friends. As generally, the relationship between a man and a woman for a single person tends not to be a relationship based on personality, but based on a sexual relationship, from the first impression, it pops up in one's mind that one does not belong to the other person. Eventually, after having sex, as this does not last long, the other person suspects that one is selling one's body to others, just like one is giving bodily permission to that person, and if a sexual relationship is not carried through, on top of it, the days of their relationship would be nigglingly brief. Therefore, as the psychological unrest is severe for a single person, when one meets Gab (The person with more power) of the opposite sex, one becomes drawn to Gab, and when one meets Eur (The subjugated) of the opposite sex, one becomes drawn to Eur, and so, could not keep one's heart focused.

Therefore, as a person is in need of another person, a lover who could undoubtedly be someone whom one could be safely at peace with, although there may be something that one becomes attached to, as long as one is a person, one seeks for one's partner. A single person who has not found one's partner for love is always lax and tottering that it is as if one is about to collapse like the telephone pole standing in the wasteland that could topple from the strong wind.

Single people, if you ever meet misfortune, in other words, lose your partner, right then and there, get a sponsor. During the time that they curse and ruminate, as the second and the third wave of misfortune come invading, unless they have the will to conquer such a misfortune, what should they do when their determination becomes fuzzier more and more to the point of its being absent, they grow to hate people, come to despise talking, and as they get cut off from the hand to hold and are losing people? Moreover, as they end up losing their health, generally, in the relationship between men and women, besides a period of rumination, rather than sexual relationship, they need the temperature of the yin (cold) and yang (heat), and are in need of the yin energy (feng shui energy of relaxation and rest). As the majority of single people feeling languid and dull is largely due to a lack of such, it goes without saying that living as a single person who lost a partner is an unnatural state.

I who once had known of the 'The Grief of Reality,' as nothing more than artistically beautiful letters, now, after comparing the past of a certain period and the present, have come to realize the grief of reality.

I think that at a certain point, I have misleadingly stepped onto a path that veered to the right or the left. As I have entered into 'failure' and have walked on considerably, even now, along with reflection, although I try to return to the path that has been divided, as I have already gone too far, it is not easy. I am merely taking the path of self-consolation.

Chastity

Chastity is not even about morals nor law, nothing, it is merely a hobby. Much like one eats rice when one wants to and eats tteok (rice-cake) when one wants to, one could do whatever one wants, without a specific standard or principle, as one intends to do, which is never about getting psychologically shackled.

As a hobby is a kind of mystique, evil could be interpreted as good, shame could be turned into laughter, and even if one could be subject to whatever shackle on the surface, one could at least psychologically move around with freedom, no pain would be there whatsoever, and without being sore and without being in pain, there would only be joy and satisfaction, in other words, as it is not objective but subjective, and it is not unconscious but conscious, one realizes an artistic taste in one's mind and one's behavior becomes artistic.

It is because in the West, earlier on, in the beginning of the 19th century, sex education was prevalent in the education of women and despite the relaxation of the public morals of Paris, rather than it seeming evil and obscene, instead, the fact that it appeared beautiful is that already, in their minds, they have become conscious of sexual relationship, simultaneously, have thought of it as a hobby, and have made such a behavior artistic.

It is just that as chastity is needed to unite character and unify life, even when an individual's mind may want to treat chastity as a hobby freely, we unfortunately have others, besides oneself, and have a life where one should keep surviving. Therefore, the more the push from society intensifies, the more it is needed for an individual to be tense, in other words, one would need to focus one's mind. Those who focus their minds are the ones who unite their characters and unify their lives. Hence, as originally, the sense of chastity has been imposed on women, it would have to be the same for men.

Now and then, in order to adhere to this chastity, we have contained our laughter, suppressed the blood that boiled, and could not say everything that we wanted to say. What an absurd irony. Therefore, as our freedom would be the liberation from chastity, we need to have people who could turn chastity into looseness at an extreme, and then, go back to adhering to their chastity. In Paris, even where there is a looseness in behavior, as there are men and women who hold onto chastity, they have a taste of everything from here and there, and afterward, take a step back once again. We also need to get a taste of everything from here and there, and then, settle down, which would not be dangerous and would be in order.

While one could on the one hand, let the flowing currents flow, they would at last stray to the other side. A youthful and intense flow would also go wrong en route. As this is nature, from whose strength could nature be blocked?

Children

While it is true that one comes to have an affection for the baby that one gives birth to, whether a mother's love is from one's nature or from one's habit, as we experience a lot, when giving birth and leaving the child to be raised by the nanny, I am of the belief that the child would not be the least bit different from someone else's child.

From a life-long separation, with the kid being raised in the other person's hands, that too forms the sense of the child being synonymous with the other person's child. Then, undoubtedly, by giving birth and raising the child, an affection is formed and the mother gets a taste of a mother's love, which is why no matter how other people raise one's own child, when one meets such a child, raised by others, fully-grown, as one is bound not to have a deep affection, emotions would be feeble and it would be awkward that if it were to be like this, without the least bit of difference from a child being a stranger, their attachment would continue in the form of self-interest.

Besides, this is a child between two people who had divorced with a great deal of heavy emotions. Starting from when the child was young, as the child was drummed into one's head the blunders of one's biological mother from adults and would have become dubious, a sense of harmony would not be easily formed after meeting the biological mother. In other words, with the principle that a woman's lifeline held onto three duties, which were to follow her father as a youngster, her husband upon marriage, and her children, after the passing of her husband, the children who had to put the focus of love on their mother and father lost the focus of their lives and simultaneously, lost the focus of their mind. How could there be a sense of nobility in a mother's love that sneaks mid-way to a child who has formed such kind of digressive habits? It is just that unless the biological mother has a great economic power with which she could conquer, the child's head would have nothing but the calculations of the gains and losses from meeting her. That is why eventually, after one's lifelong separation from the husband, legally, the children become the children of the ex-husband, and also, one ends up becoming a stranger to the children. Therefore, starting from the origin of an old custom, when the woman would separate lifelong from her husband, she would get out, bringing a child with her, and end up becoming shackled there for a lifetime that because this is a pitiable circumstance of trying to form an affection, comparably, the mother would get a lot of resentment from such a child rather than being treated with filial piety, which is why it is all in vain, and at the same time that she divorces, she would be estranged from her child and would wait for the destiny of the later days.

I knew of this well and was all prepared for it. So, when people said to me,

"When the children are grown-up, where would they go? They are all bound to be looking for their mother."

I would let out a snort. What would be the point of finding the mother, and what would be the point of finding the children?

Unless I had a lot of money, where I could be of benefit to them, I would always be a stranger to them. It is merely that for the ten months, I had the baby in my stomach, and had undergone hardship, but that too turned into a past, and looking at it, it is nothing more than a single story of one's experiences.

Whether one sees it as imaginary, everything has become things that have all already lived. The light of the sky that is facing ahead is high and blue. The foggy place on the horizon would be at most where one cries out for a bright future and hope. In my heart, which yearns for something heavily, there is a world that I do not know so much about. There, anxiety that causes hesitation and horror creeps up. As someone who unknowingly set foot into the flower garden and got intoxicated by the sweet atmosphere, I came to realize that in fact it was a bed of roses within a thorny bush and I cried. Let's find happiness from misfortune.

I say to whoever it is.

"There is no one as unfortunate and as happy as a single person."

A woman gets married, gives birth, gets worried about the side dishes of the breakfast and dinner, and when she leaves the scope of such a livelihood, she is said to be unfortunate. Yet, being flustered from such a scope is happiness. Try getting out of the scope for once and look at those within the scope. Rather, it could be felt that those within the scope are the unfortunate and one is happy, and so, compared to the stagnant life that repeats the same livelihood every day, look at oneself that has a life of sensation that changes from moment to moment. Day by day, how much one would develop one's view on life and feel the value of life. The time that a lifeline is attached to a person is not the period of living, but it is the movement of emotions that is living. In this world, how many people are there who get tied down by society, get restrained by friends and family, and get so shackled by life that their body becomes shrunken and they become incapable of running? This is truly unfortunate. Try to live in the body of a single person. Such a body seems to be capable of flying up in the sky, capable of even rolling on the ground, and as the back and front, the left and right are cleared, without it being rough, the body and the mind are free. Such a person could do things that those within the scope could not do, could think of things that they could not think of, which is why there are a number of instances of the person becoming the greatest figure of all time, a hero, and a creator of a masterpiece. Therefore, I occasionally say this.

"K, my ex-husband saved me in that I became a human being. He is someone that I could not be more thankful to. As he made me leave my family life, I was able to get my title piece selected and was able to write several excellent reports. Although I may die now, I have gotten all the tastes of living. I do not have the least bit of grudge against K. Rather, I consider him a savior whom I am grateful to."

As I say this, I find happiness from my misfortune.

Regardless of what circumstance it is, if I work hard to make everything credible, I unexpectedly find happiness in the midst of misfortune.

That is, first, it is I, myself that ought to chase after the environment, second, to make the environment chase me, third, to find the environment from other places. If I were to put this into practice, I could discover a new, wide world and it would not be that much of a difficult thing to find happiness from misfortune.

Whatever kind of blunders and disgrace, if one has the strength alone to prevail over them, they would become precious experiences, in other words, turn into brilliant decisions, and fill the person's body with happiness.

What Kind of Person Should I Be?

As a person who had been exuberant and vocal, I ended up subdued, downtrodden, like being salted down. I became devoid of spirit, sluggish, without the energy nor the stamina. Although being 40 years of age, it may be like that at the time, still, if I had not been so gravely hurt, I would not have so easily aged. However, the ideal alone that I would want to be such an exuberant and vocal woman still continues, as long as I want.

When the other person treats me with logic, let me treat the other person with feeling. When the other person treats me with justice, let me treat the other person with elegance. When the other person treats me with courage, let me treat the other person with dignity.

Let me continue an ascetic life. With the unification of the spirit, and the preservation of health. This is not because my character is heartless, but rather, because it is passionate. Although I may at glance seem strict, this is not because I am cold-hearted, but because blood boils in my chest. At the same time that I want to be spiritual, I wish to be sensual. At the same time that I want to have a strong self-esteem, I wish to be truthful. I demand great love from other people. No, rather, I try to bestow great love to others. It goes without a doubt that enjoying oneself and bestowing happiness to others would be profuse, profound, and perpetual. At the same time that I am someone's lover, I am going to be as much of a mother. In other words, blazing a trail to the happiness of life would be my kind of religious effort. At the same time, I am going to have a profound notion of responsibility and make a precise judgment of others. I will indefinitely make all the things appealing, with the feeling of being youthful. That is because that always beautifies my existence and because when I think of all the things I do as my everything, I come to feel a sense of ecstasy.

I have known of the appeal of the soul being deep and therefore, I will create a new life that is colorfully profuse with one's own characteristic elegance. Even when I would come forward, in front of people, I would abandon formality, habit, and restraints, and by being noble, face a life of service. I will speak fewer words than others. However, the silence and the smile would be rather more eloquent than speaking many words, and no matter how it may seem like a running stream on the surface, underneath it, it would have unity with a strong rhythm. Whether I would be gleaming with happiness or would be getting a fatal blow, be stable or suffering, be heartless or passionate, be happy or crying, in whatever environment, I would be a woman of a multitude of sides, and simultaneously, one woman.

I know of various kinds of delusions that men have about women. They demand for women who are fostered in many ways, in other words, a perpetually feminine woman rather than a woman with toned muscles. As men enter into society, they are coming into touch with a great deal of complexity. Hence, their circulation of emotions is intense. According to what they feel, their sorrow and loneliness are mountainous and deep. On the contrary, they are nothing but fretful that women lie dormant in such a simple household that in fact, they end up in a slump. Not only does it go without saying that they feel that such women wreak frustration in men who call for provocativeness but they also cannot help themselves in feeling that to be a responsibility of women.

Oh, gentlemen! How could they ever feel satisfaction? Oh, ladies! How could they ever give satisfaction? Satisfaction merely depends on making up one's mind. This is the lesson of the Buddha that I am always memorizing.

As life seems endless, I would like to understand it.

As there seems to be no end to anguish, I would like to break away from it.

Thus, a woman with a deep sorrow brings the realization of the unrest of emotions upon men's hearts, a kind that could not be spoken of, and a woman with complaints brings pain upon the hearts of men, which cannot handle it.

My Life

Since I was eighteen, for 20 years, I have been pretty much on everybody's lips. That is, the incident of graduating top of the class, the incident of going out with M, the incident of going mad after being parted from him by his death, the incident of going out with K, the incident of marriage, the incident of playing an active role as the wife of a diplomat, the Whang-ok incident (Assassination scheme in 1923 against the Japanese governor general by the Eyyeoldan, the Korean Independence Patriotic Activists, where Na Hye-seok aided the activists by providing a hideout in the residence of the vice-consul at Andong Japanese Consulate), the incident of the trip to the West, the incident of divorce, the incident of the release of *Confessions of a Divorcee*, the incident of the lawsuit, and like these, I experienced all sorts of things.

In terms of life, going from someone who had held a banquet along with the representatives of each country as the highest class to rolling around in the corner of the room on the opposite side in other people's house, in terms of the economy, going from someone who had ridden a train, the first-class steamboat, and taken a special seat for watching a motion picture to stepping into places where I could borrow money by having my property seized, in terms of health, I went from a person who had been exuberant and valiant to almost slipping all the way into paralysis, and in terms of the mind, I went from someone who had been bright and prodigal to winding up as a fool. As a person who had been likeable to anyone, now, I am afraid of people, fear meeting people, and hate people. As I would be like this when I see others, I bet others would also be like that, when they see me.

Consequently, after having suffered through all that could be undergone within a person's ability, what remains is a person at a loss. How could I get back the ingenuous, honest, gentle, tender, diligent, and smart character that had been my nature?

It is all destiny. We have a destiny that we, with the strength of a human are helpless against. However, the more we obediently comply with destiny, the more it grows and comes to strike us. When we face it hard, we end up unexpectedly toppling down, devoid of strength.

Where Should I Go?

One day, while taking a walk, I discovered an underground shack. I intentionally pulled the straw mat and looked inside. And, as I was turning around and heaving myself up, these words flowed out of my mouth.

"You guys are happier than me. It is because you at least have an underground shack. Where should I go in the future? Besides, after this incident (Choe Rin lawsuit; as Na Hye-seok was accused of adultery in her relationship with Choe Rin, it led to her divorce from her husband, and so, Na Hye-seok filed a lawsuit against Choe for his part in wreaking havoc to her family and defaming her in society), I could not come forward and lift my face with composure."

Tears sprang, as I muttered like this.

"Let me go to Paris. No, after leaving my homeland, what could

I do about the sorrow and loneliness? No, after going there and coming back once more, empty-handed, wouldn't I be straying again? No, what should I do about the responsibility of maternal love?"

Now that I think about it like this, once again, my thoughts become stuck.

Let's go, Let's go to Paris not to live, but to die. The place that killed me was Paris. The place that really made me into a woman was also Paris.

I will go to Paris to die.

I have nothing to find, meet, nor gain. I have nowhere to come back to. Let's stay there eternally. I, with a past and present that are nil, let me get out into the future.

What should I do?

As a person who has become this much, I have gotten a lot of favor of Joseon. I ought to have a calling that would definitely repay the kindness. Isn't this the time that one waits for a figure in the field of education, agriculture, commerce, media, literature, and art? Isn't it too selfish not to do a single thing to be of help for Joseon and just go somewhere?

No, no. Because of me, everyone's patience would be lost. To speak of more broadly, as for all the single men and women of the Joseon society, to speak smaller, as for Mr. Cheonggu, as for his second wife, as for my four children, sons and a daughter, as for my relatives from both sides, and as for my close friends, they would get anxiety and would come to lose patience. Therefore, while me being here could be an object of nuisance, it would be difficult to be an object of benefit.

I happened to have in my clutch XX won. Although this could be the fruit of blowing off my steam, it is not that refreshing to me, as well, and so, really, how would C (Choe Rin, with whom Na Hye-seok was accused of committing adultery and this is referring to the Choe Rin lawsuit, where as a result of the divorce, Na Hye-seok filed a lawsuit for financial compensation against Choe for his part in wreaking havoc to her family and defaming her in society) have felt?

"I'm going to take this and go to Paris. I'm going there not to live but to die."

As I set off, this is what I am going to say.

"Mr. Cheonggu, certainly, when you are in a moment of regret, call out my name once. My four children, sons and daughter, don't blame mother, but blame the social system, the morals, the law, and the outmoded custom. Your mother, as the pioneer in a period of transition, became a sacrifice from the rope of such a destiny. In the future, if you come to Paris as a diplomat, please find the grave of your mother and put a flower there."

> *The swallow, which flew fluttering*
> *into the cruel hand of a human*
> *two of its shoulder blades two of its legs*
> *have all been snapped.*
> *While in order to live again*

it squirms and struggles

at last, it cannot endure

and ends up drooping.

Yet, one does not know

that the swallow

still has a warm spirit

that the sound of its breathing could be heard.

Once again to float midair

vigor and courage

perseverance and efforts

would it get them back

Who would know with ease?

From an old manuscript

⟨*Samcheonri* (Magazine; 1929~1950)⟩ (1935. 2.)

My Time as a Lady Teacher

It was an incident that happened 20 years ago. It was when R (Referring to Na Hye-seok) was abroad to Tokyo. R's father was a yangban (Upper class in Joseon), an affluent man, and a great man who had the brains that her father sent word about R's soon-to-be marriage with M, told R to promptly go home, and because her father went so far as to not pay for her school expenses, R could not help but return home, and yet, R already had a lover and it was a time when R had made a solemn promise.

After R came back home, every day, R's father pleaded with her to get married to M, even brought a cane and whipped, telling her to get married. Yet, R could not dare tell her stern father face-to-face that she had already given someone her word and

when she said, "I'm going to live alone,"

"You bitch, how are you going to live alone?"

"I'm going to live alone by making money on my own."

"What an absurd world."

Uttering this, he was dumbfounded and as it seemed like he would not be listening, it was a time when things ended up going awry.

R wrote a letter to teacher Y of her alma mater, school C that she would be paying a visit for a while. Teacher Y was a teacher that she greatly favored during R's attendance in school. Teacher Y soon came down.

"Teacher, please listen to my request."

"What? Would I do no more than listen to it?"

"As I cannot be at my house in this state, please send me somewhere off to school to teach."

"How would that be difficult? As just in time, I have a place where I put in a claim, it is fortunate."

"Then, please do so."

R told teacher Y what ought to be told to her father. A little while later, her father stepped in.

"Ah, is this teacher Y? When did you come?"

"I came this morning."

"Then, did you eat breakfast?"

"Yes, I ate. But I came, because I had something urgent to say."

"What is it? Please tell me."

"It is for no other reason than that the education and the management bureau spoke of choosing a lady teacher and as your esteemed daughter has come home just in time and is leisurely spending her time in the house, I'm requesting that you send her."

"Are you talking about my daughter? Now, she needs to be taught how to weave and to get married."

"As for weaving, when she's faced with it, it is bound to be the case that she would know how to fend for it all."

In return, my father said,

"If I were to send her, where should it be?"

"Yeoju."

"Then, for how long?"

"As for that, how could I tell right now?"

"Hey, R."

"Yes!"

"Come out here."

R stepped inside where teacher Y and her father were having a conversation.

"Will you be going to Yeoju public school as a teacher?"

"As teacher Y is speaking of it like that, how can I not go?"

"Then, go."

R winked her eyes at teacher Y and smiled.

After teacher Y came up to Seoul, in just a few days, a document that informed of R's appointment and travel expenses were passed down. R went to Yeoju public school as a teacher and was lodging in the house of the friend of R's father, governor K.

It was the first month of the year. The members of the educational affairs in the house of Mr. C were asking every one of the schoolteachers over and treating them to tteokguk (rice-cake soup). As the sole lady teacher, R stepped inside. The wife of Mr. C passed away and was not there, and only young people were there. Among them, there were H and I, the two maidens who were cousins, of the same age as R. Since then, the two maidens have argued with each other over their love for R. When they boiled soup, they asked R to eat, and when they made tteok (rice-cake), they ordered their younger brother, T to pack it up and sent it to R. R who was lonely, being far away from home and the two maidens, in the absence of their mother, found affection in one another and so, every day, R and the two maidens would meet and see each other.

One day, it was a moonlit night. When R was about to lay, sprawled, sleeping, a moon rose up in midair and reflected on the window of the room of R. At this time, there was someone who knocked on the window. At first, R thought that the wind was blowing at a paper weather strip but realizing that it was not that, she opened the window. There was I who was standing with her hair hung down, reminiscent of the ninety days of spring, braided and extended.

"What is the matter here?"

R abruptly heaved herself up and grabbed I by the wrist.

"Were you surprised?"

"No, but what are you doing in the middle of the night?"

"How can I bear it when I miss you?"

R at last set her heart at ease and said,

"Come in."

"Can I come in?"

"Yes, you have to come in!"

I made her way into the room.

"But how did you come here? The gates would've been all closed."

"I climbed over the wall that had burst."

The wall at the back of the house of the governor had been low and had been slightly burst.

"What if it were a thief, climbing over the wall? White-collar crime."

"Enough of that!"

"Hahahaha······."

"Eat this!"

"What is this? Again!"

"Because we made a little bit of Songpyeon (half-moon-shaped rice-cake) at home, I brought them, thinking of my friend."

I put heaps of Songpyeon (half-moon-shaped rice-cake) inside the bowl, put the lid on, and untied the package of tteok (rice-cake), wrapped in a piece of cloth. Without a word of gratitude, without saying anything, R stared at the warm-hearted, emotional I.

"Why are you staring at a person like that?"

I pinched the knee of R.

"It's because I am so grateful."

"I brought the tteok (rice-cake) because it would harden after to-night, so hurry up and eat."

"I'll eat."

R smiled brightly, while eating tastily.

"This is as awesome as something to die for."

"I don't know who is making someone die."

"Drink some water and eat."

She held up the water bowl that was there and made her drink.

"It is tasty. I've been slightly hungry."

"Have plenty of it, okay?"

I was satisfied. At this time, the sound of a rooster crowing from afar could be heard.

R was astonished.

"I, you should get going, you must not be late. If your father knows, we will get into big trouble."

R thought of an occasion when I had gone back after seeing R and was chided about how a big girl kept going back and forth through the street (although I did wear a head-dress).

"It doesn't matter."

"It would be a big trouble if the sound of the door opening is heard."

"As my father has gone to a banquet, he'd come back late, and because I came here after planning it all with H, it doesn't matter."

Still, R could not put her mind at rest and said,

"Just go, we could meet again tomorrow."

"I'm going to sleep here before I go."

"While I'd want to hold onto you more than you do, just go."

Under the moonlight, the two ladies parted their ways and there was no way that they would let go of that resolute affection. When not seeing each other, they missed one another, and when they met, not knowing how to separate, they went back and forth, seeing each other, coming and going again, and so, after the classes were dismissed, R found huge delight in meeting the two maidens, and I and H waited around solely for the afternoon. It had been one year since she had been spending her time, day in, day out. R saved her earnings and in preparation to go back to Tokyo and continue her studies, she submitted her retirement in one year and left. The two maidens and R cried every day. However, the fact that she was leaving was callous. She had no choice but to free herself from the two maidens, who cried, clinging to her, and to leave. What R left solely in the hands of the two maidens were the one photograph of R and a single paper with an address written. Since then, while the letters traveled back and forth countless times, besides R focusing on her major, during the time that she came into contact with this or that incident, in other words, as someone who was desperate in the present, she could not afford to think of her friends of the past. Thus, naturally, they stopped contacting each other. The thoughts that had come up once in a while also became void in her memory.

After 10 years, when R was living in Gyeongseong Sungui-dong, unexpectedly, I's younger brother, T came over. He who had been a little boy grew up into a young man. R passionately welcomed him. While T spent a couple of days in R's house, through the arrangement of R and her husband, he got into business school. At this time, she heard news of H and I that they already became married women and even had children. After that, once again, there was no news of them. R had been scampering around from this life to that life, from that life to this life, and seeking out her home again, came to Suwon, and at the center of a five-compartment straw-thatched house, she lay face down, in the middle of recovering from a new illness. One day, after dinner, she was about to lie down when her sister's son came in, holding a piece of a business card.

"Ma'am, this person came to see you," he said.

On the name card, it was written, 'Vice-president of Hwaseong Financial Association, C.O.T.' R did not know right away. And then, she thought again.

"Okay, I know, I know, where is this person?"

"He is currently standing in front of this door."

R rushed outside.

"What is the matter here?"

T looked carefully without saying anything. It must have been that the countenance of R, who was old and sick, was shabby.

"Come in."

She guided him into the room.

"How have you been in the meantime?"

"Right, I have been living well. You have become such a gentleman."

"Yes, I have grown."

"But how long has it been?"

"After seeing you at the house in Sungui-dong at that time, I haven't seen you."

"Has it been ten years?"

"That's right."

"By the way, what happened to your cousin and your sister?"

"Cousin H lives in Seoul and is the wife of the head of Dongil bank in the branch of the Dongdaemun Gate, and sister I lives in Icheon and at the age of thirty-two, she became a widow."

"Really? It's a shame for her."

"So, do you take pleasure in the Association?"

"I am always busy. While in someplace like the city, I could just take care of my office work hours and it would be enough, in the rural area, as I have to be responsible for even the minute office work, if it is fun, it is fun, and if it is tiresome, it is tiresome."

"If all things are made into art, there would be no trials."

"Sure."

"Anyway, couldn't I see your sister?"

"She will come soon if she's told to come."

T played for about an hour and left. The following day, R wrote a letter to I.

> *To my dear friend!*
>
> *Hasn't it been 20 years? From your faithful younger brother, Mr. T, who has sought me, I came to know of my friend's news. How thankful this gentleman is to us. According to your younger brother, if I request you, my friend to come, you could come soon, and so, please come over to see me. Let's talk about the rest after we meet.*

After two to three days, a notification arrived that she came. R ran out. I was not a maiden with her fleshiness, glossy, and smooth face, with hair braided and extended, but a middle-aged madam with her wrinkles, charred face, and her hair done up in a chignon.

"Oh my."

The two people held each other's hands and tears glistened. The two pulled each other into a tight embrace. The two cheeks made contact with each other.

"How many years has it been?"

"Has it been 20 years?"

"How come I haven't heard that much news from you?"

"It has become like that naturally."

"Although I've heard through the newspaper, magazine, and by means of someone that my friend has proudly succeeded, I ought to know where you are. It was just that once in a while, I'd be looking at your picture, crying, and laughing alone."

"Okay, how have you been? But you've become single?"

R caressed I's cheek. I's tears brimmed. R's tears also sprang. For some time, they were silent. Every day, coming and going, coming and going, travelling around the Suwon castle, sight-seeing Seoho model farm, and after coming and going to a temple, they went into each one's bathhouse, found their way to the place where R did her sketch, carrying the painting materials, went to a bank around a field and a ridge between rice paddies, plucking out wormwood, which was made into tteok (rice-cake) and ate it, came and went for a sleepover, and like this, the friendship between the two people became more solidified day by day. I brought her younger sister and due to itchiness, she said she was going to head off to a hot spring in Onyang. As R's body was also itchy right in that moment, she accompanied them. After being in a hot spring, when they lay, stretched out in a row at night, the three women rapturously stirred up a ruckus. It was as R halted the sleep of I's younger sister whom I held in between her arms, sprawled out. Like this, for two nights, they spent their time laughing until their backs might break. Due to I's housekeeping, she could not stay for long and left. Meanwhile, R once again became mired in longing.

In the world, there are all sorts of close friends. Friends for work or friends with the same hobby. The bonding between I and R was a friendship that transcended all these conditions. With the merging of R, who had an affection that could not be poured elsewhere and I, with an affection that could not be poured elsewhere, it would only form into a beautiful friendship. However, what is regrettable is that they were so far away from one another that they could not frequently see each other. Doing everything in the world as much as one wanted, without complaint nor dissatisfaction nor resentment, and without having to shift the blame onto a person, one would want to live in the world comfortably. Yet, it was the way of the world that it would not turn out whatever one wanted it to be.

Still, we are not trying to preserve a phenomenon until the end of the world. One did not want to live under too much of a restraint. Amid living in closeness for how long, certainly, a chasm was bound to appear with the sentiment of haughtiness. We want to see big, deeply, and widely with huge eyes. We want to look at every side. Over the time that they have not been seeing each other, I and R were once again wandering in their world of oblivion, gaining and pursuing.

We have the world of physicality and the world of the spirits. While the world of physicality is narrow and shallow, the world of the spirits is wide and humongous. Although we go on living in the world of physicality, because we have the world of spirits, which is beyond that of physicality, there is a significance in living as a person. I and R, who play around, I and R, who go out together in the world of spirits, where they could ceaselessly live on to whatever extent, I and R, bearing the affection of loneliness and longing in their physicality, after a friendship formed by soulful means. Who would know which way they would go and how they would come to help each other's lives?

In the midst of the silence alone, R would merely be doing her painting, and clever I, who had gotten into a difficult marriage, brought with her children in clusters and having borne in her mind some kind of determination amidst the silence, she worked every day in pursuit of hope. God, please bestow a long and healthy life upon these two lonely daughters.

⟨*Samcheonri* (Magazine; 1929~1950)⟩ (1935. 7.)

A spinster who was a member of the Suffragette Movement by Mrs. Pankhurst from England was a teacher from whom I learned English, and so, this is a Q & A with her about women's issues.

Na Hye-seok(R): Who first started the suffragette movement?

Teacher(S): 20 years ago, when we were going around doing protests, there was one elderly lady, too old to come out, who opened the window, sat there, looking out, and then, closed the door and meditated. This was namely the progenitor of the women's rights movement in England, Mrs. Fawcett, the 2nd generation is Mrs. Pankhurst, and she was the first to start doing protests in the city. 40 years ago, there were 10,000 women all marching in the street to the Albert Hall. At the time, I was young and my mother attended.

R: What was written on the flag?

S: 'Fight for Women's Independence. Fight for Women's Right.' was written.

R: Certainly, many would've been caught.

S: Of course, all of them got caught, and they went on a hunger strike, causing an uproar.

R: Is there something different about the mark of a member?

S: There is. 'Votes for Women' sign was written on the hat, on the buttons, and on the band. This was what we wore at the time. (The madam revealed a band whose indigo color was all run down with gold letters written on it)

R: Please give it to me.

S: What are you going to do with it?

R: Who knows if I become the progenitor of the women's rights movement of Joseon?

S: Okay. Have it as a memento.

R: What is the purpose of a suffragette movement?

S: At last, it's because men don't reflect and are full of themselves. Every time they open their mouths, they ask what women know. Yet, no matter how heroic they present themselves as, there is not one of them who doesn't play into the hands of a woman, and it's because wisdom and academics are the exterior of life and the interior of life is overcome by compassion. At this time, women thought. We wondered as to how people who have the wits and the brains like us could ever be satisfied with the laws made by those foolish men, which was how the beginning of the women's rights movement took place.

R: What does Mrs. Pankhurst mainly argue about?

S: About labor issues, chastity issues, divorce issues, and voting issues.

R: By the way, didn't you, teacher, also give a speech during the protest?

S: Right, when I went on top of a chair in the street and gave a speech, one woman asked why I was doing this. "I am doing this for you and your daughter. God made you and men equally. Why couldn't you do what men do?" The tens of thousands of people passing by gathered and watched, saying, "Here, here," and applauded.

R: Were there lots of women's organizations during the protest?

S: While there were a lot of organizations, we divided them into groups according to the professional occupations and protested.

R: Aren't men actually victorious over women?

S: Why is that? Although men chatter about themselves being strong and well-to-do, actually, they are nothing but foolish. While women weakly shut their mouths, if they have something they want to do and just use their wits, there is nothing they can't do. Here is an example. When a husband suggests to his wife to go somewhere, suppose the wife says that she doesn't want to for just no reason. The husband would insist on going in a group. Yet, what if the wife clutches her head and says that she cannot go because her headache is too severe? Wouldn't the husband instead call it quits with a face of sympathy? Can't it be seen how foolish and weak men are, and how witty and strong women are?

R: How is the relationship with the children?

S: Whoever they are, as children, they think of their mother as bigger than the whole world. However, look at them when they grow up and get married. To the wives, the husband takes the place of their mother and the wives become a mother. This is what happened. A beloved mother of the husband who gave all her affection passed away. At this time, the husband became ill, bedridden. As a matter of course, the wife was going to pay a visit to the grave instead, but ended up not going, because dear husband was ill. Yet, after a few days, the mother of the wife passed away. At that time, the husband and the wife, in her ill state accompanied each other and went to the grave. Although this would be mistaken according to the imposed human ways, the strength of a woman is such. That is why there is a saying in our common speech, 'a woman laughs in her sleeve.'

R: Is gender discrimination also severe in England?

S: It was. Before, the daughter was ordered to wash the clothes of the son, but now, it is not like that. Before, the wife did all that the husband was supposed to do, but now, the husband does all that he could do by himself.

R: Among the father and the mother, whose responsibility is greater when it comes to their child?

S: If there is a slip-up among the children, the responsibility doesn't fall on the mother but the father. If the father dies first and the mother would be there, the mother would do all that she could do to foster her child. However, if the mother dies first and the father would be there, at the same time that another woman comes in and does the housekeeping, the education of the child becomes neglected. Therefore, for the sake of the child, it is good for the mother to be alive and the father to pass away first. Then, if only the mother is there, without the father, the responsibility would be on the mother, but when both parents are there, the responsibility would be on the father. After the husband dies, if she has another husband, the responsibility would be on the man, and if an unmarried woman has a child, the responsibility is shifted to the woman. When the couple has a child and a divorce lawsuit takes place, the court, based on its observation of the parents, makes the responsibility of the child fall on whichever side would be favorable.

R: Commonly, from what circumstances does divorce take place?

S: Usually, there are a lot of divorces that arise from economic issues. And, there are a lot of cases that arise from the misconduct of the man and the woman.

R: What do you think of the labor issues?

S: When I was a teacher, I had 60 students, the male teacher of the classroom next to it also had 60 students, but while my sewing hours were greater, I got a lower salary than his. So, I made a complaint. However, now, for the most part, the difference is gone.

R: How did the voting age turn out?

S: Until last year, the earliest voting age for men was 21, and for women, 30, but from this year, the earliest voting age of women has become the same as that of men.

R: Teacher, how is your single life?

S: Like married women taking pleasure in things and being lonely, single women also take pleasure in things and are lonely.

R: Then, what would be better?

S: In youth, a single life would be better.

〈Samcheonri (Magazine; 1929~1950)〉 (1936. 1.)

Translator's Notes

I remember when I first read Virginia Woolf's *A Room of One's Own* in my freshman year of university and came to terms with who I was in my musings over my identity as a Korean woman. At that time, I was filled with wonder and amazement at how during when women writers had been generally overshadowed and obscured, Virginia Woolf helped dig out many of their voices, thoughts, and talents hidden throughout history. By the time *A Room of One's Own* was published in 1929, it had only been a year since the earliest age for women to vote, first granted in 1918 in the United Kingdom, which had been over the age of 30 became equal to men's voting age, over the age of 21. Thus, as much as the literary world restricted equal access of women writers, the basic human rights to live as a female citizen in a democratic society, such as the freedom of voting and participation rights in social workplaces outside of domestics had been under constraint. And yet, despite the discriminatory default, where women had been born into a society that did not fully recognize their potential, Virginia Woolf still dreamed of a potential female Shakespeare in society. While throughout the past, the lack of female literary giants had been attributed to women's talent paling in comparison to men, Woolf turned this around by thinking that it would have been because the stories of talented women whose potential had not bloomed due to their dire socio-economic circumstances either got lost or burned, cast into oblivion from the chaotic whirlpool of history.

After reading *A Room of One's Own*, I wondered if there were any women writers in Korean history like Virginia Woolf. Surely, England had inspiring women writers of the 19th and 20th century, like Virginia Woolf, George Eliot, and the Brontë sisters. Then, what about in Korea? Even though there could have been many other Korean female writers existing in history, I could not think of anyone from my Korean Classic Literature school textbook. Even, in Korean history class, as a high school student, I wondered as to why the biographies of the historical figures recorded only a few great names of women relative to other big names of great men out there. In other words, growing up, it was hard for me to find a Korean female role-model from history that I wanted to take after.

During my sophomore year in Ewha Womans University, in Modern History of Korea, a class taught by professor Jeeha Yang, I first learned about Na Hye-seok and fell in love with her life stories and her literary pieces. That was not only because her stories were the stepping stone to the improvement of women's rights, but also because of lifting the veil of ignorance surrounding the diversity of humanity. For example, Na Hye-seok dug up a diverse cast of stories of those 'Otherized,' 'The Untouchables,' and the 'Fallen Eve,' once buried and invisible. Strangely, even as a 21st century Korean woman, I felt that the stories of Na Hye-seok, born 103 years earlier than me did not end at the past, but rather, they continued to have a life of their own through stories that later reproduced different versions of those 'Otherized,' 'The Untouchables,' and the 'Fallen Eve' as Korean women in today's society are simultaneously overcoming and facing new challenges. At the same time that the stroke of the pen reproduced and recreated story after story, the lost voices have been found, the unrecorded lives have become recorded, and the burnt pages have been pulled from the heap of ashes and restored. As a translator, in my mission to help make Na Hye-seok become recorded as a great figure in the Korean historical biography, I plodded my way through a months-long grueling process. It was a hard process where I had to actually learn all the scarce Korean expressions used in the past and decipher zillions of unfamiliar Hanja. However, the biggest struggle was in really understanding the feelings, thoughts, and intentions of Na Hye-seok underlying even the simplest of words, and sincerely conveying her heart and soul that had been poured into her works. The most precious lesson from overcoming such struggles was the importance of reading between the lines, because the implicit depths to a story beyond the surface are where the authenticity of the author is buried and shines through as the readers dig them out with all their might. If I were to go back in time and meet the author, Na Hye-seok herself, I want to say, "Thank you for being my first-ever Korean female role-model that I could look up to. All this time that I translated, I was so happy because it was like having conversations with you as I listened to your words and spoke to you. Thank you."

번역자의 말

나의 기억 속에는 대학 새내기 시절 한국 여성으로서 정체성을 고민하던 때 버지니아 울프의 『자기만의 방』을 처음 접하며 나 자신을 알아갔던 모습이 있다. 여성 작가들은 그림자의 베일에 덮여 존재감조차 없었던 그 시대에 버지니아 울프가 역사 속에서 감춰진 수많은 목소리, 내재되었던 생각과 재능들을 캐내기 위한 헌신적 노력에 나는 놀라움을 감출 수가 없었다. 『자기만의 방』이 1929년에 출판되었을 시절은 1918년부터 투표권을 처음 부여받은 영국 여성의 투표권 나이가 30살 이상에서 남성의 투표권 나이인 21살 이상으로 동등해지고 겨우 1년밖에 되지 않았던 때이다. 따라서, 여성 작가들이 불평등한 문학계에서 도약이 지극히 제한되어 있었던 것만큼 민주주의 사회에서 살아가는 시민으로서 기본적인 인권, 예를 들어, 참정권과 가정 밖 사회에서의 일자리 참여권조차도 보장받지 못했던 것이다. 하지만 완전한 잠재력을 인정하지 않는 사회에 태어나면서 처음부터 남녀 역할을 배정해 사회적으로 정해 놓은 젠더 규범, 그야말로 차별적 디폴트에도 불구하고 버지니아 울프는 사회 속 잠재적 여성 셰익스피어를 꿈꾸어 왔다. "여성 문학 거인들의 부족함의 이유는 여성의 재능이 남성과 비교해 상대적으로 열등하기 때문이다."라는 프레임이 과거에서부터 이어져 왔지만 버지니아 울프는 이를 다른 시점에서 보았다. 재능이 있는 여성들이 불우한 사회, 경제적인 상황에 의해 잠재력을 꽃피우지 못해 그들의 이야기가 잊혀 왔거나 태워져버려 역사 속의 혼란스러운 소용돌이 속 무지에 휘말려 들어갔기 때문이라는 생각이었다.

『자기만의 방』을 읽고 한국 역사 속 버지니아 울프와 같은 여성 작가들이 존재하는지 궁금했다. 분명히 영국은 19세기, 20세기의 감명 깊은 여성 작가들, 버지니아 울프, 조지 엘리엇과 브론테 자매 등이 있었다. 그러면 한국의 경우는 어떨까? 사실 충분히 역사 속에 한국 여성 작가들이 여러 명 있을 수도 있지만, 한국 고전 문학 교과서에서는 도저히 한 분도 생각이 나지 않는다. 심지어 고등학교 한국 역사 수업 시간에 위인전에 남성 위인들의 이름들은 많이 새겨져 있지만, 여성 위인들은 몇 명 밖에 떠올릴 수 없을 만큼 적게 기록되었다. 다시 말해, 자라면서 내가 따라가고 싶은 역사 속의 한국 여성 롤모델을 찾기 어려웠다.

그런데 대학 2학년 때, 본교인 이화여자대학교 양지하 교수님의 근현대사 수업을 듣고 나혜석 선생님에 대해 처음 배우면서 그분의 인생관, 풍부한 삶이 담긴 이야기(비문학, 문학 작품)에 빠지게 되었다. 이는 나혜석 선생님의 작품들은 단지 여성 인권의 개선에 발판이 되어서인 것뿐만 아니라 인류의 다양성을 덮고 있었던 무지의 베일을 벗기셨기 때문이다. 예를 들어, 나혜석 선생님은 '타자화된 사람,' '언터처블'과 '타락한 이브'의 파묻혀져서 감춰져 버렸던 다양한 이야기들을 하나둘씩 캐냈다. 희한하게 나보다 103년 전 일찍 태어나신 나혜석 선생님의 이야기는 과거에서만 끝난 것이 아니라 오늘날 21세기 사회에서 한국 여성들이 동시에 극복하고 새로운 도전을 하면서 계속해서 '타자화된 사람', '언터처블' 과 '타락한 이브'의 다른 버전들이 새롭게 재현되어 나아가는 생명체와 같다. 펜의 획과 동시에 하나하나의 이야기를 재현, 재창조하면서 잃어버린 목소리를 되찾게 되었고 기록되지 않았던 삶은 기록되고 태워져 버린 종이들은 재 덩어리에서부터 꺼내어 복구되어왔다. 번역자로서 한국 역사 위인전에 나혜석 선생님이 위인으로 기록될 수 있도록 일조하는 나의 미션을 펼치면서 몇 개월간 번역이란 고군분투의 길을 걸었다. 희소한 옛날 한국어 표현과 친숙하지 않은 무수하게 등장하는 한자어까지 모두 해독해야 하는 힘든 과정이었다. 하지만 가장 큰 시련은 단순한 단어 속에서

도 내재되어 있는 나혜석 선생님의 감정, 생각과 의도를 이해하고 그분이 자신의 작품들에 쏟아부었던 열과 성을 진심으로 전달하는 것이었다. 이러한 시련을 극복해가며 또 하나의 소중한 배움이 있다면 행간의 의미를 읽는 중요성이었다. 겉면을 넘어 내포된 이야기의 깊이에서 작가의 진정성이 묻어 있고 독자들이 힘껏 그것을 캐내면서 감춰져 있던 작가의 목소리가 빛을 발하기 때문이다. 내가 만약에 시간여행을 해서 나혜석 작가님을 만나게 된다면 나는 꼭 이 말을 하고 싶다. "제가 마음껏 존경할 수 있는 첫 한국 여성 롤 모델이 되어 주셔서 감사합니다. 이제까지 번역을 하면서 나혜석 선생님의 말씀을 듣고 제가 선생님께도 말을 건네며 마치 대화를 할 수 있게 되어서 행복했습니다. 감사합니다."

Acknowledgements

Thank you, mother for your constant advice that helped the direction of the book to flow well, for the hours we spent day and night discussing and debating about Na Hye-seok's stories. Thank you, father for your mental support that helped me stand back up whenever the translation process got emotionally draining, for the encouragement that made me recover my confidence and self-belief. Also, thank you, professor Jeeha Yang for first introducing me to Na Hye-seok and thereby broadening my horizons on the gender issues in Korean history, as well as helping me find a Korean historical female role-model. Lastly, thank you, designer Amelia Tan for creating the design of the book that wonderfully captured the essence of Na Hye-seok as a writer and a New Woman, 100 years ahead of her time, which helped to blaze the trail for Na Hye-seok's rebirth in the 21st century.

책이 좋은 흐름의 방향으로 갈 수 있도록 지속적인 도움을 주시며 밤낮으로 나혜석 선생님의 이야기에 대해 함께 토의, 토론하는 저의 말동무가 되어주신 어머니, 감사합니다. 번역과정에 지쳐갈 때 제가 다시 일어설 수 있게 자신감과 저 자신에 대한 믿음을 되찾을 수 있도록 든든한 버팀목이 되어주신 아버지, 감사합니다. 그리고 저에게 나혜석 선생님을 처음으로 소개함으로써 한국 역사 속의 젠더 이슈에 대한 저의 시야를 확장할 수 있도록 하며 역사적 한국 여성 롤 모델을 찾을 수 있도록 도

움을 주신 양지하 교수님, 감사합니다. 마지막으로, 100년을 앞서간 작가, 신여성인 나혜석 선생님의 깊은 뜻이 담긴 디자인을 멋지게 만들어서 21세기에 나혜석 선생님의 재탄생을 빛나게 해 준 Amelia Tan 디자이너에게 감사 인사를 전합니다. 감사합니다.